GW00702191

An Ungodly Child

A novel by
Rachel Green

Copyright © Rachel Green 2008
Cover Design by Discovered Authors
Original Watercolour "An Ungodly Child" by Rachel Green

This first edition published in Great Britain in 2008 by
DA Diamonds - a Discovered Authors' imprint

ISBN 978-1-905108-64-0

The right of Rachel Green to be identified as the Author of the
Work has been asserted by her in accordance with the Copyright,
Designs and Patent Act 1988

All rights reserved.
No part of this publication may be reproduced, stored in a
retrieval system, or transmitted, in any form or by any means
without the prior written permission of the Author

Available from Discovered Authors Online –
All major online retailers and available to order through all UK
bookshops

Or contact:

Books
Discovered Authors
Roslin Road, London
W3 8DH
0844 800 5214
books@discoveredauthors.co.uk
www.discoveredauthors.co.uk

Printed in the UK by BookForce Distribution
BookForce Distribution policy is to use papers that are natural,
renewable and recyclable products and made from wood grown in
sustainable forests wherever possible

BookForce Distribution Ltd.
Roslin Road, London
W3 8DH

www.bookforce.co.uk

Acknowledgements:

This tale would never have emerged but for the patience of my partners DK and Luisa during the long labour and birth, the help and editing advice of Miranda and the encouragement of Feath and Tam at MuseMuggers, who posted the writing prompt that netted Jasfoup. Thanks, folks, I pawned your souls.

Chapter 0
The Company of Angels

The incubus coiled in the semi-darkness of the bedroom, the woman's soft snores encouraging it to be bold enough to coalesce despite the noise from the television in the corner: a reality show where the last twenty-something to survive won the prize.

He dropped from the air onto the bed, his foetid breath curling like a living creature around the woman's head. His breath was supposed to be a mild anaesthetic, designed to prevent his victim from waking up.

He stared at her face, puzzled. She looked too old to be receptive of his demonic seed, but her body smelled young and ripe for the taking. He shrugged, putting the disparity down to hormone pills and began to pull back the bedcloths. He gave a startled yelp as her eyes flicked open, staring into his own fire-flecked orbs.

'Haven't you heard of foreplay?' she asked. 'It's no fun if you just jump straight in. I hope you brought a condom.' Her hand snaked out and grabbed his wrist, eliciting another shriek. 'Or three…'

***

In a small anteroom just behind the broom closet on the fourth Dome of Heaven, three angels scowled at the mortal plane monitoring equipment.

'Is she allowed to do that?' Sansenoy looked up at Senoy, his brother, who shrugged.

'She can do as she likes, I suppose,' he said. 'She's already carrying the spawn of the Fallen One, isn't she? What does it matter if she insists on a condom?'

'Is she Catholic?' Semangalof ran a whetstone along the edge of his sword, producing a hiss reminiscent of a snake about to strike.

'I doubt it.' Senoy scratched himself and examined his fingernails. 'I doubt it very much, given her heritage. Why?'

'I thought we might get her on condom use. Catholics aren't allowed artificial birth control.' Semangalof returned to the sharpening of his sword.

'Even if she was, it's not for birth control, is it?' Senoy yawned. 'Not if she's already expecting. It'll be for the prevention of diseases. That's quite sensible if you ask me.'

'We'd have her on that one, then. Disease is part of God's ineffable plan. You can't go around stopping yourself from catching diseases. We worked hard on them.'

'We?' Sansenoy laughed. 'Pestilence did, maybe. He gets all the interesting jobs.'

'She, you mean.' Senoy leaned forward. 'She decided that she's tried everything as a man, now she's swapped to being a woman.'

'Really?' Sansenoy frowned. 'When did that happen?'

'During the Renaissance, just before the plague. I'm surprised you didn't hear about it. She was shacked up with a demon for ages, a young one. What was his name?'

'Jasfoup.' Semangalof held his sword up to the light. 'Knocked about with that inventor bloke.'

'What happened to him?'

'He went back downstairs when she dumped him. I think he got promoted to minor tempter or something.'

'Doesn't matter anyway. They'll all die come the apocalypse.' Semangalof grinned. 'I haven't done any killing for ages.'

'We don't do badly for work.' Senoy switched off the viewer and sat back in his armchair. 'We burned Sodom and Gomorrah to the ground as well as our ongoing task with Lilith.'

'Ha!' Semangalof snorted. 'When we catch up with her. I haven't seen her in years.'

'Wherever she is, she's not producing children or we'd know about it.' Sansenoy glared at his brother. 'Why did you turn off the viewer?'

Senoy grimaced. 'There are some things we just aren't meant to see,' he said, 'and what that woman was doing to the poor incubus was one of them.'

'I'm surprised he was allowed to answer the summoning,' Semangalof said. 'If she was carrying my kid she wouldn't be allowed to shag anyone else.'

'That's not going to happen, is it, Mangy?' Sanoy laughed. 'You weren't issued with the right tackle.'

Semangalof glowered. 'Nor were you. The boss had more important stuff for us to do.'

'I've just thought of something.' Sansenoy held up his hand to stop them bickering. 'If she's up the duff by the Downstairs King, she's going to give birth to the antichrist, isn't she?'

'Nah.' Senoy picked up his book and turned to the page with the folded corner. 'It stands to reason, doesn't it? The antichrist will be diametrically opposed to Big J, won't he?'

'Yes.' Sansenoy nodded. 'Sired by Lucifer, born of a woman who's had more sex than hot dinners, on the other side of the world.'

'This woman fits all the criteria,' Sansenoy said.

'Except one.' Senoy looked over the top of his novel. 'She's definitely carrying a boy and to be the opposite of Big J you'd have to be a girl.'

The room fell silent. Sansenoy's mouth worked silently for a moment, his brow furrowed as he tried to fit this information into his world view. He looked up at Senoy. 'A girl?' he repeated. 'Whoever heard of the antichrist being a girl?'

Senoy shrugged. 'It's a sign of the times, isn't it? Women are getting to be as powerful as men these days. Look at England: They had a woman Prime Minister in the eighties, and look at what she achieved: the destruction of British socialism and a minor war.'

'Are you saying she was one of theirs?'

'Who knows? We're not privy to that sort of information, are we? We just destroy what we're told to.' Senoy settled back in his chair and lit a cigar. 'It stands to reason though, if you think about it. For two thousand years men have upheld the tenets of the Church, drawing all the money and power toward God and crushing all the little Goddess worshippers, then bang! Women start lobbying for the vote, then they become leaders and spokespersons and before you know it the balance of power has shifted in their favour.'

'That's disgusting, that is.' Semangalof spat onto the floor. 'We should have the apocalypse right now and get rid of all the women.'

Senoy laughed. 'We can't do that, Mangy.'

'Why not? The boss would be grateful. He hasn't liked women from the beginning. They all get uppity.' Semangalof counted on his fingers. 'First there was Lilith. She wanted an equal relationship with Adam. Then there was Sharon, poor sod, then finally Eve and we all know what she did.'

'She was led astray by Samael,' Senoy pointed out.

'She didn't have to say 'let me taste that fruit and let the juices dribble down me chin' though.'

There was another silence. 'Did she really say that?' Sansenoy asked.

Semangalof nodded. 'Yeah, she did,' he said, 'though it might have been in a different context, now I think about it. Anyway, the point is, women can't be trusted.'

'Agreed,' said Sansenoy.

'Look,' Senoy was patient. 'We can't kill all the women because there would be no-one left to gestate the babies, and then there would be no men either.'

'He has a point.' Semangalof sighed and put his sword away. 'We can't do it until men have learned how to do it without women.'

Sansenoy sneered. 'Adam worked that one out.'

Semangalof laughed. 'I meant to have the babies, not just to shag everything that moved and some that didn't.'

'We can't have the apocalypse,' Senoy said, enunciating every syllable, 'because we haven't had the antichrist yet.'

'Oh.' Semangalof digested this. 'People don't generally know that it has to be a girl, do they?'

'It's not general knowledge, no.' Senoy took a long puff of his cigar. 'What are you thinking?'

'Does it matter if we don't have an actual antichrist, if everyone thinks we do?' Semangalof waited for Senoy's reaction.

'No,' said the leader of the three. 'I don't suppose it does.'

Chapter 1
A Beautiful Boy

Ada woke early, needing the toilet. In the dim light that filtered past the curtains, she could make out the spent form of the incubus and gave it a nudge. 'It's nearly dawn,' she said. 'I'm not paying you overtime.'

The minor demon groaned and rolled onto its back. 'You got a ciggie?' it asked, sitting upright to uncrease a wing.

'No. I don't smoke.' Ada batted it with the back of her hand. 'Go on, clear off. I need to use the pot.'

The incubus yawned. 'I'm knackered. When did we get to sleep?'

'You went to sleep at three. Before I was finished.' Ada glared at it. 'Now sod off, before I open the windows and let the church bells in.'

'All right.' The demon held up its hands to placate her. 'I'm going. I don't know what the hurry is. It's nothing I haven't seen before.'

'It jolly well is.' Ada pulled the pot from under the bed. 'I'm not that sort of girl, you know.'

'Huh. Some people would offer me breakfast' The incubus drew a circle on the ground with its forefinger. Upon completion, the line turned red and a portal opened, allowing it to go home. Ada waited until the circle had faded before lifting her nightie. You couldn't trust demons. Sometimes a portal out doubled as a portal in.

Squatting was difficult when you were eight months pregnant, but Ada managed and used the water in the basin to wash her hands, pulling on her dressing gown and slippers to venture downstairs. The fire had gone out overnight, leaving the house cold and frost on the inside of the windows.

An Ungodly Child

Ada waddled into the kitchen and filled the kettle, lighting the gas on the second-hand cooker Louis had got for her. She hadn't asked from where, having learned early in their relationship that the police were often interested in things that her fiancé stored in the cellar and the less she knew about them the better.

At least it was Saturday and she didn't have to go to work. Louis said she shouldn't have to at all in her condition, but Mr Braithwaite at the grocers didn't hold with paying wages when you weren't there, especially in the run-up to Christmas.

She warmed herself on the heat from the ring as the kettle boiled and made herself a cup of tea, braving the cold of the back step to fetch in the partially frozen milk. The blue tits had already pecked away the foil to get at the cream.

Ada took her tea into the living room and put the cup on the mantelpiece before lowering herself to the linoleum. Louis had left her plenty of kindling and refilled the coal scuttle before he'd left and she raked out the cold ashes ready to relight the fire.

Paper, kindling, sticks, coal. She lit a match and touched it to the paper, sitting back as it flared. Her hope was short-lived when the flames died down and left the kindling untouched. She sighed and began again.

A knock at the door startled her and she rose, crossing to the bay window to see who was there. At least it wasn't the police.

Three men in white suits stood at the door, apparently unaffected by the cold. Ada sniffed the air for traces of brimstone. Nothing. What were they here for, then? She pulled her gown more tightly around her and made her way to the door, opening it a crack.

'Mrs Waterman?' The leader of the three raised his hat.

Ada glowered. 'It's Miss. What do you want? It's cold.'

'Then perhaps we could come in?' His smile was that of a film star: all white teeth and no warmth. Ada shivered.

'How are you with fires?'

'What?' The smile faltered for a moment, but the slightly pudgier one behind raised a hand. 'I can set fires,' he said.

Ada looked him in the eyes for a moment. 'You can come in then,' she said, pulling the door open wider. 'But you can set that fire going before you do any talking.'

'As you wish, Miss.' The leader of the three raised his hat again as he entered. Ada closed the door behind them.

'Who are you anyway?' she asked as the portly one began poking at the fire. 'What do you want?'

The leader answered her. 'You can call me Sensen – Er, Mr Duke,' he said. 'This here is Mr Mange, and Mr Patch is seeing to your fire. As to why we're here, well, have you read your Bible, Miss Waterman?'

Senoy looked up. 'I though you said I could be Mr Duke?' he said. 'Why do I have to be Mr Patch?'

'Because you've got that Maker's mark on your bum.' Semangalof grinned. 'Think yourself lucky anyway. At least you got a good name.'

'That's enough, Mr Mange.' Sansenoy wagged a finger at them both. 'We all need ordinary names for down here.' He smiled at Ada. 'Just forget all that,' he said. 'Where was I?'

'You were asking me about the Bible.' Ada stared suspiciously at all three.

'That's right.' Mr Duke composed himself. 'Have you read it?'

'Yes, as a matter of fact. If you're here about the position of three wise men, you're a bit early.'

Mr Duke laughed. 'Very droll,' he said. 'We've come about one of the later books in the volume, that of the Revelations of St John. Are you familiar with them?'

'The end of the world stuff? I suppose so.' Ada picked up her tea and cradled it in her cold hands. 'I'd offer you a seat but...' Her voice trailed off as she indicated the sparsely furnished room.

'It doesn't matter, Miss.' Mr Mange led her to the only seat in front of a blazing fire that reeked of brimstone. 'Nice job, Mr Patch.'

'Thank you.' Mr Patch stared into the flames. 'There's something very uplifting about a fire,' he said.

'Cleansing,' added Mr Mange. 'Don't you think so, Miss?'

Ada looked from one to the other, unsure of her position. 'Very nice, I'm sure,' she said. 'Now what do you want?'

'You must have seen the portents, Miss Waterman.' Mr Duke squatted by her chair and touched her arm. His fingers felt warm against her skin, and she wondered what it would be like to have those fingers wander up her body until they reached —

' — Ahem.' Mr Duke coughed and stood. 'What was I talking about?'

'The signs, Mr Duke.' Mr Mange placed the tips of his fingers together and smiled.

'Oh yes.' Mr Duke nodded. 'Miss Waterman, did you know that the end is nigh?'

Ada narrowed her eyes, one arm curled over her stomach to protect the child inside. 'How could I? Your trousers are too loose.' She laughed and tapped him on the shoulder, leaving a sooty print from where she'd picked up pieces of coal.

'Very droll, I'm sure.' Mr Duke brushed away the mark.

'You couldn't have a go at my kitchen, could you? There's a hell of a stain on the counter top.' Ada grinned. 'Would you like some tea?'

'No we wouldn't.' Mr Patch took out a gladius and began cleaning his nails.

'The signs of the apocalypse have begun to make themselves known,' Mr Duke continued. 'Babylon rises and the Devil's horns awaken in the west'

'The war in Israel, you mean?' Ada asked. 'There's always a war over there. If it's not about oil its about who owns which bit of land. If you ask me, they should just draw lots for it.'

'It's the Holy Land,' said Mr Mange. 'You can't just draw lots for the Holy Land. It belongs to God's people.'

'And which of them is that then?' Ada sniffed, wishing she'd got dressed before coming downstairs. 'I thought God loved everybody.'

'Well yes, He does.' Mr Mange shrugged. 'Some more than others, obviously.'

'That's what every religious leader says,' said Ada. 'They can't all be right.' She turned back to Mr Duke. 'What Devil's horns are you on about? I haven't seen any.'

'The twin towers in the accursed city.'

Mr Mange nodded. 'They're devil horns all right. The seat of greed and avarice.'

'The World Trade Centre?' Ada nodded. 'I saw that on the news. I thought you meant something supernatural. You can't go round counting buildings as signs of the apocalypse. If God didn't want a building up he'd send some of his minions to knock it down again.'

'That's a good idea.' Mr Mange put away his knife. 'Can we?'

'No.' Mr Duke composed himself. This was going badly. People were supposed to take everything an angel said as Gospel, not argue the point. He turned back to Ada. 'You, madam, are carrying the antichriSt The seven seals will be broken when he comes of age.'

'He'll get a damn good hiding if it's him that breaks them.' Ada laughed. 'You're having me on, aren't you? My little baby, the antichrist? I don't think so.'

'What about the new star in the sky?' asked Mr Mange. 'That's a sign if ever the was one.'

'It's a sign of a new satellite, that's all,' Ada said. 'What is it you three want, anyway? Have you come here to stop him being born?'

Mr Duke took a step backwards. 'Not at all,' he said.

'We want him born,' said Mr Mange.

'We want the apocalypse,' added Mr Patch.

***

Harold was born at one minute after midnight on Winter Solstice, in the maternity room of Laverstone Hospital. Contrary to expectations, Ada refused the gas and air and insisted on watching the whole procedure, delivering the child with less pain than she endured after a good curry.

The doctor, handing the seven pound silent child to his mother, leaned in to whisper into her ear. 'The Devil looks after his own,' he said.

Ada looked up into the pale eyes. 'Damn right he does, Doctor Duke,' she said. 'You wouldn't get a good Christian girl to give birth so easily, would you? Any chance of a cup of tea now?'

An Ungodly Child

In the ward, Ada was treated to the company of Ruby, a woman twice her age who had given birth to her fourth son. The attention Ada received from the doctor made Ruby believe there was something going on between them.

'Is he your boyfriend?' she asked.

Ada laughed. 'Not in a million years,' she said. 'Louis will be here soon, you'll see.'

'A foreigner?' Ruby raised her eyebrows, but made no judgement.

'Not really,' Ada said. 'I think he comes from the East End, though I've never actually asked.' She looked at Harold, wondering whether to tell Ruby that Louis was black, but decided not to. You'd never have guessed it from Harold.

'Well, if he doesn't show up, you've got that doctor. He seems very sweet on you.'

'He just likes my baby.' Ada smiled and kissed her son on his forehead, noticing a black mark under his hairline as her lips puckered. Smoothing back the dark fronds she could see three numbers and beckoned over Doctor Duke.

'See?' he said, with a triumphant grin. 'He has the mark of the Beast on him.'

'In biro,' Ada replied, licking her thumb and rubbing the numbers away. 'Besides, the number of the Beast is actually 616. You should know that.'

'Um, I do.' Doctor Duke blinked. 'I just didn't think you did.'

Ruby waited until he had left. 'He's a funny one, that one. I don't think he's a real doctor. I asked him to look at my episiotomy stitches and he turned green.'

Ada laughed. 'He knows his anatomy all right,' she said. 'It's funny really. It's usually the nurses who are angels.'

'That's a relief,' Ruby said, 'but I shall be glad to get out of here all the same. When are you out?'

'Tomorrow, I think.' Ada smoothed down Harold's hair again. 'Truth be told, there's no need for me to be in here at all. They just wanted to keep an eye on me.'

'I'm out tomorrow as well.' Ruby scribbled her address on a piece of paper. 'Fancy going to bingo on Thursday night?'

Ada was doubtful. 'It depends if Louis will look after Harold,' she said.

'Just drop him off with my Albert,' Ruby said. 'One more won't make much difference.'

Ada smiled. 'It's a date then,' she said.

She left the hospital the following day with Ruby, Albert giving her a lift home with Harold. She found the house exactly as she had left if five days before, the festive decorations serving to enhance the emptiness rather than provide any cheer.

The only difference was the presence of two large packages wrapped in brown paper and an envelope with her name on the front in neat copperplate script.

Ada shivered, and not just because of the weather. Setting Harold down on the one easy chair, she set the fire, her determination sending the flames soaring and the wood crackling as it caught, giving enough time for the chunks of coal to catch and begin warming the room. In an hour or two there would be enough hot water to have a bath as well.

She checked on Harold, who looked up at her and giggled, his blue eyes open wide, taking in the details and colour of the paper chains strung across the ceiling, kicking his legs and reaching out to touch them.

'They're too high to reach, Harold,' Ada said, letting him hold her fingers. 'Even for a beautiful little boy.' He laughed and she leaned down to kiss him, putting his toy rabbit, a gift from Ruby, in his arms. 'Mummy's just going into the kitchen to make a cup of tea,' she said. 'You be a good boy for a few minutes, and we'll see about something for you to eat.'

Harold chuckled and used his rabbit to extend his reach, still trying to get the coloured paper hanging from the picture rail, and Ada went into the kitchen.

When she returned, she was surprised the see her five day old son playing with the paper chain. 'Clever Harold,' she said, putting her tea on the hearth and picking him up. 'Did the heat from the fire loosen the sticky tape then?' She sat down with him on her lap and unbuttoned her dress so that he could feed.

Unable to put it off any longer, she picked up the letter and opened it. It was, as she knew it would be, from Louis.

> *My dearest Ada*
>
> *I love you.*
>
> *Trust me on this, for if anyone understands love, then it is I, and I know that I love you as much as anyone has ever loved anyone else. You are my Juliet, my Guinevere, my Mary Magdalene. Alas then, that I am the doomed prince, forced by circumstance away from your arms. I have had to leave suddenly, for a crisis in my home country requires my presence and supervision, though why my foes have chose this moment to act I shall never know. Rest assured they will find me wrathful that they have driven me from your arms.*
>
> *I will return when I can, though it may be years before the matter is settled. I will watch over you from unexpected places and give aid when I can, so leave a candle burning for me.*
>
> *I leave you with two gifts. The first is for you, my princess. Use the contents wisely. The second is for our son, but he will not need it for a long time yet. Hide it from his curiosity and give it to him when he reaches despair, for he deserves to live without the knowledge of his heritage until such time as he is ready to embrace the truth.*
>
> *Finally, fear not for your basic needs. In the box are the details I have set out with Isaacs the solicitor. The house is yours, fully paid and in your name, as is the freehold for the six houses around you. The income from them will mean you need never work. The gas and electricity have also been retro-engineered by one of my staff, and you will never have*

to worry about bills from that department. In the hall you will find a telephone, though the bills from that are your own problem.

Tell Harold that it was not my desire to leave him, and I will always be devoted to him.

With everlasting love,
Louis.

Harold reached up, surprised that water was falling from his mothers eyes and screwing his face up when he tasted it. Ada held him tightly to her chest, rocking him as silent tears poured from her broken heart.

'Daddy's gone away,' she told him. 'He says that he loves you, but we won't be seeing him for a bit.' Harold gurgled, happy that he was loved and not caring, at least at present, that his father was gone.

Ada's tea went cold, despite the heat of the fire.

She was jarred from her introspection by a knock at the door. Remembering what Louis had said in his letter, she no longer feared the bill collectors and opened it, happy to see her brother on the doorstep.

Frederick took one look at her tear-stained face and came in, closing the door behind him. 'What's wrong, Ada?' he asked. 'Why are you all alone with the baby? I thought Louis — '

'He's gone,' Ada sobbed, burying her head against Frederick's bony shoulder. 'He didn't want to go, though.' She pulled away and showed him the letter. Frederick scanned it and put it on the mantelpiece.

'He'll be back, love, I'm sure of it. It's like you said; he didn't want to go.' Frederick rubbed Ada's back, holding her until the dry heaving of grief had stopped. He wiggled his eyebrows over her shoulder and Harold giggled.

'So this is Harold,' he said.

Ada turned and wiped her eyes, the sight of her son enough to forget her tears for a moment. 'Yes,' she said, picking him up. 'Harold, this is your uncle Frederick. He'll teach you all about...' She stopped, wondering what her brother could teach him.

'Cars,' Frederick said. 'You can help me look after Betsy.'

'I don't know why you bought that thing,' Ada said, showing him how to hold his nephew. 'Fancy buying a Beetle. They'll never catch on, and then you'll be stuck with it.'

'Don't pout, Adantia.' Frederick mimicked their mother's voice. 'You'll be glad of it when there's shopping to be fetched.'

Ada laughed and touched his arm. 'Thanks for coming round,' she said. 'I needed a friendly face.'

'Anytime, sis.' Frederick smiled at her. 'I'll look after you.' He smiled at the baby in his arms. 'I'll look after you both.'

Chapter 2
Bringing up the Baby

Frederick put more coal on the fire and sat down on the stool from the kitchen, a cup of tea within easy reach. It was the great British tradition, tea. Whatever the calamity, it was always easier to bear after a cup of the brown brew, preferably with several sugars.

He looked at Harold, nursing from his mother. 'He's going to be a big lad, isn't he?' he said. 'He's got a hell of an appetite.'

Ada smiled. 'He's my beautiful boy,' she said. 'Thanks for coming, Fred. I don't know what I'd have done without you here.'

Frederick nodded, gazing into the fire. 'Aren't you going to open the box he left you?' he asked. 'He obviously meant it to be useful. Perhaps it's another chair.'

'In a minute, when he's finished.' Ada looked into Harold's bright eyes and would have kissed him again if she could have reached without disturbing his meal. Harold reached up to her face with a pudgy hand and she kissed that instead. Harold detached himself and giggled, chewing on one of the toy rabbit's ears.

'All right,' Ada said, passing Harold to his uncle. 'Let's have a look at what Louis left for me.'

She pulled the first box to her chair and fiddled with the knots, rolling the string into a ball and setting it to one side before unwrapping the brown paper, careful not to tear it so that it could be re-used. The box she revealed was made of wood, unadorned but for the word 'bananas' stamped upside down on one end. She turned it so that the clasp was toward her and opened it.

'Oh.' She stared at the folds of silk.

'What is it?' Frederick craned his neck, but couldn't see over the open lid without disturbing Harold.

Ada pulled the silk out, fold upon fold that shimmered with reds and oranges, a spark of blue a counterpoint within the deepest crimson. 'It's a dress,' she said, standing up to hold it against her. 'It's beautiful.'

Frederick nodded. 'Go and put it on,' he said. 'It'll cheer you up.'

Ada laughed. 'I can't,' she said. 'I wouldn't want to get it dirty. It's a special occasion dress.'

'Bringing your baby home isn't a special occasion?' Frederick's eyes twinkled in his slender face. 'Go on. You'll look a million dollars.'

Ada grinned and hurried out. Frederick listened to her excited feet on the bare boards of the stairs. Her progress down them again a few minutes later was a little more stately.

'You look stunning,' he said when she returned, the dress clinging to her slight frame and falling in waves from her arms and hips. 'It's a bit risqué, but that's the fashion these days.'

'Father would never have approved,' Ada said, trying a few dance steps.

Frederick laughed. 'No, but he's not here, and Mother would have loved it. You take after her, you know.'

'That's kind of you, Fred. I often wonder if we'll see her again.'

'We will.' Frederick's smile left him. 'You know she had to go. It was only to protect us.'

Ada nodded and sat down, the flowing dress echoing the flames licking around the coal. 'There's more in here,' she said, changing the subject.

'More?' Frederick made an effort to smile again. 'Louis must like you or something.'

Ada laughed. 'I think he does.' She took out a small metal box about the size of one of Frederick's paperback books and opened it, almost dropping it when she felt the heat. 'It's a piece of coal,' she said.

'That's traditional,' Frederick replied. 'It's almost new year.'

'Two months ago.' Ada smiled, referring to Halloween, the pagan new year. 'This piece is hot, though.' She showed the box to her brother.

'Best put it on the fire,' he said. 'Especially with the little chap about.'

Ada put the box on the hearth and used the fire tongs to pick it up. As soon as it was released from the confines of the box the coal began to burn with a blue flame.

'It doesn't smell like coal,' Frederick said, holding Harold's hands to stop him reaching for the pretty stone. 'More like matches.'

Ada shrugged and put it on the fire where it blended in with the rest of the coal. 'It's a thoughtful gift,' she said. 'I would have been glad of that if I was trying to light the fire.'

'Like the tradition of carrying home a piece of the bale fire in a hollow turnip,' said Frederick. 'Very thoughtful chap, your Louis. I don't know how it stayed alight in that box though.'

Ada shrugged and returned to her present, pulling out a cylinder wrapped in tissue paper. 'It's a candle,' she said. 'He said to keep a candle burning in his letter. He must have meant this one.'

'What's it made of?' asked Frederick. 'That doesn't look like any wax I've ever seen before.'

Ada sniffed the candle. 'It's tallow,' she said. 'Rendered fat. Let's not think about what from.'

'Fair enough.' Frederick watched her light it by taking a coal from the fire and put it in the middle of the bay window.

'Come back, my love,' she said. 'I'll be waiting.'

'He likes that,' said Frederick, directing her attention to Harold who was gazing at the single flame. Ada kissed his forehead. 'Are you all right on that stool?' she asked. 'I don't even have a cushion for it.'

'Fine,' Frederick lied, wishing he had a bit more padding. 'Finish opening your presents. You know you can stay with me in the manor whenever you want.'

'No.' Ada was harsh, but her voice softened again. 'Thanks for the offer, Fred, but I can't. There're too many memories there.'

Frederick nodded. 'I know, but the offer's there if you ever need it.'

Ada nodded. 'Thanks, but I have my house.'

'I just wish you'd at least take some furniture,' Frederick laughed, but Ada shook her head.

'I don't want to pay the price that would be attached to it,' she said.

'Do you still have the nightmares?'

'Sometimes.' Ada took out the next package. 'Not so often now, though.' She unwrapped the paper and fell silent, her mouth open wide.

'What is it?' asked Frederick, unable to see. He held Harold securely and half stood to see over the lid. 'Stone the crows!'

'There must be hundreds,' said Ada, putting the three bundles on her lap and taking one to examine more closely. She riffled through the stack of banknotes.

'Thousands,' Frederick agreed. 'You're rich, girl!'

'Is it stolen, do you think?'

'If it is, it won't be traceable,' Frederick said. 'Louis wouldn't put you in danger.'

'I suppose.' Ada put the money back in the chest and took out the last gift. 'It's a jewellery box,' she said, opening it. The strains of 'Für Elise' filtered through the room. 'He was playing that the first time I met him,' she said. 'Do you remember?'

Frederick nodded. 'On mother's piano in the drawing room, before everything happened.'

'I fell in love with him then,' Ada said, remembering. 'He played it with such passion, as if his heart was broken.'

'I remember.' Frederick nodded, staring into the fire. 'If you hadn't gone for him I would have.' He grinned, pulling Ada from her reverie.

'You're incorrigible,' she said, looking inside the box. Her mouth fell open again and she held the box for Frederick to see.

'Wow,' was all he could muster at the sight of so many jewels and gemstones.

Ada shut the box, leaving the room silent but for the crackle of the fire. She looked at Frederick. 'I don't think I'll be going back to work for Mr Braithwaite,' she said.

Frederick smiled. 'He said he'd look after you.'

Harold reached out to her, sensing that his mother was available again, and Frederick passed him back. He looked at the fortune in the trunk. 'You missed one,' he said, reaching inside for the final tissue-wrapped present. He passed it to Ada. 'It's the smallest one.'

Ada unwrapped the tiny grey candle. 'I wonder what this one is for,' she said.

Frederick shrugged. 'Light it and see.'

Ada passed it to him and he lit it from the tallow candle on the windowsill.

'It's a bit cramped in here,' said a voice from the fireplace.

Frederick groaned. 'Tell me it's not him!' he said.

A scaled head poked out from the flames 'Wotcha,' it said. Long, spindly arms and a torso and legs to match followed it, the creature swaying from side to side on the hearth as it extricated its tail from the flames. 'Frederick!' it said. 'You've grown since I saw you last'

'I was right,' said Frederick. 'Sorry, Ada love.'

'Ada?' The creature tuned to her. 'Surely not? You were just a girl when I saw you last and now you're a lovely young woman with a child of your own.'

'Flatterer,' said Ada, shielding Harold from the creature. 'You take your normal form. You're frightening Harold.'

'Harold, is it?' The creature drew closer. 'A newborn? Unbaptised?'

'Yes,' said Ada, half turning to keep the baby away from the creature. 'Now sheathe yourself in skin, tormentor.' She spoke some words in the creature's native tongue and it hissed and drew back. Far from being frightened, Harold was trying to touch this new person, merely curious about the different features it held.

The creature stood erect, shifting through several forms before settling upon a tall, dark-skinned male. It stretched a few times, working its mouth as if to get the feel of the new flesh. 'Is that better?' it asked.

Ada looked away.

'You might want to put some clothes on,' Frederick suggested.

'Should I?' The demon flashed through dozens of pieces of clothing, settling upon a colourful shirt with a wingtip collar and brown three-quarter length leather jacket over brown corduroy slacks. 'Better?' it asked, as its hair grew to a rakish length.

'Much.' Frederick sat down again on the stool. 'What are you doing here, Jasfoup?'

'I was summoned.' The demon smiled, replacing the three rows of needle-sharp teeth with those more appropriate to a human mouth. 'It's nice to feel wanted.'

'We didn't summon you.' Ada scowled. 'Haven't you done enough damage to this family?'

Jasfoup looked hurt. 'Firstly,' he said, 'you did summon me.' He pointed to the stubby candle that Frederick had placed next to the large one. 'I came in through the brimstone, since you hadn't bothered with a circle. Most undignified, if you ask me. I thought I deserved better.'

He walked around the room, inspecting the bare walls. 'Secondly, I resent the implication that I was anything to do with the disaster at the manor. I didn't get there until it was too late. If you'll cast your mind back, it was me who did the clearing up and the...' he coughed, 'arrangements afterwards.'

'The funeral with no body, you mean,' Ada said, shifting in her seat so that she could watch him.

'Amongst other things,' Jasfoup conceded. He returned to her side. 'So this is Harold.' He tickled the baby under the chin.

'Don't you dare try to corrupt him,' said Ada. 'I want him to grow up properly, without your influence.'

'But I can influence him for the good,' Jasfoup protested. 'There's been some talk of him being the antichrist...'

'Huh! I can guess who from.' Ada stood and faced up to him. 'You tell those interfering angels that he's not the antichrist and this is not the end of the world.'

'I know that.' Jasfoup put a hand on her shoulder. 'I know that and they know that, but they're trying to use him to bring it about. You need me to look after him.'

'And who's going to pay for your services?' asked Frederick.

'All taken care of.' Jasfoup smiled.

***

By Harold's first birthday the house was a home, and Ada had managed to splash out on one of the new colour televisions with a nineteen inch screen. The house had filled with people, including Rudy and Albert and their four boys. Harold, temporarily forgotten, was sat on Ada's armchair, his eyes fixed to the television.

'Horsies,' he said, pointing at the screen.

Frederick laughed. 'That's right, Harold. Horses. This is the 2:15 from Kempton. I've got a flutter on the white one.' He pointed to the horse at the starting gate.

'Lucy's Pride?' Albert laughed. 'You haven't got a chance. It's at fifteen to one.'

Harold giggled and clutched his toy rabbit. It was still his favourite, despite all the others that Ada had bought him.

The race started, the six horses piling out from the stalls at breakneck speed. Within moments the favourite was in the lead by a length, closely followed by two others with Lucy's Pride in fourth place.

'I told you,' said Albert. 'You should have bet on Silver Hammer.'

'Ah well.' Fred sighed. 'It was a whole pound, as well.'

Harold shook his rabbit at the screen. 'White horsey,' he cried, giggling as he buried his face in the threadbare fur.

'Good lad,' said Frederick, stroking his hair.

'Look!' Albert pointed at the screen. 'I don't believe it!'

Frederick looked back. Lucy's Pride was creeping up to the leaders. By the end of the race she was a neck ahead and clearly the winner. Frederick beamed.

'Good lad, Harold,' he said. 'He's my lucky charm.'

Ada looked at Jasfoup, who shook his head and shrugged.

Harold giggled, waving his rabbit. 'Nice white horsey,' he said.

***

By the time he was three, Harold had begun to collect the cards that came with tea packets. Frederick took an interest as well, showing him how to arrange them and buying the albums for him to keep them in. He gave Harold any that came his way, along with a red biscuit tin full of cards from cigarette packets. Harold loved them, delighting in the pictures and arranging them into numerical order. Frederick looked through his collection. 'Too bad you've got one missing,' he said, pointing to an empty space in the album. 'You can't get these any more. They stopped making them years ago.'

'I've got it here. Mummy is getting me some glue. Patch got it for me,' Harold said, pointing to the toy rabbit. Even with an ear missing and, thanks to age, a patch over half of its head it was still his favourite toy.

Frederick raised an eyebrow and picked Patch up, but the rabbit showed no sign of sentience.

'What did you expect?' asked Jasfoup, watching from the door. 'A demon in disguise?'

***

When Harold was four he began to play with action figures. Frederick brought him the very latest ones from the shops along with their spaceships and vehicles, helping Harold to make vast battlegrounds in the garden and attic. Often the missions would involve the rescue of the giantesses: three dolls that were sent as an anonymous gift on his fourth birthday and that were built at a different scale to his space cowboys.

When he was alone, Harold would forget about guns and battles and concentrate instead upon the three dolls, making up complex stories about monsters and princesses. The three figurines were his first introduction to the unique anatomy of women, and he was amazed to learn that their legs were proportionately half as long again as a mans, their waists as thin as a wasp's and their necks almost too long to support their heads.

'Why are women a different shape to men?' he asked his mother.

'They have to make babies,' she replied, her hands soapy from washing up after dinner. 'That requires wider hips and breasts to feed them with.'

'But my dolls are thinner than real women, and their necks are longer.'

Ada laughed and sat down, pulling Harold up onto her lap. 'That's because they were made by a man and are his ideal vision of a woman. Do you remember the story of the Garden of Eden I told you?'

Harold nodded. 'Adam and Eve and Lilith and Cain?'

Ada nodded. 'That's the one,' she said. 'After Lilith left him and before Eve came along, Adam's sole companions were the animals and he loved them very much.' She plucked one of the dolls from his hands and stood it upright. 'Now God wanted Adam to fall in love with Eve and live happily ever after, so he designed her to look like an animal from behind. See how her long hair falls just short of her bottom?'

Harold giggled. 'You said bottom!'

'It's a perfectly ordinary word,' Ada replied. 'Now look how her long legs look like a horse, especially in those high heels, and her hair looks like a tail. Do you see it?'

Harold nodded. 'So God made women to look like horses, so that men would want to marry them?'

'That's right,' Ada said, 'but Eve ate the apple and realised that her shape was no good for childbearing, so she made herself look like women do now. Men, though, still think women more beautiful when they look like an animal from behind, so they make dolls to encourage girls to grow up believing that.'

Harold gazed at the doll. 'Patch says that I can be a girl when I grow up. Can I, mum?'

'Did he now?' Ada looked at the threadbare rabbit, her eyes thoughtful. 'You can be whatever you want to be,' she said, 'but don't let that silly rabbit make your decisions for you.'

'Are all dolls like this?' Harold asked.

Ada shook her head. 'Not all of them. Some dolls are made with realistic proportions.'

'Will you buy me one?' Harold asked, the eagerness in his voice making Ada smile.

'Perhaps for your birthday,' she said. 'Dolls cost a lot of money.'

'An old one will do,' Harold protested.

'Old ones cost even more,' she said. 'They're called antiques, and because they're not very easy to get, people pay a lot of money for them. That goes for anything old, not just dolls.'

'When I'm older, will my dolls be worth a lot of money?'

Ada laughed. 'A little bit,' she said. 'But to be worth a lot, they have to be in pristine condition. If they're still in the box they came in they're worth even more.'

'Cor.' Harold gazed at his dolls. 'Can I have two dolls for my birthday, then? One to play with and one to keep Plasticine?'

'Pristine.' Ada laughed. 'We'll see.'

***

When Ada had put him to bed with the tale of Gawain and the Lady Ragnall, explaining that the woman was not a nasty creature like the book said, but just a woman who had been driven from her home by a greedy landlord and forced to live off the land, thus appearing ugly to the rich knights, she went around his room picking up his toys.

Patch the bunny had somehow ended up under the chest of drawers, forcing her to kneel on the floor to retrieve it. She looked at it thoughtfully. She had thrown it away twice in the past year thinking Harold had grown too old for the scruffy thing, but he had retrieved it from the dustbin both times.

'I'll sort you out, Mr Patch,' she said, throwing it into the fire. It burned as if it were stuffed with straw, leaving the two eyes staring at her in accusation. She shook her head, poked them down into the embers and put on more coal.

Ada made two cups of tea and went to the window, touching the candle that was still burning for Louis. In four years it had only burned down by an inch, leading her to wonder again what animal the fat had been rendered from. She lit the smaller candle and remained looking out of the window until the hissing behind her stopped.

'What have you just burned?' the voice asked. 'It stinks in there.'

Ada spoke without turning. 'Are you decent?' she asked.

It was a few moments before she heard affirmation. 'Right,' she said, handing Jasfoup one of the cups of tea. 'I want some protection.'

He took a sip and sat in her chair. 'What for?' he asked. 'I thought you said you wanted to bring him up without interference?'

'I've changed my mind,' she said. 'He needs someone he can trust, and I need someone to make sure that no-one's getting to him without my knowledge.'

'I always offered to help,' Jasfoup replied.

'I know, and I'm taking you up on it.' Ada stirred her tea, the spoon sliding across the china like the sound of a choir. Jasfoup winced.

'What can I do?' he asked.

Chapter 3
Turning a Profit

'I can't call him 'Scroat', you daft bugger.'

Ada looked at the imp: eighteen inches of green skin and prehensile fingers and toes. It regarded her in return, hissing softly through serrated teeth, its forked tail flicking backwards and forwards like a cat's. It looked up at Jasfoup. 'Is she allowed to change my name?' it asked.

Jasfoup sat back in the chair, one leg draped casually over the arm. His leather jacket hung open to reveal the garish paisley pattern of his shirt. 'She's your mistress now. She can call you whatever she likes.'

Ada scratched her temple. 'Stinky. I'll call him Stinky, then if anyone hears me call for him they'll think it a mild swear word.'

Jasfoup laughed, more at Stinky's expression that at the name itself. 'Stinky it is, then.'

Ada nodded. 'You're sure that Harold won't see him.'

'Yes.' Jasfoup sat forward. 'All kids are born with a bit of the Sight, but I've taken Harold's away. It can be restored if he ever needs it. He would have lost it soon, anyway, now that he's five.'

'Good.' Ada sat down, leaning forward to talk to the imp. 'Your primary duty is to warn me about any angels or devils that try to get near Harold.'

'Yes, Ma'am.' Stinky nodded so hard his teeth clashed.

'Also sprites, ghosts, pixies, elves and fairies,' Jasfoup added.

Stinky nodded again.

'Anyone or anything not native to this plane, in fact,' Ada clarified.

'Also vampires, werewolves and other nephilim,' Jasfoup added again.

'Anyone not human,' said Ada.

'Right, Missus.' Stinky grinned. 'Is that all?'

'I'll think of other duties,' said Ada. 'You can light the fire in the morning, for one thing. I'm going to move the brimstone to the outside lavvy. It'll keep it warm and be more convenient to Mr Jasfoup to use.'

'Good idea, Ada.' Jasfoup nodded in approval. 'I hated the cramped conditions you were forcing me to endure in that fireplace.' He stood, zipping up his jacket. 'I must be off now, though. Places to go, people to damn.'

'Just as long as it's not my Harold.' Ada sat back. 'Do you know how to make cocoa, Stinky?'

***

Ruby called round on Saturday. 'Are you going to the jumble sale at St Jude's? It'll be starting in ten minutes, and you have to be at the start to have a chance at the best stuff.'

'Can we, mum?' Harold tore his gaze from the television.

'I've got washing to do,' Ada replied. 'Thanks for the offer though.'

'Albert's got the car,' Ruby said. 'I'm sure your washing can wait an hour.'

'Please, mum.' Harold stood up. 'I'll use my own pocket money.'

'All right.' Ada laughed. 'It's a conspiracy. I'll get my coat.'

Harold pulled his shoes on, the heels flattened by the haste and he hopped on one foot to pull them upright again before getting a pound out of his piggy bank. Ada locked the door behind them and squeezed into the back of Albert's car with two of Ruby's boys. They arrived at the church in time, and managed to join the queue just as the doors opened.

Harold darted between legs and got inside without paying the tenpenny entrance fee, running to the toy stall first 'How much is this?' he asked, holding up a bag of plastic bricks.

The tall man behind the counter looked at him and smiled. 'Fifty pence, to you,' he said. 'A bright lad like you could be an engineer with a bit of encouragement.'

Harold grinned and handed over his money, than made his way over to the book stall.

Tom, Ruby's son and only two days older then Harold, pulled him back. 'I wanted that,' he said.

Harold shrugged. 'I got there first,' he said.

'Only because you pushed in,' said Tom. 'Give it to me.'

Harold looked at Tom and then at the bag of bricks. 'I'll sell it to you,' he said. 'A pound.'

'I've only got 50p,' Tom replied. 'That's all you paid for it.' He raised his fist

Harold looked round for his mum, but she was buried beneath a pile of old ladies at the clothes stall.

'Is there a problem, gentleman?' The man from the toy stall interrupted.

'He wants a pound for the bricks, and he only paid fifty pence for it,' said Tom.

The man laughed. 'Mr Waterman is a businessman,' he said. 'Turning a profit is every man's goal. I think that a pound is a fair price for the bag, don't you?'

'I suppose.' Tom was already sulking. 'I've only got fifty pence though.'

'Then I expect he'll let you buy half the bag.' The man smiled. 'Now shake hands and be friends. This is the house of God, you know.'

'All right.' Tom held out a reluctant hand and Harold shook it.

'I'll get you another bag,' said the man. Harold grinned and began to sort out the pieces. 'I want some wheels too,' Tom said. 'I can't make cars without wheels.'

Harold considered. 'Wheels are worth four bricks,' he said. 'You can have the wheels if you have fewer bricks.'

'You're a rotten swindler,' Tom said, but accepted the price.

The man waited for Tom to leave before approaching Harold again. 'You're quite the entrepreneur,' he said, offering his hand. 'I'm Reverend Duke. Pleased to meet you.'

'Harold Waterman,' said Harold, shaking the hand. 'But you knew that.'

'I make it my business to know everyone in the parish,' replied the vicar. 'I don't see you in church, though.'

'Mum's not very religious,' Harold said. 'She says that I don't need to be indoctrinated and that I'll make my own mind up when I'm older.'

'A sensible woman, your mum.' The reverend smiled. 'It pays to be aware of God, though. You can learn a lot from the Bible. It even tells you that the world will end soon. It's best to be prepared.'

'Really?' Harold looked up at the kindly face. 'I thought God didn't approve of making a profit, though? They told us that story about the rich man in school.'

Duke laughed. 'The Lord likes those who can think for themselves,' he said. 'There are many ways of praising Him, and not all of them are in poverty.'

'Cool.' Harold nodded, his gaze roaming around the room. 'How much for those encyclopaedias?' he asked.

Reverend Duke smiled. 'A pound,' he said.

***

Uncle Frederick arrived the next morning in his best suit. 'Come on, Harold,' he said. 'Get your coat on.'

'Where are we going?' Harold scrambled for the jacket his mum had bought him at the jumble sale. 'We don't usually go out on a Sunday morning. All the shops are shut.'

'We're going to church, Harold.' Frederick mussed Harold's hair. 'It's about time you learned about God.'

'We learned about him in school,' Harold said. 'He strengthened Man by putting him through endless trials, destroying cities and crops so they had to learn to fend for themselves. Then when everyone was really fed up he sent his son down to get them all to worship him again, only the original lot didn't believe the new lot and they've been fighting ever since.'

Ada came out of the kitchen, tutting at the state of Harold's hair. She began brushing it. 'There's a lot more to it than that, Harold,' she said. 'He does lots of good things, too.'

'Like what?' Harold asked.

Ada, standing behind him, looked blankly at Frederick.

'He saved all the people from the Pharaoh,' he said.

Harold snorted with the derision only a five-year old could muster. 'Only by releasing a wave of terrorism,' he said. 'Plagues? Biological warfare if you ask me, never mind the wilful murder of children.'

'Well, he destroyed the sinners in Sodom and Gomorrah,' Frederick said.

'He destroyed two cities because he didn't like the people that lived there,' replied Harold. 'That's an atrocity. Even Hitler didn't kill as many as that.'

Frederick smiled. 'God is allowed to do that,' he said. 'It was for the good of his people.' He put an arm around the boy's shoulders and led him out of the door. 'We can say hello to God and worship him through Jesus.'

'I'd rather watch television,' said Harold.

'Television isn't anything to do with God, though.' Frederick opened the car door and let Harold sit in the front. 'Sunday is the day we should be thanking God for all that we have.'

'Like television,' said Harold. 'Mum says that I should show how grateful I am for presents by playing with them, so isn't watching television showing God that I'm grateful for it?'

Frederick laughed. 'I can't fault your logic,' he said, 'but how do you show God that you're grateful for being alive?'

'By continuing to breathe.' Harold stared out of the window at the approaching spire of St Jude's. 'Why do you have to go to a church to worship God?' he said.

Frederick thought about it while he parked. 'So that there's nothing to distract you from thoughts of him,' he said. 'What if you loved a girl? Wouldn't you want to think about her?'

Harold considered the idea. 'It depends what she collected,' he said, 'or if she had some army figures.'

Frederick laughed. 'You'll change your mind when you're older,' he said. 'Look, there's the vicar.'

Harold approached Reverend Duke. 'I've come to learn about God,' he said.

'You've come to the right place, Master Waterman,' said the vicar, extending his hand to shake the boy's. Harold thought his skin felt like old leaves. 'It's all in the good book.'

'The Bible?' Harold looked dubious. 'I've read that already. There're loads missing from it.'

'Well, that's true,' Reverend Duke replied, nodding at some of his parishioners as they walked up the path, 'but we have to believe that God decided which bits to leave in because they were important. Have you read 'Revelations'? You might find that exciting.'

Harold shrugged. 'It's a prophecy open to interpretation to give the followers of God hope that they will be redeemed to enjoy everlasting life,' he replied. 'Like giving an annual bonus to employees at the end of the fiscal year.'

'Yes, I suppose it is,' Reverend Duke laughed. 'I would be interested in debating the point with you. Perhaps you would be of the opinion that God should be overthrown by the forces of darkness.'

'That's just another myth designed to keep his followers in tow,' said Harold.

The vicar laughed and ushered him into the church. 'He's very bright, isn't he?'

Frederick nodded. 'Too bright for his own good, sometimes. I've never seen anyone read the amount that he does.'

***

Ada was waiting for them when they got back. Harold was bouncing with excitement.

'Mum!' he said, getting out of the car. 'I love going to church. Can I go again next week?'

Ada smiled. 'Of course you can, Harold.' She let him indoors and smiled at her brother. 'Thanks for taking him. I was expecting him to hate it.'

'So was I,' said Frederick, 'but the vicar does a half-hour session for the kids afterwards. That's the bit Harold liked best The rest of us had a bit of a chat over coffee and biscuits. Did you know that that Sylvia from number thirty four,' he nodded in the direction of her house, 'is on her third husband?'

'You know I don't listen to gossip, Frederick.' Ada led him into the house.

'Can I have my pocket money on Sundays in future, mum?' Harold was emptying his piggy bank.

'I suppose so, Harold. Why?'

'I've joined 'Christian Collectors' he said. 'If I save my money with the church, I get an eight percent return at Christmas. That's two percent more than the Post Office.'

Ada frowned. 'What happened to the story of the moneylenders at the temple?' she asked Frederick.

He shrugged. 'They didn't need a new roof,' he said.

***

Reverend Duke was surprised the following week when Harold deposited thirty pounds. 'That's as much as some people earn in a week,' he said. 'Where did you get all this money?'

Harold smiled. 'I've started a Christmas club at school,' he said. 'Other kids give me their pocket money, and I pay them a dividend at the end of the term.'

'Clever.' Reverend Duke wrote the amount in Harold's pass book. 'What dividend are you offering?'

'Seven per cent,' Harold replied. 'More than the Post Office, but leaving me with a margin of profit.'

'You're taking advantage of the church to make money for yourself?'

Harold shrugged. 'I happen to know that you get a twelve percent interest because you're a registered charity,' he said. 'I'm only following your lead.'

'Where did you find that out?'

'I asked at the bank,' said Harold. 'They told me.'

'They shouldn't have done,' said the vicar. 'It must have been a clerical error.'

***

Within three months Frederick had lost interest in going to church. Despite wanting to be a good influence on Harold, he found that it conflicted with his ideals, namely that of having a long lie-in and breakfast in bed.

Harold shrugged and went on his own, pedalling his new (second-hand) bike along the edge of the high street. They had had a policeman in at school who told them it was an offence to ride it on the pavement and had arranged a cycling proficiency test Harold had passed with 98%, having lost two points by exceeding the 30 mph speed limit when he freewheeled down Quarry Bank. PC Jenkins had elected not to prosecute a six-year-old on a chopper.

He paid in another £29 to the savings scheme, Emily Perkins having been off school with mumps and thus forfeiting half her bonus. Harold kept meticulous records.

'I noticed you fidgeting during the service,' Reverend Duke said, signing his passbook.

Harold shrugged. 'It was boring,' he said. 'I know all the words and the organ needs re-tuning.'

'Does it?' the vicar was surprised. 'I'll see if Mr Jenkins can have a look at it in the week. I'm gratified that you still come to service, though. Most boys your age would rather be playing football.'

'I don't like football,' said Harold. 'I like football cards, though.

I've got the whole collection and I only need three more for a second set.'

'Is that all you collect?' The vicar put down his pen and steepled his hands, gazing intently at the young boy.

'I collect anything,' Harold said. 'I started with tea cards, though.'

'Then you follow in God's teachings by doing that.' Reverend Duke smiled. 'Is it not said that Jesus was a fisher of men, and that God collects lost souls?'

'Matthew 4 verses 17-23,' Harold replied, 'but you made the other bit up.'

The vicar laughed. 'You get my drift, though. You needn't come to church if you're following in His footsteps already.'

Harold looked at his passbook. 'What about my savings account?'

'You can keep that up,' Reverend Duke replied. 'Drop in anytime for that.'

He waved as Harold left, bicycle clips around his trouser legs.

'Well done, Mr Duke.' Senoy stepped out from the life-sized bronze of the angel that graced the apse. 'You've got him to renounce the path of righteousness and still think he's doing God's will.'

'Thank you Mr Patch.' Sansenoy smiled. 'He has good intentions.'

'And we know what road is paved with those.' Senoy laughed. 'We'll have him thinking he's the antichrist before he know it.'

'What about the hell hound? He's supposed to have one on his next birthday. Where are we going to get one from?'

Sansenoy checked the church for lingering parishioners and shrugged off his disguise. 'How should I know?' he asked. 'It's not like we can put in a requisition for one, is it?'

'We could buy one.' Senoy grinned.

'No we could not.' Sansenoy frowned. 'Those below wouldn't sell one to us, and there are none in the mortal realm.

'It doesn't have to be a hell hound though. He just has to think it's a hell hound.'

Sansenoy thought about it. 'You're right,' he said. 'We could get him a Doberman. That would look the part.'

***

Harold's seventh birthday was a quiet affair. He'd elected not to have a party, mostly because he didn't want Tom to come. Instead Ada had made him a chocolate cake to go with his birthday tea. Having a birthday so close to Christmas meant that he was also able to negotiate bigger presents.

'You said that I could have a dog!' he said.

'I said 'We'll see',' Ada corrected, looking with dismay at the discarded construction kit with working motor.

Harold glowered and stared at the television, fighting the tears that threatened to spill down his cheeks, oblivious to the despair of his mother or the two angels across the road.

'Did you get it?' asked Mr Duke.

'Right here,' replied Mr Patch.

Mr Duke sighed. 'I thought we'd agreed on a Doberman?' he said. 'That's a Jack Russell.'

Mr Patch looked down at the little dog, which wagged its tail. 'It's all they had in the shop,' he said. 'It was either this or a rabbit.'

'Very well. Let it go to its new master.'

Mr Patch leaned down and whispered in the dog's ear, pointing to Harold's front door. He undid the collar and sent it on its way.

Stinky was looking out of the window. 'Oh oh,' he said, beckoning to Ada. 'There's two angels over there.'

Ada crossed to the room and looked out. 'Where?' she said. 'I can't see them.'

'See what,' asked Harold, looking up from the television.

The dog ran across the road, just as Frederick pulled up. He felt the bump as he ran it over. 'Bugger,' he said, getting out and seeing the little black and white body. 'No collar, either. That'll be somebody's Christmas present that's got out.'

Ada looked back at her son. 'Your Uncle Frederick's just arrived,' she said. 'He's carrying something.'

'A dog!' Harold shouted and ran to the door. His face fell when he saw what his uncle was carrying.

An Ungodly Child

'I wanted a live one!' he said, his feet pounding the stairs as he ran to his bedroom. 'I hate you.'

***

Azrael, the angel of death, looked across at his two brother angels. Mr Duke shrugged and pulled Mr Patch away. He looked down.

The little terrier barked and wagged the stub of his tail. Azrael leaned down to pat its head. 'I've got a bit of string somewhere,' he said, patting his black robes. 'You should have been more careful about crossing the road.'

Indoors, things were not as peaceful. Stinky watched all three angels disappear and turned to look at the dead dog. 'What do you want me to do with it?' he asked. 'I could re-animate it if you like, or cook it.'

Ada shook her head. 'Just bury it in the garden,' she said. 'Plant a rose bush over it.' She sighed and looked up the stairs. 'Harold?' she called. 'Frederick's very sorry that he ran over your dog. Would you like a rabbit?'

Chapter 4
A Twist of Fate

It had taken Harold twenty years to build up his shop. His entrepreneurial childhood and constant love of collecting had led him, through market stalls and business school, to open a shop: Harold's Emporium.

He'd been exclusive at first, following the market trend of memorabilia and selling old comics, books and games to the never-grow-old crowd of people (mostly men) who wanted to recapture the lost innocence of youth, if they ever had any. When the economy slumped in the nineties, he'd expanded to second-hand furniture and antiques, though any of the latter he acquired were usually sold at auction.

With the turn of the century his customer base began to dwindle as people looked toward the brave new world of credit and refinancing, and bought new furniture instead of old.

Harold's shop began to lose money.

***

'What can I find for you today, Mrs Clarke?'

She hobbled to the counter, scenting the air with lavender and mothballs. Harold could tell she was wearing her best coat, in case she was seen coming in, in which case she could say that she was looking for antiques. 'I'm looking for a wardrobe, Harold. Ada said you'd got some in'

An Ungodly Child

'I have, Mrs C.' Harold held out a hand to guide her. 'Let me show you.' He led her through a archway to what used to be the shop next door. He'd bought the lease when the demand for ironmongers had dropped with the opening of the DIY superstore in the retail park. 'Here you are. A good selection of well-constructed period pieces.'

'Thank you Harold.' Mrs Clarke began opening the doors and looking inside each of them.

'Are you looking for anything in particular?' Harold asked.

'You did a house clearance for old Mrs Williams in Fold Street,' she said. 'Which one is her wardrobe?'

'I'll have to get my stock book.' Harold went back to his desk to see a familiar figure. 'Reverend Duke,' he said, offering his hand. 'I haven't seen you for years.'

'Hello, Harold.' The man who had set Harold on the road to business hadn't seemed to age a day. 'I was just passing with my friend, and we thought we'd drop in and see if you had any religious artefacts. Jedith is something of a collector.'

Harold turned to the woman beside him and fell in love. She was the epitome of everything he valued in a woman. Long red hair flowed over a travelling cloak of russet brown, a counterpoint to dark brown eyes in a face the colour of sweet coffee. Perfect cupid's-bow lips, their surface the texture of satin.

'I'm sorry,' he said, remembering where he was. 'What were you saying?'

'I said that I've heard a lot about you, Mr Waterman.' She removed her glove and held out an elegant hand. Harold shook it automatically.

'Nothing bad, I hope.' Harold smiled, holding the hand just longer than was polite. 'What do you collect?'

'I am interested in religious memorabilia, Mr Waterman.' Jedith smiled at him, and Harold felt a distinct contraction in his chest 'Are you religious at all?'

'A little.' Harold smiled back. 'I believe in God and the devil, but that's about it.'

'Nothing is ever so black and white, Mr Waterman.'

'Call me Harold.' He looked up as shadows flickered across his vision, expecting to see a moth in front of the overhead light, but there was nothing.

'Much as I hate to interrupt,' said the vicar, 'but we really must be going, Jedith.'

'Of course.' Jedith nodded to him and turned back to Harold. 'It was good to meet you. I hope we can talk more on my next visit.'

'Oh.' Harold deflated. 'You're not staying then?'

'Jedith has business all over the world,' explained Reverend Duke. 'She's a very busy woman.'

'I see.' Harold made a half bow. 'I hope to see you again soon,' he said.

'I'm sure you will.' Jedith turned to leave. 'I'll tell my brother, Asaem, to say hello when he comes here.'

'I'd like that.' Harold waved, then winced as Mrs Clarke collided with the love of his life. There was a brief exchange of apologies before the old lady demanded his attention.

'I'm sorry,' he said getting out the stock book. 'I got distracted.'

'Your lady friend.' Mrs Clarke gave him a knowing smile and touched his arm. 'You like her, don't you?'

'I hardly know her,' Harold replied, colouring.

'She left her glove,' Mrs Clarke said. 'You'd best get after her.'

'Oh.' Harold picked up the glove, holding it as if her hand was still inside. 'She'll need this.' He hurried out of the shop to catch her, but there was no-one in the street. 'That's odd,' he said. 'They must have gone into another shop.'

He returned to the counter, where his customer was working her way through his book. 'It's not here,' she said.

'It must be in the back then,' he replied. 'I haven't put the stuff there in the book yet.'

'Show me?' she asked, looking up at him like a child wanting an ice-cream.

Harold sighed. 'Come this way.'

***

When Frederick brought him his sandwich at lunchtime, he couldn't face it. 'I don't feel well,' he said.

Frederick finished his beef and onion and began to unwrap Harold's egg and cheese. 'That's not like you,' he said. 'I've never seen you ill in your life. You never even had measles when you were little. What's the matter?'

'I've got a horrible pain in my chest,' he replied. 'I don't know what it is.'

'Probably wind,' said Frederick. 'Why don't you go home? I can look after the shop for the afternoon. You'll feel better in the morning.'

'Will I?' Harold patted his uncle on the back. 'I'll take you up on that. Don't forget to lock up.'

Ada was surprised to see him. 'You're supposed to be at work,' she said, switching off the television. She noticed his pale face. 'Harold? Are you all right?'

'Not really, mum,' he said. 'I don't feel well at all.'

Chapter 5
What Fate of Men?

Harold slept, his dreams interrupted by the sensation of something alien growing inside him. For once, he couldn't put it down to late-night television and when Ada woke him in the morning she found his cup of tea untouched. She knew there was something seriously wrong.

'How are you this morning?' she asked. 'Any better?'

Harold groaned. 'No, mum. I'm worse if anything.' He staggered to the bathroom, not certain whether he was going to be sick.

'You need to get to the doctor's,' Ada said, tapping on the bathroom door.

'I can't,' Harold replied. 'I've got to open the shop.'

'Nonsense.' Ada went back into Harold's bedroom and picked out some suitable clothes. 'You're in no fit state to run the shop. It won't hurt for it to be closed for a day, will it?'

'I can't afford to have it closed, mum.' He sighed and sat on the edge of his bed. 'It's losing money. I'm not going to be able to keep it open if business continues to decline.'

Ada lifted his face to meet his eyes. 'Why didn't you tell me sooner?' she said. 'I've got a bit of money put away. We'll get by.'

'I can't eat into your savings, mum. It's all you've got.'

'The business will be closed a lot longer if you fall ill,' she said, appealing to his business sense. 'It's better to be closed today and open tomorrow.'

'All right.' Harold held up his hands in defeat. 'I'll go to the doctor.'

***

Three men watched him climb into his van.

'It looks like he's suffering, Mr Duke,' said the first

'I didn't want that.' Sansenoy looked at his two brother angels. 'It needs to be quick. If he refuses to be the antichrist he should be disposed of quickly and efficiently. I've become quite fond of him over the years.'

'He began to suffer when we warded his shop,' said Semangalof. 'People could only see it if they had it in mind already. His business has declined to the brink of collapse.'

'I didn't mind that,' said Sansenoy. 'That was just economics. He would have found some other means to make a living. I'm not sure that killing him is right, though.'

'Of course it is.' Senoy hissed. 'It will snuff out any power that he has and enable us to invest our efforts into someone more worthy of our attention. We've wasted enough time on this one. He has no potential to be the antichrist we need.'

'Still...' Sansenoy shrugged.

'Would you have us rain fire and brimstone upon his house?' Senoy scowled. 'It would bring too much attention upon us. It's better this way.'

'Deniable,' added Semangalof. 'Jedith could have bumped into him on her own.'

'I wish we'd used Menna instead.' Sansenoy shook his head. 'A terrorist attack would have been much quicker.'

'War on a poxy second-hand shop?' Senoy laughed. 'No-one would have believed it was random. There would have been all sorts of enquiries. No. Pestilence was better.'

***

Harold was distinctly worried now. Doctor Patel had sent him straight round to the hospital for tests. He felt like his arm was empty after the number of blood samples he'd had to give and his head was spinning from the three X-rays. The CAT scan had been the worst experience of his life; having to lie perfectly still in a steel tube might well have made him claustrophobic.

He looked up as a white-coated doctor approached. The name tag, Dr Jarvis, gave nothing away.

'Would you like to come into my office, Mr Waterman?'

Harold gulped. Nothing good ever came from a private consultation with a doctor. He'd seen enough television programs on the subject to know that. He followed the doctor into his office.

'What's wrong with me?' he asked. 'Is it cancer?'

'Not exactly.' Doctor Jarvis opened a medical textbook and turned the page to face Harold. 'It's a very rare infection that attacks your internal organs. Apart from today I've only ever seen it once, and that was in the Middle East'

'You can cure it, though, can't you?'

'We can treat it.' The doctor began writing a prescription. 'Unfortunately, there's no actual cure, but these will keep the symptoms in check, at least for a while.'

'A while?' Harold looked at the piece of paper the doctor had given him. 'How long is a while?'

'Three months, perhaps six if you confine yourself to your bed.' Doctor Jarvis pressed his arm. 'I'm sorry. Your condition is too rare for there to have been any research done on it. Tell me, have you travelled to the Middle East recently?'

Harold shook his head. 'No. Never.'

'I don't know how you contracted it then.' Doctor Jarvis stood and offered his hand. Harold shook it automatically. 'It normally takes six months to show up. You must have the constitution of an ox not to have noticed the symptoms before now.' He opened the door to show Harold out. 'I suggest that you drop in once a week to let us monitor your progress.'

'Will that help?' Harold asked.

Doctor Jarvis smiled. 'Indeed it will. I could get a paper out of this. Have you considered donating your body to medical science?'

***

'Take your tablets, Harold. They'll make you feel better.' Ada pressed a glass of water into his hand. 'I'll make you some scrambled egg later. That's your favourite.'

'Thanks, mum.' Harold stared at the two red and black lozenges. 'Why me? What have I done to deserve this? I've never been ill in my life.'

'I know.' Ada cradled her son's head. 'You don't deserve this, Harold. Not at all. You've never done anyone any harm.'

'Well, I've made a few financial deals that might not have been considered socially favourable,' Harold admitted. 'I've never gone back on a promise though.'

'No, love.' Ada stroked his hair. 'Would you like a cup of tea now?'

'The British answer to everything.' Harold sighed. 'I suppose so.'

Ada went into the kitchen and put the kettle on. 'Stinky,' she said.

The imp appeared. 'Yes Mistress?'

'Get me Jasfoup's candle. I need to talk to him.'

She lit the stub of the candle on the gas burner. 'I'm just popping outside,' she called. 'I left the washing on the line.'

'Okay mum.' Harold swallowed the tablets.

Outside, Ada hurried to the toilet. They'd had an indoor one for years, and Harold never understood why they kept the old one outside lavatory, though he was glad of it when he got locked out at night, because for some reason the floor was always warm.

'Jasfoup!' Ada hissed.

The demon, still wearing the wide-collared leather jacket, emerged from the toilet. 'I've heard,' he said. 'What a crappy thing to happen.'

'I want it fixed.' Ada fixed him with a steely glare. 'At any cost'

'Any cost?' The demon smiled. 'That's easy then. Give him the box.'

'What box?'

'The one that Louis left for him when he was born.' Jasfoup folded a wing around her. 'He'll figure it out.'

***

Frederick patted Harold's hand. There isn't much he could say that didn't sound either flippant or condescending. Just what do you say to a man that's just been given three months to live? Asking him about holiday plans wasn't really appropriate. He cleared his throat.

'At least you won't go grey,' he said, smoothing his unruly mass down.

At least it raised a smile. 'I'll go to my grave with the comfort of that,' Harold said.

'Will you be wanting a church burial?' asked Frederick. 'Only say if you do, because I'll have to see if they've got a plot free. There's stiff competition for them, you know.'

'Har-de-har.' Harold laughed politely, turning it into a cough as Frederick frowned. 'You didn't mean that to come out as a joke, did you?'

'What joke?' Frederick pulled some pamphlets out of his pocket. 'I stopped off at Jenkins' on the way and picked up some brochures.'

Harold took them off him. 'Caskets and budgeting plans?' I've only just been diagnosed, Uncle. Don't you think it just a tiny bit tactless to pick up funeral leaflets?'

'It's best to be prepared, Harold.' Frederick patted his hand again. Harold pulled it away.

'Will you stop doing that? It's un-nerving.' He opened one of the brochures, more to amuse himself than keep Frederick happy. 'I don't want a cardboard box and a tree,' he said. 'That may be what hippies want, but I want something traditional.' He turned the page. 'That's more like it,' he said, pointing to an oak coffin carved with angels. 'I'll have that one.'

'Are you sure, Harold?' Frederick took the brochure and turned to a different page. 'You wouldn't prefer something plainer and er... cheaper?'

'No, Uncle Frederick. I want to be interred in the mausoleum at the manor, anyway. Don't worry about the cost, I've got life insurance, remember?'

'Not against Acts of God, Harold. That voids the policy.'

'How can a disease be an Act of God?'

'Well, you never go to church, do you?'

'The vicar told me I didn't have to.'

'He's been retired for years, Harold.' Frederick continued to look at the brochure. 'It's Reverend Mackenzie now.'

'I didn't know that. I saw Reverend Duke yesterday, actually, just before you came in. He had this foreign woman with him. Jenny, I think her name was. She was a stunner.' Harold fell silent. 'Wait a minute,' he said. 'Do you think my illness has something to do with her?'

'How could it have? You said that the doctor reckoned you've had it for months.'

'True.' Harold lapsed into silence. 'I might pop up there anyway, though. I could do with confessing my sins and whatnot.'

'That's Catholics, Harold. You're C of E. What have you got to confess, anyway?'

'I've coveted my neighbour's wife, for a start.'

Frederick looked shocked. 'Mrs Farthing? She must be ninety if she's a day.'

'Not Mrs Farthing, per se, no. I mean generally. Girls that come into the shop, that sort of thing.'

'Oh.' Frederick smiled. 'Everyone does that, Harold. Even the angels did that.'

'Yes, and look what happened to them.'

'They had babies?'

'They were condemned to everlasting torment.'

'Ah.' Frederick fell silent. 'Well, you know more about it than I do, Harold. You're the reader of the family.'

'I was.' Harold sat back again. 'Shall we have fish and chips for tea?'

'Can you manage it, do you think?'

'Of course I can. I'm not an invalid.' Harold stood up. 'If I'm leaving this mortal coil I'm going out dancing.'

Frederick laughed. 'Good for you, Harold.' His face clouded again. 'You can't dance though.'

'Who can't dance?' Ada's voice sounded from the kitchen.

'Harold,' Frederick said. 'He wants to dance off the mortal coil.'

'Huh.' Ada came back in carrying Harold's tea. 'I've seen his dancing. It'll earn him no favours.'

'I am still here, you know,' said Harold. 'I haven't died yet.'

'Sorry, Harold.' Ada patted his arm in exactly the way her brother had. 'There's something for you in the kitchen.'

'What?' Harold asked.

'You'll have to go and see.' Ada paused. 'Actually, you might not be able to manage it. Frederick, would you mind?'

'Of course not, Ada.' Frederick stood up and fetched the box

'Where's that from?' Harold asked. 'It hasn't got any way of opening it.'

'It was your birthday present,' said Ada.

'Six months early?' Harold asked.

Frederick put it onto the coffee table. 'Thirty years late. Not a mark on it in all that time, either,' he said. 'That's good workmanship that is.'

'Thirty years?' Harold repeated. 'You've kept a present for me for thirty years? Who was it from?'

'Your father,' said Ada. 'Louis.'

Harold sat down. 'Why have you kept it for so long? It's probably full of toys.' He shuffled forward in his chair and touched it. There was a click as it opened for the first time since he was born. 'What's in it?'

'I don't know, Harold. Your father said to keep it until the time that you were desperate.'

Harold hesitated. 'I'll open it later,' he said. 'It's waited this long, it can keep until tonight.

Chapter 6
The Birthday Box

When Frederick had left and Ada had gone to bed, Harold sat alone with his thoughts, looking at the photograph of his father on the mantelpiece.

It showed a sunny beach with two figures in the foreground. The smaller, rounder figure was his mother wearing a rather daring, for the time, bikini and a straw boater. On her right was a tall angular figure, slightly blurred, that she claimed was the only photograph she possessed of his father, Louis. Harold took after him, though it was difficult to see from a slightly blurred black and white photograph, in his darker than average colouring. All that he could really tell from the photograph was that his father had towered over his mother and that he had a large amount of very white teeth.

Harold wondered what had happened to his dad. It had been hard to grow up without one, and he had depended on his mum for the support that both parents normally gave to a child. She had never married, though she had 'gone dancing' with a fair number of suitors, claiming always that no-one could match up to her Louis and he had spoiled her for other men. His closest male role model had been his Uncle Frederick, and although he meant well enough, Harold had known by the time he was eight that he had been standing at the back of the queue when brains had been given out. Even so, Harold adored him, and after the fashion parades of his younger years, first dressing as a hippy, then cropping his hair in the punk rock style, and finally the velvet and leather of the Gothic crowd, he'd adopted the style favoured by his Uncle Frederick: baggy corduroys and warm cardigans. Harold had never had a girlfriend – or a boyfriend, come to that – and had always attributed this lack of a soul mate to his superior intelligence and self-protective aloofness.

He'd had friends, certainly, though none he would have called 'close'. What friends he had were more of the kind that asked for his help on their homework in exchange for tea cards or cereal-packet toys. He'd never been one to pass over reading a new book to play a game of football at the back of the old garages on Princes Road, or miss a trip to the local museum to lounge on the swings in the council park. By the time he was twelve he had already had a thorough knowledge of all the subjects he was taking for his exams, and was well on the way with his self-assigned extra-curricular lessons in Latin and Greek, the better to read the Classics of literature. By the time he was fourteen, he was making a decent amount of pocket money by handing out photocopied sheets of the week's homework, though that quickly ceased after the English teacher queried why fourteen pupils had all handed in identical essays on the 'The Preposition and its Place in Language'.

He looked at the box again. The oak was bound with iron, looking exactly like a pirate chest There was a part of him that didn't want to know what was inside.

Harold hesitated for a few moments before swinging open the lid. There were no glittering doubloons, no bolts of fine silk, and no handfuls of mixed jewels. Covering the rest of the contents was a faded white linen cloth. He removed it to find a long wooden box that fitted the chest perfectly. Harold lifted it out, noting that there was a second cloth beneath it protecting whatever was on the bottom of the chest He examined the box, admiring the intricate inlays and carvings of fantastic beasts. It was obviously old. The craftwork had been executed with considerable dexterity and bore remarkable similarities to medieval woodcuts. He set it on top of the linen and opened it.

He was looking at a brace of exquisitely carved daggers. The blades were eighteen inches long and inscribed with complex sigils that

Harold, despite his eclectic reading, had never seen. The handles were of carved ivory in the shape of grinning gargoyles, their protruding feet doubling as quillions. Harold picked one of them up. This was more like the treasure he'd been thinking of. The figure appeared to be actually clinging to the handle, and he could imagine them coming to life at a moment's notice. He almost had a heart attack when he saw that the eyes glittered, but with a smile he noticed that they were tiny inset rubies.

He tested the blade against his finger, and pulled it away with a yelp when the blade sliced through the fleshy pad like a hot knife through runny jam. Gingerly he replaced the dagger in its box and sucked his finger, turning his attention once more to the chest

He lifted away the second piece of linen to expose a book. His heart began to pound with excitement. He loved books, especially old ones, and this one looked to be a rare copy of something. He felt a tingling throughout his body as he studied it, the flesh wound on his finger forgotten for now. It was a large book, full eighteen inches by twelve even when closed. The binding was old, cracked leather of an animal that he didn't recognise, and he was very careful as he lifted it out.

There was no lettering on either the cover or the spine, though there were indentations in the leather as if it had rested upon something jagged for a prolonged period. There were four long horizontal stripes on the front cover and a matching, though shorter, one on the back. A handprint, perhaps, Harold thought, indicating that the book had been held in one position either for a very long time or else by someone with immense strength.

Carefully he opened the cover, noting with fascination the letters 'LCF', his father's initials, in faded brown ink on the inside cover. The paper inside was fine vellum, scraped so thin as to be translucent, enabling him to see a ghost of the first page underneath the flyleaf. He turned the page and felt a thrill of anticipation as he read the title.

Manipulating the Ethereal
Eagerly he turned the page but was disappointed to find it written

in the same language as on the blades of the daggers. He turned a second page and a third, with a growing sense of disappointment. If the book was in this strange tongue, he thought, then why was the title written in English, and modern English at that?

He flicked through the rest of the book, noting that the vellum, although probably the thinnest he'd ever seen, was still thick enough to prevent the book from having more than forty pages or so. Several pages contained illustrations and he shuddered at the depiction of a medieval demon with a ledger. It was probably, he surmised, an early heretical text discussing the nature of damnation, written by a monk bored with his work in the scriptorium. He held open a second illustration with his left hand whilst he tried to decipher the accompanying text with his right, in the misplaced hope that running his finger over the words would somehow make them more legible.

With a muffled curse he saw that the cut on his left finger had bled onto the vellum and he pulled his hand away, wondering if he had reduced the value of the book or increased it. He riffled through the book backwards again before putting it away.

When he got back to the first written page, he was astounded to see that the text was now legible and in English. It was like magic.

Actually, he thought, the reason that it was like magic was that it probably was.

His heart pounding with nervousness and holding his breath with anticipation, he made himself comfortable and began to read.

On the Summoning of Demons
Like the other denizens of the Lower Planes, Demons are devious little buggers. Rest assured that if they see a loophole they will take full advantage of it and drag the would-be sorcerer down to the planes without so much as a by-your-leave. The solution to dealing with such an entity is to exploit any loophole in any contract (whether verbal or written) before the demon has any idea of what you're up to.

An Ungodly Child

Harold frowned. With any other book of such age he would have expected the phrases to read more like: '*Alike unto other infernal Hellspawn negotiation is fraught with such difficulties as cannot be understated,*' with the occasional lump of punctuation thrown in seemingly at random, and spelling optional. This book, though obviously old, seemed to be written entirely in modern colloquial English. He flipped the book over again and looked at the spine. He knew for a fact that it was at least thirty years old, and by the looks of it far older than that: no later than seventeenth century by his own estimate. There was only one plausible explanation: Magic.

It really galled him to admit that. Harold was always loath to accept any conclusion unless he had a reasonable argument to back up the theory. The idea of something being a magical artefact was contrary to everything he believed in. He sighed, his thirst for knowledge battling this time with his innate suspicion of anything that he didn't understand. The book, however, was like a bottle of water to his thirst

He resumed reading.

> *The average demon will always want something of value in exchange for their services. This applies to even the lowliest of intelligent form from the humble, hardworking imp to the greater demons of the pits. Value is relative, however, for something deemed worthy to the eye of a mortal may be a useless bauble to a demon if he would gain no prestige for the possession of it. Gold or jewels, for example, would mean nothing to a demon, which could at any time gather such things for itself. Notable exceptions, for there is a loophole to every clause, are when the mortal offers so much gold that he is forced to commit sin to remain in the lands of men, or when the desired demon is of the order of succubae, who are suckers for a pretty jewel.*

***

The appearance of a footnote was a little disconcerting, and Harold quickly scanned to the bottom of the page where there was writing in a markedly different hand:

***

Ensure that the jewel in question is of perfect clarity and a minimum of forty carats. Rubies for preference, followed by sapphires, emeralds and pearls. Offerings of compressed coal will do you no favours whatsoever, unless you want them rectally inserted.

He rubbed his eyes, which had inexplicably begun to water. He knew where he could get his hands on a decent sized ruby, though it would cost him a pretty penny if his mum discovered the loss. However, that was for later. He sill had no idea how to go about getting any of these creatures to come to the house. He found his place on the page and continued.

The sacrifices rendered for the services of demons vary in cost An imp might ask only for the severed limp of a warrior, which can easily be obtained by the simple expedient of walking through the site of a battle with a jar or two of formaldehyde or a box of salt. A being of a higher order will require a significantly greater gift. Those of the lower levels of the infernal pits might ask for the heart of a sovereign, for example, or the head of a saint, to prove to them that the summoner risks his own infernal damnation in pursuit of his aims. There are lesser creatures of both the lower and higher planes that require smaller sacrifice and semi-sentient beings, such as this book, require the simplest of arcane ingredients, such as blood, though increasing amounts are required to retain such a creatures cooperation.

An Ungodly Child

Harold nodded. He was far more ready to accept the supernatural if there was a defined order to it. He examined the book again. The concept that it was actually a living being was surprising, though the twisted logic of it needing a sacrifice of blood in order to be read made a kind of sense. Harold grinned. Knowing the rules would enable Harold to bend them. The pursuit of the infernal would be an interesting challenge to occupy his final days and he made a mental note to locate a war zone for some necessary parts, though a trip through Brixton on a Saturday night might well enable him to procure the artefacts he needed.

> *As ever, look for the loopholes in every ritual and contact. A demon has a strict code of conduct, and will honour every bargain made if it is (a) in its power to do so and (b) solely within the letter, if not the spirit of the contract made. No doubt the resourceful and intelligent reader has already surmised a method of applying this fact to the reading of the remainder of this book.*

Harold nodded again, grinning. He was way ahead on that one.

> *Thus he has an accurate and provable method to test the truth of the text, and will not, therefore, dismiss the remainder as idle fairy tale. Note, however, that dismemberment of the book will result in the bound entity being freed and the pages returning to their original unensorcelled state.*

He laughed aloud, abandoning the thought of closer examination of the tome with the aid of a scalpel and pot of glue. That such a thought had occurred to the writer was indicative of their relative intelligences.

> *One final word of warning, then, for the would-be practitioner of the darkest arts before you delve further: Do it to them before they can do it to you.*

Harold laughed again. The concept of hell plagiarising television dramas didn't surprise him in the least He turned the page to see a drawing of the traditional pentagram within a pentacle and continued reading.

The summoning of a demon can be performed most easily to begin with by the use of the pentagram. Demons are very traditionalist, and once they use a particular idea for a century or two they are loath to adapt to a new concept. Although it is not strictly necessary to construct a portal, since any demon worth his membership badge will be able to construct his own with the merest thought, the casting of one is akin to the opening of a door for a lady you wish to court. Although it is not required, it is also a point of manners to invite the demon to enter, since it affirms your free choice to join the ranks of the damned. Dancing about naked on hilltops is also optional, though it can be amusing to watch.

To the North give the element of Earth. A handful of mud from the garden will do, although again it is polite to use a pinch of dirt from the grave of your grandmother; intention being part of the spirit of the contract. Widdershins to the West place a gift of Water. Again, tap water will do, unless you can be bothered to collect the dew from a spider's web at midsummer. East relates to Air. Though it is tempting to leave this blank, under the premise that air is already there, it is again good practice to think of something a little more creative. Collect a jar of baby's breath, for example, or place a handful of cloud in an open bowl. South, being opposed to West, is fire. A candle will do fine, although making one of the rendered fats of a loved one will gain you a big tick in the ledger. Finally, in the centre, place the element of Spirit. A cheapskate would drop a little blood and a sycophant would bind a ghost to serve as fodder. Stay within those extremes for success.

An Ungodly Child

Next you must perform the summoning itself, and I advise these simple precautions:

Choose a decent time. Although midnight on a dark moon is traditional, it is not strictly necessary. When the kids are out will do just fine. Nothing buggers up a summoning more than a child asking for a bowl of cornflakes at an inopportune moment, and it isn't easy to explain the absence of milk in a three-mile radius when you've accidentally summoned the Infernal Devil of Wheaty Bricks.

Choose a decent place. Graveyards are traditional; cellars are adequate. The back room of a pub on Saturday lunchtime is right out. It provokes a lot of difficult questions, and there is a good chance you will be Barred For Life.

Choose a decent language. Arcane Latin has a lovely feel for it and it's very tempting to perform a version of the black mass, but cock up an inflection and you're history. Trust me: use whatever language you're reading this in.

Choose a decent gift. If the demon insists upon the head of a saint, it won't be fobbed off with the cranial cavity of the head of the local PTA. Check your local pope for the definition of 'saint' if you're uncertain.

Choose the words. Flowery language is often pleasing to a denizen of the pit, but bandy about words like 'your eternal servant' and you'll be taken literally: you'll be mucking out the stables for a hundred millennia with no tea breaks. Stick to plain language and you'll avoid most of the loopholes. Write it down first. Better still: consult a lawyer to read through it as well. Tell him you're a writer doing research.

You now know everything you need to summon your first demonic entity, except one. You need to know the true name of a demon. There are two ways of going about this. The first involves thirty years of research in ancient libraries examining dusty tomes relating the names of the Fallen as written in the collected manuscripts of the ancient texts. The second method is to pour blood onto the box below. There is a rota of demons willing to be summoned and the name of the next on the list will be revealed. Note that this has to be your own blood. No amount of rats' intestines will do the trick.

Harold looked at the carefully inscribed box marked on the page. It was fairly small, considering the size of the book, and he estimated between six and ten drops would cover it. He hesitated then reached for the dagger. 'What the hell?' he thought, realising immediately how ironic the phrase was in the circumstances.

He pricked his little finger this time, making a tiny cut so that the blood would drip freely, watching carefully as the blood was absorbed into the page and vanished to leave behind a name.

Jasfoup.

Chapter 7
The Attic Room

Harold sat in the darkness, the only illumination coming from the fire and the candle still burning on the windowsill. It had been lit for as long as he could remember, and he had always assumed that his mum changed it regularly. Now he wasn't so sure.

Knowing that his father trafficked with demons was a revelation he was having a hard time coming to terms with. Although he had never been devoutly religious, Harold had always accepted the existence of Good and Evil as opposing supernatural forces in an abstract way, believing that even if there wasn't a higher power it was better to be safe than sorry. To find out that there really were beings from Heaven and Hell and that he could actually meet one was something he would have to get used to.

He glanced down at the ritual again. If he wanted to summon this Jasfoup, it would have to be done tomorrow. Although he could rustle up the ingredients required, they wouldn't be exactly right, and the book had made the point that it was the intent and thought behind the offerings that made a difference.

He had three months to live. Summoning a demon could wait until tomorrow.

Harold yawned and went to bed. The pain had subsided with the tablets that the doctor had prescribed, and he could open the shop tomorrow, and begin the process of closing it down. He didn't want that job to fall to his mum after he died.

***

'Will you look after the shop for the afternoon, Uncle?'

Frederick looked up from his book and made an exaggerated show of looking around the empty shop. 'I think I can manage this rush of customers, Harold. Are you really certain about selling everything for half the marked price?'

Harold nodded. 'It all needs to go,' he said. 'I don't want you and mum lumbered with the business after I'm gone.'

'Don't talk like that, Harold.' Frederick took out a handkerchief. 'It's upsetting.'

'How do you think I feel? It's me that's going to die.' Harold instantly regretted the words and laid a hand on his uncle's arm. 'I'm sorry,' he said. 'It's a bit difficult, you know.'

'That's all right, Harold.' Frederick patted his hand. 'You must be going through a lot of emotions. I can't imagine how I'd fare under the same circumstances. Have you taken your tablets today?'

'Yes, uncle, thank you.' Harold rolled his eyes. 'Mum asked me that three times before I left the house, and then phoned me to make sure.'

Frederick forced a smile. 'Don't mind your mum,' he said. 'She just worries about you. What are you going to be doing this afternoon then?'

'Just a walk in the sunshine,' Harold replied. 'I spend my whole life in this shop, and I think that I'm missing out on the beauty around us.'

'In Laverstone?' Frederick laughed. 'Sorry. I know what you mean, Harold. I'll be fine here, you just take your time and I'll see you tomorrow.'

'Thanks, Uncle.' Harold put his jacket on and picked up the canvas bag he'd prepared earlier. 'If you get a chance, would you start photographing the memorabilia? I'll put them up for auction online.'

'Will do.' Frederick put a finger in his book to mark the page. 'You go and enjoy your walk. I'll be fine here.'

Harold closed the door, took in a deep breath of the High Street and coughed for five minutes. When he recovered he walked down to the traffic island at the bottom. It was difficult to get to. In order to cross the busiest intersection in Laverstone you had to either climb over the railings on the roundabout itself, or else walk on the roadside of them for fifty yards. Only then could you dodge the traffic to get to the centre. He wondered if many motorists knew of the existence of the little hermaphroditic cherub that spent all year pouring algae-ridden water into a concrete shell. The cherub didn't seem to care. Under the dark grime of years he still laughed, despite having lost his nose to corrosion.

Harold patted the dirty stonework and took an empty jam jar from his bag, filling it with the water that dribbled from the cherub's vase. The microbe infested filth that passed for water in what was once a drinking fountain would, he hoped, be a suitable offering for his demon.

He worked his way back to the pavement and went up Latimer Row to the butchers, where he purchased a pound of sausages and a hot pork sandwich which he ate in the churchyard of St Jude's. Feeling a little guilty at what was bound to be a heinous sin, he used his time there as an excuse to gather a jar full of dirt from the grave of William Brimming, 1796-1852, the founder of the town and original owner of the manor where his uncle now lived. Not exactly his grandmother's grave dirt, but at least it was chosen with due consideration.

A brief visit to the supermarket yielded a loaf of bread, a box of candles, a packet of salt and a box of matches for the princely sum of £1.68 and Harold walked to the park feeling that even if life was coming to an end he was embarking upon his greatest adventure in it.

At the park he sat on a bench overlooking the lake, drinking cappuccino from a cardboard cup with a straw. A pleasant ten minutes were spent feeding the loaf of bread from the supermarket to the ducks, something he hadn't done since he was a child. When the bag was empty, he threw both it and the cardboard cup into the litter bin, but used the straw to suck air from the second jam jar. Clean park air would probably be appreciated by a denizen of the lower depths.

He screwed on the lid and put it back in his pack. All was now ready for the summoning. The only things left to collect were a few embers from the fire after his mum had gone to bed, and his own blood.

***

'Don't stay up too late, Harold.' Ada kissed his cheek on the way to bed. 'You need your beauty sleep, remember.'

'I need about a hundred years of it to do any good.' Harold laughed. 'Goodnight, mum. I may do a bit of sorting out in the attic before I go to bed, though. It's still early.'

'Well...' Ada patted his shoulder. 'I know you want to settle your affairs and everything, but don't be too late.'

'I won't, mum.' Harold smiled up at her. 'Goodnight, sleep tight.'

'Don't let the incubi bite,' his mother finished.

Harold frowned. 'I thought it was bed-bugs?'

'Not in this house,' Ada replied. 'I won't have them in.'

She was wrong, of course. Several had come in over the years, dormant and attached to pieces of old furniture Harold had brought from the shop. Stinky treated them as snack food.

Harold gave her ten minutes before making himself a thermos of tea in the kitchen to take upstairs. When he was sure she was in bed, for he could hear her television, he scooped some embers from the fire into an empty soup tin and headed up to the attic.

Although it had come ready floored when Ada had bought the house, the attic was unused, except by Harold for storage of his collections. The house had been bought for cash for £600 in 1972 and according to the deeds held the lease on the land for three hundred yards in all directions. This was handy for Harold and Ada, because the payments on the leases of the four adjacent houses went rather neatly to pay the council's increasing taxes upon this one.

Harold had visited the solicitor, Mr Isaacs, several times over the years, marvelling how the old prune, who was ninety if he was a day, still managed to continue practising. He was very reasonable in his rates as well. He had been happy to take on Harold's own legal requirements, and the file relating to the Emporium had grown steadily over the years. His last visit to the old attorney had been curious, though, for as he put the papers into the folder, Isaacs had said, almost to himself, 'We shan't be needing those again.' When Harold had asked why not, the solicitor had looked blankly at him and denied saying anything at all. Harold had left the office feeling a little uncomfortable, as if everyone but he could see the scything rotors of the helicopter of doom whirling at his heels.

Setting his tea and his thermos flask to one side, Harold opened the book and drew the pentagram within a circle, aligning the top point to North and outlining the chalk with a circle of salt. The salt was a personal addition. Although the tome had made no mention of it, it was such a common practice in all the horror films he'd watched that he thought it was a good idea. He was pleased with the effect, as it wasn't easy to draw a perfect circle freehand: it had taken him several days, and three reams of paper, to perfect the skill as a child.

Following the directions, he placed the jar of grave dirt on the northern edge of the circle, the water to the west, the air to the east and the embers to the south, mentally marking them off and moving his finger down the page as he did so. He placed a candle at each of the points of the star and stepped back to pick up one of the pair of gargoyle daggers, which he placed in the centre of the circle.

Harold took a deep breath and consulted the book, satisfied that he had, at least so far, done everything correctly. He took the box of matches and lit the candles then turned out the electric light and picked up the blade. The gargoyle's ruby eyes seemed to glitter in anticipation. He gulped, suddenly at a loss for words, and was forced to make something up, the speech he'd carefully written and memorised earlier in the day forgotten.

'Um,' he began, 'I, Harold Waterman, Magician of the First Order, do solemnly declare this portal to the pits to be open and, um, bless all those who sail in here.' That could have sounded better, he thought, as he sliced along the base of his thumb. He was expecting it to hurt, and was pleasantly surprised when it didn't. He resisted the urge to suck it and instead allowed the blood to drip to the floor in the exact centre of the circle.

'I summon a demon to bend to my mastery. I summon a creature from the infernal pits. I summon a being of power that will grant to me that which is mine by right. I summon Jasfoup.'

Harold paused, his hair standing out at odd angles on his arms and neck, as if he was in a field of static electricity. Several sparks arced from the air onto the blade he held and he felt a roaring in his ears as the air pressure in the room changed. He took a step backwards and looked around. Nothing had changed. The pentagram was still there, all the candles were still lit and the jam jars were in the correct spots. The air pressure equalised and his ears popped. The sparks died, and his hair flattened again.

Harold lowered his arms, disappointed. Had he really been so gullible to believe that it would work? Magic was just for fairy tales.

'Sight.'

The tiny voice seemed loud in the stillness of the room. Harold, startled, looked down. The carved gargoyle on the dagger blinked its ruby eyes and spoke again.

'Sight.'

'What?' Harold didn't understand, and his confusion was evident. The tiny creature grumbled to itself and uncoiled from the handle.

'You don't have the Sight,' it explained, its shrill voice sounding loud despite its size. 'You can't see the creatures of the outer planes without the Sight. Bring me up to your face and look me in the eyes.'

Harold did as he was asked, staring the ugly little creature in its tiny red eyes. The creature stared back, then drew back its paw and poked Harold in both eyeballs in quick succession.

'Ow!' Harold instinctively dropped the dagger and covered his eyes with his hands, not moving then until the sudden pain had diminished and the stars he was seeing had faded.

'There's gratitude for you,' said the tinny voice from the level of his feet.

An Ungodly Child

'Tch! You can't please some people no matter what you do,' said a similar voice from the dagger case.

Harold opened his eyes ready to shout at them, but instead of speaking his mouth opened and closed in gaping astonishment.

The demon had come.

***

Ada looked up at the ceiling. 'He's done it,' she said. 'I can feel the portal.'

Her companion nodded. 'He took his time,' he said, black wings wafting away the smoke from his cigar.

'I told you he'd unlock his potential one day.' Ada pulled the duvet over her chest 'Why are portals so cold, when the place they open from is so hot?'

Masculine hands ran up her arm. 'I can warm you up again.'

Ada giggled.

***

Harold shivered and took a step backwards. The demon was big, though not so large that it didn't fit into the attic. Part of him wondered if the demon changed its size according to its surroundings, and whether, in that case, if Harold had performed the summoning in, say, the downstairs toilet it would have appeared less formidable.

He regarded the demon in silence for a moment. It was reminiscent of a chimera, with a lion's body and a scorpion tail, but its head was more like a dragon than an eagle. Leathery bat wings were folded across its back and its black scales were slick and oily; light playing across it in the way that that a flame licks at paper before it ignites on an open fire. Dark eyes glittered with malevolent intelligence beneath brows of ebony scale, and a mouth of ivory daggers let forth the stink of sulphur and brimstone. Harold gulped, certain that he was out of his league.

A tinny voice sounded from floor level. 'Ha!' it said, 'that'll teach him drop me hilt first onto a hard floor. I could have broken my arm, falling like that. It may not be much to him, but that was thirty body lengths to me. I might have reached terminal velocity, falling from that height.'

Its pair joined in. 'Bite his foot. That'd be a lesson for him. Mind you, look what he's called up! Looks like he might have reached terminal summoning.'

Both voices cackled, and Harold was tempted to kick the first dagger, but didn't know if it was a personal friend of the demon. Politeness, he felt, was the order of the day.

'Um.' He was at a loss for words and cleared his throat before trying again. 'Greetings, O Demon from the Pits. I have summoned you.'

The creature shifted, smooth muscles rippling under skin that changed to feathers, then to fur and back to scales, as if it couldn't make up its mind as to what it wanted to be. It turned its baleful stare at Harold and spoke; its voice rumbling like subterranean earthquakes.

'I can ssseee that,' it said, rolling the sounds, 'though it was a pitiful amount of blood ssspilt. Why hassst thou summoned me thusss?'

'Um, I thought we could strike a bargain. You know: my immortal soul for unlimited wealth and power, that sort of thing.'

The demon chuckled. 'You sssoul is already forfeit for daring to invoke me, ssso it ssseems that you have little to bargain with.'

Harold bowed, playing for time while he thought of something else. The demon waited expectantly, its tail flicking backwards and forwards and then arching over its head. It stretched its wings out, and they fitted neatly into the exact width of the roof space. Harold calculated that if the normal laws or aerodynamics applied they were insufficient to carry the creature aloft.

'Assuming I can think of something to bargain with,' he said, 'What is it that you can offer me, exactly?'

The demon shimmered in the candlelight, jaws dripping with blood and gore that vanished as it hit the floorboards It regarded the magician standing before it. 'I can ssshow you the sssecrets of the

Universe,' it hissed. 'There are none more powerful than I in all the bowelsss of Hell.'

Harold grinned, sensing a shift in the balance of power. 'If you're the most powerful,' he said, 'then why does it say 'level 5, second class' on your nametag?'

The demon growled and looked down, craning its neck so that it could see the offending article. It groaned and deflated, folding its wings until they were the merest shadow, its tail disappearing as its body shrank until a tall man stood in the circle, skin as ebony-black as the creature's, but far easier on the senses. He wore a paisley shirt and a seventies-style brown leather jacket over a pair of corduroy jeans and loafers. He sniffed and checked the state of its fingernails, tutting as he picked a piece of dirt from under one of them.

'You've got me there, mate. People expect the dramatics and I don't like to disappoint.' He nodded to the thermos flask next to Harold's bag. 'Is that tea in there?' he asked. 'I haven't had a cup of tea in ages.'

He stepped out of the circle, forcing Harold to take a step backwards in fear. 'How do you do?' he said. 'You can call me Jasfoup. You must be Harold Waterman.'

Chapter 8
A Bargain Struck

Harold sat down on the little table, knocking his canvas bag to the floor. 'How did you know that?' he asked. 'Some sort of magic?'

Jasfoup shrugged. 'Maybe,' he said. 'We call it a DNA spectrograph. We lost too many contracts through not learning the client's true name.' He paused. 'That was your blood you spilled, wasn't it?'

'Yes.' Harold narrowed his eyes. 'Could I have used someone else's?'

'Of course.' The demon grinned, displaying for a moment the same mouthful of ivory daggers that he had had in his other form until they were replaced with a normal human set. 'Wait till you want to summon a really big one that calls for eight pints of blood. You won't be so keen to use your own then.'

'I suppose not.' Harold opened the thermos. 'I hope you like sugar. I've put it in already.'

'All demons like sugar,' Jasfoup said. He pointed back at the circle. 'That ring of salt? Rubbish. Make it a ring of sugar and you'll buy yourself ten seconds while the demon eats it.'

'Ten seconds? To do what?'

'Say a few memorable words. Void your bowels, that sort of thing.' Jasfoup took a sip from the plastic mug. 'This is good,' he said, 'though a little stale from being in plastic. I prefer china, personally.'

'Now you owe me something in return for the tea,' replied Harold, grinning.

The demon laughed. 'Good try, but we struck no bargain. You

gave it willingly and without promise of reimbursement.'

'Then what if I offered you,' Harold paused, purely for dramatic effect, 'the head of a saint?'

The demon smiled. 'That's the ticket, old bean,' he said. 'That's a much better bargaining tool. For the head of a saint I would offer you a service. Just the one, mind, or perhaps a pair if it's a travel ticket you're asking for.'

Harold considered his request carefully. 'My immediate problem is that I'm dying.'

'Everyone's dying,' Jasfoup replied. 'That's the nature of life.' He picked up a fashion magazine and flicked through it. 'Is this current?' he asked, looking at the cover.

Harold glanced at it. 'It's last month's,' he said. 'My problem is that I'm dying rather quickly,' he said. 'I have only three months left to live.'

'And you want me to cure you?' Jasfoup opened a page of men's suits. 'Would this suit me, do you think?'

'I suppose so,' said Harold. 'If you had better cheekbones and lost the sideburns. Yes, I want you to cure me.'

'All right.' Jasfoup put the catalogue down. 'Take off your clothes.'

'What?' Harold shrank back. 'Is that necessary?'

'Only if you want me to see what's wrong with you.'

'Oh.' Harold began to unbutton his cardigan. 'I see. Don't look.'

Jasfoup chuckled. 'I can see into your soul,' he said. 'Why are you bothered that I see your mortal flesh?'

'You're right, I suppose.' Harold still turned his back as he undressed, presenting the demon with a good view of his flabby backside.

'Turn around then.' Jasfoup approached the naked mortal, sniffing at his skin. He gave an experimental lick. 'You've had curry,' he said. 'I haven't had curry in years.'

'Can you tell how to cure me from a lick?' asked Harold.

Jasfoup stood back. 'Yes,' he said. 'You can put your clothes back on.'

'You only licked my shoulder,' Harold protested. 'Why did I have to take my trousers off?'

'It amused me,' said the demon. 'Did you want me to lick you a bit more? We could negotiate that.'

'No.' Harold coughed and dressed again, feeling humiliated. 'Can you cure me?'

Jasfoup hesitated. 'I can stop you from dying,' he said. 'I know what's wrong with you.'

'What?' asked Harold. 'The doctor at the hospital said it was a very rare disease that they have no cure for.'

Jasfoup nodded. 'You have Amalakitis,' he said. 'The scourge of Israel. It's very rare indeed.' He stared at Harold for a moment. 'You haven't met a beautiful woman lately, have you? Red hair, likes to touch things?'

'I have, actually.' Harold remembered the woman the Reverend Duke had brought in to the shop. 'Do you know her?'

'I should do,' said Jasfoup. 'She's my ex-wife.'

'She's a demon?' Harold shuddered, thinking how much he had desired her.

Jasfoup laughed. 'Oh no,' he said. 'Quite the opposite. She's an angel.' He stepped forward and placed the plastic cup on the table, helping himself to another cup of tea. 'The angel of Pestilence.'

'Oh.' Harold sank down onto a cardboard box full of old comics. 'I'm the victim of God's hitman?'

Jasfoup laughed. 'In a way,' he said. 'You must have annoyed someone high up.' He took a sip of the tea. 'You're lucky I got here in time.'

'I summoned you, remember.' Harold grinned, the weight of his imminent death lifted. 'Go on then. Cure me.'

Jasfoup hesitated. 'It's not as easy as that,' he said. 'If you had a cold, perhaps, but you're asking me to circumvent the will of those above.' He pointed upwards. 'It's going to be tricky. Besides, I didn't say that I could cure you. I said I could stop you from dying.'

'How is that different?' Harold paused. 'You're not going to turn me into a zombie, are you?'

The demon laughed. 'No. You watch too many horror films. I can't rid you of Amalakitis but I can make you able to live with the disease and go on to live an exceptionally long life.'

'How exceptional?'

Jasfoup shrugged. 'Five hundred years. Maybe more.'

'That's great.' Harold was so pleased that he clapped the demon on the back. 'Do it.'

'It's not easy,' Jasfoup replied. 'It requires a complete transfusion of blood.'

'That shouldn't be too difficult,' Harold said. 'We can get that from the hospital.'

'It has to be your father's blood.'

'Oh.' Harold was crestfallen. 'I don't know where he is. I've never even met him.'

Jasfoup smiled and put his arm around Harold. 'Not to worry,' he said. 'We can deduce half of it from the DNA in your blood. We'll need to extract twice the amount, though, so start eating plenty of red meat for the iron. The rarer the better.'

'And the other half?'

'We'll have to find a sibling of yours,' Jasfoup said.

'I'm an only child, though.'

Jasfoup nodded. 'I didn't say it had to be a current one, did I? This is going to be a great adventure for both of us.'

'I can't leave the shop, though. I can't afford to.'

'Then we'll pick up some money on the way.' Jasfoup smiled. 'How much do you need?'

'That depends upon how long it's going to take,' said Harold. 'If it's a couple of weeks, then a few grand will cover it.'

'A few grand?' Jasfoup whistled. 'I have been gone a long time. Where would I get that sort of money?'

'I thought demons could grant you anything?' Harold said. 'A bank vault?'

'All right.' Jasfoup produced a roll of parchment from his jacket pocket. 'Do we have a bargain?'

Harold teetered on the brink of destiny. 'I suppose so,' he said, taking the paperwork. He unrolled it and began to read. 'What does this clause mean?' he asked, pointing to a particularly nested loop of 'party of the first part' clauses. The demon glanced at it over his shoulder. 'Don't worry about it,' he said. 'It just means that should you attempt to negate the contract by confessing your sins on your deathbed, the act of confession becomes a falsehood unto God and condemns you anyway.'

'Oh.' Harold sighed. 'You think of everything.'

'I try to,' said Jasfoup. 'You should have seen the Reformation. Contracts were flying like confetti, then one person recants his sins on his deathbed and they all follow suit. We had to reword it after that.'

Harold patted his pockets. 'I don't have a pen.'

'Here,' said the demon. 'A quill made from an angel's wing tip. Think of it as a head start into damnation.'

'Gee, thanks.' Harold looked at it. 'There's no ink.'

'Very funny.' Jasfoup picked up one of the daggers. 'Guess what we use.'

Harold sighed again. 'You keep some traditions alive then.' He signed where Jasfoup indicated and the demon countersigned it, also in Harold's blood.

'It wouldn't be a tradition if we didn't,' said the tinny voice of the dagger.

Jasfoup rolled up the contract and put it back in his pocket. 'Now to business,' he said. 'I believe you mentioned the head of a saint?' The demon narrowed his eyes. They were nearly as formidable as his mum's. Visions of wooden spoons came to Harold's mind.

'Wait a moment, then,' Harold said. 'I'll just nip and get it.'

Harold crossed to the other side of the attic and switched on the overhead light to look through his collections. He located the right box and opened it, flicking through the contents until he found what he was looking for. 'Thank God for efficient filing systems,' he thought.

He walked back to the demon, who had picked up the two daggers and was letting the gargoyles climb up his arm and swing off his fingers. 'Nice daggers,' he said. 'I haven't seen a pair like that in forty years.'

'Oh?' Harold was suddenly struck dumb. Perhaps the demon knew his father. 'When was that, then?' he asked.

'When I was summoned last,' Jasfoup grinned.

'Did you know my father?'

'Probably. We see just about everyone, eventually. Who was he?' The demon made a high pitched noise and the two tiny gargoyles climbed back onto their respective daggers.

'Louis de Ferre.'

The demon coughed. 'Nope,' he said. 'I've never heard of him. Is he still alive?'

'I don't know,' Harold replied.

Jasfoup patted his shoulder. 'That must have been hard on you when you were a nipper.'

Harold nodded. 'It wasn't too bad,' he said. 'I'd never had a dad, so it wasn't like I missed him or anything, and there was always Uncle Frederick.'

'Uncle Frederick?' repeated the demon with a bark of laughter. 'You're going to tell me that you've got a mum called Ada in a minute!'

Harold couldn't have been more surprised if he'd sprouted wings. 'That's right, she is; I mean, I have,' said Harold. 'How did you know?'

The demon narrowed his eyes for a moment, then shrugged. 'Just a lucky guess.'

'That's a complete lie! You know my mum!'

The demon shrugged. 'It's my job to lie,' he said. 'Also to cheat, steal, use sacred language, burp, pass wind, eat, covet, and fornicate, when I can be bothered. I'm extremely good at that, as a matter of fact. Mostly, though, I lie, and that's the honest truth. Or not, as the case may be.'

'Next time I summon you,' said Harold, 'it'll be for knowledge.'

The demon sniffed. 'If you get to summon me again, which looks doubtful as you don't appear to possess the aforementioned head.'

'That's where you're wrong,' replied Harold, holding out a small card. The demon took it.

'What is this, mortal man?' he asked; his tone just a little deeper than before.

'It's a tea card of Peter O'Toole as John the Baptist, in the film Salome of 1959. Very collectable.'

'It is not sufficient. It must be a real head of a real saint.' The demon glared at him.

'That's not what the book says, and you agreed to the price. This is the head of a saint, is it not?' Harold was firmly on the right side of the loophole here.

'I suppose so.'

'And you required the head of a saint to fulfill the contract?'

'Yes...' The demon looked doubtful.

'Then technically, the contract is filled.'

'Technically? I suppose so, but Hell was not built upon technicalities. I shall ponder upon this.'

'Ponder away, but I require your part of the deal.' Harold said, whilst in his head he sang 'I'm a Believer', realising that it was now lodged in his brain and it would be days before he would be rid of it. Evidently, Hell was no stranger to the addiction of catchy tunes.

The demon, still examining the tea card, looked up. 'Close your eyes and count to ten,' he said. Harold was suspicious.

'You're not going to welch on the deal, are you?' he asked.

'Certainly not. This is just the way it's done. Look, if it makes you feel any better, I'll keep a hand on your shoulder the whole time.'

Harold nodded. 'That sounds reasonable,' he said. 'Okay, here I go.' Harold closed his eyes and felt the weight of the demon's hand on his shoulder. It smelled of dirt and graveyards, and put images of rotted flesh into Harold's thoughts. He did his best to ignore it and counted. 'One... Two... Three...' By the time he got to nine, the demon told him to open his eyes, and he gave a yelp of fright as a severed hand fell from his shoulder.

An Ungodly Child

The demon, who squatted on the floor draining the last of the tea, grinned. 'I couldn't help it,' he said. 'It was in the vault as well.'

'As well as what?' Harold kicked the limb away and looked around, and his mouth fell open. 'Oh my Go—' he stopped himself just in time, 'Goodness,' he said. 'I'm going to prison!'

The demon looked up from where he was licking out the thermos flask, his long tongue flicking quickly in and out of the warm opening, seeking the last traces of sweetness. 'Why?' he asked. 'I thought prison was something people tended to avoid going to if they could, like carpet warehouses?'

'I never thought that there would be so much money in one vault,' replied Harold, feasting his eyes on the piles of banknotes.

'It's what you asked for, isn't it?' said the demon smugly.

Harold looked at the stacks of notes all carefully sorted into rubber-banded packages. 'How much is there, do you think?' he asked.

Jasfoup sucked air through his teeth. 'Hard to say,' he said with an easy air. 'If you pressed me, I'd say it was just short of a quarter of a million.'

'Pounds?' Harold asked, incredulous.

'Of course pounds. It was an English bank. You owe me another two cards, by the way.'

'Why's that?' Harold asked, suspiciously.

'On the last visit, I left your business card on the floor of the vault,' said Jasfoup. 'One card and I pick it up, the other is for going there in the first place.'

'You traitorous wretch!' exclaimed Harold.

Jasfoup shrugged. 'I never denied that I was anything but,' he said.

Harold brightened. 'They're very collectable, aren't they?' He went back over to his collection and extracted another tea card. 'This one is Ingrid Bergman as Joan of Arc in the 1948 film,' he said.

Jasfoup took the card and sighed wistfully. 'She was so pretty,' he said, his voice soft and distant.

'Who was? Ingrid Bergman?'

'Joan d'Arc. She was so gullible too.' Jasfoup mimicked using a telephone. 'It was easy. 'Hi Joan. It's God again. Just do me a teeny favour and destroy the English, will you. They're barbarians, and they ate your poodle when you were a little girl.' She fell for it every time.'

'You're despicable,' said Harold, fascinated despite himself.

'It worked out well enough for her,' said the demon, amused. 'She got her sainthood, though ironically, she now works as a gopher for Saint Swithin, who's English.'

Harold barked a laugh. 'Won't they notice all this is missing?' he asked, indicating the money.

Jasfoup shrugged. 'What if they do? They won't be able to trace it to you. The vault wasn't broken into.'

Harold grinned. 'More tea?' he asked.

Jasfoup nodded. 'That'd be lovely. I'll be right down after I've cleared up that loose end.'

As he passed the door to his mum's bedroom, Harold noticed that there was still a light shining under the door, and he could hear that the television was still on. He debated knocking on the door but as it was half-past one in the morning, he decided against it. It was quite likely that she had fallen asleep in front of the television.

As he passed her door, however, her voice rang out.

'Harold? Is that you?'

He debated telling her that it wasn't him, but a demon from the lower planes of hell come to grant them with immortality in return for a video of Coronation Street, but decided against it. If she was in the wrong mood, such a blatant untruth would result in a visit from Mr Spoon.

'Yes, Mum, 'tis I, Harold, your first born and beloved son.'

'Don't come in! I'm not decent.' Harold had had no intention of doing so.

'Okay, Mum. Did you want something?'

'Have you finished playing in the attic now? There's a hell of a draught.'

'Yes, mum. I've just got to put a few bits and pieces away, and I'm done for the night.'

'That's good. You were keeping me awake.'

'Sorry, Mum'. Harold rolled his eyes. Fifty channels of television were more likely to be the cause of keeping Ada awake. Especially the adult channels she subscribed to. He moved on past her door.

When he got to the kitchen, Jasfoup was already there waiting for him. 'That was quick,' said Harold. The demon laughed.

'Of course,' he said. 'If we took as long as mortals to do things, we'd still be bickering over whether Lucifer fell or was pushed.'

'Which was it?'

Jasfoup shrugged. 'A bit of both, really. Current theory is that Michael tripped him by tying his shoelaces together.' The demon grinned.

Harold laughed. 'Tea?' he asked.

Jasfoup nodded. 'Show me how to make it,' he said, 'and I'll give you a lollipop.'

'Deal,' said Harold automatically. 'Why have you got lollipops?'

'Because all the tubes of sherbet went past the sell-by date,' Jasfoup grinned. 'Four sugars, please.'

Chapter 9
Revelations of the Past

Harold woke to the insistent ringing of his alarm clock the next morning and had to fight the seductive embrace of sleep to open the shop. It was several moments before he remembered his condition, and he almost wondered what the point of getting up was.

He threw off the duvet in the hope that the sudden cold would rouse him and rubbed the sleep from his eyes. He yawned and stood, wondering, as he scratched his testicles, if the events of the night had been a strange dream, but the stink of sulphur and brimstone emanating from his washing basket testified to the reality of the demon.

Harold shuffled to the bathroom, brushing his teeth first and then having a wash and shave before getting dressed and going downstairs.

His mother, with her instinctive sense of timing, awoke just as he was making tea, her voice drifting like poison gas down the stairs.

'Harold ?'

Harold sighed and went to the bottom of the stairs. 'Yes, Mum?' he called.

'Have you taken your tablets?'

'Yes, Mother.' He hadn't yet, but a little white lie wouldn't hurt. 'Do you want a cup of tea?'

'Yes please. I'll be down in a minute.'

Harold went back to the kitchen and made two cups. While the tea brewed he took his tablets and made up a bowl of cereal then carried it through to the living room.

An Ungodly Child

He stopped short in the doorway. Sat in front of the fire was a short creature with green scaly skin, satyr legs and a monkeys arms. He couldn't see its face, as it was busy adding small pieces of coal to the flames, building up the fire to an even burn.

'Who the hell are you?' he asked.

The creature turned, revealing a reptilian snout and tiny black eyes. It looked at Harold for a moment then followed his gaze to the fire and back again.

'Me?' it asked. 'You can see me? That's not right.'

'Of course I can see you,' he said. 'Why wouldn't I?'

'You never could before.' The creature stood, unfolding its legs so that Harold could see its hooves, and flicked its tail like a hairless cat. 'You've got the Sight,' it said. 'When did you get that?'

'Last night,' Harold replied. He came further into the room and sat down. 'How long have you been here?'

'Since you were wee,' replied the creature. 'I look after you and the mistress.'

Harold put his bowl on the coffee table and sat down. 'I always wondered when mum made up the fire,' he said. 'I always thought that she lit it and went back to bed.'

The creature grinned, showing a double row of needle-sharp teeth. 'That's my job,' it said. 'I've never missed a day yet.'

'No, I know.' Harold nodded, details of his life that he'd thought strange clicking into place. 'You're the one that stopped Tommy hitting me, aren't you?'

The creature nodded. 'That was a long time ago,' if said. 'He'd been bullying you, and mistress asked me to put a stop to it.'

'No-one ever bullied me again.' Harold smiled and held out his hand. 'Pleased to meet you,' he said. 'I'm Harold.'

'I know.' The creature wiped coal-blackened hands upon its scales and put it in Harold's. It was surprisingly warm for a reptile.

'And you are?' Harold prompted.

'Sorry. I'm forgetting my manners.' The creature smiled. 'I am referred to as Collector-of-Flotsam but your mother calls me Stinky.'

'Stinky?' Harold laughed. 'I always thought she was swearing when she said that. What, er, breed of demon are you?'

'An imp, sir. A lowly class but the backbone of the Inferno. We do all the crappy jobs the other demons don't want, like mucking out the souls.'

'Mucking them out? I thought that souls were metaphysical?'

'They still leave little piles of sin about though, and the occasional lump of goodness.'

'Did you bring my tea in, Harold?' Ada bustled through the door and stopped short. 'Oh.'

'Stinky and I were just catching up,' said Harold. 'Funny how you never mentioned that we had a house guest'

'Oh, Harold.' Ada dismissed his indignation with a wave of her hand as she sat down. 'Stinky isn't a guest He's part of the family.'

'Then how come I've never had a birthday present from him?'

'You've never given him one, have you? It's better to give than to receive and all that.' Ada picked up her tea. 'So what did you summon?'

'Summon?' Harold took great interest in his cereal, which had gone soggy.

'Yes, summon.' Ada fixed him with a glare. 'I know you opened a portal last night, Harold. I could feel it. Besides, you've got plasters all over your hand.'

'Oh, that.' Harold moved his hand out of her line of sight. 'I summoned a demon. Only a little one, mind.'

'I hope you know what you're doing.' Ada rested her teacup on the saucer. 'I daren't imagine what goes on in your head sometimes. Do you remember that time you set fire to the house because there was a spider in the bathroom?'

'That was a long time ago,' Harold protested. 'I was only seven. It seemed like a good idea at the time.'

'That was a case of too much late-night television that you weren't supposed to watch.'

'I used to watch those with him,' Stinky said. 'I liked the ones where the two mortals would roll about on a bed.'

Harold coughed. The best defence in such situations was not to argue, and to change the subject. 'I found a loophole in the contract, though. He's working for tea cards.'

'Will he help you with your problem?'

'Sort of.' Harold picked up a spoonful of cereal and let them fall back into the sludge. 'He can't cure it, he said, but he can extend my lifespan beyond my natural years to negate its effects.'

'Good.' Ada could have easily been talking about his school report as a demon in her attic. 'What was its name?'

'Jasfoup,' said Harold.

Stinky rushed to clean up Ada's dropped tea.

***

Harold was well settled into his second cup of tea and was contentedly trawling through the small-ads in the newspaper when his uncle Frederick turned up, smoking a pipe filled with his usual brand of foul-smelling tobacco. 'Morning, Harold,' he said. 'How's business today?'

Harold put his pen down and picked up his tea. 'Afternoon, Uncle. Slow as usual. Even the half price sale isn't drawing any customers in.'

'No.' His uncle shook his head sadly. 'I blame it on the economy,' he said. Harold nodded encouragingly.

'When the economy is rising, people won't buy old stuff,' continued Frederick. 'They only want the new-fangled furniture and what-not. When the economy goes down, people can't afford to buy anything but the basics.'

'So what we need,' Harold extrapolated, 'is an economy that's stable but only just above poverty level, so that people can afford to buy what they need, just not at new goods prices.'

Frederick nodded. 'It's a shift in the social unconscious that we need,' he said, 'in the old days, you wouldn't dream of buying anything new unless you'd seen everything that the local shops had to offer second hand. Nobody thought about throwing money away if they could help it, and second hand was always the first choice. And if you finished with something, then you passed it on to someone else who needed it.'

Harold agreed, and passed him the packet of tobacco he'd bought that morning. 'I read a story about these on-line auction houses yesterday,' he said. 'People are buying and selling everything on there. There was one case where a chap was selling his son's soul, and made hundreds of pounds on it, even though none of the people bidding believed in souls. There was another where a woman was selling access rights to her own breasts, like selling off land with a title attached to it.'

Frederick shook his head. 'The things you see nowadays,' he said.

Harold smiled and didn't argue. Part of last night's conversation with the demon seemed applicable to Frederick, and he poured them each a cup of tea from the pot.

'Funny you should say that, Uncle,' he said. 'Do you believe in angels?'

Fred looked at him over the top of his pipe. 'Perhaps,' he said. 'Why do you ask?'

'What if I'd told you that I'd seen a demon?'

Fred sucked the end of his pipe thoughtfully. 'What sort of demon?' he asked, eventually. 'A big one? Little? The night-time sort?' he winked.

Harold shuddered and considered. 'It was big and scaly to start with,' he said, 'but then it changed into a normal person size.'

'Are you sure you weren't just dreaming it?'

'Yes.' Harold pulled out a wad of fifty pound notes. 'I'm pretty sure. He offered to help me out with my medical condition.'

Fred nodded thoughtfully. 'In exchange for something worthwhile, I'll bet. They don't do something for nothing, do demons. I had a deal with one once. It offered me a wife in return for something I hadn't used for years.'

'Oh?' Harold leaned forward, fascinated. 'What did you do?'

An Ungodly Child

'I accepted, of course. She was a pretty little thing, if you ignored the tentacles.'

Harold gulped. 'What did you give in return?'

'That's the tricky bit; the demon didn't tell me what it would be, you see. He took me todger.'

'What?' Harold was astonished. 'What did you do?'

Fred gave a bark of amusement. 'There wasn't a lot I could do, was there? I couldn't even pee standing up. She left me, of course. I couldn't perform me' wedding duties. I still miss my little darling Ngnol.' He sighed. 'Still, that was a long time ago. What did this one want from you?'

'Tea cards.'

'Tea cards? Like you used to get in with the tea?'

Harold nodded. 'Not at first, exactly, but once I'd convinced him about how collectable they were, he was all for it.'

'Did you learn his true name in all of this?' Fred asked, giving an air of superior experience.

Harold nodded and leaned forward conspiratorially. 'His name is Jasfoup,' he whispered.

Fred nodded and smiled. 'I always wondered what had happened to him,' he said. He used to pop in and out of your ma's outside lavvy when you were a nipper.' Frederick took a swig of the yellow sludge he referred to as tea.

'You've seen the demon before then?' asked Harold.

'Yes. He was all right, that demon. Used to give sherbets to the kids.'

'Sherbets?'

'Yes, yellow tubes of sherbet with a stick of liquorice in them.'

'I know what you mean, it's just that the concept of a demon from Hell handing out sweeties to itinerant children is a difficult one to grasp.'

'Oh, it was his nature. We just had to sign our names on his autograph album and he'd give us a sweet.'

'Sign your name in his autograph album?' Harold laughed.

'Aye. They were all the rage then. So he's come visiting you, has he? It must run in the blood.'

'What blood?' Harold knew that there was a pattern here, but couldn't quite grasp it.

'My dad, your grand-dad, God rest his black heart, was a bit of a dabbler in the Black Arts. Haven't you ever wondered how a humble coal merchant made enough money to buy Laverstone Manor?'

Harold nodded. It made sense. 'So it was Granddad that first summoned up Jasfoup, then? He wouldn't talk about it.'

'He probably didn't want to scare you off, after what happened to Dad.' Frederick said. Harold waited for him to continue.

'So what happened to Granddad? I don't even remember him. In fact, I don't think I've ever seen so much as a picture of him.'

He died before you were born, Harold. Nasty business, it was. I'm not surprised that Ada doesn't have any pictures of him.'

'Go on. What happened?'

'It was in 1962 when he told me what he'd been doing. I think that he knew that his time was nearly up, and he wanted to pass on the knowledge so that it didn't go to waste. I was just a young lad, then, with dreams of being a writer and a poet, and I thought he was being a bit optimistic. I could see the sort of creatures that were hanging about at the time, and I didn't much like the look of some of them. Demons and devils and ghosts and what-not used to be all over the house. Not any more of course, except for one or two that have been there for a long time anyway. These were all attracted to what Dad was up to. He was trying to find a loophole in the contract.'

'What sort of contract?'

'The usual,' Frederick said. 'All the money you could ever spend in exchange for your soul when you die. The obvious loophole, see, is not to die, and that's what he was trying to achieve. There were dead things all over the place, where he'd tried to take their life essence for his own.'

'What sort of dead things?' Harold was shifting radically between intensely curious and absolutely disgusted.

'Mice, rats, dogs; small creatures he could easily get hold of. If he could have, I'm sure he would have started on people as well. Not that he had the chance. I saw the demon called Jasfoup a few times. He was always polite to me. Helped me with my poetry, he did, on more than one occasion. I've still got the book of sonnets he gave me for a birthday present once. All handwritten on really thick sheets of paper. Really old, too. Sonnets, mostly, though there were a few bawdy limericks mixed in amongst them.'

'But what happened to Granddad?' Harold asked.

'I'm getting to that.' Fred stared at his pipe for a moment and re-lit it, puffing on it several times until the bowl began to glow brightly. 'That was the problem, see. Too many dead things. Lord knows, if you'll forgive the expression,' Fred chuckled, 'what sort of spirit Gods that these critters had, but they certainly weren't very pleased with him. When he read a book which told tales of cats being the repositories of spirits that was it; he decided that he had to sacrifice a whole load of cats to extend his lifespan. Jasfoup warned him that it wasn't a good idea, and even came to me to ask for my help in preventing him, but he locked the door to the cellar and wouldn't let anybody inside.'

Harold waited with bated breath as his Uncle Fred stared into the distant past, reliving the day.

'Jasfoup went back inside, because doors didn't really mean a lot to him, and I could hear a lot of shouting, then there was this really intense bright light shining under the door and everything went quiet. I nearly died of fright when the lock clicked and the cellar door opened, but all that came out was this orange tabby cat, sauntering past as calm as you please, tail held bolt upright with just the tip of it flicking the air.'

Fred shook his head and gave a bark of a laugh. 'You could have knocked me down with a feather,' he said. 'There was I, expecting all manner of fearsome demon to come charging out and instead I'm confronted with this cute little pussycat. Well, what could I do? I was as tense as a watch spring with fear and suddenly there's nothing to be afraid of. I laughed. And do you know what? That cat turned back to look at me and winked. I swear it! Funny things, cats. I've respected them ever since.'

Harold leaned back in his chair and took a biscuit from the packet. 'Is that why you always put out a saucer of milk and some cat food at night?' he asked.

Frederick nodded. 'Take care of the cats and they'll take care of you,' he said. 'I've yet to find one that's prepared to go up and fix the roof, mind.'

'So what had happened to Granddad?' Harold asked.

Frederick put down his pipe, the merest tickle alluding to tears gathering in his brown eyes. 'There's the rum thing,' he said. 'I plucked up my courage and went down into the cellar, and the only thing there was Jasfoup, packing things up into a wooden chest There was no sign of my dad, nor of the cats he'd taken down there, nor even of all the ghosts that had been cluttering the place up for weeks. I looked around and there were a few scorch marks on the wall, and a big splash of blood on the floor, but nobody else was there. 'Where's me dad?' I said to Jasfoup, and he looked at me with those big red eyes and he said: 'Gone.' 'Where?' I said, and he pointed down. 'That's it then,' I said and he handed me the crate. 'These are yours now, Frederick,' he says. 'if you want them.' Then he was gone.'

'What was in the crate?' asked Harold, suspecting that he knew all too well.

His uncle looked at him. 'If you've met Jasfoup, you already know. The book, the altar cloth and the ritual daggers.'

'When did you next see Jasfoup?' Harold asked. 'When you wanted a wife?'

'Aye.' Frederick nodded. 'I used the stuff in the box to call him up, and he put me on to a mate of his to arrange the marriage, like. I tried one of the incubuses first, but that didn't work out.'

'Succubus, you mean?' prompted Harold. 'I was thinking of summoning one of those myself.'

Frederick looked at him strangely for a moment. 'Succubus, aye,' he said. 'Mind you, be careful around them, young Harold. Comely they might be, but remember what they are underneath the fur.'

'Skin.'

'Aye, or skin. They're still demons, and if they can get you to agree to a little bonus on the side then they will. They've got a bigger agenda than a quick roll in the hay.'

Harold leaned forward again. 'What sort of bonus on the side are we talking about here?'

Fred shrugged. 'That depends,' he said. 'It could be that they exchange a night in your body for the skill to write poetry.'

Harold laughed. 'What would a succubus get out of this deal? Why would they want to borrow your body?'

Fred leaned forward conspiratorially. 'Haven't you ever wondered why so many demons look human?' he asked. Harold raised his eyebrows, and Fred sat back again, nodding and tapping his nose with his forefinger.

Harold changed the subject. 'Where was Mum during this?' he asked.

'She turned a blind eye to all of it,' replied Fred. 'She didn't want to know what was going on, and wouldn't believe me when I told her that Dad had been devoured by all the demons of Hell like a plate of scampi and chips without the lemon. She thought he'd run away like Mum did when we were little. That's why she has no pictures of him. She said that since he'd run out of her life, she would have nothing more to do with him.'

'But my dad ran away, too,' Harold interjected.

'That's different. He had business to attend to, he said. I was the last one to see him, when he asked me to give those boxes to your mum.'

'What has Jasfoup got to do with my dad?'

Frederick shrugged. 'I don't know. They were friends, I think. He was always hanging about, peddling his sherbet, and to be honest, I always thought that he was keeping an eye on me and your mum, making sure we were all right. I think your dad asked him to.'

Harold nodded. 'So you inherited the house, then?'

Fred nodded. 'For all the good it did me. We did it properly, of course, and had it valued first Your mum didn't want the house, and I didn't want to leave, so we divvied it all up, taking the value of the Manor into consideration. Fat lot it did me, mind. There wasn't much money left after the taxes, and now it's in a bit of a mess because I can't afford to keep it up. Want to buy a Manor, Harold? One tenant, no trouble?'

Harold laughed. 'Only if Mum would come and live there, too, and there's precious little chance of that.'

Frederick shook his head sadly. 'She wouldn't,' he said. 'She's always hated the place.'

'Because of Granddad?'

Frederick nodded. 'Partly,' he said, 'But mostly because she's worried that Louis won't find her again if she moves.'

Chapter 10
A Devious Pact

Frederick had left Harold with significant food for thought. After Frederick had gone home, still driving Betsy after all these years (though to be fair he'd changed all the bodywork twice and the engine three times) and Ada had gone to bed, he brewed another thermos and went up to the attic.

Harold renewed the pentagram, omitting the salt since it served little purpose, and laid out three more of his precious tea cards. He picked up one of the gargoyle daggers. The little creature opened a ruby eye and winked.

'Can't resist it, can you? Once you have a little taste of power you can't put it down. Slip me a little of that scarlet nectar, boy, and summon away your soul.'

The twin to the voice rose from the box. 'Why did you pick him again? You used him yesterday; it should be my turn today. Use me, and I'll give you fashion advice.'

Harold paused. 'What sort of fashion advice could a semi-sentient piece of animate bone give me?' he asked.

There was a scuffling from the knife case, and a tiny bone head poked out over the side. 'Well, for a start, cardigans should only be worn with a pipe and slippers, unless you're a teacher of the very young and need somewhere to keep your handkerchief,' it said. 'You're a sorcerer now so you need to look the part. A long black robe, perhaps, or a decent selection of leather. Green wool does not go with the profession, trust me.'

'Don't listen to him,' the first gargoyle hissed. 'He has no clue about fashion for the discerning killer. What you actually need is a leather bikini and a pair of fish-net stockings and high-heeled boots. You'd look the part then rightly enough.'

The second gargoyle barked a laugh. 'Can you really see him in a leather thong and thigh-high boots? This is Harold the Magnificent; he wouldn't want to wear that sort of stuff. Not without pay-per-view.'

'Wouldn't I?' Harold looked from one gargoyle to the other. 'I mean, I wouldn't, no.' He looked at the figure on the dagger he was holding. 'Sorry, chum,' he said, 'but I think that the evil twin is right on this one.' He put the dagger back into the case and picked up the second, its occupant winding itself quickly into place on the handle.

'Good man, you know it makes sense,' said the second gargoyle. 'You really haven't got the figure for hard-sell sexy.'

Harold rolled his eyes and before he could talk himself out of it, strode into the middle of the circle and cut a nick into the base of his thumb, just below the cut he'd made the previous night.

'I call thee, great Jasfoup. Attend me, O being of mighty power from the depths of Hell.'

He stepped back as the candles guttered and the mists swirled, watching them coalesce into the familiar form of the black skinned creature he had enlisted the aid of the previous evening. The demon blinked.

'Good evening, Harold,' he said. 'Is everything well?'

'Yes, Jasfoup,' Harold replied, stepping back into the open area of the attic. 'I have further need of your services.'

The demon grinned. 'Always happy to oblige,' he said. 'What can I do for you?' His eye fell upon the tea cards arranged neatly next to the circle. 'Usual rates, I see, and you've made tea, too!' He picked up the cards and studied them happily for a moment while Harold poured the tea. 'So what would you like this time?' he asked, adding sugar to the cup.

'You knew my grandfather,' said Harold. Jasfoup chewed and

looked at him with raised eyebrows. 'Yes,' he replied, pocketing one of the cards.

'What happened to him?'

Jasfoup shrugged, his wings opening momentarily as stabilisers. 'He tried to make a deal with the Powers That Be to extend his lifespan,' he said. 'It backfired a little bit.'

'How much is a 'little bit'?' Harold sat on one of the cardboard boxes and Jasfoup sat opposite him.

'He was dragged kicking and screaming into the pit of the heretics, whilst another entity took advantage of the distraction to come out of the pit for a while.'

'What other being?'

The demon shrugged again. 'One of the higher ones. No harm done though, she was due some leave. Schedules and rotas had to be rearranged, and we lost the inter-planar Infernopoly Cup that year, but nothing serious, unless you count the fine for landing on a hotel on the Happy Hunting Grounds as excessive. She did quite well in politics for a while, as I recall.'

'What about Uncle Frederick?'

'The poet? He was left alone until he required our services. I gave him some advice about sorting out the estate before I left, though.'

'And mum? You mentioned her yesterday, and then said you didn't know her.'

'Did you expect me to give out information for free? I've known your mum for years, though she hasn't summoned me since you were ten.'

'Why then?' Harold sat forward, his tea almost spilling from the cup.

Jasfoup smiled. 'Do you remember Mr Parsons?'

'My social sciences teacher? He was horrible. I was glad when he left to join a monastery.'

Jasfoup grinned and polished his nails on his jacket collar. 'I can't say I was surprised when you summoned me, though. There's always been a deep well of power in your family. It goes back centuries, you know.'

'Uncle Fred said that you used to pop in and out of mum's toilet.'

The demon laughed. 'True enough. I used her outside lavvy as a portal for a while, until the deal I made with your grandfather expired. Technically, I should have stayed at the Manor but with the death of the father, I had no wish to impose on the son. Besides, that housekeeper of his...' Jasfoup shuddered.

'Uncle Frederick doesn't have a housekeeper.'

'Just because you've never seen her.' Jasfoup laughed. 'Now you have the sight you'll meet her soon enough. Molly is a ghost'

'You were scared of a ghost?'

'Not at all. She used to tut very loudly whenever I put a cup down. There's a limit to the number of times you can feel comfortable when there's someone polishing the rosewood every time you lift your cup.'

Harold raised his eyebrows. 'You didn't know mum very well then, did you? She still does that if I forget to use a coaster.'

'It was easier with your mum,' Jasfoup said. 'She just never let me have a drink.'

Harold refilled their tea from the flask. 'You know, Jasfoup,' he said. 'I've never really had someone I could talk to like this. I was always a bit of a loner.'

'Billy no-mates,' said Jasfoup, sympathetically. 'Or Harold no-mates, in your case.'

'I wish you were always around.' Harold looked for the sugar, but the demon had finished the packet.

Jasfoup grinned. 'It could be arranged,' he said. 'We could do a deal.'

'I'm not giving my soul up.'

'I told you: it's already forfeit.' Jasfoup grinned. 'Don't worry, we'll come to some arrangement.' He stood and stretched, his wings extending like an umbrella in a force five gale.

Harold stood too. 'I'll drink to that,' he said, and they smiled as their plastic cups thudded together.

***

An Ungodly Child

Harold woke very early the following morning. He and Jasfoup had had an eclectic conversation the previous night, from the culture of Florence in the fifteenth century, where Jasfoup had learned much of his formal education amongst the minor court magicians and sorcerers, to the recent cinematic releases of modern special effects films, particularly those which edged closer and closer to a reality that Harold had never before dreamed possible. The cinematic fantasies of angels and demons upon the streets of modern London were, he had assumed, flights of childish fantasy, but now that he had joined the ranks of those with the Sight, he found it un-nerving just how accurate such adventures were, and he was led to wonder just how many of these writers had the Sight themselves.

Jasfoup, on the other hand, had cited the snowball effect. Once one film had used the premise successfully then others would follow suit.

What Harold found strange was that although he'd ended up going to bed at a ridiculously late hour, he'd awoken bright and fresh and significantly earlier than usual. It was, he surmised, a consequence of being exposed to someone who didn't appear to sleep at all.

Harold took advantage of the early hour by taking his tea in the attic. He recalled a passage in the book that had mentioned the summoning and binding of a menial servant, which held a certain appeal. Although the servant was mentioned, there was no spell in the chapter he'd revealed which gave details of the necessary rituals.

Selecting the less abusive of the two gargoyle-headed daggers and holding it for a change in his left hand and cutting his right just below the thumb, Harold allowed blood to drip onto the book until the text was revealed. He gave a satisfied smile and settled down to read.

> *On the Introduction of a Servant*
> *No sorcerer is complete without a servant of the lower planes to fetch and carry and perform the menial tasks with which the sorcerer does not wish to concern himself. This leaves him free to indulge in the higher function of life; of*

amassing the knowledge that he will need, the fortunes with which to perform his work without interference, and the pursuit of sin.

To summon the servant, one requires the use of a sanctified area and a bribe, normally of food. One need not know the name of the creature, for many are willing to answer, giving as it does a certain prestige amongst their own kind. The binding of the servant for a period of time to be determined requires the use of a suitable gift, but fortunately one of proportionally lower value than that required to summon a being of higher power. The brain of a warrior, if one can be obtained at reasonable cost, or the hand of a hero should be considered sufficient to entice the creature into service.

Harold closed the book with a grin. He knew exactly what he could use as bait. He went downstairs to the kitchen and made a cheese sandwich, then returned and took care to sanctify the ritual circle again, lighting the candles before preparing his payment, keeping it carefully out of sight for the time being.

With a grimace, he reopened the cut under his right thumb and dripped more blood onto the floor, then added the cheese sandwich. He stood back.

'Um... I hereby summon a servant of Hell that is willing to be bound for a term of service. I offer food with no thought of return as a measure of faith.'

He paused and waited until, with the sound of a pane of glass being cut, a tiny hand appeared and stretched a hole through the air as if it were a tent flap. A face soon followed: a snout full of teeth followed by tiny red eyes and a long forehead topped with pointed ears. Harold was put in mind of a goblin and expected the creature to hiss like a kettle when it spoke.

He was a little disappointed when it pulled its little hoofed feet through the gap and looked around the room. 'You're an imp!' he said.

'That's right.' The creature narrowed its eyes, its brow ridges deepening into craters. 'Greetings, Sorcerous One,' it said cautiously. 'I have answered your summons, and thank you for the gift of food.' It nodded as if it had ticked something off in its head and picked up the sandwich, folding it once before stuffing the whole thing into its mouth and swallowing.

The imp looked around. 'It's a bit of a dump here,' it said. 'You could do with a spot of decorating, if you ask me. I could help you out with that if you like.' It paused and for the first time looked at Harold directly. 'For the right price, naturally.' It grinned, showing the amount of needle sharp teeth that Harold was beginning to think of as representative of the creatures of the lower planes.

'It's funny you should say that,' said Harold enthusiastically. 'I had in mind something of the sort when I asked you to come.'

'Oh yes?' said the creature with a grin. 'You do know that there is a price attached to the service of an imp, don't you? Especially an imp of my stature.'

Harold suppressed a laugh. The imp was all of eighteen inches high. 'Indeed I do,' he replied without hesitation. 'I believe the price of the hand of a hero was suggested as appropriate?'

'It would, yes,' said the imp, continuing to view the room. 'Not that they're easy to come by these days. They used to be ten for a goat, of course, but these days they're worth a sheep each.'

Harold smiled, sure of his loophole. 'I have not only the hand of a hero, but an almost unending supply of them.' A phrase from the small ads in comics came to mind. 'You too could be the envy of your friends.'

'Friends?' said the imp, his interest suddenly awakened. 'I could have friends?'

'Indeed,' said Harold, with a salesman's smile, 'envious ones.'

'Will I have to call you 'Master'?'

'We can negotiate that,' said Harold, 'but it would be nice if you did.'

'How many hands are we talking about here?' asked the imp.

Harold considered. 'Forty, perhaps,' he said, thinking of the size of the box he kept them in.

The imp nodded. 'I could call you 'Master' for that,' he said. 'We're talking a lifetime of service, I presume.'

'My lifetime, yes,' said Harold, unsure of the longevity of imps. The imp nodded in agreement. 'As short as that?' it asked. 'I agree.'

'Excellent!' exclaimed Harold. 'How do we seal the bargain?'

'You just have to give me the hands,' said the imp, 'and we're done. I don't stay with you when you're not actively requiring service, though. I do have my own work to get on with as well.'

Harold nodded. 'Terms agreed,' he said, and picked up the box he'd made ready earlier.

The imp took it and looked inside. 'These are no good,' it said. 'These are plastic. What kind of low down trick are you trying to pull here?'

'We agreed upon the hands of heroes, did we not?' said Harold with a devious smile.

'I suppose so.' The imp replied cautiously.

'These are the hands of merchandising products from a dozen films,' said Harold. 'They are the hands of superheroes. We didn't specify in the deal that they had to be the hands of human, or even once living, heroes. The contract is still valid.'

The imp raised himself to his full height of eighteen inches. 'You're Harold Waterman, aren't you? I've heard about you. I knew that I should have checked who was calling, but then with the promise of a cheese sandwich, I forgot altogether. You've already got a reputation, you know.'

'A good one I hope?' said Harold. The imp shook its head.

'Not at all,' it said. 'It is by far the opposite.' It grinned again. 'It would be an honour to serve you, Master,' it said.

Harold smiled. 'Glad to have you on board,' he said. 'Um… what's your name, anyway?'

The imp thought about it. 'In honour of the way you tricked me,' it said, 'you can call me Devious.'

An Ungodly Child

They shook hand to tiny paw, and the deal was done.

'Devious?' said Harold.

'Yes, O bountiful Master?' said the imp.

'Tea. Earl Grey. Hot.'

Chapter 11
In Search of Style

The well-dressed gentleman took a seat opposite his brother and pulled his cup toward himself. 'How's the plan progressing, Mr Patch?' he asked.

Senoy took a moment to spread jam and cream onto his scone. 'It progresses well, Mr Duke,' he said. 'Our Mr Waterman has decided to follow the path we predicted. A life-threatening disease has forced him to confront his heritage. Even as we speak, he dabbles in devilry, with not one but two denizens of the pits.'

'Excellent.' Sansenoy filled his cup from the pot. 'What are you doing, Mr Patch? If I didn't know better, I would think you guilty of gluttony.'

Senoy wiped a trace of cream from his upper lip. 'Only if I was enjoying the process, Mr Duke.' he said. 'Know your enemy. Mortals eat such things all the time. The more we understand them, the better we can manipulate their reactions.'

'A good point indeed.' Sansenoy inclined his head and signalled for the waitress. 'Then purely in the pursuit of knowledge, I'll have the triple-choc gateaux.'

***

Devious sighed and sucked his fingers. The bars of his prison were well designed: cold iron blessed with holy water that burned if he touched them. They were arranged in a circle just wide enough for him to stretch his arms out to the sides without hitting them. Fortunately, the floor was only blessed on the outside so that he could stand on it without damaging his feet. The front of his prison had a wider gap, though not large enough for him to get his head through. He scratched his ragged ear in frustration.

'Please, sir, let the poor suffering little fellow out. I've learned my lesson.'

Harold looked across at him. 'Less of the insubordination, you. You were warned of the consequences of your actions, and yet you persisted.'

'Yes, Master. Sorry.' Devious chewed on toenail cheese and fell silent. His new master could order his destruction if he chose to; the long contract that he and his family had made with him had that written in the small print. It was the demon's fault, of course. The Master would have quite happily signed anything, but his companion had looked it over and had crossed out more than a few of the invalidation clauses.

The Master meant well, naturally, which was a shame. He really needed to work on his image. At the moment he looked like one of the old-school geography teachers that wandered in from time to time, following the golden paving slabs of Good Intentions. Shirt and tie tucked in below an old cardigan, tweed jacket arranged over the back of his chair, shiny brown trousers and polished shoes. It was smart, true, but hardly the attire befitting a future Lord of the Damned.

Devious looked across at Jasfoup. Now there was a figure to stop an execution. Jet-black skin encased a seven-foot tall frame, not counting the huge wings folded in repose as he sat at the small table. Long claws thrummed upon the wood as he waited his turn, and he cleaned a tiny piece of eggshell from the gap between his seventeenth and nineteenth incisors.

Devious backed away from the front of the cage as Jasfoup turned to him. He knew the words that were about to be spoken, and dreaded them.

'Devious?' The deep voice rumbled through he iron bars, taking on an edge that made his blood chill. 'Do you have any sevens?'

Devious sighed and held his two remaining cards out through the gap in the bars, much to Jasfoup's delight. 'That's me out, then,' he said dejectedly, and sat on the floor of the cage to wait out his sentence.

Harold grinned at Jasfoup, trying to distract him. He was up by six sets to three, and one more would ensure another victory. He moved his cards about between his hands, and winked.

'You're just trying to put me off.' Jasfoup looked at his six cards and took a gamble. 'Do you have any nines?'

'Ha!' shouted Harold happily. 'Go fish!' He began humming. Jasfoup hated humming, he always maintained that it was worse than the sound of ice cream freezing.

'Have you, Jasfoup, Soul collector of the Fifth Level of Hell, got any sevens?'

Jasfoup slammed down the three sevens he had in his hand, knowing that Harold had now won for the fourth time in a row. It was unfair. Why couldn't he win for a change? 'How did you have a seven?' he asked, petulantly. 'You didn't have any when I asked you last time.'

'No, but I'd picked one up since then; when I had to fish after asking you for fours.'

'I'm never going to get the hang of this game, Harold. Why can't we play Blackjack instead?'

'Because you always cheat at gambling games,' replied Harold, shuffling the cards.

Jasfoup glared at the imp in the cage. 'I can't help it, Harold. Avarice is as much a part of me as gluttony and pride. I'd have won if Devious hadn't kept gating about to look at the cards.'

'Of course you would have, Jasfoup. It was a tiny, menial imp that prevented you from winning, and I shall tell your superior so if he asks.'

'That's below the belt, Harold. I shall pretend that I didn't hear you.'

Harold would not have been surprised if Jasfoup had sucked his thumb. He looked across at Devious, who was staring intently at him. 'What?' he asked.

'Not my place to say.' Devious sat on his haunches and wrapped his thin arms around his knees.

'Go on, Devious. I expect you to be, well, devious to be frank, but honest would be a pleasant change.'

'Master, it's just that you don't look the part. When I point you out and say 'That's my Master', it's really annoying when they say 'Where? Behind that fuddy-duddy schoolteacher?' You need to look a bit more like a great sorcerer.'

Harold was taken aback. What he wore had always suited him very well in the shop. 'The daggers said something similar,' he said. 'What sort of thing should I be wearing?'

'Leather.' Both Devious and Jasfoup said in unison. The imp fell silent under the demon's withering glare.

'It's traditional,' Jasfoup added. 'Black leather, chain mail, steel plate, velvet cloak. Dye your hair black… or white… and, um, lose the moustache…'

Harold raised his hand to his lip in horror. 'Lose my moustache?'

'Or grow a goatee, if you really want the facial hair. Nasal fur is all very well for seventies porn actors, but you ought to have more…' Jasfoup searched for the word, clicking his fingers.

'More what?' asked Harold.

'More of that thing that celebrities have.'

'I don't follow,' said Harold, perplexed. 'Spandex?'

'He means style,' supplied Devious.

'Ah, I see.' Harold held out the cards. 'Another round?'

'No,' said Jasfoup, a crease lining his brow. 'Time I took you somewhere, I think.'

'Really? Are we to visit the fabled Hanging Gardens of Babylon? The High Tombs of the Egyptian Pharoes? The fiery depths of the Pits of Hell?' Harold could hardly contain his excitement.

'No, Harold. Better than any of those.' Jasfoup smiled. 'We're going to Milan.'

***

Travelling with Jasfoup was certainly a convenience. Harold had panicked when the demon had told him they were going to Italy. The furthest he'd ever been before was a weekend in Paris and he wasn't sure if his passport was still up to date.

Jasfoup had waved away his protestations with a confused grin. 'Why do you need a little book to tell you who you are, Harold? Don't you already know?' He leafed through the passport, chuckling at the image of Harold six years previously.

'That's not the point,' said Harold. 'What it's for is so that the authorities can see that you are who you say you are, and not somebody nameless.'

Jasfoup frowned. 'All this to travel from one bit of land into another? Mortals are a strange lot, Harold, even Hell doesn't have as much bureaucracy as you do, and we like our paperwork.'

'How will we get there, though?' Harold asked. 'Should I book a flight or a train?'

Jasfoup laughed. 'It's quicker to go through Hell, Harold, and from what I've seen of aeroplanes and cross-channel trains, a lot more pleasant, too.'

'Hell?' Harold paused. 'Is this some trick to take me down there early? I'm not prepared to die just yet.'

The tall demon laughed. 'You're so suspicious! You've time left yet, Harold. What I'm proposing is just a shortcut between here and there. The fact that it goes though Hell is coincidental.'

Harold laughed. 'A bit like airports, then,' he said.

In fact, it had been nothing like airports. If anything, it was more like subway tunnels. Jasfoup had opened a portal in much the same way as Devious did, peeling back a section of air as if it were wallpaper, motioning Harold through, and then climbing in himself. Harold was a little disappointed to find that the space behind the portal looked more like Covent Garden Underground than anything that Breughel had imagined.

'This way,' said Jasfoup, turning left and humming along with the tune that was being piped through the intermittent speakers. Harold followed him, taking note of the posters pasted one on top of another in a fabulous jumble of images and lettering. He hurried to catch up with the demon.

'There's something odd about the posters,' he said, 'but I can't quite decide what.'

Jasfoup grinned. 'You mean the way that they're posted over the top of each other and yet none of them are actually on the top?'

'Yes! That's it exactly!' said Harold.

'It's enough to drive you mad, isn't it?'

Harold fumed and stumped along behind the demon. 'This music is getting on my nerves, too,' he said after a short while.

Jasfoup nodded and broke off his humming. 'Don't blame me,' he said. 'This is a torture designed specifically by mortals, for mortals. We had nothing to do with it.'

'Apart from emulating it, you mean.'

'True. We conducted a poll once, amongst ten thousand schoolchildren, asking what they thought Hell might contain. We implemented the top thirty answers, except for number twenty six, because even we aren't that depraved. Piped music was number seventeen.'

'What was number twenty six?'

Jasfoup grinned. 'I can't tell you.'

'You devil! Why not?' Harold was beetroot with frustration.

'Because we were never told. The Powers That Be decided that to release the information would cause us all to defect.'

'You know that's going to drive me mad, don't you?'

'Not far to go now, Harold.'

'Don't be rude!'

Jasfoup stopped and pointed ahead towards what appeared to be a cluster of railings. 'I meant that we're nearly there,' he said with a grin.

'Oh.' Harold looked ahead. 'It looks like a London Transport ticket barrier.'

'Why reinvent the wheel?' Jasfoup asked.

'Do we have tickets?'

'They're just like the real thing,' the demon said proudly. 'We don't need a ticket.'

They reached the turnstiles and Jasfoup climbed carefully over them. Harold followed suit, and found himself in a huge round room with turnstiles going off in every direction. 'Where are we?' he asked.

Jasfoup gestured expansively. 'This is the terminus. From here we can go anywhere.'

'Oh.' Harold considered this. 'Do we need a ticket?'

'Not for this journey, no.' Jasfoup pointed to a tin sign, reminiscent of a London Underground sign in the same way that a building site is reminiscent of the wooded glade it used to be. 'That shows all the routes you can take from here.'

'It looks a little complicated,' said Harold dubiously.

'So does the alphabet until you learn to read it,' said Jasfoup. 'It shows the routes we can take now, without a ticket, and all the other routes into the past, which we do need a ticket for.'

'We can go into the past?'

'No. We haven't got a ticket.' Jasfoup grinned. 'Today, we're going to Milan, which is this direction.' He pointed in one direction and Harold hurried after him down the white tiled corridor in which the posters became increasingly unintelligible.

After a few minutes' walking, Jasfoup stopped and pointed to the wall. 'Here we are,' he said, tracing a doorway with his fingertip.

Harold looked closely. 'How do you know?' he asked. 'The wall looks exactly the same here as it does everywhere else.' He looked up and down the corridor, but could see no change in the walls for the whole of its length.

Jasfoup's forehead creased. 'It just is,' he said. 'This is the doorway that we need, thus we go through it.'

'I can't see a doorway.'

'You can't?' Jasfoup looked perplexed. 'It must be training or something. I bet you'll say that you can't see auras next, or mathematics.'

'That would be stupid,' said Harold wondering how it was done.

An Ungodly Child

Jasfoup opened the door, and bright sunlight flooded the corridor. 'After you,' he said.

Jasfoup put on his sunglasses. He liked Italy. All sorts of great things had come from here: art, literature, ice cream; and he loved them all. Milan was a far cry from his beloved Florence, though, and they were a few centuries past the ideal. He noted with pleasure the increase in rubbish and general city filth, and made a mental note to congratulate whoever it was that had thought of takeaways.

Harold was reduced to trailing along after Jasfoup, uncertain of where they were going, or, indeed, why. At least Jasfoup was easy to follow. Even though the general populace could only see a rather confused Englishman, Harold could see in front of him the exceptionally tall figure with the telltale black wings. Harold trudged along, listening to the local language which he could tell was Italian but couldn't follow.

Jasfoup turned off into a boutique. Harold paused, uncertain. Did he really want his image to be that of an Italian film star? He was in an inner turmoil, debating the concept of an Italian style with that of his comfortable, but, and even he had to admit it, somewhat shabby chic.

'Harold, we're here. Come, your destiny awaits.' Jasfoup had appeared in the street again to chivvy him along. Harold sighed and followed him inside, but was surprised when Jasfoup walked straight through the boutique and into the courtyard behind. The courtyard was cool, and formed a space shaded by potted trees bearing oranges and grapefruit. He caught up with Jasfoup, who was knocking upon a small door set into the side of the six-storey wall opposite. The door opened just as Harold arrived, and he followed the big demon inside.

'Air elemental servant,' said Jasfoup, noticing Harold searching for the doorkeeper.

Harold nodded and pretended he knew that already.

Jasfoup held out a hand, indicating that he should go ahead, and he began walking up several flights of stairs. It didn't bother him, as he was fit enough with all the lifting and carrying he did at the shop, but his interest rose stair by stair as his surroundings grew in opulence from bare stone and wooden floors to marble tiles and Renaissance paintings.

He paused and inspected one, unsurprised to find that it was a genuine Raphael. He was taken aback to see that the subject, although subtly different from the version before him, was Jasfoup himself copulating with a woman of dubious honour. He looked back at Jasfoup, who grinned and mimicked the pose. 'It was a long time ago, Harold,' he said. 'It's not easy to maintain that pose for three hours at a time.'

Harold studied the painting carefully. 'Didn't her neck hurt?' he asked, eventually.

Jasfoup laughed. 'It wasn't her neck she was worried about at the time,' he replied.

The stairs ended at a dark doorway, through which was a round room with an ornate glass dome. Although Harold could see the blue sky, and the sun, the room was refreshingly cool. He turned to Jasfoup in puzzlement. 'Where now?' he asked.

'We wait.' Jasfoup sat on an elegant regency chair and crossed his legs primly.

'For what?' Harold examined the wall; a carefully painted fresco of a woman in a garden, surrounded by animals. He would have sworn it was a Michelangelo.

'For whom.' The voice as high but melodious, and Harold turned to behold a woman. She stood a little over six feet high and was dressed in green robes. Her hair hung down her back in a curtain of black, though it shifted colour continuously, like oil on water.

'I've been expecting you for a long time, Mr Waterman,' she said, 'Picture yourself for me.'

'Picture?' Harold frowned. 'What sort of picture?'

Jasfoup leaned forward and tapped him on the arm. 'She will pick the clothes that suit your mental image of yourself,' he said. 'She's the best in the business. All the major figures came here: Da Vinci, Judas, Monroe. You name them, and if they had style, they got it here.'

'Oh, clothes.' Harold's confusion eased as he tried to think. 'Leather?' he ventured. 'We thought leather would be appropriate.'

'Leather is timeless,' the woman agreed. 'It looks as fashionable now as it did five hundred years ago.' She waved a hand and Harold's clothes vanished leaving him naked and holding his hands in front of his genitals in embarrassment. Another wave, and several garments flew across the room and he was redressed, lifted into the air several times so that underwear, trousers and boots could be applied. A mirror shimmered into existence in front of him and he beheld his new image.

He was adorned in soft, supple black leather of the consistency of silk, highlighted with accents of silver. He certainly looked the part of the charismatic mage, though he couldn't help wondering what the customers in his shop would think. He rather liked the white linen shirt, though; that looked very chic and rather complimented the skin tight leather trousers. The heels on his boots gave him a couple of inches of extra height, and the overshirt fitted him like a shroud. He wondered how he would ever sit down.

'Try,' said the woman, startling Harold out of his thoughts. A chair appeared by his side, and he bent gingerly, expecting the fabric to rip, but remarkably it expanded slightly, allowing him the freedom to move as he desired. 'Clothing fit for an angel,' he said in amazement, and laughed.

'Not exactly,' Jasfoup said.

'It suits you well.' The woman walked slowly around him, 'But your face needs altering.' 'I'm very attached to my face, thank you,' replied Harold indignantly, but again the woman waved her hand, and Harold felt his face freshen, as if he'd just washed and shaved with a diamond-edged razorblade. He looked in the mirror again and was startled by the visage. Jasfoup moved out of the way. Harold's new look was clean-shaven, despite his fondness for his moustache, and his hair shimmered in a silver that complimented the accents of his clothing. He nodded and grinned. The Dark Mage look was definitely in.

'All I need now is a silver-topped cane,' he said, turning back to Jasfoup, who was waiting with breath bated and fingers steepled hopefully, 'and I'll look like a pimp.'

'You look just the part, Harold.'

'You do indeed,' said the Empress with a low bow. 'Perhaps, though, I might suggest one or two accoutrements?'

'Such as?' Harold waited for her to wave her hand again, and was rewarded by the feel of a hat settling on his hair, a cane in his hand, and a light cloak settling on his shoulders. He nodded at his reflection, and adjusted the tilt of the top hat. 'I look as if I'm going to the opera,' he said. 'Is there an alternative that's a little less formal?'

The top hat was replaced by a fedora, and the cloak by a top coat in the same soft leather. He nodded at his reflection. 'Much better,' he said, turning to the Empress. 'How much do I owe you?' He began to take out his wallet, unsurprised that it had appeared in the pocket of his new jacket.

The woman smiled. 'His Lordship is having a little joke,' she said. 'How very amusing.'

Harold turned to Jasfoup.

'Not money, then. What do I pay with?' Jasfoup grinned. 'The usual currency for our kind, Harold: blood.'

'Blood? I probably don't have enough for all this.'

'Just a little, Harold. Your blood is valuable; having some is like having insurance'

'Insurance?'

'In case you become really powerful, and forget who helped you along the way.'

'I'm not sure I like the sound of that,' said Harold. Nevertheless, he rolled up his sleeve, and let Jasfoup partially fill a small goblet and present it to the Empress, who smiled.

'What about my favourite model?' she said. 'Included in the price, naturally.'

Harold held a handkerchief over the cut on his arm and looked at the ebony-skinned demon. 'Something conservative, I think. A business suit in dark grey, perhaps?'

An Ungodly Child

'An excellent suggestion.' The Empress waved her hand again.

Jasfoup allowed the ministrations of the elemental servant and was soon dressed in a classic Armani suit. He looked at himself in the mirror and straightened his tie, then turned to Harold and smiled. 'Who's your daddy?'

Chapter 12
Angelic Disharmony

Harold led the way back down the stairs, getting used to the feel of the new clothes and relieved that his wallet and loose change were exactly where they should be. When they re-emerged into the bright Italian sunlight, Jasfoup reached into his top pocket and took out a pair of expensive sunglasses, pointing across the street to a small café. Harold nodded and they commandeered a pavement table, enduring the derision of the owner as she served the tourists. Jasfoup, appearing to the mortals as a well-to-do businessman, made the order in fluid, pitch-perfect Italian.

'You know what?' asked Harold when they were served. He admired the way his leather caught the glow of the sunlight as he reached for a sugared pastry.

'What, Harold?' Jasfoup stirred sugar into his tea, careful not to spill any on his new suit.

'Even with all of the paintings, and the architecture, and the rich history of the country, I don't really like Italy very much. Do you know why?'

Jasfoup was getting used to Harold's way of thinking. 'They don't speak English?'

'Exactly.' Harold dunked the pastry into his tea and ate it. He was reaching for a second when his face paled. 'Oh, bugger,' he said.

'What's the matter?' The demon paused, a morsel of pastry landing on the napkin he'd placed on his knee.

'Mum's going to kill me!'

Jasfoup grinned.

'Finish your tea,' he said, 'and we'll head off home. We'll have to find somewhere to open the portal, though, because they'll be suspicious if they just see you vanish into thin air, and that's if we're lucky.'

Harold drank down half of his remaining tea. 'What if we're unlucky?'

The tall demon looked all around and then leaned in close. Harold leaned it too, expecting Jasfoup to impart some sensitive information, but the demon just grinned and pinched the last of the pastries.

'If we're unlucky,' he said, spraying Harold with slivers of lightly baked filo pastry and crunchy sugar, 'we'll be spotted by one of the other side.'

'One of the dead?'

'Pah!' Jasfoup spat out a lump of currants, which sat hissing in the hot sunshine of the pavement. 'The dead? Don't make me laugh. Not really known for their acute powers of observation, are the dead. Apart from the ones that can see really well, of course. No, I meant—' his voice changed to a whisper and he surreptitiously pointed upwards, 'the other side.'

'Oh,' Harold said, 'you mean the heavenly hosts?'

'Shh!' Jasfoup looked fearfully around. 'You don't know who's listening! You could get away with that in say, Clapham, but here in Italy is a different vat of Pisceans.'

'You mean 'kettle of fish'?' Harold finished his tea.

'No, Harold. You're forgetting where I live.' The demon grinned and Harold looked away. Jasfoup continued. 'Italy is full of them,' he said. 'Angels that meddle in the affairs of mortals and honest demons alike. It's all very well having an 'ineffable plan', but the trouble with it is that it needs constant tweaking to make sure that everything goes your way. You have the white-suited chaps running all the church religions, sowing seeds of diversity as they go so that everyone benefits from the healthy competition, then they have to run the Satanist churches, which are really Christian under another name, and then—'

'Hang on,' interrupted Harold. 'How can angels be running the Satanist churches? Isn't that a bit out of their jurisdiction?'

Jasfoup laughed. 'Not really,' he said. 'What happens when you're at war?'

'A lot of people get killed.'

'Apart from that.'

'Rationing?' Harold had listened to long speeches about the subject from his mum. 'You're only allowed one packet of tea a week. No wonder they didn't like it much.'

'Rationing, yes, that's good. What else?' Jasfoup was waiting for Harold to say a keyword, which was all very well unless you didn't know what the lock looked like.

Harold thought of the books he'd read about the war. 'Bombs,' he said. 'Lots of bombs flattening cities.'

'Good.' The demon was getting excited. 'And what happens to the cities?'

'They get rebuilt.'

'What does that do?'

'Creates jobs and a growth in industry.'

'Which fuels?' Jasfoup coaxed the argument out of his protégé.

'An increase in technology and invention, and a re-interpretation of the social and political mores of society as a whole.'

'Excellent.' Jasfoup grinned. 'So what if there isn't a war?'

'Society stagnates, growth slows to a snail's pace and people bitch about petty issues and demand a change of government.'

'Exactly. So what would be the best thing to do to encourage growth in the absence of war?'

Harold looked at him, noticing the fine aquiline set of his nose and fashionably chiselled chin. 'You're not talking about a change in social policy to promote growth in the community, are you?

Jasfoup shook his head.

'You start a war.'

'Bingo!' exclaimed the demon. 'But what if the other side doesn't want to have a war?'

'Then you have to invent an enemy, naturally, just as the Americans did in the sixties.'

'And if there is no enemy that you can put the blame upon?'

Jasfoup could see the change in Harold's face as realisation dawned. 'Then you have to rename part of your own force as the enemy, even though they're really your own troops underneath the different uniforms.'

Jasfoup nodded. 'Thus we have The Fall. What happens to the splinter group thus created?'

'They become cut off from their home, disillusioned and eventually become the enemy you invented in the first place.'

'Quite so.' Jasfoup tapped his claws on the table. 'For your bonus point, then, what happens if your people are apathetic towards the war and no longer believe in the enemy?'

Harold guessed the conclusion he had been cleverly led towards. 'You start up factions of the enemy amongst the common populace, engendering confusion and vilification and shock value to rally the people to your own cause.'

'Thus we have the people upstairs starting and running the Satanist churches.'

'Wow.' Harold was amazed. 'I've never reasoned it out like that before.'

Jasfoup grinned. 'It's easier to reason out if you know the answer to begin with,' he said. 'Now, since you've finished your tea, it's time to go.'

Harold nodded. He was tempted to leave a tip for the waitress, who had looked quite strangely at him when he said how much he liked her buns (*'Mi piace il tuo fondo'*), but all he had was a few English pounds.

'Don't leave a tip,' cautioned Jasfoup, seeing his hesitation.

'Why not?'

'It will make her day a little worse, causing her to be more volatile, which in turn makes her treat her other customers badly, which snowballs into a whole tangle of snarls and petty sins and does us all a little good.'

'Wouldn't a big wad of English money make her feel more justified in snarling at those customers who aren't English, though?'

'Good idea,' Jasfoup smiled, 'but no. She would be excessively nice instead, hoping to repeat the good fortune.'

'No tip then. I'd never thought that saving money was furthering the cause of the Infernal Majesties before. ' Harold stood up and followed the demon out. 'Incidentally, why are the people from upstairs more prevalent here than at home?'

'Oh that.' Jasfoup stopped in the doorway of a footwear shop. 'Home turf. This is where the major churches are, you see, though it's nowhere near as bad in Milan as it is in Rome, of course, with all the blatant consumerism here.'

'And there's no Pope here.'

'Ah,' Jasfoup laughed. 'He's one of ours.'

'Really?' Harold was surprised.

'How do you think he got to be Pope in the first place?'

'That makes sense.' Harold laughed, and was followed the demon back into the throng of people going about their business.

Jasfoup led Harold through the streets of Milan. Everywhere he looked there were people, which made it entirely unsafe for Jasfoup to open a portal for them to go home.

After they had walked for half an hour in the heat, he purchased a bottle of full fat, full sugar cola from a street vendor, along with an ice lolly for each of them.

Jasfoup had to intervene when Harold was confronted by a string of Italian.

'He says that he can't change your stupid English money,' he said, 'and why can't you use Euros like everyone else?'

Harold shrugged. 'I didn't really have time to go to the bank when we came,' he said. 'Tell him to keep the change.'

'From a twenty?' Jasfoup raised an eyebrow. 'I thought you were more careful with your money than that.'

'That was when I hadn't got any,' Harold laughed. 'It's easier to be altruistic when you have plenty to spare.'

An Ungodly Child

Jasfoup told the vendor to keep the change, and he was suddenly all smiles. 'The English are the nicest people in the world,' Jasfoup translated as they resumed their walk. 'Thanks for the lolly.'

'That's all right.' Harold sipped his cola. 'This is disgusting,' he said.

The demon laughed. 'There are fewer restrictions here,' he said. 'You've probably got a stronger bottle than you'd get in England'

'I'll save it for emergencies,' replied Harold, dropping it into his pocket. 'At least the ice-cream's good.' They were winding through the back streets now, and the general populace was getting poorer. Harold was a little uncomfortable, since he was obviously a well dressed Englishman with a substantial amount of ready cash and kept a watchful eye on the people around him.

'Jasfoup,' he said, after noticing a particular child several times. 'Have you seen the urchin?'

'I've seen lots of urchins,' the demon replied. 'Are we talking small Victorian children or simple sea creatures?'

'The former. I keep seeing one particular boy.' He pointed.

Jasfoup laughed. 'You would do, Harold, we're following him.'

'We are? But he's behind us.'

'Yes. He's taking us to a safe place to open a portal.'

'Oh. That's good. Why can't we just go into a toilet or something? It's unusual for you to rely on someone else.'

'He's one of us, Harold. Can't you see his wings?'

'To be honest, Jasfoup, no. They're sort of misty and vague. He does have eyes that light up in a sort of amber, though.'

The demon snorted. 'You need your eyesight tested, Harold. Perhaps you need your Sight spell renewed.'

Harold flinched. 'I hope not,' he said. 'That hurts!'

Jasfoup laughed. 'You just had a vindictive little animate. I can renew the spell for you at any point without poking you in the eyeball. In fact, when we get home I'll teach you the spell. It's only a little cantrip.'

'That would be good, Jasfoup, thank you.'

'No problem, Harold. You can make me a cup of tea in return.'

Harold laughed. 'Deal,' he said.

The boy had stopped at a wall and seemed to be waiting for them to catch up. They increased their pace and soon stood next to him, staring at an iron grill.

'We're supposed to climb through there?' said Harold. 'I would have thought a quick trip to the gents' would have been less suspicious.'

'Hush, Harold.' Jasfoup took something shiny out of his inside pocket and gave it to the boy, who stashed it into his shirt before opening the grate and motioning the two through.

Jasfoup went first, crouching to fit through the gap then helped Harold through. They were in a dark tunnel, and Harold jumped when the grating clamped down behind him. The demon's eyes glowed red when he took off his dark glasses.

'That's better,' said Jasfoup. 'Now I can open the portal without anyone seeing us.' There was a ripping sound, and he tore away a section of the air to reveal the inter-world corridor again. Harold hadn't imagined that he would be relieved to hear the piped music again.

'After you, Harold,' Jasfoup said. Harold stepped into the light of the tunnel and turned to wait. Jasfoup was just stepping through when Harold heard a splash and the demon shrieked, leaping through the gap with a speed to rival his mother calling bingo.

'The little bugger!' the demon exclaimed. 'He appeared at the grating just before I came through and lobbed a water bomb at me.'

Harold laughed. 'Boys will be boys,' he said. 'Even little boys who are really demons in disguise.'

Jasfoup sat on the floor and examined his leg, twisting it fully to inspect it in the same way that Harold's stomach twisted to see it. The flesh was smoking a little.

'Quick, Harold. Give me the bottle of cola.'

Worried, Harold passed it to him, and the demon unscrewed the cap to pour a little of the drink onto each of the smoking areas of flesh.

An Ungodly Child

'It's not terribly funny when the water bombs are full of Holy Water, Harold,' the demon muttered.

'Why cola?' asked Harold. 'Why did it stop the burning?'

'Opposite substance,' explained the demon. 'It's like acid and alkaline. One will prevent the harm from the other. The cola, being demonic in origin if not in manufacture, counters the harmful effects of the Holy Water. It's a bit like urinating on a jellyfish sting.'

'I see.' Harold was glad of the purchase now. 'What are you up to?'

'I'm looking for the little blighter.' Jasfoup was stalking along the walls of the tunnel, his hand pressed against the cold tiles. 'Ah!' He opened another door and stretched through a hand, yanking the small boy into the corridor. Harold hurried to relieve him of his remaining Holy Water bombs.

Jasfoup held the boy at shoulder height at arm's length. He looked ridiculous and forlorn hanging there, and Harold almost pitied him. Jasfoup, however, deftly recovered the small glowing object Harold had noticed earlier. 'Why the murder attempt?' He shook the small child by the shoulder.

The boy stared at him sullenly. Harold, viewing from the other side, made an observation. 'He's had his tongue cut out. Look at his feet, Jasfoup,' he said. 'They're all scarred and burned, and his wings are shadowy, like I told you.'

Jasfoup took hold of the boy by the ankle and turned him upside down. 'Martyr's feet,' he said, 'and his wings are in flux.'

'What does that mean?' asked Harold, retrieving the cola and taking a drink.

'You've seen Heaven, haven't you, boy?' asked the demon, shaking the child again.

'I thought he was a demon?' asked Harold. 'How can a demon go to Heaven?'

'There are some doors that take you there,' said Jasfoup, darkly. 'This little chap has gone through one, and liked what he's seen.' He shrugged. 'It suits some, I suppose, just as some of the angels would rather be in Hell.'

'But why did he try to kill you?'

Jasfoup shrugged again. 'Perhaps he thinks he'll earn a place there if he kills a demon or two. He's a little misguided, though, because the taint of Hell will forever bar him from Heaven. Jasfoup muttered something, and the boy shrieked.

'You've removed his wings?' Harold was surprised. The demon nodded.

'He has chosen his path,' he said, 'much good that it will do him. He is now forever barred from the paths below.' He opened the door again and unceremoniously dumped the boy through it. Harold lobbed the water bombs through, too, and heard another shriek as Jasfoup closed the door.

The demon brushed off his hands. 'Let's go home, Harold,' he said, and led the way to the turnstiles.

***

'You were right, Mr Duke.' Senoy wiped the blood from his sword and looked up at his brother.

'On this occasion, perhaps.' Sansenoy nudged the remains of the demon child with his shoe, watching it dissolve into the dusty street. 'A bribe might have been better than torture.'

'Still,' Senoy slid the long sword into his jacket pocket. 'It did the trick, I think. At least we know where Mr Waterman's sympathies lie.'

'Indeed we do, Mr Patch.' Sansenoy smiled. 'Aiding and abetting a demon, using travelling tunnels, consorting with elementals. It makes a good case to put forward to the Council of Twelve.'

'Excellent. Then can we go to war?'

'Soon, Mr Patch, soon. We need evidence that he intends to begin the apocalypse first'

'How will we do that, Mr Duke?'

'Mr Mange is handling it. Perhaps we should see how he's getting on.'

***

'What the bleedin' 'ell are you wearing?'

Ada looked at Harold, disbelief written on her face. 'What have you done with the cardigan I gave you for Christmas?'

Harold smiled, a nervous tic already appearing at the edge of his right eye. 'I've been to a tailor, Mum. Do you like it?' He gave her a slow twirl.

'It's leather,' she said. 'I've never seen you wear leather in your life before. I thought you were a vegetarian?'

'That was for three weeks when I was thirteen, and only because I fancied Gloria Steerbuck.' Harold held out his arm and looked at the cut of his suit. 'Don't you like it?'

'It's that demon pal of yours, isn't it? Leading you into bad ways.'

Harold frowned. 'Jasfoup's teaching me a lot about the world,' he said. 'I should have summoned him years ago. We needn't have struggled all these years.'

'We never struggled, Harold. You struggled. I always got the bills paid, I just never told you.' Ada felt the leather. 'It's good quality, though. Is it Italian?'

'Yes, Mum. Jasfoup got a new suit, too.'

'That's good. That jacket of his looked like it came from a charity shop when it was new.' She looked up. 'What have you done to your hair?'

Harold grinned. 'I had it coloured. I think it makes me look enigmatic.'

'It makes you look something,' Ada agreed. 'It's a shame you shaved your moustache off, though. You've got a stiff upper lip.'

Harold grinned. 'That's because I'm an Englishman.'

Chapter 13
Revelations and Genesis

'Swallow this.'

Jasfoup tossed what appeared to be a marble to Harold, who caught it in one hand. 'What is it?' he asked, putting down the newspaper to examine it. 'A pill of some kind?'

'In a way.' Jasfoup smiled and sat down. 'It's the pineal gland of a vampire. It'll help you regenerate blood and tissue.'

'Thanks, I think.' Harold grimaced. 'Do I really need to swallow it? Shouldn't I keep it for emergencies?'

'This is an emergency, Harold.' Jasfoup patted him on the arm. 'You've only got a few months to live, remember? We've got a lot to do before then.'

'Such as?' Harold swallowed the object, washing it down with a swig of lukewarm tea.

'I've got to extract some blood from you, Harold. You need a complete transfusion.'

'What's the point of giving me my own blood?' Harold asked. 'The disease will be in it.'

'It will and it won't,' Jasfoup was deliberately enigmatic. 'I can separate it into its components and find out which of your DNA comes from your mum and which from your dad. Then I can use blood from them to construct replacement blood for you.'

'Clever.' Harold nodded. 'How will we get my dad's though? I have no idea where he is.'

Jasfoup coughed. 'This might come as a bit of a shock, Harold, but I do actually know who your father is.'

'You do?' Harold stood up so quickly that his chair skidded across the floor. 'Who is he?'

'Shh.' Jasfoup motioned Harold to calm down. 'This has to be kept quiet. It's very important.'

'All right.' Harold picked up his chair and sat down again. 'Why didn't you tell me that you knew who my dad was?'

'Because it could put your life in great jeopardy.' Jasfoup tilted his head to one side. 'Well, more than it is already.'

'From what?' Harold's brow creased.

'Not what. Who.' Jasfoup pointed upwards.

'Mum?' Harold was even more puzzled. 'Why would I be in danger from mum?'

'Not her, idiot.' Jasfoup snorted. 'Further up. '

'Heaven?' Harold's voice dropped to a whisper. 'Why would I be in danger from there?'

'Because you're the son of Lucifer,' Jasfoup said. 'Lord of the Fallen, Master of Hell.'

Harold laughed. 'You're having me on,' he said. 'Good one, Jasfoup.'

The demon frowned. 'This is no joke, Harold. I'm utterly serious. Didn't I tell you that magic ran in your family? This is why. All your family have been magicians so when your grandfather summoned the Lord of the Pit it was a complete surprise to everyone when Ada fell in love with him, and he with her.'

Harold sat back in his chair. 'I can't take this in,' he said. 'My head's spinning like a top.'

Did you never wonder about his name?' Jasfoup asked. 'You've heard it often enough.'

'I just thought it an odd coincidence,' Harold said. 'Just like some people are really called 'de Vil'.'

'Well your father is really called Louis C Ferre,' Jasfoup replied, 'though I have it on good authority that he was known as Lu before the Fall.'

'So I'm really the son of the Devil?' Harold said. 'Doesn't that make me the antichrist?'

'Not really.' Jasfoup laughed. 'If you'd been a girl, perhaps. Have you never noticed the way that things always turn out the way you want them to? That's part of your innate powers.'

'Really? I thought it was just luck.'

'You're a very lucky person, Harold. You didn't even make the pentacle right. That thing about the salt being useless? I was lying. You hadn't used enough. I just strolled right through the grains.'

'Is that why you're helping me?' Harold asked. 'It's not because of some loophole that I took advantage of at all, is it? You're helping me because I'm the boss's son.'

'A bit,' admitted the demon. 'Though I do like the tea cards, honest'

'Wait a minute.' Harold stood again and began to pace the kitchen. 'If I'm the son of Lucifer, who was once an angel—'

'Shh!' hissed the demon, motioning upward. 'He was a seraph, the most beloved.'

'Sorry, a seraph.' Harold struggled to regain his train of thought. 'Then that makes me a nephilim, doesn't it? A half-angel.'

'Not exactly.' Jasfoup grinned.

'Why not? That would explain why I'm hated by God, and why that woman infected me with this disease.'

'It does explain that, yes,' Jasfoup admitted, 'but you're still not a nephilim.'

'But I must be,' Harold protested. 'I'm half angel.'

'But not half human.' Jasfoup shrugged and grinned.

Harold frowned. 'Of course I'm half human,' he said. 'Mum's my mum.'

'You're one-quarter human,' Harold. 'Your mum is half human.'

'But…' Harold's mouth opened and closed in silence. 'Is Mum a nephilim too then?'

'Not in the least, Harold.' Jasfoup was beginning to enjoy this. 'Your mum is half fey.'

'Fey?' Harold frowned again. 'Elf, you mean? They don't exist'

'I beg to differ, actually, Harold,' Jasfoup said. 'But no. Your mother is half fairie.'

'She hasn't got any wings or anything, though, and she's my size, I mean tall.'

'So are most fairies, Harold. Mankind couldn't cope with the idea that there were visitors to this plane that were better than them so they pretended that fairies, though dangerous, were only a few inches high and could be charmed by children.'

'And can they?' Harold smiled. 'I always wished I could see fairies.'

'No. They'd sooner slit your throat. The only exception is their own children. They'd do anything to protect them. This is why you were never told who your father was, and why your Aunt Tatiana never came to a birthday party.'

'Why live here though? Why live in the squalor of England? Why not live in the fairy kingdom?'

'Because your mum is not a pure blood,' Jasfoup said. 'They're a supercilious lot, fairies.'

'So where are all my powers?' Harold flexed his muscles. 'Shouldn't I be able to have everything go my way?'

'More than they do already?' Jasfoup laughed, then sobered. 'Your power will increase, now that you've begun to use it,' he said, his red eyes like burning like potatoes in a bonfire. 'The more power you gather to yourself, though, means an increase in the number of entities that want to remove the power from you.'

'How would they do that?'

'It's a fairly simple extraction, and doesn't hurt a bit.'

'It doesn't?'

'Not to the extractor, no. The extractee dies a horrible, bloody, painful mess.' The demon grinned.

'Oh, har-de-har. I nearly fell for that one.'

Jasfoup patted him on the shoulder. 'Trust me,' he said. 'You'll know when you fall. It's true about the power, though. You're going to have to be careful. The more you learn, the bigger your presence will be. Sooner or later you'll get a whole slew of creatures who want to take advantage of you. You'll find that they're attracted to you, and half of them won't even know why. I'll bet that you've seen an increase in the number of entities that are around even in the few days you've been practicing magic.'

'I have, as a matter of fact, though only in the street and the shop. I've not noticed any here.'

Jasfoup nodded. 'That's because I'm here, and that stupid imp you hired.'

Harold looked around. 'Have you made wards around the house then?'

Jasfoup shook his head. 'No need,' he said. 'My presence is enough to scare away all but the most tenacious.'

'Are you sure that that isn't your cologne? It's very strong.'

'I'm not wearing any…' Jasfoup frowned. 'Oh, har-de-har.'

Harold grinned. 'Are they dangerous?'

The demon shook his head. 'Not yet. They're just drawn to your power like houseflies to rotting meat.'

'This is a lot to take in, Jasfoup.' Harold stared into his teacup, willing it to be full again. 'How does all this help you to get my dad's blood, though?'

'Because you can help me to get some of your brother's.'

Chapter 14
Traces of Blood

'My brother?' Harold looked odd with his top lip raised, exposing his teeth. Jasfoup was put in mind of a rodent. Perhaps a chipmunk.

'Yes,' he said. 'Half-brother, anyway. Remember how old your dad is. You didn't honestly think you were his first, did you?'

'Well, no.' Harold relaxed his incredulity at last, returning his face to its normal, though to Jasfoup's mind equally comical, state. 'I just wish someone had mentioned him.'

'I doubt anyone thought about it.' The demon patted him on the shoulder. 'You'd recognise him if you saw him, though. He looks like you except his skin is darker. His mother was from the Middle East'

'Was? Is she dead then?' It was odd, Harold thought, that after being told your father was a demon and your mother a fairy, how easy it became to accept the idea of an unknown brother.

'Hell, yes.' Lucifer grinned. 'Though she was very famous in her day.'

'Who was she then?'

'I can't tell you that just yet.' Jasfoup held his hands up against Harold's glare. 'You'll find out in good time, though, I promise you.'

'What about my brother, then? Can I meet him?'

'Soon.' Jasfoup sat down. 'First I need to take some of your blood and compare it to your mum's. Then I'll know what part of your DNA came from His Unholiness. Then I do the same with your brother and his mum. When I compare the two, I should have enough DNA to construct your dad's, then I can use that and your mum's to synthesise enough to give you a transfusion.'

'I thought you said that my brother's mum was dead?'

'She is.' Jasfoup coughed. 'Remember when we travelled to Milan and you asked about tickets? We'll have to get some.'

'Tickets?' Harold frowned. 'You said that tickets were only needed to go into the past You mean we're going to time travel?'

'In a way yes.' Jasfoup lowered his voice. 'It's not an authorised journey, though, so we're going to have to get the tickets on the white market.'

'The white market?' Harold lowered his voice. 'I've heard of the black market for stolen goods. What's the white market?'

'The same thing, except that when the society deals with stolen goods all the time, prohibited items become white. Leaving Hell is frowned upon, see, so the white market caters for those desperate souls wanting to avoid detection. Time travel is prohibited except with the express permission of the dukes and above.'

'That's all right then,' said Harold. 'We'll just ask my dad for the tickets.'

Jasfoup shook his head. 'No, we can't,' he said. 'It would put him in a terrible position, breaking the rules to help his own son. It would be enough to start a civil war and we can't afford that.'

'No, I suppose not.' Harold chewed through the plan in his head. 'Why do you need me to come? Wouldn't it be less risky to go alone?'

'It has to be you,' Jasfoup sighed. 'Your brother is so closely aligned with the folk upstairs that I'd probably combust just by approaching him.'

'Ha.' Harold laughed. 'It's Jesus, isn't it?'

'Don't be stupid, Harold.' Jasfoup batted him across the head. 'Didn't I tell you that your brother is still alive? If it was... Him... then the whole resurrection story would be wrong, and the mortals would have no hope of gaining the glories of the place upstairs.' He laughed. 'No, Big J would be your cousin at best'

'Sorry.' Harold rubbed his head. 'I let my imagination run away with me there. When do we meet my brother then?'

'We'll do him at the same time as his mum,' Jasfoup said.

'Back in time? Why can't I meet him now, in the present?'

Jasfoup shuffled on his seat. 'He's changed a bit,' he said. 'He's not the same as he once was. His blood would be no good to us now.'

'How do you mean, changed?' Harold asked. 'Blood's blood, surely?'

'Usually,' Jasfoup admitted. 'Just not in this case. You'll have to trust me on this.'

'Do I have a choice?' Harold didn't mean it to come out so bitterly, but Jasfoup laughed.

'No,' he said.

***

Later that evening, when Harold returned to the attic, Jasfoup was already waiting for him. 'I thought I had to summon you,' he said, taking in the glowing pentagram on the floor and the cold in the room.

'Not any more,' said the demon, clearing the top of a box so that Harold could sit down. 'We have a contract now and I can appear autonomously. It's time to take a little of your blood.'

'How much is a little?'

'A pint or two.' Jasfoup grinned. 'Are you all right, Harold?'

Jasfoup may as well have talked to the wall for all it changed his friend's grimace. He clicked his fingers in front of Harold's face.

Harold jumped. 'What?'

'I asked if you were all right.'

'Not really.' Harold frowned. 'You're all too cheery for someone about to take a pint or two of blood from me. I'm not sure I can spare that much.'

Jasfoup shrugged. 'Don't worry,' he said. 'That pineal gland will have kicked in by now. You'll replace it in an hour.' He looked around the attic. 'Where's your imp?' he said. 'I haven't seen him today.'

'I haven't called him.' Harold clicked his fingers and waited for the imp to arrive. 'What do you want him for?'

'Tea,' said Jasfoup. 'I looked it up. Apparently it's traditional to give a blood donor tea and biscuits.'

'That's true.' Harold sat down in time to see the imp cracking open a window in the air.

'You called, Master?' Devious asked, looking around the room. 'You still haven't cleaned this place up, you know. It'd look a lot better with a lick of paint.'

'Two cups of sweet tea please, Devious,' Harold said.

'And some biscuits,' added Jasfoup. 'Chocolate ones. Be quick about it.'

'You summoned me from the depths of the Infernal City just for that?' asked the imp. 'I was right in the middle of sweeping the Plain of the Desolate. I'll have to start again now.'

'Them's the breaks,' grinned the demon. He watched Devious vanish again. 'Sometimes I love my job,' he said. 'I'd have its babies.'

'All right. Let's get on with this blood donation,' Harold said. 'Where's the needle and tubing? It has to be sterile.'

Jasfoup grinned. 'I don't stand on ceremony,' he said. 'I've got a knife and a bucket. Hold your arm out.'

***

Ada opened her bedroom door and looked out. 'Harold?' she said. 'Is that you?' There was no reply.

She picked up her cocoa tray and made her way to the stairs. There was a light on in the attic which explained the absence of Harold. She stopped at the bottom of the attic stairs and listened. A smile lit her face as she heard their voices, apparently discussing theology. It was good that Harold had a friend at last, even if it was a demon. She didn't mind how close their relationship became. Although she would have liked to have grandchildren, she would be content if Harold was happy.

The kitchen, although dark, was not silent. It took a moment for her to identify the sound of a kettle boiling and she frowned. She knew that Harold was in the attic with Jasfoup, and there was no-one else in the house. Burglars, as far as she knew, did not make tea.

She switched the light on to make sure, and there was indeed no-one there. Harold or Stinky must have left the kettle on, she reasoned, and it had been boiling and cooling down all night.

She went to the cupboard for a fresh cup, depositing her cocoa mug in the sink on the way, and saw that Harold had set out a tray for her already, though oddly with two cups. She added tea to the teapot and filled it with water from the boiling kettle, added a plate of four biscuits and went to the fridge for a small jug of milk.

She stopped in front of the tray, confused. There were only two biscuits on the plate, and she was sure she had put four on. She put the milk down and added another two biscuits, then went for the sugar, stopping again and looking around the room when she saw that there were again only two biscuits on the plate.

From the drawer she added a teaspoon and her largest wooden spoon. Balancing it on one arm so that she could hold the wooden spoon in the other, she walked towards the kitchen door, holding out the wooden spoon to flick off the light switch.

Ada spun sharply, bringing the wooden implement, which Harold referred to as Mr Spoon, down over a tiny paw that was reaching for her biscuits.

Devious let out a howl and sucked his injured hand. Ada glared at him, wagging the wooden spoon.

'I see you, little mister demon, and I'm watching you. I don't know where you came from, or how you got in, but you mind your own business, or it'll be more than your hand I bash; you mark my words.' Ada paused and regarded the imp. 'Are you Harold's?'

Devious nodded. 'Yes, missus,' he said. 'Lifetime contract.'

'I see.' Ada smiled; a sight that made the imp shudder. 'You just remember that I know your boss personally,' she said. 'And I don't mean Harold.'

***

'Fair's fair, Harold.' Jasfoup grinned as he wound up the tubing. 'If we didn't have an agreement I'd have hung you by your ankles and slit your throat.' He kicked the bucket, which made a dull resonance. 'As it is I didn't take much.'

'You took enough,' Harold said. 'I feel weak.'

'Don't be such a baby.' Jasfoup grinned. 'Look, here's the imp with your tea.'

'You took your time!' Harold glared at Devious, who walked, crab-like, into the room through the door. The imp set the tray onto the table, pushing the cocoa mugs to the side, and coughed.

'I er... caught my hand in the door,' he said apologetically. 'It stings too much to open a gate at the moment. I've brought your tea, though.'

Harold frowned, unsure this was regular behaviour for an imp, but Jasfoup ignored it. 'Fetch me a ruby,' he said.

'But my hand...' Devious began.

Jasfoup gave him a nudge with his foot. 'I'll break the other one if you don't hurry up,' he said. Devious opened a gate and vanished.

'What's the ruby for?' Harold asked, taking a sip of his tea before dunking his biscuit.

'It's to summon a succubus,' said Jasfoup. 'They can separate out the blood.' He reached across to the tray and took the remaining biscuits. 'You only need one,' he said.

Harold scowled. 'You'll get fat,' he warned.

Jasfoup patted his belly affectionately. 'Demons don't get fat, unless they actually want to,' he said. 'Magic takes an awful lot out of you, you know, so the more magic you perform, the more you need to eat. I bet that you've lost a few pounds yourself over the last day or two.'

Harold brightened and felt his stomach. 'Do you think so?'

'Not really, no.' Jasfoup grinned. 'It could as easily be the disease, eating its way through your body, but it's early days yet. You'll be doing magic with a wave of your hand before long.'

'Will I? What sort of magic?'

'Summoning a succubus, for one thing.' Devious appeared with the ruby and he threw it across to Harold. 'Get on with it.'

An Ungodly Child

'I won't ask where this ruby came from,' Harold said. 'It must be at least forty carats'

Jasfoup laughed. 'Never ask a question you don't want the answer to,' he said. 'That's the standard rate.'

'You're really not very nice, are you, Jasfoup?'

The demon looked closely at him, the light refracting off the demons black skin in an oily gleam. 'I'm a demon, Harold,' he said. 'You summoned me, remember? If you'd wanted to summon the Fluffy Bunny of Happiness, you should have made your desire a little clearer.'

'Is there a Fluffy Bunny of Happiness?'

'No. Nobody believed in him, and he died three and a half minutes after he was thought of.'

'That sounds tough.'

Jasfoup racked his memory. 'Very tender, actually, poached in white wine.'

'Oh, har-de-har.' Harold shook his head in an exaggerated manner and took another swallow of tea. Jasfoup tapped his fingers impatiently.

'Are you going to summon this succubus or not?' he asked. 'Much as I'm enjoying the conversation, that blood will congeal soon.'

Harold laughed. 'I'm going, I'm going,' he said. 'Who am I supposed to be summoning?'

Jasfoup gave it a moments thought. 'Ask for Marisuel,' he said.

Harold nodded and went to his circle, still intact despite Jasfoup's repeated use. He set out fresh candles and checked the contents of the jars, deciding that he really needed to refresh them and resolving to do it tomorrow.

'Do I use blood for this, or the ruby?' he called across to the demon.

Jasfoup stood to watch the summoning. 'The ruby. You don't want to bind her to you.'

Harold nodded. 'Okay,' he said. 'Are there any particular words I should say?'

Jasfoup shook his head. 'Just say whatever you think best; it's worked for me.'

Harold turned toward the circle and cleared his throat.

'Um… I summon thee, lady of darkness. Queen of the dark realms of desire, Whore of the infernal pits. I summon thee to do my bidding for the standard rate of one flawless ruby weighing forty carats, inclusive of overtime. I summon you, Marisuel.'

He stood back and waited for the succubus to appear. Jasfoup patted him on the back. 'Nice bit of rhetoric, Harold,' he said.

'Thanks, Jasfoup. I'm doing my best to get into the spirit of all this. It's not as easy as it looks in the films, is it?'

'Indeed not,' agreed the demon. 'You need to combine just the right amount of flattery with just the right amount of command and presence, and mix in just a smidgeon of obeisance and charm as well.'

'Yes, I'd sort of gathered that much. Do you think it would be better if I researched the Latin for the summoning of the infernal?'

'It would help,' Jasfoup replied. 'We're all sticklers for tradition downstairs, after all. Mind you, just between you and I, some of the succubae are suckers for a little Spanish.'

Harold grinned. 'Really? I'll have to brush up on a few choice phrases then.'

'It comes from the time of the Inquisition. Very popular, they were then.'

'I thought the Inquisition was merely a political tool to suppress the poor, and women in general?'

'Don't forget the primary purpose of acquiring wealth for the Church, Harold. Less that a quarter of one percent of the witches found 'guilty' by the Inquisition were actually summoning demons. More demons, especially succubae, were summoned by the members of the Inquisition themselves under the heading of 'know thine enemy.''

Harold laughed. 'I can't say I'm surprised. I bet that they didn't send them back very quickly, either.'

Jasfoup laughed. 'You'd get good odds,' he said.

There was a cough behind them, and they turned to see a beautiful woman tapping her foot.

An Ungodly Child

'I do hope that I'm not interrupting anything,' she said. 'I can see that you're very busy having a little bonding ritual together. Would you like me to find you some ale?'

Jasfoup was instantly all charm. 'My dear Marisuel, how kind of you to join us. I trust the journey was unpleasant and eventful?'

'Would that include being totally ignored once I got here?'

Jasfoup coughed. 'My apologies,' he said. 'My friend here has just started his travels upon the left hand path and I was giving him a little instruction in the summoning of the denizens of the Nine Hells.'

Marisuel raised a delicate eyebrow. 'So I heard,' she said, 'though personally I find Spanish a little distasteful, having been so regularly summoned during the period you refer to.'

Jasfoup bowed. 'Of course, though if I recall correctly, you sired a number of homunculi during that difficult era, so your efforts were not entirely without recompense.'

The she-demon nodded. 'True,' she said, 'though I have no idea what happened to them, or the mortals who bore them into the lands of men.'

Jasfoup grinned. 'They probably became politicians or priests,' he said .

Harold coughed, and drew the attention of both demons.

'May I introduce my mortal protégé, Harold,' Jasfoup said. Harold extended his hand in greeting. 'How do you do?' he asked.

Marisuel smiled and took his hand in a light grip. 'How pleasant it is to make my acquaintance,' she said with a smile. 'I've heard so little about you.'

Harold smiled. With the exception of the redhead in the shop, the succubus was the most delightful creature he had ever seen, and touching her hand was like being caressed by a fairy tale princess with a piece of soft rabbit fur. His senses were flooded with contentment and desire, and he could detect the faint scents of patchouli and custard, with the not unpleasant bitter undercurrent of tea.

Jasfoup's voice cut into his reverie. 'If you're finished with grinning like a loon, Harold, we'll get on, shall we?'

Harold shook his head to clear it. 'I'm sorry,' he said, 'I was miles away.'

Jasfoup grinned. 'Yes, we saw the blood rush three feet downwards.' He looked across to Marisuel and nodded to her. 'Sorry, ducks,' he said. 'This has to be done.' He placed his hand over Harold's face. 'Sight,' he said. 'You see and not see. Now see, and see again.' He took his hand away.

Harold screamed.

Marisuel wasn't quite as pretty as she was a moment ago. The pleasant scent of vanilla custard and patchouli had been replaced by the charnel scent of blood and faeces and the soft velvet of her skin had become the coarseness of chitin and scales. Her face, so delicately Edwardian a moment ago, was now oozing with pus from dozens of boils in the suppurated skin and bones showed through her flesh in several places.

'Oh, Jasfoup,' she said, her black tongue flicking out from between her elongated jaws, 'he was all but captivated by me. We could have got along famously.'

'Famous like the Black Plague,' muttered Jasfoup. 'Harold? Stop screaming now.' He slapped Harold lightly across the cheek.

Harold stopped screaming. 'Sorry about that,' he said. 'It was a bit of a shock. I was... um... feeling all sorts of emotions there.'

Jasfoup shook his head and turned to the succubus. 'Be a dear and separate that blood out into paternal and maternal DNA, would you?'

'Why?' Marisuel wrinkled her nose in distaste.

'Because you can, and it will save me hours,' Jasfoup replied. 'Your kind have a knack for it.'

'The better to take the shape of a dream lover,' she replied.

'How does that work?' Harold asked, still queasy at the sight of her true form.

'Most people, whether they know it or not, want to make love to themselves,' she replied. 'So I separate out their DNA and construct their perfect mate.'

Jasfoup handed her two jars, and she filtered the blood through her hands until both were full. 'There,' she said. 'One is the father's and one the mother's. I cannot tell which.'

'That's fine,' said Jasfoup. 'We'll get the comparison samples.' Jasfoup waved as the long-legged demonette faded from view.

Harold watched her go, pleased that the stench that accompanied her had gone as well. He turned to Jasfoup, who was delicately wiping his nose on his sleeve.

'So how do we get mum's blood?' he asked. 'I'm certainly not asking her for it.'

'Well, someone has to,' said Jasfoup.

'Devious?' Harold asked. Jasfoup laughed.

'No,' he said. 'We'll use an incubus. That will get it for us.'

Devious let out a sigh of relief.

***

The incubus coiled in the semi-darkness of the bedroom, the woman's soft snores encouraging it to be bold enough to coalesce and drop onto the bed.

He stared at her face and his mouth fell open. 'Oh no,' he murmured. 'Not again.'

Chapter 15
The Protection Business

Harold could find no trace of the wound Jasfoup had inflicted upon his arm when he showered the next morning, but the skin around the area felt a little less sensitive than he remembered. He clicked his fingers.

The sound of a diamond cutting glass was almost lost above the spray of water, but Harold turned in time to see Devious peering at the flow of liquid. The imp looked up at him.

'I'm not getting out here,' he said. 'Look at all that stuff. It's disgusting.'

Harold followed his gaze. 'It's only water,' he said. 'I have a shower every morning.'

Devious shuddered. 'Water's for drowning in,' he said. 'Do you really get into that and let it flow all over your body?'

'Of course.' Harold crossed the bathroom. 'Let me show you.'

'No!' Devious shrieked. 'Don't be so cruel! If you want me to wash, just say so and I'll bathe in the lake of blood.'

Harold grimaced. 'I'll let you know,' he said.

Devious tore his gaze from the liquid. 'What did you want me for?' he asked.

'Look at my arm,' Harold said, 'and tell me if you can spot anything odd about it.'

Devious looked from Harold to the bath. 'You'll have to come closer,' he said. 'I can't see it from here.'

Harold sat on the edge and showed Devious his forearm. The imp prodded it a few times. 'What am I looking for?' he asked.

'The skin feels thicker here.' Harold pointed with his free hand. 'It's where Jasfoup cut it to take some blood yesterday.'

'You let a demon take blood from you?' Devious shook his head, tutting. 'Did he say why?'

'It's to help give me a blood transfusion to arrest this disease,' Harold told him. 'The tablets allow me to carry on as normal, but it's going to kill me in three months or so.'

'I know,' Devious muttered. He prodded the skin with a claw. 'You've grown thicker skin over the wound,' he said. 'Have you been taking vampire blood?'

'Sort of. Jasfoup gave me a little marble to eat.'

'That'll be it, then.' Devious nodded. 'Vampires have thicker skin than humans, an extra three to five layers, depending upon the age and power. It helps them to survive damage from sunlight.'

'That's useful,' said Harold, rubbing at the toughened area.

'It certainly is,' agreed Devious. 'Vampire skin makes great leather when it's cured properly. Much better than human.'

Harold felt slightly sick. 'I didn't need to know that,' he said.

Devious looked at the water again. 'Can I go now?'

Harold yawned. 'I suppose so. I need to take my shower.'

Devious grimaced again and closed his portal, leaving Harold to revel in the cascade of water.

***

Harold left the house early and drove to the shop. He was surprised by the number of people on the streets, since he rarely saw anyone other than the postman on his way to work. He parked under the solitary plane tree at the back of the Emporium and got out. It was sheer luck that he glanced in the window of the car as he locked it.

The reflection showed a figure hurtling toward his back and Harold ducked out of the way just it time. Glass shattered as a fist the size of a pineapple went through his van door and Harold scrambled out of the way.

Facing him was a demon easily ten feet in height, though without wings. 'Who the hell are you?' Harold shouted.

'Death!' the figure replied, crouching on legs that would have been too powerful to attach to an elephant. Two pairs of arms reached forward over the bonnet. Harold danced backwards.

'You're not Death,' he said. 'Death is an angel, or was, at least What was his name again? I don't remember.'

'I am your death.' The demon shifted sideways and lunged. Harold scrambled further round the van, trying to keep it between the demon and himself.

'You should look like me then,' Harold said. Although he was quite fit from the years of lifting furniture, he regretted eating that second bowl of cereal. 'You don't look a bit like me. Are you sure that you're not… what's his name, the angel of Death? Azimuth?'

'Stand still, mortal, and I will give you a quick death.' The demon drew a blade. Where it had come from, Harold had no idea, since the demon appeared to be naked.

He patted his pockets, seeking something he could use as a weapon. 'Jasfoup!' he called.

'That weakling will not help you,' said the demon. 'He has no means of defeating me.'

'Hasn't he?' Harold pulled out the quill Jasfoup had lent him the first night. 'I bet he'd win a battle of wits with you. You're unarmed.'

'Enough prattle.' The demon advanced again. 'Do you think to defeat me with a feather?'

'They say that the pen is mightier than the sword,' Harold replied, his fingers trailing across the tail lights of the van. 'I didn't expect to have to prove it though.'

The demon sliced down and only missed cutting into Harold's shoulder because he skipped backwards. Metal shrieked as the blade sliced off a corner of the van.

Harold risked a brief glance over his shoulder. He was out of reach of the van now, on the service road at the back of the shop. He might get a few yards' head start if he began running, though he was sure that the demon would soon close the distance.

An Ungodly Child

The demon closed again. Another few feet and Harold would no longer be worried about his disease. He raised the sword again.

'Azimov!' Harold shouted, pointing behind the demon. 'At last!'

The demon twisted to see who had come, and Harold darted in, stabbing him with the quill. The demon shrieked and vanished, the sword clattering to the tarmac.

Harold rested his arms on his bent legs to catch his breath. He looked at the feather in his hand and kissed it. 'Wingtip of an angel,' he said. 'Who knew that petty theft could save your life?' He put it back in his pocket and bent to retrieve the sword. He knew very little about them, other than they were sharp and pointed, and was glad that he hadn't got to know this one better.

'That was a lucky escape,' said a voice. 'I thought you were a goner for sure.'

Harold stood, using the sword for balance as he waited for his heart to stop hammering. 'Mrs Peters,' he said. 'It's a little early for you to be out shopping, isn't it?'

The old lady laughed. 'It's a little late, if anything, Mr Waterman,' she said. 'I've got a funeral to get to.'

'I'm sorry to hear that,' Harold replied. 'Anyone I know?'

'Mine,' she replied. 'I died yesterday.'

'Oh.' Harold wasn't quite sure what to say. 'I'll cancel that wardrobe you ordered then, shall I?'

'You do that, Harold,' Mrs Peters replied. 'Now could you tell me the way to Mr Jessop's funeral parlour? Every time I try to get there I end up here again. It's most inconvenient.'

'Go left at the end here, round past the front of the shop and take the second right.' Harold stepped toward her. 'Are you sure you're all right?'

'I've never been better, Harold, thank you.' Mrs Peters smiled. 'My arthritis has gone and I can breathe God's clean air again now that my bronchitis has cleared up.'

'I see.' Harold gave a little wave. 'I'm glad you're up and about, Mrs P.' He wondered what the air was like for ghosts, because anyone calling what he was breathing 'God's clean Air' should be prosecuted under the Trades Description Act.

***

Harold, after making sure all the doors and windows of the shop were locked and bolted, put aside his tea and lit the candles.

It was a makeshift pentagram, formed from straightened paperclips, a rubber band and a packet of birthday cake candles, but he'd aligned it properly and pricked his thumb with a drawing pin. He almost laughed when Jasfoup appeared. The demon was all of two inches high.

'I know I said 'call me anytime', Harold, but this is just ridiculous.' The demon's tinny voice was far removed from his normal husky tones. 'Let me out, would you?'

Harold lifted off the elastic band and the demon began to grow to his full size. When he felt that he was tall enough, he hopped off the table onto the floor. He looked at the improvised circle.

'Clever,' he said. 'What was the urgency?'

'A demon attacked me in the car park,' said Harold. 'I very nearly died.'

'What did he want?' Jasfoup picked up a magazine from the table and began leafing through it.

'He wanted me to die,' said Harold. He put his hand over the magazine to stop Jasfoup reading it. 'You don't seem very concerned. You should see the damage to the van!'

'I don't need to, Harold. You obviously dealt with the matter.' Jasfoup smiled. 'You're still alive.'

'Only just,' Harold glared at him. 'What was he after?'

'I told you, Harold. The more powerful you get, the bigger a target you'll be. You know that vampire's pineal gland I gave you to eat?'

'Yes. What about it?'

'Your pineal gland would be prized highly. The more powerful you get, the more valuable it will be, but a potential user has to decide when the balance between power and vulnerability occurs. Leave it too late and you'll fry all comers with a whisper.'

'If I live that long.' Harold folded his arms. 'He said you were a weakling.'

Jasfoup frowned. 'Did he? We'll see about that. Come with me and bring that sword.'

***

Harold followed the demon down the road. 'Where are we going?' he asked.

'To a hostelry,' Jasfoup replied. 'You'll see.'

'I don't really drink, Jasfoup.' Harold hurried to keep up. 'Besides, it's a bit early for the pubs to be open.'

'This one will be.' Jasfoup stopped outside the old bakery, which had been abandoned and boarded up for as long as Harold could remember.

'Here we are,' said the demon. 'Mind what you say, and don't stare at the clientele.'

'This is the old bakery,' said Harold in puzzlement. 'What are you talking about?'

Jasfoup grinned, showing more than one set of teeth. 'Your Sight has lapsed again, Harold. You should get into the habit of renewing it every morning.'

Harold nodded and muttered the words of the simple spell, drawing his fingertips over his closed eyelids and looked again at the disused shop. This time, the sign that hung out over the pavement was not that of 'Ye Olde Bakery' but a carefully painted rendition of the moon. He looked at the building, darkened glass windows showing where he was expecting faded boards covered in posters for musicians long since disbanded.

Jasfoup pushed open the door that no longer appeared to be nailed shut although, curiously, it still sported the sign 'Danger: Keep Out.'

Inside, the building looked similar to a hundred pubs that Harold had entered over the years. Partially stained glass windows allowed a little sunlight to enter, although there were heavy wooden shutters that could block out the light completely. Oak floorboards led the way to the bar, behind which were arrayed various glass jars and bottles, only a few of which Harold recognised. A chilled cabinet held wine and a heated one held food that Harold didn't want to look closely at.

There were only three people patronising the building, two stocky-looking men in animated conversation, and an older man in a suit at the bar. The two swarthy fellows ceased talking and watched as the pair entered, but seemed to relax when the door closed again behind them.

Jasfoup made his way over to the barman, a heavy-set man in a black suit who watched the demon's progress through black, sunken eyes.

'Jasfoup.' He nodded to the demon. 'It's been a while. What'll it be?'

'The usual.' Jasfoup smiled. 'I'd like to introduce you to a friend,' he said, beckoning to Harold. 'This is Harold —'

'de Ferre.' The barman finished the sentence for him. 'How do you do? The Moon is always open to you, sir. I knew your grandfather, may the devils gnaw his bones.'

'Actually, it's 'Waterman',' corrected Harold. 'I was named for my grandfather, though I never knew him, rather than my father, whom I've never met.'

'I'm sorry to hear that, sir,' said the barman. 'You can call me Bernard. What'll you have? The first drink is on the house.'

Harold smiled. 'That's very decent of you. Um… do you do tea, perhaps?'

'Indeed I do, Mr Waterman.'

Jasfoup took a tall glass of what Harold suspected was blood.

'Just a minute or two for the tea, Harold,' Bernard told him. 'Is there anything else I can get for you?'

'Have you got a minute?' Jasfoup leaned forward across the bar.

'I have two.' Bernard leaned forward to meet him. 'What do you want?'

Jasfoup lowered his voice. 'Do you still do your special trades?'

Bernard nodded. 'It depends upon what you're looking for, of course, and what you have to offer in exchange.'

'Do you have any contact with the folk upstairs still?' Jasfoup gave an upward nod of his head, causing Harold to wonder who it was that rented the flat over the top of the pub.

Bernard nodded. 'A little. Why? What is it that you're after?'

Jasfoup lowered his head even closer to the barman's, and forced the merest whisper through his jaws. 'Harold needs a weapon,' he said, 'one that he can use against both sides.'

Bernard gave a low hiss. 'What are you offering in exchange?'

Jasfoup smiled. 'My thanks and a favour owed?'

Bernard laughed. 'I don't think so,' he said. 'Anything else?'

Jasfoup grinned. 'How about this sword?' He motioned to Harold, who put the demon's blade onto the counter.

Bernard gave a low whistle. 'A bound soul, eh? Yes, I'll trade you for it.' He spat into his palm and held out his hand. Jasfoup grimaced and did likewise. They pressed their palms together, Bernard holding the grip a little more tightly and a touch longer than Jasfoup would have liked. He retained a smile until the barman had stood and gone back to his customary place behind the counter.

Jasfoup shook his hand as if to cool it, then inspected the palm. There was a small patch the size of a tuppence that smoked.

'How did that happen?' asked Harold. 'There's not much that can damage you.'

Jasfoup turned his palm over and showed it to Harold. There was an irregular circle where they had shaken hands which looked burned, over the top of a pair of similar circles that had healed in the past 'You always get that reaction when you mix my kind with his,' he said.

Harold looked across at the bartender, who felt his gaze, turned and smiled. 'You mean he is an a—' Jasfoup shushed him. 'One of the people upstairs?' Harold corrected.

Jasfoup nodded. 'Use your Sight, Harold.'

Harold looked more closely at Bernard, and could discern the ethereal wings sprouting through the jacket. Unlike Jasfoup's, they were feathered rather than leathery, but instead of the expected white they were iridescent with the colours of flame.

'I see the wings,' he whispered to the demon, 'but why are they orange?'

He's what we call a wounded soul,' explained Jasfoup. 'He has earned enough to go to the big cricket-pitch in the sky and done enough to warrant a place downstairs, too, but since neither outweighs the other he is doomed to endure the Middle World until such time as the balance significantly tips one way or the other. Thus he has the wings of an angel, tainted with the fires of the Inferno.'

'So he's a sort of wheeler-dealer of the three worlds?' Harold surreptitiously took another glance at Bernard.

'Yes, in a manner of speaking, but don't hold it against him. It's certainly doing us a favour. He's usually got a bit of stock to pick through.'

'Here's your tea, Mr Waterman.' Bernard placed a china cup on the counter. 'What sort of sword are you looking for? Backsword? Broadsword? Shortsword? Rapier? Sabre? Epee? Soul-sucking vampiric blade of doom?'

'I was thinking of something sharp and pointy,' admitted Harold. 'The last one sounds fairly splendid, though.'

'Out of stock.' Bernard rubbed his eyes with the heels of his hands. 'I can do you something in the sharp and pointy line. What's it for?'

'Just general protection from overly enthusiastic parties,' interrupted Jasfoup. 'Something to suit his image would be best, something he can easily conceal.'

'I have just the thing,' said Bernard with a smile. 'I'll be right back.' He went through the oak-panelled door at the back of the bar and returned a few minutes later bearing a black cane. He handed it to Harold with a smile. 'I think this will suit you very nicely,' he said.

'I already have a cane at home,' protested Harold.

'Not like this one, I think you'll find.' Bernard took the cane back and demonstrated how to twist the silver handle to allow the blade to slide from the rest of the cane. Harold whistled.

'Very nice,' he said. 'I'll take it.'

Jasfoup examined the blade. 'What is it made of?' he asked.

Bernard leaned in close again. 'Iron shot with silver. That'll sort out your ghosts and—' he glanced toward the two burly men and lowered his voice still further, '—werewolves. You'll have to make up the rest yourself. If you spread the blade with a paste made of garlic, demon blood and holy water it should prove sufficient for your needs.'

'Why?' asked Harold. 'What's the point of that?'

Jasfoup backed away from the naked blade. 'The point,' he said, 'as you so cleverly punned, is that you would have a weapon that is effective against ghosts, werewolves, vampires, angels and,' he gripped Harold's wrist, 'demons.'

Chapter 16
The White Market

'No, no, no,' Jasfoup said as Harold brought the cane over his head for a downward strike. 'You have to twist from the wrist. The way you're doing it exposes your arm as you turn. You'll have your arm cut off before you can say "scoundrel".'

'I never say "scoundrel",' Harold replied, relaxing. 'Can we stop now? My arm hurts.'

'That's because you're using new muscles,' Jasfoup said. 'They'll hurt less as you practice. How are your legs?'

'My legs?' Harold looked down. 'They're fine, thanks.'

Jasfoup chuckled. 'Wait until tomorrow,' he said. 'Then you'll notice that you've been using different muscles there, too.'

'Oh, great.' Harold sat down. 'Any chance of a tea?'

'Certainly.' Jasfoup turned to the imp on the kitchen counter. 'Devious? Stop sitting on that egg and make some tea.'

'Huh.' Devious stood and an egg rolled off the counter top onto the floor. Devious hopped down to inspect it. 'I was nearly there,' he said. 'Another hour and I'd have hatched it.' He held up a partially formed creature that looked nothing like a chick.

Harold pulled a face. 'What on earth is it?' he said. 'I thought eggs were unfertilised.'

'They usually are,' said Devious, 'but this one was free range, so there was a good chance it wasn't.' He showed Harold the partially grown creature. It was a form of lizard, as far as he could tell.

'What was it going to be?' he asked.

Devious shrugged. 'A toad would hatch a cockatrice,' he said. 'I was hoping for a basilisk.'

'Aren't they a bit dangerous?'

Jasfoup took the lizard from the imp and swallowed it. 'Only to mortals,' he said. 'I remember a chap in the fifteenth century who made superb statues. Nobody knew how he did them so fast, until they caught him using a basilisk on his models.'

'What happened to him?'

'He's part of the fixtures of Canterbury Cathedral now,' Jasfoup said. 'His peers thought it fitting that he should join his victims.'

'Well, I don't want one in the house,' Harold said. 'No more egg sitting, Devious.'

'No, master.' The imp grinned and winked at Jasfoup. 'Here's your tea.'

Harold took a sip. 'Thanks for the lesson, Jasfoup,' he said. 'I feel a bit more confident with it now.'

'Good.' Jasfoup grinned. 'You might need it where we're going today.'

'Oh?' Harold put down his cup. 'Where's that then?'

'The White Market.'

'Good. I've been looking forward to that since you told me about it. Where is it?'

'Birmingham.' Jasfoup laughed at Harold's face. 'The best place to hide a market is where no-one would bother to go,' he said.

'Maybe,' Harold replied. 'But Birmingham?'

'Trust me.' Jasfoup drank his tea down in one gulp. 'If we can't find what we need there, we never will.'

'All right.' Harold left his cup half full and stood. 'I'm ready.'

***

They emerged into the city under grey skies. Harold dusted off his jacket from the limed plaster of the tunnel walls. 'Those are really useful,' he said. 'It would have taken us hours to get here on the train. Could I use them on my own, do you think?'

'Sorry, Harold. You'll have to be with me to access the tunnels.' Jasfoup turned a full circle to get his bearings. 'It's this way.'

'Surely it's just a matter of having extra-planar blood,' said Harold, hurrying to keep abreast of the demon. 'If that's the case, then I should be able to use them as well as you.'

Jasfoup stopped. 'You've proved that you can use them, Harold. I could even teach you how to open a gateway into them. What I can't teach you is how to get out again. That's a matter of skill and genetics. If you went into the tunnels on your own you'd be stuck there until someone came along. Then you'd probably be killed.'

'Not when they found out who my father is, surely?'

'Especially when they found out who your father is. Not all the demons of Hell are as kind and considerate as me, you know.'

Harold sighed. 'They aren't? I don't suppose you could teach me?'

'No, Harold, I couldn't. You'd have to be a fully-fledged member of the demonic legion first'

'That's that then. I'll have to stick to the van.'

Jasfoup patted his shoulder. 'I've seen the way you drive, Harold,' he said. 'You're not far off being a full demon.'

Harold smiled. 'Thanks, Jasfoup, I think.'

Jasfoup pointed to an archway leading to a covered indoor market area. 'Here we are,' he said. 'The White Market.'

Harold followed him inside. 'It looks just like any other market to me,' he said, looking at the cheap tee shirts and bolts of cloth. 'I could do with picking up some buttons for mum, though. She likes buttons.'

'I didn't know that.' Jasfoup smiled. 'You go and get your buttons then, and I'll wait for you here.'

'Aren't you going to look for tickets?'

'We've plenty of time for that. Did you take your tablets today?'

'Yes, Mum.' Harold wandered off into the stalls and made several purchases. Jasfoup waited patiently for him to return.

'Are you finished?' he asked when Harold stood by him again.

'Yes,' Harold replied. 'It's only a little market. I bought some figs, though. Do you want one?'

Jasfoup shook his head. 'No,' he said. 'The seeds get stuck between my teeth. Now we'll go to the White Market.'

'Where is it then?' asked Harold. 'Is it on a different day?'

'Not at all.' The demon grinned. 'You forgot to renew your Sight again, didn't you?'

'Oh.' Harold performed the cantrip. 'Why is it that I can see you and Devious, then, if my Sight has worn off?'

'Your brain has become used to seeing us and created the pathways so that you can. That's all very well, but you'll never see something that you're not expecting if you don't renew the spell. Eventually your brain will adjust to the new information from your optic nerve and you won't need the spell.' Jasfoup motioned behind Harold's back. 'Look.'

Harold turned, his eyebrows raised in surprise. Where there had been a dozen mundane stalls selling ironmongery and office supplies, there now stood five times as many selling things that Harold didn't know the use of.

One stall sold animals in cages: cats, rats, birds, lizards and goldfish, though how the fish survived without water was anybody's guess; another sold candles made from tallow in any shape you wanted; another sold glassware: retorts and alembics, test tubes and jars; and another sold bolts of cloth that shimmered with colour that made his eyes hurt.

'Where have all the ordinary stalls gone?' Harold asked. 'They were right here.'

'They still are, Harold.' Jasfoup began threading through the stalls. 'They occupy the same space. If you took your Sight away now you'd be at the stall selling broken biscuits instead of—' he paused to peruse the stall in front of them '—body parts. How much are the fingers?' This last was to the stallholder.

Harold looked away. There were some parts of the demonology business that he couldn't face just yet.

Jasfoup proffered a paper bag. 'Would you like a finger?'

Harold was torn between revulsion, curiosity and innuendo. He opted for a curt 'No thanks.'

'Your loss.' Jasfoup munched on a biscuit.

'Wait a minute.' Harold held his arm. 'I thought you'd bought body parts.'

Jasfoup grinned. 'I can see both stalls at the same time, Harold. You shouldn't judge by appearances.'

'What point is a fortune teller in a market of demons?' Harold asked, pointing to a purple tent. 'Surely you all know what's going to happen?'

Jasfoup laughed. 'It's a fortune giver's tent,' he said. 'Very clever. They can actually alter your life path, for the right price.'

'Could they stop my disease?'

'That would be good, Harold, but no. You've been touched by a power higher than theirs.'

They passed a stall that sold books stacked spine-upwards in crates and another that had a display of dozens of jars, each containing a different alchemical substance. Jasfoup stopped at this one. 'What do you want for holy water?' he asked.

'What have you got?' The woman on the stall asked. She looked quite normal but for a splash of fur around the jowls, though Harold couldn't tell what she looked like beneath her robes. 'One of your claws, perhaps.'

Jasfoup thrust his hands into his pocket. 'I don't think so,' he said, moving away.

Harold caught him up. 'I can get you some holy water,' he said. 'There's a font of it at St Jude's.'

'Splendid, Harold. Can you pick up some garlic as well? I want to make that paste for your sword.'

'Certainly.' Harold grinned. 'Does that mean I get to drain off some of your blood, too?'

'Good idea, Harold,' Jasfoup said. 'No.'

He led the way around a stall selling tiny boxes and stopped. 'Here we are,' he said.

An Ungodly Child

Harold looked at the stall, which was the kind made from a suitcase on legs. He wasn't sure that he trusted the demon either. There was something shifty about the way he was looking through his customers, as if he was calculating the resale value of their body parts.

Jasfoup leaned in to whisper. 'I'm looking for a pair of travel tickets,' he said. 'Both ways, for preference.'

The salesdemon looked him up and down. 'Oh yes?' he said. 'What are they worth to you?'

Jasfoup shrugged. 'That depends,' he said. 'What do you want?'

'Show me what you've got,' said the demon, stroking out his whiskers. 'An' I'll tell you if I want it.'

Jasfoup shrugged and put his hands in his pockets. 'Pocket watch?' he asked. The demon shook its head. 'Biscuits? A coronation mug? Tea cards?'

'You'll have to come up with something a bit rarer,' said the demon. 'You're planning an unauthorised trip out, else you'd be going through official channels.'

Jasfoup tried his other pockets. 'How about an apple from the Tree of Life? He said.

The demon narrowed his brow ridges. 'They're rare,' he said. 'All right then.'

Jasfoup paused, one hand in his pocket. 'Show me the tickets first,' he said.

The demon spat. 'You can't trust anyone these days. Here they are.' He waved a pair of purple tickets in Jasfoup's face. Harold thought them reminiscent of the cardboard bus tickets he remembered as a child.

'Run, Harold,' shouted Jasfoup, snatching the tickets.

Harold paused, not sure what was happening, and Jasfoup grabbed his wrist

'Stop, thief!' shouted the demon. The cry was taken up by several people who had been standing near, and heads began to turn.

'Quick,' Jasfoup said. 'Through that tent there.'

Harold saw the fortune giver's tent ahead and dashed inside, Jasfoup hard on his heels.

'What's your game?' asked the woman inside. 'I've got an appointment in five minutes.'

'We'll just be a moment, madam.' Jasfoup smiled and opened a gate. 'Come on, Harold.'

The tunnels were free from pursuit. 'Why did you steal the tickets?' Harold asked.

'I didn't,' Jasfoup replied. 'Or I won't, anyway. I just traded him something that I haven't got yet.'

'So what happens now?' Harold looked across at a poster advertising the apocalypse: 'Coming soon to a plane near you', and then back to Jasfoup.

'Simple,' said the demon. 'These are time tickets, see, so we turn up the moment before we ran and pay for the tickets. We have what we want, he has what he wants and everybody's happy.'

'But we ran,' said Harold. 'You can't change the past'

'Yes you can.' Jasfoup waved the tickets at him. 'That's why these are so hard to get without authorisation. You could easily nip back and kill off your own grandfather if you're not careful.'

'You did that for me,' said Harold.

'Oh har-har,' retorted the demon. 'Here's the turnstiles, look.'

They inserted their tickets and walked through. The tunnels changed. The posters were replaced by graffiti in a score of languages. Harold recognised one as Latin and, as the walked further, ancient Hebrew. Eventually the tunnel walls became sandstone instead of mosaic or tile, and dwindled down to nothing.

'Here we are,' said the demon.

'Where?'

'The tunnels start here,' Jasfoup said. 'Where do you think we are?'

Harold considered. 'If the tunnels start here,' he said, 'then we must be at the start of time.'

'Correct.' Jasfoup fished about in his pocket. 'Star prize,' he said. 'Have a walnut.'

'It's covered in fluff,' Harold said. 'I can't eat that.'

'Shh!' Jasfoup put his finger over his lips. 'Be quiet now. Don't let anyone see us.'

He opened the gate and crept out. Harold followed, pleased to feel grass beneath his feet after the long walk through the tunnel. 'Where are we?' he asked.

'This is a quick stop,' whispered the demon. 'Just give me a minute. I want a pomegranate.'

'We could have got one at the market,' said Harold. 'Why didn't you say?'

The demon had gone.

***

Jasfoup crept toward the big tree. There was a naked woman asleep under it, and Jasfoup paused to admire her. Her dark skin was satin under the early morning sun, but she didn't wake as Jasfoup stepped over her. He stopped and drew a hypodermic from his pocket. With the utmost precision he drew as much as he dared from her and stepped back.

He turned to the tree and reached upward for a fruit, plucking the ripest he could see. He couldn't resist smelling it, taking a step backwards as the scent tempted him to take a bite.

''Ere, watch where you're treading!' The woman woke as he trod on her hand. 'Who are you? You don't look like an angel.'

Jasfoup grinned, realising that she had the Sight. 'Er, Samael,' he said. 'Pleased to meet you.'

She stared at his hand and he took it back after a slight pause. 'Why do you have an apple? They are forbidden.'

'An apple? Nah.' Jasfoup grinned. 'These are pomegranates. Do you want one?'

'Oh.' The woman hesitated. 'It's apples that are forbidden. I must have got it wrong.'

'No problem.' Jasfoup passed her the fruit and took two more for himself. 'I must get off. Nice to have met you.' He dashed away back to where he had left Harold.

***

Harold had his own problems.

He had looked for Jasfoup, but upon emerging from the bushes where the demon had left him, he had run straight into a wall of light.

'Who are you, and what do you do here?' said a voice. It seemed to surround Harold, and he looked around, trying to locate the source.

'You are mortal. How can a mortal man be here?' The wall of light coalesced into the figure of a winged man. 'Where did you come from?'

'Er...' It was the first time Harold had ever met an angel. 'Birmingham?'

'You should not be here.' The angel drew a sword which burst into flame along its blade. 'Prepare to be here no more.' The sword described a lazy loop and Harold held up his cane to deflect it. The angel seemed surprised.

Harold used its momentary confusion to unscrew the sword section from his cane. This time, as the angel brought the sword round for another cut, he darted forward and stabbed it.

The angel laughed. 'No mortal can harm an angel,' it said. 'Especially not the mighty Samael.'

'Samael?' said a voice behind him. 'Oh, shit.'

The angel turned just in time to be bowled over by Jasfoup, who had his head down as if he were an American footballer. 'Thrust', shouted the demon as the two came hurtling toward the mortal swordsman.

Harold held out the sword at full length and closed his eyes. He felt it pierce the angel's body, and then the pressure increased.

'What manner of being are you?' gasped the angel. 'Alike to an angel but not so.'

'Push harder,' Jasfoup shouted. 'Push it into me.'

Harold pushed, feeling the increased resistance of the demon flesh.

'Ow!' said Jasfoup, hanging on to Samael for dear life. 'Now pull it out.'

Harold withdrew the blade to a squeal of pain from the angel.

'Quick,' said the demon. 'Back to the door.'

Harold ran with Jasfoup, holding his stomach where Harold had cut him, close behind. They reached the spot and the demon pulled open the door. 'Inside,' he said. 'Hurry.'

He slammed the door shut behind them and collapsed to the sandy floor of the tunnel. 'That was a close one,' he said.

Harold looked at his friend. 'You're burned,' he said. 'And cut.'

Jasfoup nodded. 'I know,' he said. 'That's contact with an angel for you.'

'Why did I have to run you both through?' Harold asked. 'Surely that hurt you?'

Jasfoup nodded. 'It did,' he said, 'but just as contact with the angel hurt me, once your sword had my blood on it you could hurt him as well.' He groaned. 'I'll be all right, though. I just need a lot of cola as soon as we get back.'

'Can you walk that far?'

'I'll have to.' Jasfoup grunted and struggled to his feet. 'We have a stop to make first, though.' They began walking, the demon leaning heavily on the human.

'For what?' Harold asked. 'Haven't we got what we came for?'

'Not yet. That was just to get the payment for the tickets. We still have to meet your brother.'

'My brother's in the past?'

'Yes.' Jasfoup groaned. 'I told you all this. We need to get blood from both him and his mother.' He patted his pocket. 'I've got the mother's, but now it's up to you to get your brother's.' He pulled out a capped syringe. 'This is the door,' he said. 'Take this and fill it with your brother's blood. Try not to let him see you, else there could be consequences.'

'What sort of consequences?'

'The sort that we got into back there.' Jasfoup nodded back down the passage. 'Now hurry. I don't like being in this much pain.'

'All right.' Harold began to step through the gate. 'What's my brother's name?' he asked.

'Oh, didn't I say?' said Jasfoup, smiling through the pain. 'It's Cain.'

***

Harold stumped through the dry brush toward the mountain where twin trails of smoke climbed into the clear sky. He could hear two men arguing and hid behind a tree.

'He liked mine better because it was meat,' said the first voice. 'God isn't a vegetarian.'

'That's all right for you, Abel,' said the second voice, which sounded closer. 'I got the job of growing vegetables. What was I supposed to do? Tell God that I didn't want the job because it was menial work?'

'No of course not. You were stronger than I was, Cain. You were the one with the ability to work the fields.'

Harold smiled. Now he knew which of the brothers were which and readied the syringe. As Cain passed his hiding place he struck, yanking out a tube full of Cain's blood. Cain spun around, but Harold ducked back behind the tree.

'What did you do that for?' Cain shouted.

'What?' Abel asked.

'Threw that... whatever it was at me.'

'I didn't.'

Cain picked up a big stick. 'That was bearing falsehood,' he said. 'I'm going to teach you a lesson, Abel.'

Harold made his way back. He was fairly certain that he knew what happened next.

***

'Well done, Harold.' Jasfoup staggered upright and headed home, leaning on Harold's shoulder. 'No complications, I hope?'

'Um... no.' Harold coughed. 'What's behind this door then?'

Jasfoup refocused his eyes. 'Good call, Harold,' he said. 'You might have the skill after all.' He struggled to open it.

'Why?' asked Harold. 'Where does it lead?'

'Atlanta, 1890.' Jasfoup grinned. 'Where they made cola with real cocaine in it.'

***

Jasfoup paused, one hand in his pocket. 'Show me the tickets first,' he said.

The demon spat. 'You can't trust anyone these days. Here they are.' He waved a pair of purple tickets in Jasfoup's face.

'Thank you.' Jasfoup produced a pomegranate. The demon grinned.

'Well done,' he said. 'I thought you were going to get out a lame-ass orange pippin. Not many realise that the apple of Eden was a pomegranate.'

Jasfoup shrugged. 'All the depictions of Eve's transgression show her with an apple. The early painters had never seen a pomegranate, so naturally they painted a grain apple as something the public could recognise.'

Chapter 17
Harold's Magic Touch

Harold swung the sword around. The veranda built onto the back of Ada's house in the late 1970s had proved to be a good space to practice in, assuming that Harold didn't mind the washing machine and the stack of plant pots on the table she used as a potting bench for her garden.

'Good,' Jasfoup said. 'Now bring the sword around in an arc, keeping the guard toward the enemy at all times so that they don't stab you in the fingers.'

Harold followed the instructions and Jasfoup nodded.

'Once more,' he said, 'but don't bend your arm this time. That gives your opponent your arm as a target.'

There was a crash as Harold put the sword through the window behind him. 'Perfect,' Jasfoup said.

'Mum's going to kill me,' said Harold, looking at the broken glass.

Jasfoup surveyed the damage. 'She won't have to,' he said. 'You're going to die soon anyway.'

'Thanks for reminding me.' Harold went up to inspect the damage. 'It's not too bad,' he said. 'At least it wasn't one of the double glazed ones.'

Jasfoup came to stand next to him. 'Get Devious to do it,' he said. 'You might as well make him work for his keep.'

'Good idea.' Harold clicked his fingers.

'Look at this,' said Jasfoup, lifting something from the wall just above the window. 'It was hidden in the brickwork and papered over. I wouldn't have noticed it if the glass hadn't cut the wallpaper.'

'What is it?' asked Harold. 'An old bottle?'

'A witch's bottle,' said Jasfoup. 'It's got an odd resonance, though.'

'Aren't they bad luck?' Harold took the bottle from the demon and peered at it. 'There's a little voodoo doll inside.'

'That's not a voodoo doll, it's a poppet,' said Jasfoup. 'They're very different. This one is designed as a protection fetiche.'

'Fetish?' repeated Harold. 'Somebody gets their jollies out of this?'

'No,' said Jasfoup. 'Well, probably not, anyway. A Fetiche is a power focus for a spell, a receptacle of spirit, if you like. Someone made this so that they can send their spirit here; either for good or ill.'

'Who put it there?'

Jasfoup took the bottle out of Harold's hands and twisted off the top. 'We'll soon find out,' he said, sitting at the potting bench and using a pair of tweezers to extract the doll.

Harold grimaced, wafting the air with his hand. 'What's that terrible smell?' he asked.

Jasfoup smiled. 'Blood, faeces, urine and—' he frowned. 'Marmalade.' He looked up. 'What we have here, Harold is a very old little poppet.'

'What was it put here for?' Harold asked. 'Does someone mean me harm?' He looked at the broken window and his mum's back garden. The bushes looked as if they might be hiding all sorts of creatures.

'I expect that hundreds of people want you dead, Harold, but that's not the purpose of this little chap.' Jasfoup held up the tiny doll. 'Look,' he said, showing it to Harold. 'It's you.'

'Me?' Harold examined it. 'I don't look like that. Why is it yellow?'

'The stuffing's leaked,' Jasfoup said. 'It's tobacco.'

'Uncle Frederick.' Harold shuddered.

'He's put it here to protect you,' said Jasfoup. 'It should go back again.' He began to reassemble the bottle.

'Could I make one of those?'

Jasfoup shrugged. 'When you learn enough about spells,' he said.

'I've learned the one to give me the Sight,' Harold said. 'Why don't you teach me a few more?'

Jasfoup frowned. 'It wouldn't hurt to teach you a few cantrips,' he said. 'Simple spells for simple tasks'

'Go on then.' Harold sat down. 'How about a spell to slow down time?'

Jasfoup snorted. 'You don't want much, do you? A spell like that takes a lot of power, and unless you want to start sacrificing you're a long way off that.'

Harold looked crestfallen. 'You really annoy me sometimes. I should cast you back into the eternal pit, you know. What can I learn then?'

'You wouldn't do that, Harold. You've a thirst for knowledge that only I can satisfy.' Jasfoup paused, looking at nothing and collecting his thoughts. 'Do you know about the conservation of energy?' he asked.

Harold nodded. 'I think so,' he said. 'Whenever something happens, a chemical reaction, say, there is always the same amount of energy afterwards as there was before, even though some of the elements of the reaction might have changed. Nothing is ever lost, just converted into other forms.'

'That's good, Harold. Not terribly accurate, but you understand the basic principle. Now I want you to speculate where the energy for a spell comes from. Imagine a fireball; an expanding cloud of plasma that will burn anything in its path. Does it go on forever?'

'No, of course not'

'That's right.' Jasfoup stood and put his arm around Harold's shoulder. 'So why does it stop?'

Harold looked up into the sparkling red eyes of the demon. 'Because it runs out of energy?'

'Quite so. It runs out of energy.' Jasfoup waved his free hand. 'So where does the energy for the fireball come from?'

'Well, I would have said the environment, but I suspect that you're going to tell me that it comes from the caster of the spell himself.' Harold followed Jasfoup with his eyes as the demon walked around the room.

'Exactly. You're brighter than you look, Harold. It comes from the caster of the spell. Now, where does the caster get the energy from?' Jasfoup raised his eyebrows.

'From food. That's where we all get our energy from,' said Harold. 'Go on.'

Jasfoup tapped his fingers on the bench. 'Food is a good answer,' he said, 'but what if there isn't any food, or you don't have time to eat it? What happens if you've got, say, a wounded angel charging at you and there's no plate of egg and chips handy?'

Harold thought about his school biology lessons, trying to take his mind off egg and chips. 'Wouldn't it come from stored body fats?'

'That's right.' Jasfoup laughed. 'So if the energy for your spells is coming from stored body fats, what happens to your body?'

'You get thinner.' Harold grinned. 'So I needn't really worry about any extra weight I've put on, because as soon as I start casting spells, I'm going to lose it again.'

'Correct,' said Jasfoup happily. He became serious again for a moment. 'There is a downside to all this, of course,' he said.

Harold looked at him. 'There was bound to be,' he said. 'Don't tell me, eternal damnation?'

'Of course, but not necessarily because of the spells you cast, but due to the intention with which you cast them.' Jasfoup mimed firing a gun first at the target on the wall, and then at Harold.

Harold shuddered. 'I'll try to remember that,' he said.

Jasfoup nodded. 'The real danger is that the bigger the spell, the more energy it needs, and if you don't have enough food or stored fats, the spell will take it from wherever it can; your muscles, your blood, your brain, your heart. That's why there are those 'last resort' spells, where the caster dies as soon as he utters them. A big spell would drain so much energy that the caster turns to dust' Jasfoup sat down again. 'Is this my tea?'

Harold nodded. 'Do I need a wand?'

'No, not for cantrips. I'll teach you the separation spell that we were doing the other day. Fetch those two syringes we collected yesterday, the jar of your mum's and the two jars of yours that Marisuel separated for us.'

'Yes, Master?'

Jasfoup looked up in surprise, but it was only Devious speaking.

'You took your time,' Harold said. 'I called you ages ago.

Devious shifted from hoof to hoof . 'Sorry, Master,' he said. 'I was very busy indeed, and couldn't stop what I was doing.'

'What was so important?' Jasfoup asked. 'I didn't think that anything overrode your Master's wishes.'

'Well…' The imp began to blush. 'It's the wife, you see. She doesn't like me to leave unfinished business.'

Jasfoup let out a howl of laughter.

'What?' asked Harold. 'What are you on about Devious?'

Jasfoup wiped tears from his eyes and spoke up for the imp. 'It must be her mating season,' he said. 'Devious was doing his husbandly duties.'

'Oh.' Harold swallowed and blushed as well. 'I see. Have you um… finished now?'

'Yes, Master. What did you want?' Devious was relieved to change the subject.

'Can you mend that window?' Harold pointed to the broken pane. 'Preferably before Mum sees it?'

The imp nodded and wrote it down on a pad. 'Anything else?'

'You can make us a cup of tea while I fetch the blood samples,' Harold added. 'That'd be useful.'

'Yes, Master.' Devious put his pad away. 'I'll make it now.'

Harold went upstairs to the attic. Jasfoup looked at the fetiche bottle. He put a tiny piece of his own fingernail inside and sealed it back up, replacing it in the wall cavity it came from.

'Here they are,' said Harold, laying out the jars on the table.

'Good.' Jasfoup checked them over. 'I'm just going to need a tiny bit more of yours, though. Hold out your arm.'

Harold rolled up his sleeve, ignoring the 'tut tut' of the imp as he carried in two cups of tea.

Jasfoup dragged a claw down his arm, gathering the trail of blood until he had enough to fill another third bottle and holding Harold's arm in a vice-like grip until it was done. Harold was looking everywhere but at his arm.

Jasfoup corked the bottle and spat onto the wound, rubbing it gently with his finger until it had healed without even a faint scar. 'All done,' he said. 'Now for the fun part.'

'I'm not sure how I feel about exchanging body fluids with a demon,' said Harold, as he watched Jasfoup set out several Petri dishes.

'I pour a little of your blood into one dish,' the demon said, 'and some of your brother's into the other.' The two looked identical to Harold, but he knew that there were subtle differences. 'Now, I cast the spell that will separate your brother's out into its two components: his mother's contribution and your father's.' He murmured a few words, and the pool of blood separated like a miniature red sea under the direction of a tiny Moses.

'That's incredible,' said Harold. 'Can I try it?'

'Sure.' Jasfoup indicated the second dish. 'Try it on your own.'

Harold repeated the words of the cantrip and watched the red-sea effect occur in his own blood. He grinned in delight.

'Now,' Jasfoup grinned. 'We cast a spell of like-to-like and add a drop of your mother's blood. That will tell us which part is hers.' The single drop veered to the left hand side of the dish. Jasfoup took a white hand-kerchief out of his breast pocket to wipe away that pool of blood since it was Ada's contribution to Harold and they didn't need it.

'Now for the second dish.' Jasfoup grinned. 'Since the portion of your blood that was your inheritance from your father is incomplete,' he said carefully, 'I'm hoping that when I isolate your shared father in Cain's blood it will be sufficiently different to make up a full sample, or near enough as makes no odds, of your father's blood.'

With a pipette, he took a drop of his Eve's blood and let it show him which of the separated halves of Cain's had belonged to her. With a nod of satisfaction, he wiped away the portion that came from her.

'There,' he said, mixing the two remaining portions together and putting the result into a separate bottle. He took out a quill and ink and marked the glass with the legend 'Harold's Father' in neat, copperplate lettering.

'Is it really that simple?' Harold asked.

Jasfoup shrugged. 'Yes,' he said. 'The hard part was gathering the components. How do you feel?'

'Hungry, now that you ask,' Harold said.

'Spells make you hungry,' said Devious, his hands full of window putty.

Harold grinned. 'How's your tea?'

'You've separated out the tea from the water, haven't you?' Jasfoup shook his head. 'Very funny. You've mastered the simplest of spells. Now mix them back up again so that I can drink it.'

Harold laughed and, taking a tea spoon, began to stir Jasfoup's tea. It swirled in the cup well enough, but as soon as he stopped stirring, the liquids separated out again, much to his consternation.

Jasfoup smiled. 'Bring me that empty glass jar,' he said.

Harold fetched it and Jasfoup poured the contents of his cup in. Within a few seconds, it had split into its component liquids: milk on the bottom, then water, then the dark sludge that was the essence of tea. Jasfoup performed the same spell as Harold had over the glass, and the milk separated out into water and grades of fat. A third spell caused the water to split into pure water and a fine layer of additives. A fourth caused a layer of sugar to separate from the sludge.

'This is what we drink so much of,' he said. 'Look at the different components that go into making a simple cup of tea. Now imagine that this wasn't a cup of tea, but something more complicated. A human body, perhaps. With enough casts of this simple, apparently harmless spell, we can cause a devastating effect on the target.'

Harold picked up the glass and looked at the liquid inside. It reminded him of the times when he was young, and a favourite experiment had been to mix up three tablespoons of soil into a pint of water and stir vigorously. Over the course of a week, as the mud settled out, you were left with layers of strata, the stones at the bottom, followed by increasing amounts of clay, rising in inverse order of density, to the lightest of plant matter at the top. He wondered if there was a market for selling separated tea, perhaps in small clear plastic animals like the one you could fill with coloured sand. He looked at Jasfoup. 'So how do I get it all back together, then? Is there a spell to do the opposite?'

Jasfoup steepled his fingers, regarding Harold though half-lidded eyes. 'There's certainly is a spell to mix things together,' he said. 'Watch.'

He performed a spell similar to the one he'd just taught to Harold, but with the actions reversed and the word 'commisceo' substituted for 'digero'. The liquids in the jar began swirling together, and within a few seconds looked just like the tea Harold had poured.

'That works well enough for liquids,' said Jasfoup, pouring the tea back into his cup, 'but look what happens when I use it for solids.' He took a currant biscuit out of his pocket and crumbled it, using the *digero* spell to separate them out, and the *commisceo* spell to put them back together. What he was left with was a pile of biscuit crumbs interspersed with currants.

'The problem here,' he said, sounding like a professor trying to explain quantum mechanics to a six-year-old, 'is that once the solid bonds are broken, it's not easy to repair them. It can be done, but that's a much more complicated spell, and one that you won't be able to perform for a long time yet.'

He grinned at Harold's disappointment. 'Cheer up, Harold. You've learned two spells today; you can't expect to fly when you've just taken your first step. You know more magic than ninety-nine point five percent of the population'. Harold smiled a little.

'That's better.' Jasfoup took a sip of his tea and spat it out again.

Harold looked at him in curiosity.

Jasfoup grinned sheepishly. 'That reminds me,' he said. 'Never separate milk from its components. It doesn't go back properly once the fat content has congealed out.'

'Would you like a fresh one?' Harold asked, turning to call Devious.

'What a splendid suggestion.' Jasfoup grinned and held his cup out.

Harold passed it to Devious. 'One thing puzzles me, though,' he said.

Jasfoup sat back in his chair. 'What's that?' he said.

'Why did you have a biscuit in your pocket?'

Chapter 18
The Corruption of Angels

Harold wasn't certain that all his customers were trustworthy. He'd taken a few bad pennies here and there over the years, but that was to be expected and besides, he often sold them on for more than the face value he'd taken them for: there was always a market for a decent forgery. He'd even made a few in his time, just for the practice, of course.

When he was small, for example, the local garage had a promotion on for the world cup, and with every gallon of petrol his uncle had bought he'd received a small medallion with a famous old-school footballer on. These medallions, Harold had discovered, were exactly the size and shape of a ten pence piece, so he began buying them from his friends for five pence each, then using them in vending machines and re-selling the products. This doubled his working capital, with the added bonus of enabling him to complete his collection in double time. Today was no exception. From his desk, where he was doing the crossword in the paper over his elevenses, he could see three customers in the shop. Old Mrs Clarke, who was perfectly harmless so long as he kept the silverware locked up; a young man who, judging from the army surplus coat and beanie hat, was probably a student, and a woman who rang a whole peal of bells on the 'oh no, not again' scale. She was dressed in a similar fashion to the last time Harold had seen her, in the company of Reverend Duke. Long red hair cascaded over the russet travelling cloak, and he could see a loose blouse tied at the neck over red leather trousers and calf length boots. What was different this time was that Harold could now see her wings.

Harold was getting used to seeing wings. Either the black, membranous ones like Jasfoup's when he chose to unfurl them, or the white feathered ones like the angel he had fought in the Garden of Eden. This woman's, though, were unusual in the way that a monkey's tail is unusual when you're used to seeing a dogs: they were prehensile.

As she walked toward him, her wings flexed and stretched, touching everything around her as if they had a compulsion to stroke every surface. They were invisible to ordinary folk, naturally; all that had happened when the other customers had walked past her was a momentary shiver as the wings caressed them. She was hanging back until Harold had sold Mrs Clarke a small ceramic cat figurine and arranged delivery of a desk and word processor (he was glad to see the back of that) to the student with a ten-pound deposit before the woman had finally approached the desk.

'Mr Waterman?' She spoke with a clipped accent, reminiscent of the old films he'd seen in his youth about the English in Victorian times, slaughtering native peoples in the name of progress and Christianity.

Harold put down his pen and backed away from her. He was stuck on nineteen across anyway: 'Down the toilet is the obvious solution.'

'Jedith,' he said. 'I didn't expect to see you again.'

She tapped her fingers on the table top. 'You remember me then.'

Harold stared at her fingers, wondering how it was possibly for anyone to have nails quite that perfect, even if she was an angel. 'How could I forget? You infected me with a disease that will kill me in a couple of months. I tend to remember people that do that to me.'

She smiled slowly, like a snake that has tempted a chipmunk to inspect its teeth. 'It was nothing personal,' she said. 'Just doing my job. You are one of the accursed.'

'Thanks to you, yes,' Harold said. 'I can't even claim on my health insurance, the disease you gave me is so rare.'

An Ungodly Child

Jedith stared at him, her gaze taking in his new haircut and clothes. 'I bear you no ill will,' she said, reaching to touch his hand.

Before Harold could jerk away, the leather of his suit stretched, seemingly of its own accord, to cover his hand. Jedith pulled away.

'You have discovered much since we last met,' she said, her eyes narrowing. 'I sense the stink of Hell upon you.'

Harold shrugged, un-nerved by the action of his jacket but more concerned with the threat before him. A glance showed him that his sword cane was out of reach. 'Heaven hasn't done a lot to help my cause,' he said. 'The first contact I have with the Heavenly Host is when they try to kill me off. You can't blame me if I ask for help from the other side.'

'Perhaps not.' Jedith smiled. 'So when will your armies obliterate the people of the earth?'

'Armies?' Harold laughed. 'You're barking up the wrong tree. I don't have any armies. All I want is my life back.'

She looked surprised. 'Even when legions of Hell are at your disposal?'

Harold laughed. 'I'd hardly call one demon and an imp a legion,' he said. 'Jasfoup is just helping me find a cure for what you gave me.'

'Jasfoup?' Jedith stepped forward, her body pressing against the glass of the display counter Harold used as a front desk. He was almost distracted by the shape of her figure under the tight leather. 'You have the aid of him?'

'He's my friend,' Harold said. 'Why? Do you know him?'

'Biblically.' Jedith seemed to find this amusing. 'Is he here? Tell him that I wish to speak with him.'

'If you insist' Harold took a sideward step, hoping to get closer to his cane. 'Can I tell him what it's about?'

Jedith rubbed a hand over her face. 'His plan is unclear,' she said. 'I must think on this.'

'Whose plan?' Harold asked. 'Jasfoup's?'

'Jehovah's,' said Jedith, turning and heading for the door. 'I cannot see the path.' Her wings folded as she strode away, her cape billowing behind her.

'Wait!' Harold called. 'What path?'

The ring of the bell above the door as it closed was his only reply.

***

'Jedith was back in today,' Harold said. 'She wants to talk to you.'

Jasfoup's eyes clouded. 'What about?'

'She wouldn't say.' Harold looked up into the demon's red eyes. 'Something about Jehovah's plan being unclear.'

'Shh.' Jasfoup shrank back. 'Don't say that name. You don't know what it will summon.'

Harold swallowed. 'What has J—' He paused. 'What does He want with me? You never told me why He would want me dead. Is it because of who my father is?'

'Probably.' Jasfoup nodded. 'That's the only reason I can think of, although it surprised me. He doesn't usually single out individuals for termination, just cities and continents.'

'What would be the advantage of killing me?' Harold was clearly upset and held a hand over his eyes to prevent tears from falling.

Jasfoup stood behind him, one hand on his shoulder. 'I don't know, Harold. It's not as if you're a threat to the Host, is it?'

'No. She said something similar. She asked me when my armies would destroy the world.' Harold looked up into the demon's face

'Why would she say that? You don't have any armies.' Jasfoup's brow creased into ridges of confusion.

'Only the two in my sleevies.' Harold grinned. 'Then she said she needed to speak to you. Do you know her, then?'

'Yes. She's neither angel nor demon, but something in between, one of the Four Horsemen.' Jasfoup shook his head sadly. 'It's not like her to become personally involved with anything.'

'I didn't see her horse.'

'Horses are allegorical. When the books of the Apocalypse were written, it was the fastest transport Paul could think of. If they'd been written any earlier, they may well have been the Four Camel Drivers of Jezreel.'

'Jezreel? Who's he?' Harold took his hand away from his face, glad to focus on something other than his impending death.

'It's not a person but a place in the Holy Land; the site of slaughter for thousands of years, and where the name 'Harmageddon' refers to.'

'I didn't know that.'

'Well, you wouldn't, would you? Unless you lived there, of course. If the books of prophesy had been written here, they may have well been 'The Four Pizza delivery boys of Deptford.' Jasfoup laughed, relieved to get a smile from Harold.

Harold frowned. 'I always thought that 'Armageddon' was the end of the world. The ultimate battle between the forces of good and evil.'

'No. Armageddon is just a place.' Jasfoup sat down on a box of comics. 'When Lucifer was cast out of Heaven, all the Hosts took sides, except for four angels who were playing cards. Guess who got picked on by the Big Bearded One? The Four are now destined to bear both the burdens of the world and the brunt of satirical humour until the end of eternity.'

'That's a place too?'

'No.'

'Oh.' Harold tried to fit this information into what he'd learned in Bible studies. 'What were they playing?'

'What?' Jasfoup tried to switch tracks on his train of thought to keep up with Harold.

'What card game were the Four playing?'

'Oh, Bridge, obviously. Death was on for a little slam in No Trumps at the time. He was a bit annoyed, let me tell you!'

'He? Death isn't a woman as well, then?'

'Not always. Death is what everyone expects him to be. These days he's usually depicted as a little Goth chick. It doesn't matter to Asaem how people to portray him; they all get to meet him in the end.'

'Hang on, though, I thought that angels didn't have sex.'

'Don't you believe it, Harold. They're at it like rabbits, all the time.'

'No, I meant... what? Really?'

Jasfoup nodded solemnly. 'In a very civilised fashion, naturally. Why do you think all the Catholics want to get there?'

'That makes a lot of sense. I did wonder what could possibly occupy someone for eternity.'

'Exactly. The downstairs action is more fun, though.'

'Isn't it always?' Harold grinned, remembering the magazines he kept in a box at the shop. His thoughts returned to Jedith. 'She looks good for her age, though. Is she single?'

'Death? Of course.' Jasfoup laughed. 'She couldn't really be anything else.'

'No...' Harold gestured to the shop.

'Oh, Jedith. Yes, she's single, but please stay away from her, Harold. She's not girlfriend material, I promise.'

'How do you know?'

Jasfoup wrung his hands. It was the most agitated that Harold had ever seen him. 'I just do. Leave her well alone.'

'Why? Are you after her?' Harold grinned.

'She's a bit out of your league, isn't she?'

'What do you mean, out of my league? I'm a very eligible bachelor, I'll have you know.'

'She's not actually allied to either upstairs or downstairs, though, as technically all the Four are impartial?'

'Oh, right. I see. I apologise, then.'

'Accepted,' Jasfoup huffed. 'Nine across is 'scatological', by the way.'

'You still haven't said why you think she was looking for you, though.'

'Didn't I?' Jasfoup coughed. 'She's my ex-wife.'

**

Harold was surprised, the next morning, to see that Ada was up before him. 'Are you all right, Mum?' he asked, as she put on her coat.

'Yes, Harold,' she said. 'Have you taken your tablets?'

'Not yet, no.' Harold kissed her cheek. 'Where are you going?'

'To see Mrs Clarke. She was taken poorly last night. There's fresh tea in the pot if you want it.'

'Thanks, Mum. She was fine yesterday. She was in the shop.'

'Well, she's not today.' Ada paused. 'You didn't drop a wardrobe or anything on her, did you?'

'Mum!' Harold was shock.

Ada put a hand on his arm. 'I'm sorry, Harold. I'm worried about her, that's all.'

'I know, Mum.'

Harold waited until the door closed behind her before rushing upstairs to the attic to summon Jasfoup.

The demon was surprised to be summoned so early. He was still eating a piece of toast and jam. 'Where's the fire?' he asked.

Harold looked grim. 'Mrs Clarke is ill,' he said.

'So what?' Jasfoup shrugged. 'I can't cure everybody.'

'Mrs Clarke is the old lady who buys all the chintz about cats that I can shovel her way. She was in the shop yesterday when Jedith came in.'

'Oh'. Jasfoup finished his piece of toast. 'Was there anyone else?'

'A student. Frederick delivered a desk and word processor to him yesterday afternoon. I'll have his address on the invoice.'

'He'll have an interesting disease too. What a waste, though. I can't accept souls culled by the Four and it'll cut into my bonuses.' Jasfoup sucked air through his teeth in irritation.

'What will we do? They may trace the disease to my shop.'

Jasfoup grinned. 'I've got an idea,' he said. 'Let's go and get that invoice.'

***

Jasfoup liked the van. It was an average three ton panel van, with 'Harold's Emporium' emblazoned in peeling gold paint along the sides, but the best bit about it was the cabin height. Jasfoup could sit quite happily on the passenger seat and not have his wings crushed by the roof of the cab. He enjoyed Harold's driving, too, and made a mental note of which pedestrians and motorists cursed and swore as his employer weaved in and out of the traffic.

It was only a few minutes before they pulled up in front of a run-down row of terraced houses. Several of the windows sported displays of liberated road signs and traffic cones, and Jasfoup grinned at the rich pickings that were on offer to a soul collector of his caliber. They climbed out of the van, and walked up the short path to the door of number thirty-two. Jasfoup knocked on the rattling glass panel whilst Harold checked the delivery note. It was opened by a girl with beads in her hair and smelling of incense. 'Of course it's incense,' thought Jasfoup, 'and I'm an angel.' She was a little taken aback at the two men at the door, but was polite enough.

'Hello,' said Harold, cheerily. 'I'm looking for a Mr John Knowles. Is he in?'

She looked at him. 'I've never heard of him,' she said.

Harold smiled. 'Sorry,' he said. 'I only ask because he bought a computer from us the other day and we owe him a small refund.'

She opened the door further. 'He's upstairs. He's not very well, though.' The girl stared at them, and Harold managed to keep his smile just long enough for her to drop her gaze and step to one side.

'Thank you,' said Harold. 'This will only take a minute.' They stepped inside into the darkened hallway.

The girl pointed upstairs. 'First door on the right,' she said, then, as Jasfoup edged past, 'Cool wings.'

Jasfoup raised an eyebrow. 'Cute soul, Annie, nice shade of grey,' he whispered, smiling at how pale she suddenly became.

He followed Harold upstairs and entered John's room. Inside the curtains were still drawn, but he could clearly see that the young man was in the grip of a deep fever. Harold went over to him and roused him from sleep. As his eyes focused, he started.

'Who are you?' he said. 'Have you come for my soul?'

'What?' started Harold, but Jasfoup stopped him.

'He can see me,' said the demon, before turning to the young student. 'You are about to die, mortal.'

John gasped. 'I can't,' he said. 'I've got an assignment to hand in on Tuesday.'

Jasfoup hissed. 'You would have got a 'D' anyway,' he said. 'Tell Jedith where to find me.'

'Who?' John's voice faded as his eyes glazed. The sweat lying on his skin slowed and stopped and was reabsorbed, leaving him encrusted with salt.

'Ugh!' exclaimed Harold.

'Can I make a small point about Lot's wife?' said Jasfoup, with a grin.

'That was in bad taste,' Harold replied. 'Time we left, I think.'

As they trooped down the stairs again, Jasfoup was humming. 'That was a great idea,' he said.

'And here I am.' A feminine voice in a clipped English accent caused then to stop suddenly upon the stairs.

Jasfoup started at the familiar voice. The spot that Annie had occupied as they went upstairs was now host to the Angel of Pestilence.

'Jedith.' Jasfoup nodded a greeting.

'Jasfoup.' She smiled in return.

'I hear you wanted to speak to me.' The demon resumed his walk down the stairs slowly.

'And now I find you, as well as your new master.' Harold was rewarded with the smile. He raised an eyebrow at the term 'master', though.

'More of a business deal,' Jasfoup corrected, his voice harsh and cold.

'What, Jasfoup? No warm welcome for your beloved Jedith?' The angel took a step forward, and Harold could see the young girl, Anne, slumped on a chair in the room behind her, her flesh already discolouring with the onset of disease.

'Hello, Jedith, how good to see you,' Jasfoup replied mechanically. 'What do you want?'

'What is this human?' she asked, indicating Harold. 'He is of the House of Lucifer and yet does not seek to conquer?'

'He's not the antichrist, Jedith.' Jasfoup reached the bottom of the stairs, and looked ate the angel. 'Why were you contracted to kill him?'

'I was told that he would start the war, Jasfoup, but he seems to have no desire to.'

Jasfoup glanced at Harold's puzzled expression. 'Who told you that?' he asked. 'Harold has neither the desire nor the power to do that.'

'I cannot say.' Jedith frowned. 'I have been misled, I think.' She turned to Harold. 'I'm sorry, mortal man. I have done you a disservice.'

Harold smiled. 'That's all right,' he said. 'Just take the disease away and we'll call it quits.'

She shook her head. 'Only Yahweh has that power,' she said. 'I do not. I will vouch for you at Judgement day, though.'

Harold frowned. 'That's not much help to me now,' he said.

Jedith gave a curt nod. 'It is all I can offer,' she said, 'apart from my friendship.'

'That's peachy, Jedith,' the demon replied, putting an arm around Harold. 'We'll let you know.' Jedith bowed, turned and walked out of the house without a backward glance.

'That was disappointing,' said Harold. 'I was hoping she'd at least tell us why I've been marked for death.'

'Marked,' said Jasfoup. 'Harold, you're a genius.'

'I know,' Harold replied. 'But why specifically?'

Chapter 19
Talking to Ghosts

Harold placed two cups of tea on the kitchen table.

'So what did you mean when you said that I was a genius back at the house?' he said.

Jasfoup added sugar. '*Digero*,' he muttered to stir it. 'You wanted Jedith to tell you why you'd been marked for death,' he said.

'So?' Harold frowned. 'She wouldn't tell me, would she?'

Jasfoup wagged a finger at him. 'But you said 'marked', which put me in mind of your brother.' He took a sip of his tea and continued. 'He was marked, too.'

'I remember,' Harold said. 'There are still debates as to what that meant, though. Some say that he was marked just to show that he was a murderer.'

'The mark of Cain,' said Jasfoup, 'is vampirism. He could no longer face the sun's light. He called it 'The Eye of God'.'

'So are you saying that I'm a vampire? I think I'd have noticed, Jasfoup. Especially when I brush my teeth.' Harold ran a finger along them, just to be certain.

The demon laughed. 'Not at all, Harold. I think you should become one.'

'Ugh.' Harold made a face. 'I don't want to be a vampire, Jasfoup. I have no interest in killing people just to survive. Besides, I wouldn't be able to drink tea any more.'

Jasfoup nodded. 'Remember that pill I gave you?' he said. 'That was a vampire's pineal gland.'

'Don't remind me,' Harold said. 'It makes me queasy to even think about it.'

'You didn't complain about the benefits, though,' Jasfoup reminded him. 'Increased healing, tougher skin.'

'And a desire to wear opera cloaks and speak with a lisp.' Harold laughed. 'So what? It still doesn't mean I want to be one.'

'But what if you had a vampire's regenerative ability, but remained human?' asked Jasfoup. 'Tell me that's not an attractive proposition.'

'I suppose.' Harold considered it. 'Would that get rid of the disease?'

'In theory, yes.' Jasfoup drummed his hands on the table. 'Where is the nearest vampire?'

Harold shrugged. 'How should I know?'

***

Semangalof looked up. 'Can we allow that?' he asked. 'He's supposed to die and make way for another antichrist'

Sansenoy steepled his fingers. 'Becoming even part vampire is an act of great evil,' he said. 'Perhaps he will step onto the path we desired originally.'

'And bring about the apocalypse?' Senoy grinned. 'The Lord has left it too long. Hell gathers in strength while we waste time. If we can bring about the final battle soon, Heaven can still win.'

'Exactly so, Mr Patch.' Sansenoy considered the problem. 'We should not interfere yet. Let him see if he becomes a cold killer.'

'It will make it more difficult to kill him if it doesn't,' Semangalof warned.

'Agreed, but it is worth the risk.'

Senoy put his sword down again with a sigh. 'I'm bored,' he said. 'We haven't done any killing for ages. What happened to Lilith?'

'She went into hiding.' Sansenoy shrugged. 'There have been no lilim born in centuries.'

***

Harold pulled onto the side of the road where Jasfoup indicated. 'This can't be right,' he said. 'This is my solicitor's.'

'Have you never wondered why Isaacs prefers evening appointments?' Jasfoup asked. 'He's been in business for seventy years. That should have been a clue.'

Harold shrugged. 'I just thought it was a father and son thing. Anyway, it's closed.'

'He's a vampire, Harold. Light is for customers. Let's have a look, shall we?'

They got out of the van and knocked on the door. The shop was silent. Harold cupped his hands against the glass and tried to peer in past the reflections of the street lamps, but could see nothing. 'He's not here,' he said.

Jasfoup frowned. 'He must be out hunting,' he said. 'We'll ring tomorrow and make an appointment.'

Harold sighed. 'You've got me all worked up over nothing,' he said. 'I thought I was going to get cured tonight.'

'Think of it as delayed gratification.' The demon climbed back into the car. 'Home, James.'

Harold slipped into the driver's seat. 'Are there no other vampires we could see?' he asked. 'He can't be the only one, surely.'

'He probably is.' Jasfoup braced himself as Harold shifted into gear. 'Vampires are very territorial.'

'Isn't there anyone we could ask?'

'I suppose so,' Jasfoup admitted. 'We could summon a ghost'

Less than ten minutes later, Harold led Jasfoup into the house as quietly as he could, careful not to disturb Ada. 'Do we need to use the circle to summon a ghost?'

'Unless you want it roaming freely about the house,' the demon replied. 'If you don't confine it you'll never get rid of it.'

'We'll go to the attic upstairs then,' Harold whispered.

'Really? Isn't that an unusual place to keep an attic room?' Jasfoup grinned, his teeth fluorescing in the light filtering in from the streetlamp in the road outside.

Harold grimaced. 'You'll cut yourself being so sharp one of these days.' He began to climb the stairs, beckoning the demon to follow.

'I'm hurt, Harold.' Jasfoup moved to follow. 'At least we make a good team. If I'm sharp, you're blunt, or dim, depending upon your interpretation of 'sharp'.'

'Will you be quiet? If mum hears us she's going to be more cutting than a bacon slicer.'

'Sorry.' Jasfoup paused. 'What sort of ghost do you want to summon?'

Harold shrugged. 'I don't care,' he said, 'as long as it can tell us where to find a vampire.'

Jasfoup stopped, his eyes flaring in anger. 'You don't care? What kind of imbecilic necromancer do you want to be? You have to know exactly who or what you're summoning. Even the most pathetic of wandering spirits can steal your body or your soul if you're not prepared for them. You need to place specific constraints within the pentagram for each class of spirit.'

Harold examined his shoes for a moment. 'How about Mrs Clarke?' he asked.

'The woman Jedith killed?'

Harold nodded.

'She'll do fine. She liked cats, didn't she?'

'That's right.' Harold raised his eyebrows. 'Does that make a difference?'

'It gives us an edge.' Jasfoup grinned.

They were suddenly bathed in light. Ada stood by the switch, glaring at them. Jasfoup let out a shriek.

'Hello, Mum,' said Harold, offering her a smile.

'Do you know what time it is Harold?'

'Er, half-past two?' Harold had hoped to avoid running into his mum. 'We didn't wake you, did we?'

'Half-past two.' Ada repeated the phrase, enunciating every syllable carefully. 'What time of night do you call this? Hello, Mr Jasfoup, How are you today? Nice suit.'

An Ungodly Child

'Hello, Ada. I'm very well, thank you, and thank you.' Jasfoup was on a back foot, psychologically speaking, when it came to Ada.

'Go and put the kettle on, Harold,' said Jasfoup, brightly. 'I'm sure your mum would like a nice cup of tea.'

'Make it cocoa,' said Ada, turning again to go back into her room.

'Yes, mum.' Harold trooped down the remaining stairs to the kitchen.

Jasfoup watched as Harold went around the corner at the bottom, and then put his arm around Ada's shoulders. He lowered his voice conspiratorially. 'Harold does look very good in those new clothes,' he said. 'Very attractive and manly, if you know what I mean...'

'Oh.' Ada wanted to sit down. Although not unexpected, it was still a bit of a shock to her. 'You mean you and Harold are...' she waggled her fingers for emphasis. Jasfoup was puzzled. 'What?' he asked.

'You're a gay couple, are you?' Ada was warming to the idea fast. She'd always liked Mr Jasfoup, and having him in the family would be nice.

'What? No! We're not gay! I just meant that he was very desirable, now. He'll soon have a lady friend, and lots of little Harolds, too, I'll be bound.'

'Oh, I see,' said Ada, relieved and disappointed at the same time. 'I did think you might be a little old for him, but the two of you spend a lot of time together these days, and I wouldn't have minded, you know.'

Jasfoup smiled and gave Ada a peck on the cheek. 'But if Harold and I were an item, that wouldn't leave room for my favourite girl, would it?'

Ada chuckled. 'Oh, Mr Jasfoup; you are a one,' she said.

Jasfoup smiled. 'I'll just go and see how my little concubine is doing with that cup of cocoa,' he said. 'Only joking,' he added at the look on Ada's face.

Harold reappeared carrying a tray with the cocoa for his mum and two cups of tea. 'What were you two talking about?' he asked.

Ada and Jasfoup exchanged a glance. 'Nothing,' they said in unison.

Harold frowned. 'Here's your cocoa, mum,' he said. 'Jasfoup and I are going to have a last cup of tea before bed.'

'Good for you.' Ada winked and went back into her room.

Harold looked at the demon. 'She winked,' he said. 'What was that about?'

The demon shrugged and took out some papers from his jacket pocket. 'How should I know?' he asked. 'Here, hold these.' The demon handed the sheaf of paperwork to Harold, who glanced at it but was unable to read the lettering. 'What language is this?' he asked.

'It's the ancient tongue of the Seraphim,' said Jasfoup. 'It's a little archaic, but still widely used in legal circles.'

'What are you going to do?' Harold whispered.

Jasfoup took off his jacket and handed it to Harold. 'Watch,' he said, 'but don't tell.'

Jasfoup shimmered from his generally human appearance into his full demonic form. Harold took a step back. It wasn't that he hadn't seen Jasfoup like this before; he had, many times; but it was one thing to spend the time he did with a vaguely human-like man (albeit with huge claws and teeth that could turn a saucepan into a colander) but quite another to see the full bringer of nightmares.

Jasfoup stretched into his real skin and spread his wings as far as the landing would allow. Harold took a quick look towards his mum's room and hoped that the television would continue to keep her occupied. He was about to speak when Jasfoup began to shimmer again. The leathery bat wings seemed to turn white, and Harold was astonished to see tiny feathers appearing and growing across the taut membrane. Jasfoup's normally pitch-black flesh paled into a milky shade, his claws retracted into fingers, and his snout into a normal mouth. Finally, with the crack of bone, his legs shortened and his hooves elongated, each changing to one large toe, then splitting into five, before finally settling into a standard human foot. Harold gasped. Stood before him was an image of true beauty. 'You're an angel, Jasfoup,' he whispered, awe-struck.

Jasfoup grinned, or rather the angel smiled beatifically. 'Only in as much as putting on a top hat makes you English, Harold. I've told you before: people see what they want to see, believe what they want to believe, and do anything an angel wants them to.' He winked. As he opened the door to the attic, Jasfoup began to glow with a golden radiance, his head changing into the shape of a cat's.

Harold followed him in, holding the papers up while Jasfoup recited the invocation. Mrs Clarke appeared as an outline first, like a cartoon that hadn't been inked in, then filled out into three dimensions. Jasfoup composed himself. 'Child of the Earth,' he began, 'thou art wandering the realm of limbo. Doth thou wish to move onwards?'

Mrs Clarke looked at him and smiled. 'Yes,' she said. 'I could see my Tommy again then.'

Encouraged, Jasfoup continued. 'Where, then, is the nearest stealer of life?'

'That could be anybody,' muttered Harold. 'Any killer at all.'

'Ghosts aren't bound by that,' Jasfoup hissed. 'Life meant blood, originally.'

Mrs Clarke shook her head. 'I'm not sure I know what you mean. Will I be going to cat heaven?'

Jasfoup opened his hands in a gesture of honesty. 'If you wish it,' he said. 'Where are the vampires, though?'

'Oh, vampires.' Mrs Clarke waved a hand. 'Christopher Lee was so dashing, you know.' She paused, her face creasing. 'There's one to the north, in Milton Keynes, I think, and another to the east She's a younger one. Very pretty.'

'Oh?' Harold perked. 'What about Mr Isaacs?'

Mrs Clarke looked straight at him. 'He's away, Harold. You know he takes August off for his holidays.'

'I didn't, actually.'

'Well, you do now.' Mrs Clarke looked at the cat-headed angel that was Jasfoup. 'Can I go to cat heaven now?'

'Of course.' Jasfoup flipped through the pages Harold was holding and spoke a few sentences in the strange language.

Mrs Clarke smiled and, a look of joy and contentment lighting her features, faded from sight.

Harold watched as Jasfoup returned to his normal form. 'That was easy,' he said.

'Yes.' The demon stepped back from the circle and took the papers back. 'It looks like we'll have to wait until tomorrow night to call a vampire here,' he said. 'Which do you fancy?' He looked at Harold's face. 'That was a stupid question, wasn't it?'

Harold grinned and stared at the circle. 'Will she really go to cat heaven?' he asked.

'If that's what she truly believes in, yes.' Jasfoup grinned. 'She's not going to like it though.'

Harold turned. 'Why not?'

'Because all the cats are twenty feet tall,' the demon said. 'She's five.'

Chapter 20
After Life

Jasfoup stepped out of the toilet cubicle to a clean and hygienic gentleman's rest room. That was one of the reasons he like Bernard's bar: privacy and discretion were assured. There were few other public places where he dared to emerge from the travelling tunnels in case one of the rare few that could see him, saw him. He nodded to a putto using the urinal, and went into the main bar area.

He stopped when he saw the old solicitor. 'Good evening, Isaacs,' he said. 'I was told you were away. Harold and I were looking for you.' He stepped around the headless corpse of an elf as it hung inverted over a barrel with nothing more than a raised eyebrow.

'I am aware of that, Mr Jasfoup,' said Isaacs, pleasantly. 'May I say what a pleasure it is to have your company once again.'

Jasfoup smiled. 'You may indeed,' he said.

Isaacs paused for a moment and gave a dry, rasping laugh. 'You were ever the source of mirth, Mr Jasfoup. How is young Harold?'

Jasfoup pushed a ghoul off a barstool and sat down, nodding to Bernard for service. 'He's all right. Doing quite well, as a matter of fact, learning his craft.' He leaned forward and lowered his voice. 'He'd be doing a lot better if he wasn't dying.'

Isaacs nodded. 'I know what you want to ask,' he said, 'and it's not my place to offer it.' He laughed at Jasfoup's expression. 'I had to employ a bit of subterfuge. I knew you'd be looking for me to take young Harold under my wing, as it were, but I had strict instructions not to bind the lad to me.'

Jasfoup looked at Bernard, waiting for his order. 'Tea, please, Bernard,' he said, 'and whatever Isaacs is having.' He returned his attention to the vampire. 'Instructions from whom?' he asked.

'His father, of course.' Isaacs smiled, the tips of his canines making slight indentations in his lower lip.

'You've seen Mr Ferre?'

'Not since the lad was born, no, but he left instructions nonetheless.' Isaacs took the glass of blood that Bernard placed in front of him, nodding his thanks.

'He knew what would happen to Harold?' Jasfoup took a sip of tea, digesting this new thread.

'All part of his ineffable plan, apparently.' Isaacs shook his head.

Jasfoup grimaced. 'I hate ineffability.'

'Don't we all.' Isaacs drained his glass. 'You'll be wanting to contact the young lady, I expect. She's been turned thirty years now, that should be about right. Not so strong that she can dominate him, but strong enough to give him what he needs.' He laughed. 'Just make sure that she gets a taste of his blood, and he a taste of hers.'

Jasfoup frowned. 'Why's that then?'

'So that she'll be bound to him.' Isaacs smiled. 'All part of the plan, so he said. Don't ask me.'

'Mr Ferre knew all this thirty years ago?'

'Of course.' Isaacs lowered his voice. 'I shouldn't say this,' he said, 'seeing as he's your boss and my grand-sire, but it wouldn't surprise me if he'd engineered it all.'

'But Harold is dying,' Jasfoup said. 'Who would arrange that for their own son?'

'Someone who knew that it wouldn't happen,' Isaacs replied. 'Someone who knew that death would be a catalyst for their son to begin to live up to his potential.' He placed his glass on the bar and signalled for another. 'You watch. Now that he thinks he's not going to die, he'll turn his life around.'

'What do you mean?' Jasfoup drained his tea and pushed the cup away.

'He'll want to downsize the shop,' Isaacs said. 'Specialise in the things that he likes best'

'There's not much of a market for used tea leaves, I'm afraid.' Jasfoup grinned.

Isaacs chuckled. 'You could probably sell them on eBay,' he said.

The bar stool next to Jasfoup scraped and the putto he'd seen in the bathroom climbed onto it. He looked up at Bernard. 'Pint of the Heavy, please,' he said.

Bernard narrowed his eyes. 'Are you old enough to be at the bar?' he asked.

The putto curled a tiny fist 'You have got to be joking, right? I'm as old as dirt. It's not my fault that He created me as a putto. Do you know how difficult it is to be taken seriously when you look like a two year old?'

'Not really.' Bernard shrugged. 'You've got cute little podgy cheeks, though.'

'Make one move to pinch those cheeks and I'll fill the whole pub with locusts,' warned the putto.

'It'd liven the place up a bit,' grinned Jasfoup. 'But you're right. Bernard, leave the poor fellow alone.'

Bernard laughed. 'Anything you say, Jasfoup.' He said, shaking his head. 'Here's your Heavy. That'll be four pounds.'

The putto scowled. 'Can I have a tab?' he asked. 'I don't have any money. Where would I keep loose change in a nappy?'

'Put it on mine,' said Jasfoup. He turned to the putto. 'What's your name? I haven't seen you in here before.'

The putto held out a pudgy hand, and Jasfoup shook it carefully. 'Arty,' said the putto. 'Thanks for the drink.' He held the pint glass in two tiny hands and tried to lift it. Jasfoup signalled Bernard over. 'A straw for the gentleman, if you would be so kind, Bernard.'

'That's an odd name,' he said. 'Where did you get it?'

The putto smiled. 'It's short for 'The Achievement of Arbitrary Targets'. He leaned in closer. 'Are you a demon?' he asked. 'Only I was told that this was the place to come where everybody could be themselves and there wouldn't be any trouble.'

'Trouble?' Jasfoup laughed. 'There's certainly no trouble in here, not unless you want to get barred for life, which, let's face it, is a bloody long time for us.'

'Does anyone get into trouble for being here? From their superiors, I mean.'

'No.' Jasfoup was dismissive. 'The Moon is protected from scrying. As long as you have a legitimate reason for being on the mortal plane, the only way that anyone could tell that you've been in here was if they came in themselves, and if they come in here they won't want anyone knowing about it either.' Jasfoup signalled for another cup of tea. 'And yes, I am a demon, if you couldn't tell by the claws and the wings.'

The putto snorted. 'I bet you don't get ridiculed by the Seraphim,' he said. 'At least you have a decent form.' He leaned in closer still. 'I want to defect,' he said, his voice barely above a whisper.

'Good for you,' said Jasfoup, adding sugar to his second cup of tea. 'But why do you think we'll take you? It's not like we have a pressing need for fallen putti, is it?'

'I know things,' Arty said with a sideways glance towards Isaacs. 'Things that He wouldn't want generally known to your side.'

'Isaacs? He's harmless enough, as long as you don't drink from his favourite vessel.'

'Not him. G-O-D. I know some of His secrets.'

'How do I know that? How do I know that you're not a plant?'

Arty looked down at his pudgy figure. 'Is that a joke?'

'A spy. I meant a spy.'

'I'm not a spy.'

'Any spy worth his salt would say that they're not a spy.' Jasfoup sipped his tea, 'Got any crisps, Bernard?'

'That would be a lie!' Arty was shocked. 'I don't lie. I'm a putto.'

'That's exactly what you'd say if you were a spy, though. Do you want a packet of crisps?'

'Thank you. How can I prove that I'm not a spy?'

'What's the secret about Him, then?'

'If I tell you, then I won't have any bargaining power left, will I?'

The putto lifted another drink, his rosebud lips sucking sweetly at the straw.

'You'll have to give me something,' Jasfoup said. 'I can't just go to my superiors and say: 'He wants to defect and he says he's got a secret.'

'All right, then.' Arty thought for a moment. 'He censors whole sections of the Bible.'

Jasfoup laughed. 'Everybody knows that,' he said. 'Even the mortals. You'll have to do a lot better than that!'

The putto frowned and thought harder. 'He eats crackers,' he said at last. 'In bed.'

Jasfoup considered the prospect. 'That could be useful,' he said. 'It's not actually a sin, but it could be useful leverage.' He thought about the proposal for a minute. 'All right,' he said finally. 'I'll pass it on to the relevant department, but I'm not promising anything.'

'Fair enough.' Arty said. 'How will I know of the decision?'

'Meet me in three days, and I'll let you know.' Jasfoup drained his tea and stood up.

'Where shall we meet, though? Here again?'

'No.' Jasfoup pondered. 'Meet me in the park. I believe that the duck pond is traditional for this sort of thing.' He grinned. 'Come in from the cold: it's warm in Hell.'

***

Harold had managed five hours sleep before having to open the shop again. Having some hope for the future had meant that his apathy towards it had decreased, although standing in the middle of all the detritus of society made him want to change the focus of the shop.

At lunchtime he clicked his fingers for Devious and waited, eventually making his own tea and summoning Jasfoup with a pentagram of wet tea bags.

'I can't summon Devious,' he said.

Jasfoup raised an eyebrow. 'So you summoned me instead? I'm not doing your menial work for you.'

Harold laughed and handed him a tea. 'You can assist me, though. Why can't I get hold of Devious?'

'Ah.' Jasfoup followed him to the desk. 'There are only two reasons for that. Either he's been discorporated, in which case I'd know about it, or else he'd in his mating season and he's busy with his wife.'

'Ew.' Harold pushed his sandwich away. 'I didn't need to think of that.'

Jasfoup chuckled and gestured towards Harold's sandwich. 'Don't you want that?'

Harold shook his head. 'Not any more,' he said. 'I thought imps and demons were, I don't know, magicked into being or something.' Harold waved his hands for emphasis.

Jasfoup shook his head. 'No, Harold. All of us, except the Third, obviously, once had mothers. Some succubae, some mortals, some animals, even; but we were all born in some way or another.'

'What was your mum like then?'

Jasfoup shrugged. 'To be honest, I don't remember. She was burned as a witch in 1376. I've had a dislike for witch finders ever since, and not just for professional reasons.'

'Do you… erm… do you have a belly button then?' Harold was almost afraid to ask.

'Of course, Harold, haven't you seen it already though?'

Harold frowned. 'I don't think so,' he said.

Jasfoup grinned and stuffed the rest of his sandwich into his mouth. He unbuttoned his suit just enough so that Harold could see the navel. It was one that poked outward.

'I don't know about a cup of tea,' Harold said. 'After that, I think I need a stiff one.'

'That's a bit further down,' said Jasfoup with a smirk. 'But I can get it out if you like.'

'Har-de-har,' said Harold. 'You know very well what I meant.'

'It was worth a shot,' chuckled the demon. He looked at the remaining sandwich. 'Is Frederick coming in today, do you know?'

'As far as I know, yes,' Harold replied. 'So don't eat his sandwich. There're some crisps in the cupboard by the sink if you want a packet.'

'I do, I do,' said Jasfoup. 'Are they salt and vinegar?'

'I bought a multi-pack,' Harold told him. 'Bring me a packet of cheese and dog-breath flavour, would you? And put the kettle on again while you're there?'

Jasfoup went to the back of the shop and Harold could hear the kettle being filled and then switched on. The demon returned bearing three bags of crisps.

'Do you know, I thought you were having me on,' said Jasfoup, sitting down again, 'but they really are 'cheese and dog-breath' flavour. How very odd. This is the sort of things that the boffins in Dis would think up, but you mortals have done it all by yourselves.' He examined the green and brown packet with interest before passing it over to Harold, who opened it and chewed.

'It's one of these special promotion packs of unusual flavours,' Harold explained between crisps. 'They do odd ones occasionally to get people into the habit of buying crisps again.'

'I thought it was a euphemism for 'cheese and onion' until I saw the packet,' Jasfoup admitted, emptying the bag of salt and vinegar into his mouth and chewing. 'I never imagined that it was real.'

Harold nodded. 'They taste terrible, actually, but they're very moreish.'

'Moreish?' Jasfoup had visions of Saracens swarming out of the ancient walls of Jerusalem.

'In that once you eat them, you want more and more of them,' Harold explained.

Jasfoup nodded. 'A bit like Chinese Dragons,' he said. 'You eat one and then an hour later—'

'You want another one,' Harold finished for him. 'That joke's probably older than you, Jasfoup.'

Jasfoup stared at the sandwich again. 'Are you sure Frederick is coming down here?'

'I told you, yes. You can't eat his sandwich.' Harold finished his crisps and grinned.

'You're right about the dog-breath.' Jasfoup waved his hand in front of his face.

'This is from a person who eats pickled eyeballs.' Harold sipped his tea.

'I prefer pickled eggs myself.' Frederick's voice came from the open doorway, and Harold looked up with a smile.

'Hello, Uncle Frederick,' he said. 'I didn't think you were going to make it. We were getting worried!'

Frederick took his watch out of his pocket. 'It's only just gone one,' he said. 'I'm not late at all; it's just that you two gannets have started early.' He sat down and dropped a packet of biscuits onto the table before getting his tobacco out of his other pocket and filling his pipe. The shop was soon filled with the aroma of Old Virgin shag tobacco. 'I hear that Mrs Clarke died,' he said. 'That's a shame.'

Harold nodded. 'She was eighty, and she'd had a good life. One day she was in here, and the next day she was gone.'

Frederick nodded. 'That's as good a way to go as any, I suppose. When I die, I want it to be quick so that I don't suffer.'

Harold nodded thoughtfully and got up to fetch Frederick a cup of tea.

Jasfoup grinned. 'You want to 'Get to Heaven before the Devil knows you're gone', eh? There's not much chance of that, I'm afraid. Everybody knows everybody else's business, and the obituaries are published a day in advance where I come from.'

Frederick laughed. 'When am I going to die then?'

Jasfoup shrugged. 'Not today, at any rate. I'd have it in my diary if you were.'

'I didn't know you kept a diary,' said Harold, returning with Frederick's tea. 'What sort of thing do you write in it?'

Jasfoup shrugged. 'This and that,' he said. 'Appointments, notes on people I come across on their way to damnation. Birthdays and anniversaries. When people are due to die. The same sort of thing that everyone puts in a diary, really.'

'There're not many who have the last one,' remarked Harold. 'Your diary must be jam-packed if you have all of those in.'

Jasfoup shrugged again and picked up the packet of biscuits, slicing through the wrapper with his sharp claws. 'I only have the deaths of my personal clients in my diary,' he said, taking out a biscuit and examining it. 'Even then, it's only the ones who have either had a contract from me or are undecided which way to go.'

Harold helped himself to one of the biscuits. 'What do you mean?' he asked. 'I thought it was a foregone conclusion whether you went up or down depending upon what you did during your life.'

'Please go on,' said Frederick, gesturing with his pipe. 'This is interesting. Doubly so at my time of life.'

'Well,' Jasfoup bit into the biscuit. 'Ooh, chocolaty bits!' he explained, showing it to Harold. 'That's true for most people, they go up and stand at the pearly gates and get judged by the Gatekeeper.'

'Is that Peter?' asked Harold, eagerly.

'It used to be,' the demon told him, 'but now it's done on a rota system. You're more likely to get judged by a swimming instructor than by one of the original Host these days.'

'Why a swimming instructor?' asked Frederick, curiosity prompting him to interrupt. 'Why not a lawyer or an accountant?'

Even Harold knew the answer. 'Because lawyers and accountants never get into Heaven in the first place!'

Jasfoup grinned, swallowing the rest of the biscuit and reaching for another. 'True, I'm afraid,' he said. 'Where was I?'

'The Gatekeeper,' prompted Frederick.

'Oh yes.' Jasfoup brushed crumbs off his suit. 'So they get judged and then walk all the way down the stairs to Hell, where they get judged again by Minos to decide upon which circle of torment they enter.'

'I don't want to be judged by a big bullock,' muttered Frederick, putting down his pipe and taking the remaining sandwich. 'Can't somebody intelligent do it, instead?'

'It's not a Minotaur, it's the Angel of Judgment,' explained Jasfoup, patiently. 'Minos the king was named after him, the city was named after the king and the bull-headed guardian of the Labyrinth was named after the city.' He waited until Frederick had nodded before continuing. 'Anyway, there are a few who have led lives of perfect balance, and these are what we call 'contested souls'.'

'What happens to them?' asked Harold, wishing he hadn't let Jasfoup eat his sandwich.

'An angel and a demon go down and reason with the soul, trying to coax them to go one way or the other. The Angel says something like 'Come to the Light, where there will be praising of the Lord on High, and much singing of hymns and happiness and well being'.' Jasfoup mimicked a falsetto voice as he said this, causing Harold and Frederick to laugh.

'What of your lot?' asked Frederick. 'How do they tempt with damnation?'

Jasfoup held up the biscuit. 'They just say something like: 'Come to the Dark Side: We have cookies!' We get about eighty percent of them that way.'

'What happens to those who don't choose at all?' asked Harold, reaching for the temptation.

'They become wanderers,' Jasfoup told him, 'and they take so much paperwork to deal with that we just let them glide around. They don't do any harm, for the most part. Do you want that, Frederick?'

'No, Jasfoup, not really. I think I'd rather be a ghost; keep an eye on young Harold here.' Frederick sighed heavily.

'I meant the sandwich.' Jasfoup pointed to the bread that Frederick had left after carefully consuming the filling.

'Oh, sorry. Help yourself.'

'Ta.' Jasfoup munched on the soggy crust

'Talking of ghosts,' Harold told his uncle. 'We spoke to Mrs Clarke last night.'

'Really?' Frederick asked.

Harold nodded. 'Yes Uncle. She was haunting the car park.'

'Is she the usual, transparent sort?'

Harold nodded again.

'I haven't seen her.'

Chapter 21
The Honey Trap

'Will this work?'

'According to Isaacs, yes.' Jasfoup finished smearing the television aerial with blood. 'It cost me a pretty penny, I can tell you.'

'I thought Mrs Clarke said that Isaacs was away this month?' Harold clutched Jasfoup's arm. 'How did you get to see him, then?'

'Ah.' Jasfoup grinned. 'Remember that I'm a demon, Harold. We're not limited to talking to people down the pub, you know.'

'I suppose so.' Harold looked over the edge of the roof to the ground below. 'Whose blood is it?'

'Your brother's.' Jasfoup followed Harold's gaze. 'Jump,' he said. 'You know you want to.'

'Don't!' Harold drew back and held on to the chimney. 'Why Cain's? Isn't it a waste after we went to all that trouble to get it?'

'Not at all. It's perfect. Besides, this is a new batch.' Jasfoup picked up Harold in his arms and glided back down to the ground. 'Do you recall that I told you that your brother was still alive?'

'Yes,' said Harold. 'I presume that was his curse, to wander the earth for eternity.'

'Well, yes and no. That's not what was intended for him, but a gift of the first woman.'

'Eve? I thought Eve never saw him again after he killed Abel?'

Jasfoup led the way back into the house. 'That's right, but Eve wasn't the first woman.'

Harold nodded. 'You're talking about Lilith,' he said. 'The first suffragette.'

Jasfoup gave a bark of laughter. 'I suppose so. Your father helped her escape from Eden and in return she gave immortality to his son.'

'Cain? How did she do that?' Harold led the way into the kitchen.

'Having eaten of the sacred tree of life, her blood was immortal. She gave it to Cain, making him immortal as well.'

'He was the first vampire, then?' Harold made them both a cup of tea.

'Yes and no.' Jasfoup rested his chin on one hand and used the salt cellar to pour patterns on the tabletop. 'Technically he was, but he was a very ethical man in those days. He survived on goat's blood.'

Harold put two mugs of tea on the table and fetched a cloth to clear up all the salt. 'So the Canaanites were a tribe of vampires then? No wonder they were despised.'

'Not at all. They were ordinary people, descended from him. He didn't change until he was well into his six hundreds, you know. He had plenty of children.' Jasfoup sighed. 'Of course, it became a bigger curse that he had to watch them grow old and die.'

'Harold?' Ada came into the kitchen. 'Would you have a look at the telly, please? The picture's gone all fuzzy.'

Jasfoup coughed. 'I'll check the aerial for you, Ada,' he said. 'There's probably pigeons on it.'

'Would you, Jasfoup? That's a dear.' Ada went back into the living room.

'So why have we smeared Cain's blood on the TV aerial then?' Harold asked when the demon returned. 'To attract vampires?'

'Exactly,' Jasfoup replied. 'Vampires are attracted to blood like sharks are in the sea, only far more acutely. The prospect of getting a mouthful of the progenitor of their race will be irresistible.'

'Won't they be a bit annoyed when they find out it's just a smear, though?' Harold glanced at the window, as if he were expecting a dozen angry vampires to come crashing in.'

'A bit,' the demon admitted, 'but once they're on the roof they'll be able to smell you.'

'I shower daily,' Harold protested.

'Your blood, I mean. It's very similar to Cain's, since you share a father.'

'So I'm the honey pot,' Harold said. 'That's really comforting.'

'You'll be fine, Harold. You'll have me to protect you, and your suit.'

'My suit?' Harold remembered what had happened when he had seen Jedith in the shop. 'I meant to ask you about that,' he said. 'It behaved very strangely the other day.'

'It was trying to protect you.' Jasfoup clapped him on the back. 'It's made of nephilim leather; semi sentient.'

'But I'm nephilim,' said Harold. 'You mean that I'm wearing family?'

'Yes,' said Jasfoup. 'Not all nephilim are born sentient. Those that cannot function independently are used to make things for those that can. Think of it as recycling.'

'That's disgusting, Jasfoup, and a little disturbing.'

The demon shrugged. 'It's common practice where I come from,' he said. 'Would you prefer that they die for no reason? It wouldn't bother you if it was cow leather, would it?'

'That's different', Harold protested. 'Cow leather wasn't a sentient being.'

'I think that the cow would disagree,' Jasfoup replied. 'Trust me; your brother there will save your life for you one day.'

'My brother?' Harold looked at his sleeve.

'All nephilim are your brothers, if you think about it,' said Jasfoup. 'Your cousins, anyway, seeing as all the angels were brothers.'

'I see.' Harold patted his lapel. 'What was his name?'

Jasfoup grinned. '23784165,' he said. 'But you could call him 'Jack'.'

***

Harold had fallen asleep soon afterwards and dreamed of having a tea party with his family. Ada was there, at the head of the table, and so were Coat and Trousers. Socks had a high chair to themselves and Underpants had been sent off to wash before eating. He awoke to the phone ringing at 8:00am.

'Harold?' His uncle's voice sounded weak and far away. 'I need you at the Manor, please.'

Harold rubbed sleep from his eyes. 'Can't it wait, Uncle? I'm due to open the shop soon.'

'Not really.' His uncle sounded apologetic. 'It is a bit urgent.'

Harold looked at his clock. 'All right, Uncle Frederick. Give me twenty minutes.'

'Thank you Har—' The phone clicked off.

***

Harold parked the van by the stone pillars and switched off the engine. There was little noise here, and he could hear the tink tink of the engine as it cooled, as well as the cheeps of the birds in the nearby bushes.

He got out and squeezed through the partially open iron gates and walked up the drive to Laverstone Manor. The sun was still low, leaving the drive in the shade of the beeches that lined it and the breeze felt fresh on his face, despite the fact that it carried with it the fumes and noise of the distant M25. Apart from that, there was little to indicate that he was in a suburb of London. Harold could imagine himself strolling up the drive of an Edwardian stately home in Kent.

The exception was that such a house would not have a battered VW Beetle parked in front of it. Harold couldn't help but smile at the sight of his uncle's old car. It was as old as Harold himself, and was in a variety of colours; various parts having been replaced by visits to the nearest scrap yard when the rust ate more of the metal than it was possible to replace with resin and fibre glass. One of the stalls in the stable block to the rear of the house held, Harold happened to know, enough body panels and engine parts to a complete second vehicle, if not a third. Frederick, with the familial eye for a bargain, had begun buying every scrap Beetle that appeared in the local paper as soon as they had stopped being made.

Harold patted the old car as he went past it, wondering if the offside wing was the same one he had helped repair when he was barely into his teens; the hole in the metal that needed attention so deep that, with the enthusiasm of the young, he'd added a dozen '00' scale toy soldiers into the mix of fibre glass to bridge the gap before sanding it smooth.

He walked past the front door and round into what used to be the stable yard, noticing the state of the roof that his uncle had mentioned the other day. It was seriously in need of repair, and Harold couldn't begin to estimate the cost He wondered if his uncle would accept money from an undisclosed source. It couldn't hurt to try.

The back door, which was the one that actually got used for everything but weddings and funerals, was unlocked and Harold went inside the house. 'Uncle?' he called out. 'Uncle Frederick?'

There was no reply.

Harold went into the kitchen where his uncle spent the vast majority of his time. Living in the Manor was all very well and Frederick would never move out into something more suitable for a single man, but the thirty-four roomed mansion was really too big for him to cope with. He had instead retreated to the rear of the house, where the kitchen was pressed into service as a comfortable one-room apartment. 'Uncle Frederick?' Harold called again, becoming a little worried about the lack of reply.

The telephone rang. Harold jumped with the sudden change from silence to noise, and looked about guiltily. He didn't feel right about answering it, since it wasn't his house, but as his uncle wasn't here he felt he should. He dithered for a further three rings before plucking up the courage to pick up the handset.

'Hello?' he said, trying to sound like a butler. 'Laverstone Manor?'

He breathed a sigh of relief when his uncle's voice came on the line.

'Harold?' Frederick still sounded quite distant, and Harold wondered where he'd got to.

'Uncle? Where are you? Did you know that the door was unlocked?'

'I'm still in the house, lad. I saw you coming up the driveway.'

'Oh.' Harold was surprised that it hadn't occurred to him. 'Whereabouts?'

'I'm in the East Wing, Harold. I've had a bit of an accident.'

Harold felt the cold hand of fear tighten his bottom. 'Where?'

'In the East Wing, Harold. I just said that.' Frederick sounded a little tetchy, but was speaking easily enough.

Harold was reminded of his mother for a moment, not that she'd be happy with the comparison to her brother. 'I meant which room are you in, Uncle?'

'Oh.' Frederick sounded surprised. 'I'm in the Mouse room.'

Harold knew the room, named for the painting that hung over the fireplace. He'd been fascinated by it as a child. It was a depiction of a number of mice, all dressed in Victorian clothes, seated around a blazing fire on a dark evening. Mother mouse was knitting and nursing a small child whilst father mouse read from a large black book. Three children were sat on the floor in rapt attention and a fourth was playing with a wooden toy by the side of a bookcase. Unbeknownst to the characters, but in plain sight to the viewer, a large cat had crept into the room and was about to pounce upon the preoccupied child. It was a painting of the everyday suffused with the absurd. It had given Harold nightmares for years.

'I'll be right there, Uncle.'

Harold put the phone down and glimpsed, out of the corner of his eye, a figure standing watching him from the shadows, but when he turned to look properly it had vanished. He stared at the space for a moment before setting off at a brisk pace through the mansion.

He went out of the kitchen and passed the cloakroom before turning left into the Long Passage, the corridor that ran the length of the main house and connected it to the two wings. He passed the paintings of his ancestors and the suits of armour that his uncle had told him were haunted when he was small. He eyed them as he went past, but none of them moved so much as a rivet.

He made another left turn into the day room, walking briskly through to the Mouse room, where his uncle was lying in a twisted heap upon the floor, his legs at an odd angle to the rest of his body.

'Ah, there you are, Harold,' he said with relief. 'I've had a bit of an accident, I'm afraid.'

Harold stood in the doorway, uncertain how to proceed. His uncle was covered in plaster dust and the three bulb chandelier lay on the floor a few feet away, next to an overturned step stool and the remains of the plaster ceiling rose. His legs were splayed at a ninety degree angle from his pelvis, and Harold could tell, from long nights as a child perusing Gray's '*Anatomy*', that the legs were not only broken but had been wrenched from the ball and socket joints. He was almost surprised that there wasn't a lake of blood on the floor.

That wasn't the primary problem, though. His uncle was lying face down on the floor. At least, his body was. His head, however, was facing the ceiling.

'Your head's the wrong way round,' said Harold, never shy of stating the obvious. 'I feel rather sick.'

'I always said that you were a sharp one, Harold. I do seem to have a bit of a crick in my neck. I'd be obliged if you could keep your breakfast to yourself, though. There's enough of a mess to clear up already, without your cornflakes.'

'I didn't actually have breakfast, Uncle.' Harold looked down at his feet and tried to take long, slow breaths. 'I was in a hurry to get here.'

Harold looked up again, wishing they were talking about any subject other than food, but relieved that he hadn't had runny eggs this morning. He heaved at the thought, and clapped his hand over his mouth.

'I suppose not. What's the verdict, then, doctor?'

Harold shook his head. 'You've got compound fractures of both legs and possibly your right arm, though since you're lying on that

I can't really tell for sure, and you've wrenched both your legs from their ball and socket joints. Then there's the rather severe problem with your head facing the wrong way.'

Frederick tutted. 'It looks bad, doesn't it?'

'About as bad as it could get, I'm afraid, Uncle.' Harold nodded sympathetically. 'Can you actually move at all?'

Frederick was silent for a few moments, except for the occasional huff and puff. 'I don't think so, Harold. It may be that my neck is broken.'

'You're probably right,' he said.

'Are you going to examine me properly and call an ambulance?'

'I think it's a little late for that, Uncle,' said Harold sympathetically, 'seeing as you're dead.'

Chapter 22
Looking Backwards

Frederick stared at Harold. 'Dead? Are you sure?'

'Your head's on back to front and I'm talking to your ghost Didn't you think it a little odd that you were looking down on yourself?'

'I did a bit, Harold, yes.' Frederick stepped over his own body, his translucent feet making no marks in the plaster dust that lay thickly around the corpse. 'I just thought that experiencing trauma was giving me a new perspective on life.'

'You certainly got a new perspective, Uncle. Look, do you mind if we step out of the room? It's a little unnerving looking at your corpse.'

Frederick nodded. 'I understand. It gave me the willies when I first saw myself.' He grinned, his spectral teeth still stained a spectral yellow from years of tobacco and tea. 'Listen! Do you need any bits?'

'Bits? What sort of bits?' Harold was surprised to see that Frederick the ghost looked exactly the same as Frederick the living person had been, right down to the few unshaved hairs on the right side of his chin.

'Well,' Frederick took out his pipe and began filling it with Virgin Shag tobacco. 'My heart's in good shape, and so are my kidneys, although I expect that my lungs are shot by now.' He grinned, pointing towards the corpse with his pipe. 'Will any bits of me help you sort out what's wrong with you?'

'I don't think so.' Harold thought about it. 'It's tempting to take some bits for my other projects, though. I'd take you up on the offer if it wasn't that I have to call the authorities and report the death. They might ask some awkward questions if I've removed several organs and a hand. You didn't carry a Demonologist Donor card, did you?'

'What's one of those?'

'Like an organ transplant donor card, only for sorcerers of the Infernal Pits.'

Frederick shook his head. 'Sorry, Harold,' he said. 'If I'd seen one I'd have got it.'

'You wouldn't have seen them, Uncle. I made them up.'

'At my expense? That was a bit tasteless, Harold, what with me being dead and all.'

Harold nodded. 'I suppose it was. Sorry, Uncle, I think my association with Jasfoup is affecting my taste. Can we go out now?'

Frederick led the way back into the Day room, with its French windows overlooking the garden. Harold sat in one of the white painted wicker chairs. 'I'm going to have to call for that ambulance,' he said, taking out his mobile phone.

Frederick nodded and lit his pipe. 'Mind you, tell them to use these doors here,' he said, gesturing to the French windows. 'I don't want them tramping through the house with their dirty great boots.'

'Will do.' Harold dialled, asking for an ambulance and the police, and ignoring Frederick's look of alarm. He gave the address, explained the scene, and directed them to the east wing before ending the call.

He tapped the handset thoughtfully against his palm. 'How did you phone me when I got to the house?' he asked. 'You must have been already dead by then.'

Frederick shrugged. 'I've no idea,' he said. 'It didn't occur to me that I couldn't, so I used the extension, there.' He pointed to the old Bakelite phone on the side table.

'Would you do it again? Call my mobile this time.'

Frederick nodded and drifted over to the telephone and reached for the receiver. His hand drifted straight through it and he grimaced in consternation.

'You did it before, Uncle, you can do it again,' said Harold.

An Ungodly Child

Frederick tried again. He felt a little resistance this time, but his hand still went through the receiver. 'I can't Harold. It's like trying to pick up air.'

'Forget that you're dead,' Harold suggested. 'Try picking it up as if you were still alive.'

Frederick concentrated and stretched out his hand to grasp the receiver. He managed to pick it up, although it slipped once or twice, sliding like warm treacle through his pale hand, but with effort he got it to his ear. He began to dial, the pause whilst the dial rotated between the numbers on the ancient telephone maddeningly slow. When it connected, he retrieved the handset from where it had seeped through his shoulder into his chest

Harold's mobile rang, showing the number of Laverstone Manor. 'You did it, Uncle,' he said. 'Well done.'

Frederick replaced the receiver, a big grin plastered onto his face. 'I did, Harold! I manipulated a physical object!'

'Well done, Uncle!' Harold repeated, grinning along with him. 'I didn't even know that ghosts could manipulate physical objects.' He attempted to pat his uncle on the back, but was faintly disturbed to find that his hand sank through to what would be between the ribcage. 'Um,' he said. 'I'm proud of you, Uncle.'

Frederick turned from the telephone, Harold's hand still inside him, so that his arm now protruded from Fredericks's chest, and looked down.

'I'm sure that there must be some sort of ghost etiquette,' he said, 'and I'm almost certain that sticking your hand inside me would not be considered something to do in polite company.'

Harold quickly removed his hand. 'Sorry, Uncle,' he said, his face turning a fetching shade of beetroot, 'I doubt that it would be considered polite in any company.'

Frederick patted his chest where Harold had withdrawn his arm. 'There's no mark left,' he said, 'though it does feel a little tingly, like putting your tongue on one of those little square batteries. I wonder why that is.'

Harold was looking out of the window, waiting for the ambulance men. 'I don't know,' he said without turning. 'Perhaps it's something to do with interacting with the living.' He turned back to his uncle. 'How come you're a ghost, anyway? And why haven't you gone on to a different plane? Isn't there supposed to be a bright light or something that you're to follow?'

Frederick shrugged. 'There was, but just as it arrived I saw my pipe on the floor under the chair, and I thought I'll just take my pipe with me so that I can have a bit of a smoke, and the light went out again. I missed the afterlife bus. At least I didn't have to go down there.' He pointed downwards dramatically.

'I'd have put in a good word for you, Uncle. I've got connections. Besides, isn't your dad down there?'

'I wouldn't be too anxious to run into dear old Pops,' said Frederick with a wry smile. 'He wasn't the greatest father when I was alive. I'm surprised I made it to adulthood, to be honest; with the number of creatures he used to summon up. I'm glad that Jasfoup was around to deal with them.'

Harold caught a flash of light out of the window. 'Look, the ambulance is here. Oh; they can't get through the gates. Are they still closed?'

Frederick thought about it. 'Were they closed when you came in?' he asked.

Harold nodded. 'As closed as they ever are. You can squeeze through the gap if you're on foot.'

Frederick shook his head. 'That was something I always meant to get around to,' he said. 'You'll have to let them in, Harold. The remote is in my car.'

'Yes, Uncle.' Harold clicked his fingers and the little window to the thousand planes opened, allowing Devious his egress.

'Yes, Master? What can your humble servant do for you today?' Devious grinned like a Cheshire cat on caterpillar opium. 'Wotcha Ghostie.'

'Hello, Devious. Go and fetch the remote from Frederick's car and open the gates, would you? There's a good lad. Hurry up, though, the ambulance is waiting.'

Devious stopped with one foot above the other, about to dash off. He turned to look up at Harold. 'Good lad?' he said with a sneer. 'Not only am I older than your grandmother, but I'm also capable of travelling to nearly all of the known planes. You send me off on an errand you could do yourself in five minutes, and all you can say is a patronising 'good lad'? You should be ashamed of yourself.' He left, opening his portal window without looking back at Harold once.

'That's your humble servant, is it?' chortled Frederick. 'I'm glad you don't have one that barely tolerates you.'

'Oh, har-de-har, Uncle,' said Harold crossly. He looked out of the window again. 'They've got fed up with waiting, look, they're going to go away... no, hang on... the gates just opened and they're coming in, followed by a police car. I'd better get out there and show them the way in.'

'You do that, lad,' said Frederick with a heavy sigh. 'Best we get it over with.' He relit his pipe and nodded solemnly. Harold opened the French windows and trotted outside, reaching the front of the house just as the ambulance men were unloading the stretcher and emergency medical kit.

'He's round here,' he said, pointing behind him.

'Right you are, mate,' said the first medic, a tall thin chap whom Harold would have assumed was under legal driving age. The second medic, an older, rounder man, unfolded the stretcher and the two of them followed Harold round the side of the east wing, and were in turn followed, unbidden, by the two policemen. Harold led them into the Garden room, where Frederick stood back to let them pass, and into the Mouse room.

'Oh dear,' said the younger medic when he saw the scene. 'Have a bit of an accident, have we?' He moved forward and checked the pulse of what used to be Frederick.

Harold nodded. 'He has, anyway. This is exactly as I found him.'

The larger of the two policemen pushed past Harold into the room. 'Have you touched anything, sir?'

'No, nothing.' Harold turned to look at him, rather than at the corpse. The policeman smelled of coffee and hair gel, and had hair growing out of his nose. Try as he might, Harold could look nowhere else but at those twin tufts of hair.

The tufts twitched. 'Are you any relation to the deceased?'

Harold nodded. 'He's my uncle,' he said. 'He phoned to say that he'd had an accident.'

'But you knew that he was dead, sir? How did you determine that?'

'He told me that he was.'

'He told you? The deceased told you that he was dead?' Tufty looked to his colleague and rolled his eyes.

'Yes.' Harold nodded before realising what he'd just said. 'Um... that is, I could tell by the angle of his neck that it was broken, and there's plaster dust on his nose and lips, which wouldn't be there if he was still breathing.'

'Oh, a medical expert, are you?' Tufty grinned and nodded at the second policeman, who took out his notebook.

'Reasonably so, yes,' said Harold emphatically. 'As much as one can be from reading all the medical texts available.'

The second ambulance man went back outside whilst the first opened his medical kit and took some samples of the body, noting the readings down on a clipboard.

'Where were you at the time of the accident?'

'I was at home in bed.'

Tufty nodded. 'What time would this be, sir?'

'Eight o'clock, just before the alarm went off.'

There was a tutting behind him. 'You shouldn't have said that, Harold. I died half an hour before then.' Frederick came to stand next to him. 'He'll think that that's suspicious.'

'But I didn't have anything to do with it!' Harold whined.

'I never said that you did, sir,' said Tufty, looking at him curiously. 'But I'd like to know how he phoned you after the accident when it seems to me that he died instantly.'

Harold backtracked. 'I don't know,' he said. 'Perhaps I'm getting confused. It's been a bit of a shock, finding him like this.'

'Perhaps you'd like a cup of tea,' suggested Frederick.

'Perhaps you'd like a cup of tea,' suggested Tufty, at the same time.

Harold nodded. 'That would be nice,' he said. 'Is it all right if I go to the kitchen?'

'As you wish, sir. PC Henderson will come with you to make sure that you're all right.' Tufty nodded towards the second policeman, who shut his notebook and put his pen away.

The second ambulance man returned. 'The doc's on her way,' he said. 'Sorry about this, mate,we have to follow procedure in these cases.'

Harold nodded and turned to Frederick. 'Are you coming?' he asked.

Frederick shook his head. 'I'll stay here, he said. 'You can never trust what people are going to do with your body when you're not looking.'

'Yes sir, lead the way,' replied Henderson, assuming that Harold was talking to him.

Harold sighed and led the way to the kitchen.

Frederick called after him: 'I suggest you get yourself some counsel,' he said. 'You're liable to say something stupid, else.'

'Yes, I'm good at that,' said Harold.

'Good at what, sir?' asked Henderson, falling into step behind him.

'Nothing,' said Harold. 'Nothing at all.'

He managed to stay silent until they reached the kitchen and had put the kettle on to boil. Henderson sat on a dining chair at the table. 'Mind if I smoke?' he asked, holding out a packet of cigarettes.

Harold shook his head. 'Not at all,' he said. 'I doubt it would make any difference to forty years worth of Uncle Frederick's pipe smoke. If you scrubbed the nicotine stains off the ceiling you'd probably have to replace the plaster as well. How do you take your tea?'

'White, please, with four sugars.'

'I tend to take mine in a cup, personally,' said Harold. He looked at Henderson's stony face. 'That was a joke,' he said. 'Ha-ha.'

Henderson said nothing and lit his cigarette from a lighter he kept in the packet. 'Did you know your uncle well?' he asked eventually, sending a plume of smoke towards the ceiling, where it danced around the solitary light fitting.

'All my life,' said Harold. 'It's a little dark in here, isn't it?' He went to switch on the light, moving the button up and down several times when the light didn't come on. 'That's odd,' he said. 'I wonder if the fuse has gone.'

Henderson leaned back in his chair and took off his cap, placing it on the table and aligning it with the edge of the wood. 'It's probably the accident,' he said. 'Your uncle pulled down the light in there, didn't he?'

'That's true.' Harold could have kicked himself. 'Then why does the kettle work?'

'It'll be on a different circuit,' said the policeman knowledgeably. 'Will you be the one to inherit this place?'

Harold considered it. 'It'd probably go to my mum first,' he said. 'She's Uncle Frederick's sister. It might come to me after that.'

Henderson nodded. 'It needs a lot doing to it,' he said. 'It's an old house. My brother-in-law's an electrician, if you're interested. I could ask him to do you a quote for re-wiring.'

Harold smiled. 'That would be kind of you,' he said, 'but I've got a friend or two that would do it at cost'

Henderson snorted. 'That's assuming you can afford the death duties, of course. Have you got any savings?'

Harold thought of the half a million in cash he still had in his attic. 'I've got a bit put to one side.'

The kettle boiled, and Harold made a pot of tea, putting the cups and saucers on the table along with the sugar and the least sour of the milk from the refrigerator.

Henderson looked around for an ashtray. Harold handed him the one from the arm of the easy chair in front of the small television, emptying it first so that the picture of the Blackpool Tower was visible.

'Would you like some tea with your sugar?' Harold asked, holding up the pot.

'That was another joke, wasn't it? You're a funny man, Mr Waterman.'

'That's terribly kind of you to say so, Mr P,' said Harold with a forced smile.

'Just 'Constable' will do, thank you. I don't know who this Mr P is, but I hope it wasn't meant to be an insult.'

Harold smiled. 'Not at all, Constable, it was merely a reference to Dickens.'

'Oh?' Henderson began to get out his notebook. 'And who might that be?'

Harold looked at him. 'No-one you need worry about. He's long dead.'

'Really, sir? Another relative who had a fatal accident in your proximity?'

Harold laughed. 'Not at all. He died of a heart attack in 1870. I doubt you could pin that one on me.'

'Pin it on you, sir? Why ever would we want to? From the way you're talking, I might think that you did have something to do with the deceased's accident, after all.'

'Certainly not,' said Harold, mustering a believable amount if indignation. 'He was dead when I arrived.'

'But you didn't examine him?'

'I didn't need to.'

'You know that if it should turn out that he was alive at the time, we would have to regard it as death by negligence, don't you, sir?'

'That won't be the case.' Harold sniffed. 'Oh, excuse me; I'm going to... ach... ach... Jasfoup! Sneeze!'

'Bless you, sir.'

'Thank you,' said Harold, wiping his nose on his handkerchief.

'Not that it will do any good, of course,' said a sibilant voice, 'seeing as you're one of the living damned.'

Harold sniffed. 'I prefer to think of it as heavenly challenged,' he said.

'Think of what, sir?' asked Henderson, puzzled.

Harold caught himself. 'I was wondering whether my uncle would go up or down,' he said, pointing with his finger. 'Have a biscuit?'

'He was actually supposed to go upwards,' said Jasfoup reaching to take one. 'But unfortunately, he missed the call of Michael. They're a bit peeved about that upstairs.'

'Don't mind if I do,' said Henderson, taking a digestive from the plate Harold set out. 'I'm glad that you're so certain of the deceased's status when you arrived, sir. It does make the paperwork a little easier.' His radio crackled, and he answered it, staring at the china plate clock on the wall as he did so. 'Two-zero... Yes, Sarge, he's quite calm... Will do, sir. Over and out.' He looked back at Harold. 'The doc's arrived,' he said. 'We'd better get back over there.'

Harold nodded and stood, carrying the tea cups to the side of the sink.

Henderson reached to take another biscuit.

''Ere,' he said, 'What happened to all the biscuits?'

Jasfoup said nothing, and munched quietly, his finger over his mouth in a shushing signal.

Harold smiled. 'Rats probably,' he said, walking out of the door on his way back to the Mouse room.

'I resent that!' replied the indignant voice of the ebony-skinned demon from behind him.

Harold entered the Day room to find a red-haired woman talking to Tufty. His uncle's body had been placed into a plastic zip-up body bag and put on the stretcher. Harold was grateful that he could no longer see the corpse; the ghost that stood peering over the lady's shoulder was bad enough.

Sergeant Tufty turned at his entrance. 'Here's Mr Waterman now,' he said. The lady looked up from her notes and turned, favouring him with a smile.

'Hello,' she said, transferring her pen to her left hand and holding out her right. 'I'm Doctor Hammond.'

Harold shook her hand amiably. 'Harold Waterman,' he said. 'Are you all done with Uncle, now?'

The doctor nodded. 'I'm sure it's all been a bit of a shock,' she said. 'I've made a preliminary verdict of accidental death, but I'd be grateful if you could fill in the details.'

Harold looked over her shoulder at his uncle's ghost

'I don't remember,' said Frederick, uncertainly. 'The light was playing up and flickering, and I climbed up on the stool with me screwdriver to see if I could fix it. Then there was a big flash and I woke up like this.' He shrugged.

'I'm sorry, I really can't help you,' Harold said to the doctor. 'I found him on the floor with his legs and neck broken.'

The doctor nodded. 'When was the last time you spoke to your uncle—' she referred to her notes,

'—Frederick?'

'That would have been—'

'Yesterday,' prompted Frederick.

'—Yesterday. He seemed fine then.'

'I see.' The doctor made another note on her paperwork. 'Well, I think that's all,' she said. 'You can collect a copy of the death certificate from the registrar any time after 10:00am. tomorrow.'

'All right, thank you.' Harold watched as the ambulance crew wheeled his uncle out of the door. 'Where are you taking him?' he asked.

The doctor frowned. 'The morgue,' she said. 'If you want to contact a funeral home, they'll make the arrangements to have the body moved. Goodbye.' She followed the stretcher out.

Sergeant Tufty spoke up. 'We'll be moving along as well, Sir. We have your address if we need to speak to you again.'

'That's nice,' said Harold, watching as Frederick made to follow his own corpse. 'I'm usually down at the shop on weekdays, though. You have my mobile number?'

'Yes, thank you.'

'Thanks for the tea, sir,' Constable Henderson said.

'And the biscuit,' added Harold. 'You're welcome.'

'Yes, sir, thank you.' The two policemen left, pushing through Frederick, who was still standing in the doorway. Harold waited a few minutes before speaking.

'Are you all right, Uncle? Apart from being dead, I mean.'

Frederick turned. 'Not really, no. I don't seem to be able to leave the house.'

Harold reviewed all the ghost stories he'd ever read. 'Isn't that normal, though? I've never heard of a ghost that wasn't tied to a particular place. Red rooms, blue rooms, bloody towers. I don't think I've ever heard of one that was free to go where they wished.'

'What about horror books, though?' Frederick asked plaintively. 'You always get creeping horrors and wandering spirits in those.'

'Tch,' said Harold, rolling his eyes. 'Fiction.'

'That'd be a bit of a bugger,' said Frederick. 'I don't really want to be tied to the Manor. There are two ghosts here already; I'll end up being a tourist attraction.'

'Now there's an idea,' said Harold with a grin. 'We could probably restore the hall to its former glory on the proceeds.'

'No! I don't want a lot of strange people tramping through the house.'

'We've got to do something to bring in a little cash, Uncle. This is a big place, you know, and the roof is in dire need of repair.'

'Why not ask the imp to help out with that?' said Jasfoup, coming into the room with a tray of tea and biscuits. 'He'd be able to do it for virtually nothing.'

'How?' Harold accepted a cup of tea and a biscuit, and sat down.

'Well, look at his abilities.' Jasfoup paused to bite into a biscuit, gesturing with the remaining half. 'He can appear and disappear at will, go anywhere, obtain anything within reason and has the strength of an ant.'

'That's not very helpful,' said Harold. 'Besides, he's much stronger than that.'

'Har-de-har. I meant proportionally, as you well know. All you'd have to do is teach him how to re-roof a building and Bob's your uncle.'

'I'm his only uncle,' said Frederick. 'Is there any chance of a cup of tea for me? I'm parched.'

'Sure, Uncle, try mine. You managed to use the telephone.' Harold indicated his cup.

Jasfoup nodded and crossed his legs. 'It's a rare ghost that can manipulate the real world,' he said, 'but it is actually possible.'

Frederick sat beside Harold, who wished he'd brought his jumper with him, and reached for the tea. His spectral hand closed around the cup and began to lift it. Frederick grinned as he lifted it to his lips and took a sip. The tea, however, poured straight through him onto the floor. Frederick cursed.

'That was a good effort,' Harold said sympathetically. 'Remember that it's your first day as a biologically challenged entity, and you've done really well so far.'

'But I've seen it done!' protested Frederick. 'On the telly, like. It's a basic stock in trade of a ghost to drink people's tea.'

'That was just television, though,' Harold pointed out. 'Special effects and camera tricks. It doesn't mean that real ghosts can do these things.'

'You'll gradually find out what you can and can't do,' pointed out Jasfoup, 'and when you've found out what your limits are you can work on extending them. Do you remember when you were little? We used to chat about what you wanted to be when you grew up.'

Frederick nodded. 'I remember,' he said. 'I wanted to be a writer and a poet, and live in a big house on my own, but Father always insisted that I concentrated on my sewing and singing so that I could attract a good husband to get married.'

'Husband?' Harold looked confused. Jasfoup scowled at him to be quiet.

'That's right,' he said. 'What did I say to you then?'

'I remember you saying 'don't worry about it because your dad's going to be dragged down to the eternal pits and tortured for eternity.' It was helpful, but not terribly comforting at the time.'

Jasfoup coughed. 'What else did I say?'

Frederick scratched his head. 'Be nice to cats?'

The demon nodded. 'That too, but I'm thinking specifically of something I told you about yourself and your future.'

'You told me that I could be whatever I wanted to be, so long as I truly believed that I wanted it, and signed on the little dotted line.'

'That's right. That's what I told you. Tell me if I was wrong.'

Frederick smiled, seemingly for the first time since his unexpected demise. 'You weren't. I did become a writer and a poet, and I lived here alone for the rest of my life.'

Hold on,' Harold interjected. 'He signed away his soul for this, did he?'

The demon and the ghost both nodded, waiting for him to continue.

'So why is it that he's here as a ghost, instead of fulfilling his side of the contract and spending eternity scrubbing off his skin in a vat of boiling brine?'

Jasfoup grinned. 'Ah. Well… I might have left a little loophole in the contract.'

Harold was stunned. 'A loophole, Jasfoup? That's not like you at all. What sort of loophole?'

Frederick looked a little shifty. 'Well, it's like this, Harold. If Jasfoup hadn't come along, and I'd acceded to Father's wishes, you'd still have had an uncle, though I don't know what his name would be, but you'd have had an Aunt Freda, too.' He waited for this to sink in.

Harold's mouth worked as he thought about this. 'You mean that you were born a woman?' he said, 'And Jasfoup arranged for you to have a sex change?' He frowned, his mouth working a silent overtime as he tried to equate this revelation with the uncle he'd been used to seeing all his life. 'I'd have known, surely? You can't hide something like that. I mean, you smoke a pipe!'

Frederick looked uncomfortable. 'I didn't exactly have a sex change, Harold. This was the 1950s, and nobody really knew about such things then. If it had been these days, that's what I would have asked for.'

'I knew all about the drag queens of the sixteenth century stage,' Jasfoup interrupted, 'who lived as women for most of their life off stage as well as on, so I thought that would be a good solution. I offered Freda the chance to live as a man for the rest of her life, and arranged it so that everyone but her family would forget that there had ever been a Freda, and treat Frederick had been a man all his life.'

'So that story about you marrying a demoness wasn't true?' Harold asked.

'Oh it was true enough, except that the reason that she left me was that she wasn't satisfied with my physical endowments. I never actually lost my todger, because I never had one.'

'We had fun trying to get you one, though,' Jasfoup grinned with the memory.

Frederick laughed and continued the story. 'Ada knew, of course, but she never had a problem with it. Once she'd got used to me being a man all of the time, she treated me like a brother, just as I wanted her to. She used to call me Fred anyway, so it wasn't much of a shift for her. As for Father...' he shrugged.

'Henry Waterman did not approve,' said Jasfoup, quietly. 'He had an idea of using the souls of his own children to extend his own life. I'm pleased to say that I intervened and suggested he try the process with cats, first Not the best advice I ever gave him.' He winked and took another biscuit.

'You killed my grandfather?' Harold asked.

'Not at all,' smiled the demon. 'He didn't have to carry out the ritual. His greed and vanity killed him, not I. Besides, there was never a body.'

Harold shook his head. 'This is a lot to take in,' he said. 'One thing that you still haven't told me, though, is how Uncle Frederick is still here when he signed one of your contracts.'

'That,' said Jasfoup with a degree of satisfaction, 'was the beauty of the loophole. Frederick never signed a contract. Freda did; and I erased all trace of her.'

Harold nodded. 'That was clever,' he agreed. He stared at the ghost 'You were a woman all those years?' he said. 'With breasts and everything?'

Frederick nodded. 'It didn't make any difference to you, did it? I still loved you whatever padding I was wearing.'

Harold felt blood colour his cheeks. 'You used to take me to the gents,' he said. 'You used the urinals and everything.'

'Pretended to.' Frederick reached out to touch Harold's arm but his fingers passed straight through. 'I'm sorry I never told you the truth,' he said, 'but once I been Frederick for a couple of years even I forgot that I'd ever been anything else.' He pointed to the sideboard. 'Have a look in there. There's a Rover's Assortment biscuit tin. Get it out.'

'Why? What's in it?' Harold dug through a pile of napkins and anti-macassars and pulled out the tin.

'Open it.' Even as a ghost Frederick was filled with trepidation.

'Photographs?' Harold leafed through them, recognising his mother as a younger woman with her parents and another, slightly older girl. 'This is you?'

'That's right.' Frederick looked at the photograph. 'That was taken about three years before Mum disappeared.'

'Where did she go?' Harold flicked through the photographs, recognising his uncle in the features of the elder sister. 'You've never talked about her.'

'She just disappeared one day.' Frederick shook his head sadly. 'Even the police don't know what happened to her.'

'I told you. She went home to Faerie.' Jasfoup beamed as he checked the teapot for another cup.

'So what do we do now?' Harold asked, putting the photographs away.

Frederick looked around. 'I'd appreciate it if you cleaned up a bit,' he said. 'I still live here.'

Harold laughed and clicked his fingers three times. With the sound of fingernails on a blackboard, Devious appeared.

'Yes, O, sweet and wonderful Master,' he said. 'How can I be of service? A light switch turned on, perhaps? Or your tea leaves individually dried?'

Harold smiled. 'A kind offer indeed, Devious, but not at present, thank you. First, I would ask of you three things.'

'Yes, Master. Three things I will do for you, then, before I return to my normal duties. Tell me these three great tasks, then.' He tapped his foot.

'Remember that your name is not Insolence, imp,' said Jasfoup, darkly.

Devious jumped and tugged on his ear. 'Sorry. Tell me your tasks, Master.'

Harold grinned and nodded his thanks to the demon. 'Firstly,' he told the imp, 'I want you to close the gates, oil them, and ensure that they are in perfect working order.'

Devious repeated the instructions, his mouth moving as he wrote the instructions on his pad. 'Yes, Master,' he said. 'What is the second task?'

'To clean up the room where Frederick died,' said Harold. 'Brush away all the fallen plaster, re-do the ceiling and make the room as good as new.'

Devious wrote down the second task and looked up again. 'And the third?'

Harold grinned. 'What do you know about roofs?' he asked.

'They're like house lids,' Devious replied. 'They keep the inside things in and the outside things out.'

'Very good,' said Harold. 'Do you know how to repair one?'

Devious shook his head sadly. 'No, Master. We don't have much use for them downstairs.'

'Then you have an extra task,' said Harold. 'First you must learn everything there is to know about roofs, by studying them and by studying books, and then, gathering the materials you need from wherever they won't be missed, you will repair the roof of this house, or replace it completely. Are my instructions clear?'

Devious nodded. 'Perfectly, Master. I shall begin at once.'

'Excellent!' Harold rubbed his hands together.

'Is that really wise?' asked Frederick. 'Asking him to do the roof, I mean. We could end up with a thatched roof on a seventeenth century faux-gothic building.'

Harold nodded. 'He'll do a good job,' he said. 'I'm certain of it.'

There was a creaking of air and Devious returned with a sack of plaster, mixing tray, and a bucket of water. He was wearing a pair of white overalls and a little peaked cap. 'Right, Guv'nor,' he said. 'I'll start task the second, if I may?' He made shooing motions with his paws, and the companions left the room again.

Jasfoup, Harold and Frederick made their way back to the kitchen, Harold carrying the tray with the empty cups. When they arrived, Jasfoup sat at the table and Frederick, after a couple of unsuccessful attempts to not sink through the chair, joined him. Harold stood at the sink and washed the teacups whilst the kettle boiled for the third time that morning.

'Will you be all right, here on your own?' asked Harold when the cups were safely draining.

Frederick grinned. 'I was all right for the last forty years; I expect that I'll survive a bit longer now that I'm—'

'—Dead?' suggested Jasfoup.

'—Blood-pumpingly challenged?' suggested Harold.

'I was going to say 'not so worried about hurting myself,' finished Frederick. 'Besides, I can still use the telephone.'

'True.' Harold nodded as he prepared the tea and brought it to the table, carefully pouring three cups. Frederick watched him mournfully.

'What's the point?' he asked. 'We know that I can't drink it.'

'I have an idea,' Harold told him. He added the milk and sugar, then carried one of the cups to the sink and poured it away. He brought the empty cup back to the table and sat down. The demon and the ghost looked at him quizzically.

'I have the idea,' said Harold, carefully, 'that if all things have a spirit, then if I have just 'killed' the tea I poured, then only the spirit of the tea will remain in the cup, and Uncle should be able to drink it.' He looked expectantly at Frederick, who shrugged.

'It sounds like a load of tosh,' he said, 'but I'll give it a try.' He carefully lifted the cup to his lips and took a sip whilst the other two watched expectantly. He smiled at them and took a second sip, and then a third.

Harold grinned. 'It worked, then,' he said happily.

Frederick grimaced and put the cup back onto its waiting saucer. 'Don't be stupid,' he said. 'Of course it didn't work.'

Harold looked crestfallen.

Jasfoup patted his arm. 'It was a good theory,' he said, 'but it's more likely that the tea was reduced to its component parts as spirits, else we'd be inundated with the souls of the tea cups of the English on a daily basis. Spirits don't work like that; they're more likely to become part of the spiritual wholeness. Sugar to the Spirit of the Canes, tea to the Spirit of the Plant, and homogenised pasteurised semi-skimmed milk... well, I don't even want to think about where that goes.'

Harold nodded glumly. 'You're right,' he said. 'It was a stupid idea.'

Frederick nodded and re-lit his pipe. 'You're a good boy though, Harold, and I appreciate the effort.'

Jasfoup held his hand up. 'Hush,' he said, looking with his eyes half closed at a space beyond Harold, near the door to the cloakroom. He lowed his voice to a hushed whisper. 'There's something there that doesn't want to be seen.'

'What do you see?' asked Harold, quietly.

Jasfoup, without taking his gaze from the spot, leaned in close. 'With this tea in evening dreary, while I pondered, weak and weary, over problems of a complex and a spiritual lore; Whilst we chattered and we nattered, suddenly there came a presence, as if our talk had somehow mattered, mattered in our verbal fore; 'Tis some stranger here, I'll wager, attracted by our oratory bore. Only this and nothing more.'

Harold flicked his eyes sideward, but could see nothing. 'Is the presence dark and gloomy, standing just inside the roomy?'

The demon nodded. 'With cloak of night and angel's wings he watches like a midnight hawk.'

'Spirit of the house, perhaps, dressed in oils of shadows' rags?'

'So well remembered, face dismembered, like a joint of finest pork', Jasfoup agreed.

'Uncle, tell me of this spirit, living here without the gibbet, does it look for something more?'

'I cannot even seem to hear it, let alone begin to fear it, tempted, I, to shut the door.'

'You're a pair of bleedin' nutters, talk in dark and whispered mutters. 'Tis only Man and nothing more,' said Frederick, emphatically.

'Who's Man?' Harold whipped his head round, just catching a glimpse of the figure before he vanished through the door and away.

'He's been here years,' said Frederick. 'He's a bit funny about visitors; especially if they can see him. He'll have liked the Poe, though. He's very fond of Poe.'

'How very odd,' said Jasfoup. 'He looks like an angel, though not one that I recognise.'

'Aye.' Frederick tamped out his pipe and relit it. 'He's not daft, is Man. Never did work out who he was an' I've known him nigh on thirty years. Where did the Poe come from anyway, Jasfoup? I haven't heard you spout poetry since I was small.'

The demon shrugged and finished his tea. 'It just felt like the right thing at the time. Well done for catching on, Harold.'

Harold shrugged. 'You don't do a degree in antiquities without doing a bit of literature,' he said. 'That was my favourite poem when I was a lad.'

'Aye,' agreed Frederick. 'I remember you memorising it and giving me a rendition when you were small.'

'He still is,' cackled Jasfoup.

'I am not!' retorted Harold. 'I've had no complaints.'

'No compliments, either,' grinned the demon.

'Oh, har-de-har,' said Harold, getting up from the table. 'We ought to head off home. Are you sure that you'll be all right, Uncle?'

'I told you I would be,' said Frederick, floating out of his chair.

'Right you are then.' Harold transferred the dirty cups to the sink. 'We'll see you tomorrow, then?'

'Right you are.' Frederick practised his object manipulation by opening the door for them.

'Thanks, Uncle.' Harold stepped through into the evening. 'Would you mind if I borrowed the remote control for the gates?' he asked. 'Unless you need it, of course.'

'I can't see me driving about just yet, Harold. You take it with my blessing.'

'Thanks Uncle. See you tomorrow then.'

'All right, lad, unless I'm transparent by then.' Frederick's laugh was spookily hollow.

Harold was halfway down the drive, with Jasfoup at his side, when he heard the ghostly voice of his uncle again.

'I might be able to move objects,' he shouted, 'but did you have to leave me with the washing up?'

Chapter 23
The Manor of a Ghost

Jasfoup watched with interest as Harold pressed the button on the remote gate control. He examined the handset. 'Is this wizardry or technology?' he asked, looking down the infra-red beam and pressing the button. He screeched and dropped it.

Harold stared at him. 'You can't have been hurt,' he said. 'That was infra-red.'

'Bleedin' hot, too,' exclaimed Jasfoup. 'I think I've cooked an eyeball. Can you have a look?'

Harold pulled his face downward. 'You'll have to bend a bit,' he said. 'You're taller than I am.' The demon obliged, and Harold peeled open an eyelid. 'I can't see any damage,' he said, 'but then again, I can't see very much at all in this light. You've definitely still got an eyeball, though, because I can see the streetlights reflecting in it.'

'There's the beginning of a sonnet for you,' said Jasfoup sarcastically. 'My friend, your eyeball is not badly burned. Streetlights are reflected by the pupil.'

Harold grinned. 'For though the love I have for you is spurned, there's a chippy round the corner open still.'

Jasfoup laughed. 'Not exactly what I had in mind, Harold, but a good riposte nonetheless. I think it's better now, anyway, the nerves have regenerated.'

'You have remarkable recuperative powers, Jasfoup.' Harold led the way through the open gates and pressed the button to close them.

Despite himself, Jasfoup flinched. 'Don't worry, I won't point it in your direction,' Harold assured him.

'I'm not worried, Harold. It's just that I don't trust this technology stuff. I don't understand it too well yet. I've been out of town for far too long. Are you driving?'

Harold nodded. 'I'm a good driver, you'll be fine. You can walk home if you prefer, though. It's only a ten minute walk. By the time I've got round the one way system you'll probably beat me there anyway.'

Jasfoup climbed in and, with a grin, braced his feet against the dashboard. 'I love your scary driving,' he said.

'Stop fretting, Jasfoup. I've never had an accident in my life.'

'I know you haven't. I read your file. You've never so much as stubbed your toe, have you?'

Harold shrugged and started the engine. 'Come to think of it, no. I've never have. I have had accidents, though.'

'Only self-inflicted ones, where you cut bread whilst you were holding it, or stabbed yourself with a pencil when you were seven.'

Harold laughed. 'I remember that. It really hurt. It soon healed, though.'

'Of course it did, boss. You have very good healing powers, don't you?'

'Yes, why? Is it something to do with my dad's blood?'

Jasfoup shrugged. 'Probably. It's powerful stuff.'

Harold pulled away from the manor into the traffic stream, ignoring the honking of horns and the flashing eyes of the cars of angry road users. 'You called me 'boss' then.'

Jasfoup began to relax. 'Yes. So what?'

Harold shook his head. 'Nothing,' he said. 'It was unexpected, that's all.'

'We have a contract. Technically, I'm employed by you.'

'Excellent!' Harold grinned and put his foot on the accelerator.

Harold pulled up in front of his house and switched the engine off. 'See?' he said. 'Home safe and sound.'

Jasfoup looked across at him. 'I've never been so scared in my life,' he said. 'you travel at sixty miles an hour over speed bumps, ignore red lights, slalom round streetlights, and treat buses like road kill. It was brilliant.' He grinned happily.

Harold harrumphed. 'Told you I was a good driver,' he said.

'Good? You're an absolute lunatic. I thought I was evil, but the expressions of those people on the number forty-seven to Temple Green were priceless! Every one of them will be dry-cleaning their trousers tomorrow.' He giggled.

Harold got out before replying. 'It's not my fault that the driver couldn't decide which way to turn,' he said.

Jasfoup giggled again. 'I'm not surprised! You were heading straight for him, going the wrong way down a one-way street!'

'I was only going one way,' Harold huffed.

Jasfoup laughed.

Harold opened the front door, relieved to be greeted by the warm and familiar smell of home.

'Harold? Is that you, Harold?'

He sighed. 'Yes, Mum,' he called. 'It's me. I've got Jasfoup with me, too.'

Ada came out of the living room. 'Harold, I've got some bad news, dear. Your uncle Frederick's dead.' Harold nodded. 'Yes, Mum, I know. I've been with him all afternoon.'

'That was sweet of you, Harold. How is he?'

'Bearing up well, I think, under the circumstances.'

'That's good. As long as he's all right.'

'Apart from being dead, you mean?'

'Yes. Is he happy?'

'Not terribly, no, we ate all his digestives. Why don't you give him a ring?'

'Can he answer the telephone? I didn't think ghosts could do that.' Ada looked vaguely worried. 'Or is he a poltergeist or a manifested entity?'

Harold shrugged. 'Just a ghost, I think, though he's a bit peeved about being tied to the house.'

'No, he won't like that at all,' Ada agreed. 'I'll give him a ring, then, that will cheer him up. You'll take care of all the arrangements, won't you, Harold? The funeral and such?'

'Yes, Mum, leave it to me. Did he have any special requests?'

'Apart from not being buried or cremated or thrown to the fishes? No, I don't think so, Harold. What was his body like? Intact or in lots of pieces?'

'Intact, Mum,' said Harold, wrinkling his nose in distaste.

'That's nice.' Ada nodded thoughtfully. 'What's for tea?'

'I'm sorry, Mum. I hadn't thought about it. Fish and chips?'

'I'll have cod and a sausage.' Her excitement over, Ada looked past him. 'Mr Jasfoup,' she said. 'Did you have anything to do with the death of my brother?'

Jasfoup shook his head. 'No, Ada, it was nothing to do with me. You know how fond I was of the little tyke.'

Ada smiled. 'You always took good care of him. Make sure that you continue to do so.'

Jasfoup smiled. 'I will, Ada.'

***

Semangalof watched from the tower window as the last of the interlopers left and heaved a breathless sigh of relief. The real world disturbed him when he had no control over it; all the mortals disturbing the house were anathema to him. He walked back to the kitchen, eschewing his normal route through the corridors in favour of the more direct route through the walls and ceilings.

Frederick was sat in his usual chair in front of the television, trying desperately to get it to work. He looked up as the disguised angel dropped slowly through the ceiling.

'Ah, there you are, Mr Mange. I was wondering where you'd been all day.' Frederick grinned.

Semangalof stood perfectly still, feeling the current of God's will eddying in the manor. 'You're dead, then,' he said, as a statement rather than a question.

'It seems so.' Frederick laughed. 'Curiously, I've found that death has brought with it a peculiar clarity of thought. I find myself remembering much of my life where, somewhat ironically, it was a haze of half forgotten memories for much of it.'

Semangalof stared at him through hooded eyes, seeing the loosening ties of Heaven on his thirty year friend. 'Death does that,' he agreed. 'It wipes away all the inconsistencies of the mortal realm, bringing clarity like a scalpel to a cancer, cutting away all that is surplus to need.'

'Aye,' Frederick nodded, 'but I can't get the telly to work. Harold tried to teach me to manipulate solid objects, but I'm not very good at it as yet.'

'It is certainly a difficult task for one of the spirit realm to influence the physical plane,' Semangalof agreed. 'But it can be done.' He reached inside the screen, manipulating a transistor here, the flow of current there, and the screen crackled into life. He sat upon the other chair, just as he had done for the last thirty years, and watched the images flicker past

'What will happen now?' he asked. 'With the house, I mean. Will it now be transferred to your sister?'

Frederick shook his head. 'I've willed it all to Harold, if he can afford the inheritance tax and the roof repairs, but I strongly doubt that Ada will want to live here. She hasn't been the same since Pops died.'

'So young Harold will live here, will he?' Semangalof almost smiled.

***

Harold sat in the attic in what was rapidly becoming his retreat. He always thought that he'd be upset when his uncle died, but mourning the dead when the dead were there to offer their own commiserations made it far more bearable. He looked up as the door opened.

'I thought you might need a tea,' said Jasfoup, 'unless you'd rather be alone with your thoughts, of course.'

Harold smiled. 'That's uncommonly kind of you,' he said. 'I'd love some, thanks.'

Jasfoup nodded and looked behind him. 'Make a pot full, Devious, and bring it up.' He came further into the room and sat on one of the cardboard boxes. 'What's in this one, then?' he asked by way of opening conversation.

Harold looked at the tag. 'They're my diaries from when I was old enough to write to when I was in my early twenties. I've kept them as an historical document for when I'm famous.'

Jasfoup laughed. 'The last thing you want is to draw attention to yourself,' he said. 'You don't last long as a powerful sorcerer when your name is on the bestseller list'

Harold grinned. 'You think that my autobiography would be on the bestseller list?'

'Well, no,' the demon admitted. 'It was just a figure of speech, but there's precious few who could claim a peerage as unusual as yours, Harold. You're a magician through and through, with a bit of fairy blood thrown in for good measure. Once you've got a few hundred years under your belt, there'll be no stopping you.'

Harold gave Jasfoup his first genuine smile of the day. 'Praise indeed,' he said. 'Thank you. It's comforting to know that you have such faith in my abilities.'

'I do, Harold. I'm counting on you.' Jasfoup looked his charge in the eye. 'You're a very rare commodity.'

Harold shrugged. 'What do you mean you're 'counting on me'?'

Jasfoup shuffled his hooves. 'I want to be proud of you,' he said. 'I've never actually had a protégé before. I've always made bargains with people who assumed that I was just a servant to be taken advantage of. It makes a change to have someone who actually respects my opinions and asks for advice.'

Harold reached across and patted him on the shoulder. 'I do, Jasfoup. I really appreciate you teaching me all this stuff. Talking of which though, is Uncle Frederick bound to the manor, or can he leave it and wander about?'

Jasfoup considered the question. 'There was no specific ritual involved with his passing,' he said, 'so we'll need to determine whether he's a ghost or a spirit. The former haunts a particular place, and the latter is free to move about.'

'He did say that he'd been invited upstairs,' said Harold, 'but had dallied looking for his pipe and missed his chance.'

Jasfoup smiled. 'Then there's a good chance that he's not bound,' he said. 'We'll have a try tomorrow, and see if he can go with you somewhere.'

'I've got to make the funeral arrangements tomorrow,' said Harold gloomily.

'What better way of arranging one than taking the deceased to ask his opinion?' grinned the demon.

'Good point,' Harold agreed. 'Here's Devious with the tea, look. I'll drink to that!'

**

Semangalof left Frederick watching television and went off to do his rounds. He followed his usual route through the house, managing, by way of light relief, to creep up on Molly and stab her through the neck with his sword. He laughed as she twisted this way and that, trying to extract the blade from its entry point without severing her neck, but she managed it eventually, brandishing the sword at him in fury.

'Ow many times 'as I told you not to do that?' she shouted, her hollow voice echoing through the empty corridor. 'It blinkin' 'urts does that. Just you wait, Mr Mange, me lad. I'll 'ave you soon enough. The Master's a ghost too now, and 'e'll put you bang to rights, so 'e will.'

Semangalof laughed, making Molly even more furious than she already was. 'I hardly think so,' he said. 'Frederick has his own problems adjusting to being dead. He seems to think that he can just carry on as he was and go about his daily business.'

'Mebbe's he can.' Molly tapped the air with the blade. 'Mebbe 'e can leave the 'ouse and go about like 'e's still mortal. You know whose blood 'e 'as in 'im.'

'Had, you mean.' Semangalof smiled, but doubt had begun to work its dark fingers into his mind. What would happen if Frederick was free to leave the manor? When he adjusted to his new state of being, he would recognise his ghostly friend as an angel?

'Get away with you, woman,' he said to hide his discomfort. 'Give me back my sword before I sunder your spirit to the winds.'

'Ha!' Molly tapped the blade against the air. 'I'll gi' it back in me own good time, Mr High and Mighty. Aye, an' buried to the 'ilt an' all.'

'Pah'. Semangalof turned on his heels and stalked away to the room at the top of the tower. He did a slow circuit of the four openings to the air, his gaze attracted as it often was by the buzz of spiritual energy coming from the park. There was a higher power there, amongst the spirits and wandering dead, although he was at a loss to guess who, or what it was doing there. He shrank back. It would not do to reveal his presence to another angel.

A heartbeat later, he was gone.

***

Jasfoup gave Harold a nudge. 'What about your mum's dinner?' he said. 'You promised her fish and chips an hour ago.'

'I did, didn't I?' Harold stood up. 'Want to come? It's only five minutes' drive in the car.'

'I wouldn't miss it for the world,' Jasfoup said. 'I love seeing the terror on other people's faces.'

Harold laughed and led the way downstairs, picking up the keys to the van on the way out of the door. Jasfoup grabbed his arm. 'Wait,' he said. 'Listen.'

Harold closed his hand around the keys to stop them jingling. 'I can't hear anything,' he said.

'Exactly,' Jasfoup hissed. 'No dogs, no birds, no small animals. It's too quiet.'

Harold laughed and stepped towards the van. 'Enough,' he said. 'You're giving me the willies.' He looked toward the bushes at the side of the path and shivered.

He was totally unprepared for the vampire that dropped off the roof.

Chapter 24
Tooth and Nail

Senoy looked up. 'What did you expect?' he said. 'Harold was bound to inherit the Manor when his uncle died.'

'But he nearly saw me.' Semangalof stalked across the cloud. 'There's another problem,' he said.

'What's that?' Sansenoy spat onto his sword blade and used the solution to polish it to a mirror finish. 'Don't tell me the resident ghost is giving you trouble again.'

'No.' Semangalof frowned. 'I could destroy her with a thought. There was a higher power in the park. It didn't see me.'

'A higher power?' Senoy took a book off the shelf and consulted it. 'It was probably just Azrael,' he said. 'It says here that he's there on official business. He's got a backlog of claims to deal with; people who never left the mortal plane since that Waterman incident.'

'Is that still going on?' Sansenoy sheathed his sword again. 'That was the reluctant antichrist's grandfather, wasn't it?'

'Yes.' Senoy closed the book and put it back on the shelf. 'They opened a drain to remove his mortal presence from the world and the town hasn't recovered yet. We get more instances of spirits in that town than anywhere else in the country.'

'So it's nothing to worry about?' Semangalof breathed a sigh of relief.

'No. He's not looking for you.' Senoy returned to his seat. 'Have you discovered anything about Lilith yet?'

'Nothing,' Semangalof said. 'Anyone would think she'd left the plane altogether, but I know she's there somewhere. I don't think that Frederick knows anything about her at all.'

'Keep watching,' said Senoy. 'Lucifer was always too fond of that woman. If anyone knows where she is, it's him. He must have left a clue somewhere.'

'If he did I'll find it.' Semangalof stepped off the edge and began the long flight back to the Manor.

***

Harold jumped back with a start. 'What?' he began to say, staring at the vampire crouching in front of him. Jasfoup had warned him this would happen, but Harold had been rather hoping any attracted vampires would stay at a suitable distance and not attack him until after a formal introduction. The vampire had a different opinion and leaped up from the ground toward him. Harold noticed, with horror akin to his recurring 'running in treacle' nightmare that her canines were elongating as she moved. She was dressed in the traditional lace shirt, but had eschewed the formal attire for the practicalities of a leather jacket and trousers, and utilitarian boots. Her long black hair was worn as a plait down her back and her eyes glittered in the light from the living room window.

Harold ducked, managing to raise his cane to protect his face, but with a speed he would never have imagined possible she ducked under his guard, attempting to bite. The nephilim leather, which he expected to protect him, peeled back for her lunge, exposing his arm and allowing her to fasten her teeth into his wrist Such pain! He'd thought that stubbing his toe was bad, but this was excruciating. Her teeth were twin points of living flame embedded in his wrist, causing the blood to flow up them and his heart to race from both adrenalin and blood loss. He was on the verge of passing out; a warm, all-embracing darkness threatening to overwhelm him. He relaxed. In an instant the dark panic was replaced by a wash of euphoria, calming him and bringing visions of sunshine on blue water. He felt as if he were flying over lakes and mountains, the shadows of terror peeling away under bright sunshine. In his mind's eye, he paused in his flight and stretched his arms wide to laugh at the sheer exuberance of power.

It had all happened in a heartbeat. Jasfoup had turned away to pull the front door shut. He could have kicked himself for not remembering the danger he had put Harold into by coating the aerial. He should have gone out first to check that the way was safe. It was probable that Harold could withstand it, but it wasn't something he'd wanted to field test. It was one thing to know that theoretically Harold had immense power inside him, but quite another to risk his life on the assumption. Rather like dropping a cat out of a sixth storey window: you knew that it would probably land on its feet, but did you really want a furry placemat if you were wrong? By the time Jasfoup had turned, she had already sunk her fangs into Harold's wrist He was surprised that Harold's nephilim leather, which should have covered his wrist and protected him, had peeled back to allow her access to his artery.

He moved in the space between heartbeats, his claws extending as he sprang to protect his mortal charge. He could feel Harold's heart pounding, sending shockwaves through the air as he spun around him. Hers he could almost see; her chest cavity expanding as her stomach acted as a vacuum pump, drawing in Harold's blood and forcing it out into her own body, her skin flushing with pink as it travelled through her heart and along her veins. His claws raked her face, sending a spray of blood spattering into the darkness, and Harold flinched as a portion of it landed on him. Within a second he stood by Harold's side, his claws like a blade, poised to separate her head from her torso with one flick. 'Cease,' he said calmly.

Harold opened his eyes and saw her own darker ones widen in surprise, and then Jasfoup was at his side, claws out and poised at her neck. He felt the pull of her power as her teeth glided back into their sockets and she let him go. He drew back his arm, curious to see the wounds, and the skin closed over them as he watched. He flexed his arm and stood up straight.

'How do you feel, Harold?' Jasfoup asked with concern showing in his voice.

'I'm all right, thank you, Jasfoup,' Harold replied. 'Nothing that a cup of tea wouldn't cure.'

'Lucky for you, vampire,' the demon hissed.

The vampire stood, extracting her neck from the tangle of blades that were Jasfoup's claws. 'No matter,' she said. 'He has my blood within him and is mine to command as a ghoul.'

Jasfoup glanced at Harold, whose face was covered in the vampire's blood. He was licking his lips.

She indicated a pack, half-hidden in the bushes. 'Man, pick up my bag from the road.'

Harold looked affronted. 'Pick it up yourself,' he said. 'I'm not your lackey.'

Her smile faded, and Jasfoup laughed. 'Harold,' he said, 'Do you feel any different?'

'I feel alive, Jasfoup,' Harold replied. 'Full of beans, in fact.'

'He has more power than you thought,' he said to the vampire, 'And probably some of your own, now. Did you have time to close the wounds?'

'No,' she muttered, fear etching her voice.

Jasfoup grinned. 'How are the wounds, Harold?' he asked.

Harold looked at his wrist The skin was as unblemished as a freshly shaved glamour model. He held it out for Jasfoup to see. The demon grinned. 'Mission accomplished,' he said, 'You took some of her blood while she was taking yours. You now carry the Mark of Cain.'

'Does that mean I'm not going to die?' Harold smiled, his eyes shining. He turned to the vampire. 'Would you like to join us for chips?'

***

Jasfoup thumped the teapot onto the table. He was obviously not happy, and stomped about like a recalcitrant child. Harold did his best to ignore him. He had sent Devious for the food, and they now sat in the kitchen surrounded by paper-wrapped packets. Harold had taken Ada's in to her on a plate.

'Would you like tea?' he asked, 'or would you prefer coffee?'

The woman sat at the kitchen table stared at him almost insolently. 'Blood.' She leaned back on the chair, one arm hooked over the back of it. Jasfoup froze. Not even he would dare to be so rude to Harold, but his charge seemed to take it in his stride.

'Blood? I'm terribly sorry, there isn't any. Tea it is, then.' He poured three cups, adding milk automatically. 'Sugar?' She shook her head, but he added one anyway. 'Have a little,' he said, 'It's good for a shock, apparently.'

'Would you like a sausage with your breasts?' he said, offering her one of the packets of food. She looked at him, and he coloured. 'I meant tea,' he said, 'with your tea?' She shook her head.

He tried again. 'So you're a vampire then? How long have you been one?'

'Thirty seven years.'

'I must say,' Harold replied. 'You don't look a day over thirty. But that's a benefit of being a member of the legion of foul undead, I suppose.'

She nodded and reached out for her tea, enclosing the cup in her hand in a most unladylike manner. Harold tutted. 'That's hardly befitting a lady,' he said. 'You should hold it as I do.' He demonstrated, resisting the urge to extend his little finger. Still she stared in sullen silence. Harold continued. 'You did give me a bit of a shock, jumping off the roof like that,' he said, 'You might have been killed.' He thought about that for a moment. 'Well, perhaps not. But you might have been hurt, at any rate.'

'Then I would have waited for another day to kill you.' She stared at him, her dark eyes betraying none of her emotions.

'You could have tried,' Harold said. 'I must say, I'm glad it was you that took the bait, and not the other vampire from Milton Keynes.'

'Bait?' The vampire sat up in her chair. 'You lured me here? Why?'

Jasfoup grinned. 'We needed Harold to ingest vampire blood,' he said. 'He has a rather nasty disease. Well, had, with any luck.'

'You planned this?' The vampire was disgusted. 'I came because I smelled the blood of Cain.'

'And you've had a swig of his brother's.' Jasfoup gnawed on a chicken wing. 'Thanks for your help. We had intended to capture you and bleed you properly.'

'Had we?' asked Harold. 'You didn't tell me that bit.'

'Oh yes.' Jasfoup reached for a sausage. 'I didn't want us to be saddled with a leech,' he said. 'A supermodel or an airline pilot, perhaps, but not a vampire with a face like a bulldog stung by a wasp.'

Harold snorted back a laugh. 'That's hardly fair, Jasfoup. I think that she's very pretty.'

'Thank you.' The vampire managed a small smile.

'You think succubae are pretty, Harold.' Jasfoup laughed. 'Looking on the bright side, though, at least she can pass as human. With your luck it could have been a vampiric German Shepherd that bit you.'

'Do they have sheep in Germany?'

'Yes, Harold, but I meant a dog.'

'Oh.' Harold grinned. 'It would have been cheaper to feed, though.'

'True.' Jasfoup looked at the woman. 'How are you about eating meaty chunks in gravy?'

She glared at him. 'I think I might have a say in the matter,' she said. 'I do not wish to stay here, and I will not.'

'I don't think that you have a choice, love,' said Jasfoup, a little harshly in Harold's opinion, but then again, good manners weren't a required class in demon school. 'You and Harold are linked now.'

'I'm not sure I like it either, Jasfoup,' said Harold. 'If I had a girlfriend, I'd want her to want to be with me, not forced by some accidental bonding.'

'That's not what you said down the fetish club last Friday night,' grinned the demon.

'That was an accident. She misplaced her handcuff keys.' Harold coughed. 'Anyway,' he continued, 'I was only talking about a one-night special. You're suggesting an indefinite period here.'

'Am I allowed any say in this at all?' the woman interjected

'No.' Harold and Jasfoup replied in unison. They looked at each other. Harold continued: 'That is to say, you would be, normally, but not in the actuality of it.'

'That's very kind of you.'

'That's all right, um... What is your name, anyway?'

'Gillian Du Point. With a 'G'.

'Du Point?' asked Harold suspiciously. 'Is that the Louisinana Du Points?'

Gillian coloured. 'I don't know,' she said. 'I took the name from the grave next to mine when I was buried. It was so much classier than "Jones".'

Haroldbreathedasighofrelief.'That'sgood.Iwonderedforamoment if I was going to be saddled with a name like 'Sharon' for a girlfriend!'

'Or 'Lassie',' Jasfoup added.

'Well, Gillian. I'm Harold, and this is Jasfoup, and the scaly little gannet under the table is Devious. Welcome to my humble abode.'

'Or 'Mr R Hand.' added Jasfoup, still on the previous conversation.

'Our hand?' asked Gillian. 'Are you two an item, then?'

Jasfoup frowned. "R' as in 'right'. No we're not an item. We merely have an understanding.'

Harold had a thought. 'If Gillian is a vampire, and I'm mortal, won't she stay exactly as she is while I get older and older?' he asked.

'Possibly, Harold,' replied the demon. 'We'll have to see what other effects the blood has on you.'

Harold rubbed his hands and looked at the remaining food. 'Are you sure you won't eat, Gillian? There's plenty left.'

'I don't eat, Harold. I'm a vampire, remember? Anything that goes into my stomach won't digest'

'Oh. What about the tea?'

'If I drink anything other than blood, I bring it up again a little later.'

'I didn't really need to know that.' Harold clicked his fingers.

'Yes, Oh mighty one?' Devious came out from beneath the table, scrunching up his empty chip wrapper.

'I need you to find some blood for Gillian, Devious,' Harold said. 'Preferable human, but nothing too... icky...'

Jasfoup rolled his eyes.

'No need to go to the trouble, really,' added Gillian. 'I can easily find my own.'

'It's no trouble,' said Harold. 'There's a hospital up the road.'

'Yes, Master. Should I take a bucket into the emergency room?'

'If you like.' Harold had a distinct blind spot when it came to sarcasm, except when it was from Jasfoup, where it wasn't so much sarcasm as The Way of the Insufferable. Devious blinked a few times, as if waiting for more, then vanished, leaving an imp-sized after-image on Gillian's retinas.

Harold stood and began to clear away the uneaten chips. Devious reappeared with several packets of blood almost immediately.

'Look, Master,' he said. 'They have bags of it free for the taking.'

Gillian took one. 'It's cold,' she said, biting off the top and draining it.

Devious winked. 'I know where you can put it to warm it up,' he said.

Jasfoup laughed, more at Gillian's expression than at the remark. Devious grinned and took left-overs under the table with him.

Harold stifled his smile. 'I'll just get Mum's plate,' he said. 'Any chance of another cup of tea, Jasfoup?'

'Sure, boss.' The demon aimed a kick under the table.

'Devious.'

Harold could have cut the atmosphere with a knife when he walked into the living room.

'Where is she, then?' Ada passed him her tray.

Harold tried a bluff. 'Who, Mum?'

'Your new girlfriend. That's who. Is she well spoken?'

'Yes, Mum, I think so.'

'English?'

'Yes, she speaks very good English.'

'No, I mean is she English? I've always said that you should have a nice, old fashioned English girl to settle down with.'

'I don't know if she's English, Mum, I haven't asked her. It doesn't matter, does it?'

'I suppose not. I'm just worried about her waltzing off like your father did just before you were born. The way you're carrying on, I can hardly blame him. It's almost as if he could see into the future.'

'Well, I wish he hadn't gone. I'd have liked to have met him.'

'I'm sure you would, dear.' Ada's tone became placatory. 'When am I going to meet this young lady of yours then?'

Harold sighed. 'I'll bring her in in a minute,' he said, giving himself time to groom her first. Jasfoup was drinking a fresh cup of tea when Harold got back to the kitchen. Gillian merely looked bored.

'Mum wants to meet you,' Harold said.

Gillian looked up. 'Isn't is a bit soon to meet your parents?'

Jasfoup grinned. 'You don't want to meet Harold's dad,' he said. 'Trust me on that. Think of it as averaging out the meetings; his mum now, and his dad never.'

***

'Mum, Gillian; Gillian, Mum.' Harold introduced the two women in his life to each other and fidgeted.

'Hello, Duck.' Ada gave the appearance of attempting to stand up by rising an inch or so and then sitting down again. Since this was a special occasion, she turned the television volume down slightly, but not so far that she couldn't hear it.

'Hello, Mrs Um... Harold,' said Gillian. 'How very nice to meet you.'

'Call me Ada, dear, everyone does. Have a seat.'

'Thank you, Um... Ada.' Gillian sat gingerly on the edge of the sofa.

'Now then,' said Ada, leaning towards her slightly. 'What's this I hear about you and my Harold?'

'Well, we've only just met…'

'And already in love? That's nice. We didn't have love at first sight when I was a girl. It must be nice.'

Gillian wanted to say 'I'm not in love with your idiot son, you stupid old bat' but surprised herself by saying, 'Oh, yes, he's adorable,' instead.

'That's nice, dear,' said Ada, patting her arm. 'You've got a lovely tan. Are you English?'

'Mum!' Harold was upset by his mum's apparent racism.

'I do have a lot of English blood in me,' Gillian replied truthfully.

'That's all right, then. I only ask because I don't like Harold to go off visiting strange countries. You never know what he might catch.'

'There'd be no-one to make the tea,' suggested Harold in a low voice.

'What was that, Harold?'

'I said I'll just make some more tea, mum,' He replied. 'Coming, Gillian?'

'Yes, you run along. I was in love once, so I know what it's like. I expect you can't stay away from him.'

'I would if I could,' Gillian replied, which came out as 'I can't get enough of him.'

'Well, I don't need to hear about that sort of thing, dear. I know he's got a very vivid imagination.' Ada paused. 'Just keep the noise down.'

They returned to the kitchen to find Jasfoup in animated conversation with Devious. Normally the big demon would have little to do with the helpful little imp, so this was quite a surprise to Harold. 'What's up?' he asked.

'Lots of people in white, composing sonnets,' answered Jasfoup. 'Trust me, you don't want to go there, Boss. All the best poets are down below, and if they write something we don't like, they get a thousand years of writing limericks. You've probably heard some.'

Harold had to stop himself from remembering limericks, but a sudden thought struck him. 'Are you lot responsible for knock knock jokes, too?'

Jasfoup was hurt. 'Of course not,' he said. 'They're not funny. Anyway,' he went on, 'Devious has pointed out that we don't have anywhere for a sunlight-fearing leech to sleep.'

'I can find somewhere,' Gillian said. 'I always do.'

'Will you come back?' Harold asked. 'I'd like to get to know you better.'

'She's bound to you, Harold.' Jasfoup grinned. 'She doesn't have a choice.'

Chapter 25
Undead and Unburied

Frederick awoke with a start. Had he been dreaming? He didn't think that ghosts slept. The television had turned to the morning news and slivers of light were creeping through the gaps in the curtains. He looked down at his hand, amazed that he could see through it to the arm of the chair beneath. It grew more opaque as he looked and he remembered the lesson on concentration that Harold had so patiently taught him. He gripped the armrest, and was satisfied to see slight indentations in the fabric. Testing himself further, he reached forwards and turned off the television, smiling as the screen dissolved to a tiny dot in the centre and then went dark.

He looked across at the sink and frowned. In the old days, and he counted yesterday as the old days because an awful lot had changed since then, he would have started the day with a cup of tea and a pipe in the garden if the weather was fine. Now he was unable to make or drink tea, but a pipe of shag was still on the cards. He stepped into the garden with a contented air, only belatedly remembering that he should have tried to use the door first, for practice.

It was a new dawn and a new day and he was feeling fine.

**

Harold appeared quite early in the morning, driving his van all the way up the drive now that he had the remote control for the gates. He parked up next to the VW and sauntered inside the Manor.

An Ungodly Child

Although there was no sign of his Uncle Frederick, he caught sight of Molly who froze at his entrance, her broom still in mid-sweep.

'Hello,' he said. 'It's Molly, isn't it?'

The ghost nodded slowly. 'You must be that one who sees us,' she said. 'Master Frederick was telling Mr Mange about how you was teachin' 'im what to do now as 'e's a ghost'

Harold sat down on one of the kitchen chairs, slowly, in order not to alarm her. 'That's right,' he said. 'How is he getting on? Do you know?'

''E seems to be doin' all right, for a new 'un,' she replied, setting her broom upright and leaning upon it as if she were still living. 'I 'ain't seen 'im this mornin' though.'

'Can you give me any tips to pass on to him?' Harold leaned forward, his elbows on his knees as if to hear confidences. 'How do you manage to affect the mortal world? I know that you keep the Manor spick and span?'

'That's kind of you to notice, Sir.' Molly smiled, and Harold realised how pretty she would have been in life, and wondered if anyone in the Manor at that time had ever noticed. 'I do me best, that's all. It were easier in the old days, when there was a full staff, like, but there's only Master Frederick now, an' 'e's easy enough to clean up after. As for 'ow I does what I do, I don't rightly know, Sir. I just does what I'd have done in life.'

Harold nodded. It made sense. To carry on as normal would enable a ghost to retain a grip upon the physical world, literally as well as metaphorically.

'Sir?' Molly's voice jarred him from his musings.

'Yes, Molly?'

'Might I ask what'll 'appen to the 'all, now that master Frederick 'as passed on? If it 'ain't too bold o' me to ask, that is.'

'Not at all, Molly. I've not seen the will yet, but I suspect that Uncle Frederick will have left everything to my mum.' Harold smiled encouragingly.

'That'll be 'is sister?' Molly voice was uncertain.

Harold nodded. 'That's right, yes. Ada, her name is.'

'I remember 'er, Sir. She don' like it 'ere much. Not after what 'appened to the old master.'

Harold nodded again. 'So I've heard. She may not want to come back here. Who's this Mr Mange? I'd not heard of him until yesterday.'

'You can't get rid o' 'im, Sir. 'E's not bound 'ere, like I am. Not that I'd mind overmuch if 'e were gone, like, murderin' bastard that 'e is. Just last night 'e wend and stuck a dirty great knife into me neck. I 'ad the devil of a job to get it out again.' Molly paused and looked at Harold. 'Sayin' that, though, Sir, e is company o' me own kind, if you know what I mean. I know Master Frederick's a ghost an all now, but it wouldn' be the same, 'im bein' the Master an' me bein' a servant.'

'I don't know how I could get rid of him, even if I wanted to, Molly. Are there no other ghosts here that would ease your loneliness? One that's more pleasant to you, perhaps?'

Molly shook her head and moved her broom in a desultory fashion, sweeping up a small pile of tobacco ash. 'There used to be, Sir, many years ago, but Mr Mange drove 'em all away. It can be traumatic to be killed over an' over, even though it does no 'arm in the long run.'

'Could we not invite them to return?' Harold was very interested in the idea that there should be more ghosts at the Hall. He had been curious about the ghosts of such an old building ever since he was a child, even though in those days he had no way of seeing them.

'I doubt it, Sir. Those that 'aven't moved on will 'ave formed new associations by now. They'll not want to move from where they be comfortable.'

Harold shrugged. 'It's all academic, anyway. I can't get rid of this Mr Mange.'

Molly leaned forward conspiratorially and lowered her voice so that Harold had to strain to hear it. 'There is a way, Sir, if I might be so bold.'

Harold was surprised. 'There is?' he asked. 'How?'

'You 'ave to kill 'im with a rod of cold iron.'

'I don't know where I could find one of those, I'm afraid.' Harold tapped his fingers. 'Do you know where his body lies?'

Molly shook her head, looking around the room to check that no one else was present. ''fraid I don't, Sir. I bin 'ere a lot longer 'n 'im, an' I ain't never seen a body. I don't think e's got one. He comes an' goes as 'e pleases.'

'I could ask Jasfoup about it,' Harold offered. 'He might know. What is cold iron, anyway?' Harold reduced his own voice to a whisper, more for Molly's peace of mind than any fear of being overheard.

'Cold iron is metal what's fell from the 'eavens,' Molly said. 'There's a spear in the Great 'All what 'as a tip made out o' it. You can tell which one it is by the shape. It 'as two curved moons back to back to make up the point. Oh, Sir,' Molly actually reached out and touched his arm. 'Say you'll do it, an' get someone nice in, instead. It'd be such a relief to 'ave someone 'ere I could talk to, an' beggin' your pardon, Sir, you an' your mum would love it. I'd take good care o' the place for you both.'

Harold smiled, touched by the centuries-old girl's plea. 'I can't promise anything,' he said, slowly. 'But I promise that I'll look into it, all right?'

'Yes, Sir, thank you, Sir.' Molly bobbed a curtsey and ran off, straight through a wall.

Harold searched the whole house looking for his uncle, waving hello to Molly again as he traversed the east wing, most of which was shrouded in dust sheets, unused since his grandfather had died. He wondered what he and his mum would do if Frederick had indeed left them the Hall. Would they stay at number twenty-two? He couldn't see why they should. The Hall was so much more his style, assuming he could persuade his mum to come. The Mouse room had been repaired perfectly, he was pleased to see, though the resulting colour scheme made him suspect that imps were colour blind, or at the very least, possessed of a bizarre sense of décor. He would have to rename it the Aqua, Cerise and Lemon Yellow room if he moved in.

As he walked through the Grand Hall he looked for the spear that

Molly had mentioned, and saw it attached to the wall above the empty fireplace. It was an impressive piece, an eight foot long oak staff to which was attached a dully gleaming point made of two crescents attached back to back, the point of each one touching the other to create the feel of a trident with the outer points a little behind the central one. He was tempted to take it down from the wall and try it out, but there was no time to play with it today.

When he had completed the whole circuit of the Hall, and had still found no sign of Frederick, Harold began to feel a little worried. He hoped that nothing had happened to him (though he had no idea what could actually happen to a ghost). It was with some surprise that, when he entered the kitchen for the third time, he happened to glance out of the window into the rear gardens and saw his late uncle enjoying a pipe of tobacco in the sunshine.

'Uncle!' he said, stepping out into the morning sunshine. 'You almost scared me to death!'

Frederick turned and regarded him, taking another puff before replying. 'I can meet you half way,' he said, 'but why?'

'I thought something had happened to you when you weren't in the Hall,' he said. 'I've just spent an hour walking round looking for you.' Harold sat down on the bench next to his uncle and unbuttoned his leather jacket.

'Harold. I died yesterday. What could possibly have happened today that could be worse than that?'

Harold shrugged. 'I don't know,' he said. 'I thought perhaps that you might have taken the elevator up to Heaven or the long spiral staircase down to Hell.'

'There'd be nothing wrong with that.' His uncle tapped out his pipe on the edge of the bench, the ashes vanishing before they hit the ground. 'I'd see a lot of old friends in either place, I should think, though Papa might be a tad annoyed to see me.' He laughed suddenly, a bark of surreal intensity in the peaceful morning air. 'No, I like it where I am, Harold. The only thing I really miss is a nice cup of tea.'

An Ungodly Child

Harold nodded. 'I'd miss you, you know, if you left,' he said. 'You've been like a father to me.'

'That's a kind thought, lad,' said Frederick, 'though knowing who your father is gives it a sour edge. Do you know what I found out last night?'

'No, Uncle.' Harold waited with baited breath for the compounded wisdom of the ages, imparted from the lips of the newly dead.

'I found out that there's such a thing as Lemmings.' Frederick nodded emphatically.

'Lemmings?' Harold was puzzled. 'Little mammals with the tendency to run off cliffs, you mean?'

'No. I mean women who. . .' he looked around and lowered his voice. 'Women who go with other women.'

'You mean Lesbians!' Harold laughed. 'What about them?'

'Did you know about them?' Frederick turned to his nephew and searched his face.

'Of course, Uncle. They've made a different lifestyle choice. There're loads of them about, just as there are gay men.'

'You always seem cheerful, Harold.'

'No, Uncle Frederick. I mean men who love men. Gay means homosexual.' Harold was embarrassed to be talking of such things with his uncle. It was like watching a 'Deep Throat' with his mother giving a running commentary: 'I wouldn't do it like that, dear, that'll give you cramp. Call that big? My Louis' was twice the girth of that. It's not as good for your skin as you think it is, dear. Go and get some proper face cream.'

'Does it? It didn't used to.' Frederick waved his hand. 'We were all gay in the sixties.'

Harold laughed. 'Why are you so interested in lesbians anyway?'

'I could have been one if I'd known,' Frederick said with a sigh. 'All those years I pretended to be a man and not a bite of the sausage. If I'd known about other women liking the same things I did, I wouldn't have been so alone.'

Harold patted his uncle's arm. 'It wasn't just that you didn't know about other lesbians,' he said comfortingly. 'You never had a partner because you were a cantankerous loony.'

'That's a bit harsh, lad. I was a poet. Poets are supposed to be moody and enigmatic.'

'I know that you were a poet, Uncle. I have both the anthologies that you were published in, as well as the issue of the Laverstone Times that carried your sonnet about the coronation. All in pristine condition, I might add, and both books are first editions.'

Frederick snorted. 'There never was a second edition,' he said, 'and by 'pristine' I presume you mean "unread".' He sighed. 'I was misunderstood, lad. They never printed any of my own anthologies the miserable bastards.'

'Perhaps we could get them published posthumously,' Harold suggested. 'At least you'd still get to see them, which is more than a lot of posthumous authors do.'

'Aye, lad, that'd be nice, but I won't hold my breath.'

'You don't need to—' Harold began before thinking better of it and receiving a glare from his uncle. 'Have I got time for a tea?'

'How should I know? What are your plans, anyway?'

'I have to arrange a funeral.'

'Anyone I know?' Frederick asked brightly. 'There might be a will.'

'I hope so, Uncle,' said Harold with a laugh. 'It's yours.'

'Oh.' Frederick's face fell. 'I'd forgotten. Have your tea, by all means. I've nothing better to do.'

Harold clicked his fingers, asking Devious to make him a cup when the little imp appeared, opening his vertical trapdoor and blinking in the sunshine.

Devious vanished, reappearing moments later with a mug. Harold stared at it. 'Is this the only mug you could find?'

Devious looked at it. It had a picture of an old VW beetle on it, the colours faded with age but made up for by the patina of years of tea drinking. If Harold hadn't known that it was his uncle's, and therefore fairly safe, he would have been wary of catching a disease just by looking at it.

'That's a disgusting cup,' he said, finally.

Devious wrinkled his snout. 'It was the one that was on the draining board, Master. I assumed that you'd already used it today, and thus it was your favourite.'

Harold looked at him. 'It hasn't been washed properly for years! Have you ever known me to drink out of anything that filthy?'

Frederick looked at it. 'It's my cup,' he said. 'Your mother bought it for me in 1969 and I've used it ever since. It's my favourite, actually.'

'And a lovely cup it is too, Uncle Frederick,' said Harold, changing tack suddenly. He paused in thought. 'Did you say it was your favourite?'

'That's right.' Frederick nodded. 'Or it used to be. I can't manage to lift it now, of course.'

'And you've been using it for years?' Harold continued.

Frederick nodded again. 'That's right, Harold. The patina it's built up adds to the taste; any germs would be killed by the boiling water anyway, so it's perfectly safe.'

Harold pressed further. 'So would you say you were very attached to it?'

Frederick thought about that. 'Well,' he said, finally. 'Your mum bought it for me, and I've used it ever since, so yes.' He passed his hand through the mug. 'I was, anyway.'

'Jasfoup talked about the spirits of objects a bit,' said Harold. 'What we need to do is destroy this cup utterly, so that it will continue to serve you. A bit like the Egyptians burying grave goods to serve the Pharaoh in the afterlife.'

Frederick considered the idea. 'A dozen slave girls would be nice,' he said. 'But will you bury me with a cup of tea then?'

'Not exactly. Devious? I want you to take the mug, still filled with tea, downstairs with you and lower it into the deepest, hottest pool of magma you can find.'

'Brilliant, idea, Master,' the imp told him, 'except for one small detail.'

'What's that?' Harold stared at the little imp until it looked away.

'It's a small thing, Master, but the lords and knights downstairs don't like you throwing stuff into the lakes, ever since someone threw in Excalibur and it melted.'

'It's a mug of tea,' Harold said crossly. 'It's hardly likely to change the fate of the known world, is it?'

Devious scuffed the dirt with his hoof. 'I suppose not, Master,' he said. 'I'll go and give it a try then, shall I?'

'If you would be so kind,' Harold replied sarcastically. 'Add two sugars to it first, though.'

Devious returned a few minutes later empty-handed. 'I did as you asked, Master, although I got some funny looks from Baphomet when I asked him to put it in for me.'

'Where is it then?' asked Harold.

Devious shrugged. 'I did as I was told,' he said. 'I've never tried to kill a mug before.'

Harold sighed. 'It was worth a try,' he said. 'Sorry, Uncle.'

Frederick shrugged. 'It doesn't matter,' he said. I have my pipe, and that's the main thing. You still haven't had you cup of tea, though, and we'll have to be going soon.'

'True.' Harold paused. 'We? Do you mean that you want to come too?'

Frederick nodded. 'Of course. Then I can tell you what I want.'

'All right, Uncle, but you have to let me make the decisions. More tea, Devious.'

Frederick nodded. 'I will. Just no burial or cremation, that's all I ask.'

'All right.' Harold was distracted by the sight of a grinning imp.

'It was by the kettle, Sir. It worked!' Devious grinned like an anorexic on laxatives.

Harold smiled and took the more solid of the two cups, pleased to see it was significantly cleaner than the previous one. He nudged his uncle.

'Tea's up,' he said. 'Welcome to your afterlife.'

***

An Ungodly Child

'You will be careful, won't you?' Frederick touched his baby tenderly. 'I don't mind you taking her out for a turn around the park, but you've got to look after her.'

'Uncle Frederick.' Harold carefully prised the old man away from the subject of such devotion. 'I promise I'll be careful. It's not like she's my first, after all.'

They both looked at Betsy. She was a child of the sunlight, and it brought out the colour in her beautifully. Frederick sighed, wiping away a tear. 'They age so quickly, don't they? It feels like only last year I was changing her and trying to steer her right, and now you're taking her away from me.'

'Uncle, she's old and cranky. You bought her in 1968. Beetles were obsolete by the eighties but you certainly wouldn't get that number plate for under five grand these days.'

***

Frederick followed Harold down to the viewing room, the attendant holding the slip of paper like a map to a lost hoard of treasure. There would be no gold at the end of this trail, though, unless you counted the fillings in the deceased's teeth.

The attendant led them to a room lined with draws stacked four high. He counted them as he went past the handles, stopping at the seventh across and third drawer down.

'This is it,' he said, pulling the drawer out. 'Frederick George Waterman.'

Harold and Frederick looked at each other, and then back at the attendant. Harold nodded.

'That's Uncle Frederick all right,' he said sadly. 'Funny how different he looks when he's…'

'Dead.' The attendant finished the sentence for him. 'You're lucky that he's in one piece. You should see the one in number fourteen! We had to scrape him up into plastic bags. Want to look?'

'Er, no thanks,' said Harold turning green.

The attendant leaned in a little closer to him. 'You did know that this is actually a woman's corpse, don't you?'

Harold nodded. 'We don't talk about that,' he said. 'It's *Uncle* Frederick.'

'Ah.' The young man nodded solemnly. 'Got you, sir. Only we had a right job last night. Thought we'd cocked up the labels on the stiffies.' He caught Harold's stern look. 'Oh, right. I'll leave you to it, then, Sir.' He gave Harold a respectful distance.

Frederick patted his arm. 'You know, Harold, it's giving me a funny tummy to see this.'

'I didn't think that ghosts had stomachs, Uncle,' Harold replied absently. 'Do you feel any connection to um…' he gestured towards the corpse.

'I don't think so.' Frederick forced himself to look carefully at his mortal remains. 'Give it a prod and I'll tell you.'

'Must I?' Harold looked faintly sick.

'It's important,' his uncle insisted. 'I don't want to remain a ghost that can feel everything that happens to his mortal remains.'

Harold sighed. 'I suppose you're right,' he said. He checked that the attendant wasn't watching and stepped towards the drawer, prodding his uncle's corpse in the arm. 'Did you feel that?' he asked.

Frederick shook his head. 'No,' he said, 'but that was very light. Try somewhere else, and a bit harder, this time.'

Harold looked at the young man, who seemed to be busying himself filling in paperwork, and prodded the corpse's leg this time.

'Still nothing.' Frederick visibly relaxed and took out his pipe. 'You know,' he began. 'I'm beginning to be a bit more comfortable with this.'

Harold went back to him. 'I'm glad, Uncle,' he said. He called the attendant back. 'Excuse me,' he said. 'We've finished now.'

The young man returned, a slight look of puzzlement upon his face at Harold's use of the 'we'. 'Righty-o, sir. There's a small packet of personal effects, if you'd like to sign for them when you collect the body for burial.'

Harold nodded. 'When will that be?'

'I don't want to be buried, lad,' Frederick interjected.

'I'm afraid I don't know, sir,' replied the attendant. 'There's got to be a post-mortem yet.'

Frederick looked slightly green. 'I don't want to be cut open,' he protested.

'Post mortem?' said Harold in surprise. 'Why?'

The attendant shrugged and looked at his sheet. 'It says here that it was an accidental death,' he said. 'All those have to be investigated to rule out foul play.'

'He might have been murdered, you mean?' Harold was shocked.

'I wasn't murdered,' protested Frederick. 'Tell him I wasn't murdered, Harold.'

Harold relayed the information. 'He wasn't murdered. He fell off a ladder.'

'I don't know anything about that, I'm afraid, sir,' replied the young man. 'We have to rule it out, see. Do you know how many accidental deaths are actually unrecognised murders?'

'No,' said Harold. 'I'm afraid that I don't.'

'Nor do I, sir, on account of them being unrecognised. The ones we do recognise, however, run into double figures. There was one last year, for example, that was run over by a bus. An accident, apparently, but the post-mortem showed an ante-mortem bruise in the shape of a hand on the deceased's back. He'd been pushed into the traffic. If I'd just let that one go a murderer would be walking about now, and who knows who she'd have killed next?'

'I can see your point,' said Harold. 'Have you any idea when the postmortem will be?'

'It's scheduled for this afternoon, sir, so all being well we can issue the death certificate and release the body tomorrow.'

'Oh. Well that's something at least' Harold seemed mollified. 'Come on, Uncle, let's go and pick out a coffin.'

They left the mortuary, the attendant watching Harold with a puzzled expression as he went through the door, then held it open, as if for a ghost.

Rachel Green

***

'Not a pine box, then.' The undertaker seemed quite affronted by Harold's reference to it as 'cheap and nasty'. 'How about this one, Sir? It's made of good English oak. Padded and lined with cream satin with the fixings made of polished brass. It's a lovely piece, Sir, and would lend respect to any august person.'

'I was born in July, not August,' said Frederick, grumpily. 'And I've never liked cream very much. It reminds me of cheap paint jobs done on houses just before they sell them.'

Harold shook his head and smiled at the gentleman. 'He doesn't... er... wouldn't have liked that one either, I'm afraid. You've done a lovely job on it, though.'

The trader stared at him. 'That's kind of you to say, Sir,' he said, acidly. 'Moving on, then, we have the deluxe model, made of beech but inlaid with mahogany, teak and ebony.'

'Tropical hardwoods,' said Frederick. 'I don't want them.'

Harold shook his head.

The undertaker sighed. 'May I ask what exactly you, or the deceased, had in mind?'

Frederick grinned. 'That's more like it,' he said. 'I want a decent sized, roomy coffin, made of solid 32 ounce bronze with cast representations of excerpts from Milton's 'Paradise' along the sides. Rounded corners with bronze accessories and fittings, and with a red leather interior.'

Harold stared at him.

'I saw one like that on television,' Frederick explained.

'Sir?' The undertaker snapped his fingers in front of Harold's face. 'Sir? Are you all right, sir?'

Harold looked at him blankly. 'I'm sorry,' he said. 'I was just trying to remember.' He relayed Frederick's request, the man writing it all down as he spoke. He shook his head as Harold finished.

'I'm sorry, Sir,' he said. 'I'd have to have one shipped in from America and tailored. The cost would be prohibitive. There's no call for metal coffins over here.'

An Ungodly Child

Harold took an envelope out of his pocket. 'Here's fifteen thousand,' he said, placing the cash on the desk.

'It'll be ready Monday.' The undertaker smiled.

***

'Good afternoon, sirs.' Bernard served them with a smile.

'Hello, Bernard.' Harold replayed the words. 'Um... You can see us both?'

'I certainly can. What would you like? The usual tea for you, Mr Harold? Mr Frederick? I have a smaller choice for you than usual. Only what's been left behind when someone of your persuasion has been taken away suddenly.'

'Taken away?' Frederick asked, puzzled.

'Exorcised.' Bernard thumped on the bar emphatically. Frederick blanched.

'Does that um... happen a lot?' he asked.

Bernard laughed. 'Only on Fridays,' he said, 'When it's throwing-out time.'

Frederick nodded, making a mental note never to outstay his welcome here. 'What have you got that I can drink then?' he asked.

'Spirits,' replied Bernard with a grin.

Harold was still chuckling when the door opened again and Jasfoup came in.

'Good afternoon, all,' he said cheerily, sitting down at Harold's table and pouring himself a cup of tea from the pot that Harold had ordered. 'Where have you been all day?' He splashed a little upon the table, and stood the teapot on top to hide it.

'We went down to the hospital morgue to view the body.' Harold signalled Bernard for another pot of tea.

'Were there any problems?' Jasfoup asked. 'They're sometimes funny about stuff down there.'

'They want to do an autopsy,' said Frederick gloomily. 'I don't want them cutting my body up and weighing the bits in plastic bags. How can I go through the afterlife knowing that my organs are in freezer bags?'

'It won't affect you,' said Jasfoup wisely. 'You no longer have a connection with your old body. What you're wearing now will do you very well, you know.'

'I suppose.' Frederick sipped his drink as Bernard replaced the teapot with a fresh one.

Harold nodded his thanks to the barman. 'Uncle,' he said, a thought occurring to him with the subject of bodies past and present. 'Is your form… um… exactly as your old one was?'

Frederick frowned. 'I don't know,' he said. 'I haven't actually looked, not having needed to go to the toilet or anything.' He put a hand cautiously to his groin, and grinned happily. 'I got the right bits!' he said, happily.

'Of course you have,' said Jasfoup, topping up his cup with fresh tea. 'Your spirit is everything that makes you who and what you are. In your head, you've always been a man, so that's what you are now.'

'Good for you, Uncle,' said Harold, raising his cup in a toast. 'Welcome to the world of men.'

Jasfoup laughed. 'It's a little ironic that you finally join the world of men just after you depart it.'

'Hilarious,' agreed Frederick without a smile.

Jasfoup looked up as the door to the cellar opened and nudged Harold. 'It's Isaacs,' he said. 'I told you we'd find him in here.' He raised his voice. 'Isaacs,' he said. 'Would you join us?' He nodded to Bernard, who brought the old lawyer's drink over to their table.

'Good afternoon, Mr Waterman; Mr Waterman; Mr Jasfoup.' Isaacs nodded to each of them in turn. 'I can see that some changes have occurred since I saw you last May I offer my condolences upon your recent loss?' Isaacs sat down on the fourth seat and took a sip of his drink.

'Thank you,' said Frederick, 'but I find the whole process rather freeing, to be honest'

'Honesty is always an admirable trait,' agreed Isaacs. 'I shall have to try it one day. Ha-ha.' He touched Harold's arm. 'That would be a joke about lawyers,' he explained.

'Very nearly,' agreed Harold

Isaacs reached a hand into his jacket pocket and drew out a manila envelope. 'I believe that this belongs to you.' He pushed the packet across the table, narrowly missing the splash of tea that Jasfoup had spilt earlier. Harold looked at the packet.

To be delivered to Harold Waterman C/o The Tattered Moon

He slit open the faded envelope and unfolded the single sheet of paper. Isaacs sat back, a half smile upon his face as he watched his new client. Harold began to read:

> *My dear son.*
>
> *Don't worry about your Uncle Frederick. He will soon adjust to his new life and no doubt you will find many uses for his new abilities. I'm sure that I don't need to warn you about strange women, for your compassion and good nature will reap you many rewards. Look out for the one with the book, he has been waiting for an opportunity to assist you in a more personal matter. I'm sorry that I can't be less cryptic, but rest assured that I do what I can to aid you. You will hear from me again soon enough.*
>
> *Louis*

'Curiouser and curiouser,' said Jasfoup. 'I wonder what that's all about.'

'That's an invalid sentence,' said Harold absently, mulling over the information.

'I knew that,' said the demon. 'That's exactly what I said to Reverend Dodgson when he read it out to me, but he wouldn't have it any other way.'

'It's a famous quotation now,' added Frederick.

Jasfoup tutted. 'It's always the errors that get remembered,' he said sadly.

'It's a bit cryptic,' said Harold, passing him the letter. 'The bit about Uncle Frederick is reassuring and I'm going to meet a woman, apparently, but what's all this about a bloke with a book?'

'Jehovah's Witnesses?' suggested Frederick.

Harold laughed. He tapped Jasfoup on the arm. 'There's something I've been meaning to ask you,' he said.

Jasfoup raised an eyebrow. 'Ask away,' he said.

'Why did my jacket roll up when Gillian bit me? Why didn't it protect me, like it did with Jedith?'

Jasfoup smiled. 'Two reasons,' he said. 'One is that, as a living entity, it knew what was best for you.'

'And the second?'

Jasfoup grinned. 'It didn't want to get bitten.' He drained his tea and stood up. 'I've got work to do. I'll see you back here later on, shall I?'

'Right you are,' said Harold. 'Does Bernard do food?'

Jasfoup sneaked a glance at the barman. 'Nothing you'd want to eat,' he said.

Chapter 25
Suicide and Murder

Jasfoup spent the afternoon working alone, increasing his supply of blood. By the time dusk began to fall he had cultured four pints of fluid that matched Lucifer's, or as near as he could get, and four of Harold's. He transferred it to the tower at the Manor, warding it from the resident ghosts with sigils of his own devising.

***

It was dark when they got back to the house and Gillian was waiting for them, sat on the small roof over the bay window.

'It's about time,' she said. 'I've been here for an hour already. I need to feed.'

Jasfoup nudged Harold. 'Are you sure you want to keep this leech around?' he asked. 'She's a difficult pet.'

Harold scowled. 'She's not a pet,' he said, clicking his fingers. He looked up towards Gillian. 'Come down, and we'll find you something.'

'You think you can train me to come when you click your fingers?' Gillian snarled.

Harold blushed. 'No,' he said, 'that was for Devious.' He looked around, grateful when he saw the imp appear. 'See?'

'Yes, Master?' Devious jumped when Gillian landed, one leg on either side of him.

'That's hardly a snack,' she said. 'Besides, imps taste revolting.'

Devious howled. 'Don't let her eat me, Master,' he said.

Harold laughed. 'I won't,' he said. 'Devious, I want you to find something for me.' He hunkered down and whispered in the imp's ear. Devious nodded and vanished.

***

The tunnel was the usual affair, and they always reminded Harold of underground railway stations with that depressing, there-must-be-more-to-life feel about it. He looked back at Gillian and was pleasantly surprised to find that he could detect her heart beating. Only once every ten seconds or so, it was true, but still, where's there's a heartbeat there's a warm welcome, as Frederick would have said in one of his more romantic poems.

'Where's Frederick?' asked Harold, suddenly noticing the absence of the spirit.

'Spirits can't use the tunnels,' said Jasfoup over his shoulder. 'Else they'd all be running about willy-nilly, and we'd never keep track of the buggers.' They stepped out into a dimly lit terrace. Heavy traffic noise indicated that they were on a side street to the main road and Devious led the way to tall four storey house. Jasfoup tried the door and, finding it locked, walked through it and opened it from the other side for Harold. There were advantages to being insubstantial at will. Devious raced up the stairs and Harold and Gillian followed at a more leisurely pace, whilst Jasfoup floated slowly upward, his midnight skin becoming pale and his membranous wings feathering. There was some activity at the top of the stairs, and Jasfoup increased speed to investigate. By the time that Harold and Gillian got up there, He was already deep in conversation with a man who was in the process of tying a rope to the roof beam.

'Suicide is a sin, you see,' Jasfoup was saying, 'but we have a special on at the moment, where you can repent your sins before the fact, as it were.' He nudged the man conspiratorially. 'It goes down very well at the annual Vatican Vacation, I must say!'

'So,' the man was grasping at this new concept, 'I can ask for repentance before I actually do the deed, and I'll be absolved?'

'One-day only special offer!' Jasfoup agreed, 'Just sign on the dotted line!'

'I'll do it. Have you got a pen?'

'Has to be in blood, like in the old days,' Jasfoup was insistent.

'Don't the... um... other side do it in blood?'

'Ballpoint pens. Haven't you ever noticed how ballpoint pens are always dry when you need them? That was an invention of Hell.' Jasfoup, for a change, spoke quite truthfully.

'Yeah, that makes sense.'

Jasfoup drew out a quill and stabbed the man's thumb.

'Ouch! That hurt!'

'It's only a little bit, and you're about to kill yourself anyway.'

'Oh, yeah.' He signed the paperwork, and Jasfoup checked it over.

'Thank you, Mr...' He looked at the signature, 'Mr, Whelp.' Jasfoup whipped the contract away. Harold had long since given up wondering how he did that. 'Off you go, then.' Jasfoup stood back expectantly.

'What?'

'You were about to hang yourself.'

'I was, yes, but since I've got a free pass for absolution, I thought I'd get even with my ex-wife first'

Jasfoup shook his head. 'It doesn't cover you for mortal sins, I'm afraid.'

'Isn't suicide a mortal sin?'

'Technically, yes, but we downgraded it to 'self-depopulation'.' Jasfoup was pleased by this invention.

'I'd best get on with it then.'

'Jolly good.'

Whelp tied the rope around his neck, but Harold interjected.

'You're not doing that right,' he said. 'Allow me. I used to be a boy scout.' He tied a perfect hangman's noose. 'Long drop or short?' he asked.

'What?'

'Long drop or short? Apparently, a long drop is quick and painless, but a short drop is very erotic. You come before you go, as it were.' Harold grinned.

'I don't know. You choose.'

'Short,' interjected Jasfoup. 'It's more fun, trust me.'

'Short it is.' Harold tied the knot and stood back. 'Jump away.'

'I'm not sure I want to, now,' said Whelp.

'Tch.' Jasfoup tutted. 'This contract will expire soon.'

'Got any food while we wait?' asked Devious, impatiently.

'Yes, there's some pizza in the fridge.' Whelp pointed, and lost his balance. Devious scampered off. Whelp was flailing in the air, slowly going purple. Jasfoup nodded to Gillian, who sprang, her incisors growing as she leaped. She sank them into Whelp's neck, just below the rope, and they swung like a macabre pair of puppet dancers. Within a minute, Gillian let go and dropped to the floor below, landing uninjured on her feet. Jasfoup dropped his disguise, his beautiful feathered wings rotting to his regular issue leatherette, and his skin turning midnight black once more. He shook himself. 'That really takes it out of me,' he said.

'Useful confidence trick, though,' said Harold.

***

Frederick walked home by way of the park, but he wasn't entirely sure that he liked it. It had already been going dark when he'd arrived and he'd watched the few departing humans with interest, amusing himself by making faces at small dogs and scaring babies. He'd had the same reactions when he'd been alive.

When the park had closed he'd sat on one of the benches overlooking the pond and watched the ducks until he'd noticed the others arriving.

With it cleared of mortals, ghosts converged upon the park like mosquitoes to a muddy puddle. They viewed Frederick with suspicion, not having met him before. He tried talking, but they just ignored him.

One spirit condescended to talk to him. An old man with a Jack Russell terrier on a piece of string stood in front of his bench where he watched the play of moonlight on the dark water.

'You're in my seat,' the spirit had said in a gruff Yorkshire accent.

Frederick had looked up at the dour prune of a face as it peered out from beneath a checked, peaked cap and elected not to argue. He got up and moved aside. The ghost sat down and lit a cigarette. Almost as an afterthought he offered one to Frederick and with a nod of his head indicated that he could sit on the other half of the bench.

Frederick sat down again. 'I've got a pipe and baccy, thanks,' he said.

The old man nodded and put his cigarettes away. They smoked in amiable silence for a few minutes.

'You're new around here.' It was more of a statement than a question.

'I am,' Frederick agreed.

''Appen no bugger will speak to you.'

'Also true.' Frederick nodded.

''Appen you're a stuck-up, toffee-nosed git who doesn't know why he's stuck here on Earth.' The spirit took a last drag of his woodbine and flicked the nub out into the pond. It flew in a perfect arc and vanished before it even hit the water.

'Now that's not true at all,' said Frederick, still puffing on his pipe.

The spirit glared at him.

'I know exactly why I'm stuck here.'

The spirit laughed.

''Appen you're worth talking to after all,' he said. 'The name's Tom. Just Tom. We don't bother with family names no more, not since our families can't see us or care. This 'ere' is Jester, on account of his motley.' Tom patted the little dog on the top of his head and it grinned and wagged its tail.

'Frederick.' They shook hands formally.

'How did you end up stuck 'ere, then?'

'I didn't want to go,' said Frederick. 'I liked it where I was.'

Jester urinated and licked his testicles.

Frederick pushed him away.

***

'There's that cat again,' said Jasfoup, nodding towards the local orange tom as they stepped out of the tunnel. 'The one you keep feeding.'

'Oh yes!' Harold fished in his pocket. 'Kitty want a treat?' he asked in a sing-song voice.

The cat sauntered over, took a sniff of the mint and flicked its tail before stalking off towards the house. Harold watched it go.

'It's quite at home, here,' he said, 'though I can't seem to get it to respond to me.'

'I can't think why,' said Jasfoup. 'It's not as if you smell of dog, is it?'

Harold brushed a stray cat hair from his leather trousers. 'Perhaps it has a higher intelligence than me,' he said.

'That's possible,' the demon chortled. 'I think that mice and bats probably have a higher intelligence than you. Come to think of it, so does a plank. Perhaps it would respond better if you got a hat with kitty ears.'

'Har-de-har,' said Harold, opening the house door.

'How's your mum?' Jasfoup asked. 'I haven't seen her today.'

'She's all right.' Harold replied. 'She's spending an awful lot of time cooped up in her bedroom, watching television until all hours.'

'Perhaps she's found herself a friend,' suggested Jasfoup, wiggling his eyebrows.

'Mum?' Harold laughed. 'I doubt it. She doesn't go in for that sort of thing any more. I doubt that you could engage her interest in that department with a rocket launcher!'

Jasfoup laughed. 'I'm sure you know Ada better than I, Harold,' he said with a smile, 'but I wouldn't rule out the possibility. Perhaps it's her that the orange cat comes to see.'

'Yes Jasfoup. Most amusing. My mother is having illicit bedroom liaisons with a cat. Pull the other one.'

Jasfoup just grinned, watching it dash into the house as Harold opened the door. His protégé had never noticed that the cat had a triple row of incisors.

***

Frederick was beginning to get the hang of manipulating objects in the physical world. He carried petrol from the stables to his beloved Betsy, careful not to spill any.

He splashed the flammable liquid over the beetle, opening the doors with the keys that he'd taken from the hook in the kitchen and climbing inside. He splashed the rest of the petrol around inside it, watching it stain the old vinyl of the seats as it pooled, and wiping away a tear as it collected in the cracks of the dashboard between the fake-wood Formica surfaces.

He stepped out of the car and returned to the house to collect the matches, shaking the box merrily as he climbed back in and closed the door. He allowed the petrol to evaporate, filling the car with fumes before drawing the match across the sandpaper.

The explosion blew the windows out and the doors cleanly off. In the midst of the sudden inferno, Frederick laughed, touching his initials carved into the dash board as they burned away. He almost felt warm for the first time since he'd died.

***

Harold climbed into bed, relishing the feel of clean sheets. His mum must have done the washing while he was out, or at least had Stinky do it. He beckoned Gillian to join him. There was a thump from the wardrobe and they both looked at it, startled.

The door opened and Devious poked his head out.

'What were you doing in there?' Harold asked.

The imp grinned, his cheek strangely distended. 'I thought that if I combined real portals into your world with the exits from the tunnels, it would be a more natural progression from one space to another, Master,' he said.

Harold nodded. 'That does make a kind of sense. Wardrobes have always held a little magic for me as portals to other worlds. It's quite fitting that it should really be that way. What are you eating?'

Devious removed a white ball from his mouth. 'I think it's a gobstopper,' he said, 'but it tastes a little strange. There're loads of them in there.' He pointed to the wardrobe.

Harold grimaced. 'They're mothballs,' he informed his scaly servant.

Devious took it out again and stared at it. 'Really?' he asked. 'I've never seen a moth that big!'

Gillian laughed and Harold elected not to explain. 'Would you give us a little privacy, please?'

'Oh.' Devious grinned. 'Right you are, Master.' He closed the door again.

Harold didn't notice the eye at the crack where the hinges joined.

Chapter 26
Inter Poet, Stage Left

It took the time of two cups of tea for Devious to bury the car. He'd tried to bury it on the drive, but Frederick had drawn the line at having the concrete ripped up, since his father had laid it and he had no desire to find out what was underneath. The three friends sat in the garden with their tea, content to watch the imp dig a deep enough hole under the rhododendrons.

'You're following in your Grandfather's footsteps, you know.' Frederick tapped the ash out of his pipe.

'Am I? I wondered whose they were.' Harold followed the trail of mossy footprints in the concrete of the garden path.

Frederick nodded. 'He wanted to leave his mark upon the world.'

'He could have found a better way than fifty yards of size eights, if you ask me.'

Frederick gave a hollow laugh. 'He did,' he said. 'He begat me an' your mum, and she begat you.'

Harold sighed. 'You can be a soppy old git when you want to be, Uncle,' he said.

'Aye, lad.' Frederick began refilling the pipe. 'Just don't follow him too far. He went about things the wrong way and got sliced open by a bunch of fiends and dragged down into the pit.'

Harold nodded. 'That's a nasty way to go.'

'You're telling me. He only wanted a bag of potatoes from the farm shop.'

Harold looked at him. Frederick was far away in the land of

memory. 'Was that as well as absolute power at the cost of any soul who happened to cross his path?'

'That too.' Frederick grinned. 'At least you're paying the dues as you go along.'

'Trying to, Uncle. Trying to.' Harold clapped as Devious replaced the bush and jumped up and down on the earth to settle it again. 'Good job, Devious,' he called out.

The imp hurried over, wiping a little sweat from his brow. 'I buried it good and deep, Master,' he said. 'In the same hole that a load of old bones were buried, too.'

Frederick coughed. 'We won't talk about that,' he said. 'The rhododendrons have been there for fifty years. Papa liked rhododendrons.'

Devious stared at the ghost for a moment before returning his attention to Harold. 'What's the next job then, Master?'

Harold took out his wallet and gave the imp the card from the funeral parlour. 'Go to this address and bring the coffin I ordered here. You'll recognise it because it's the only one made of metal. I've already phoned to check that it's in. Just make sure that no-one sees it going, and mark off his records to say that we've taken delivery already. Put it in the Green room.'

'Yes Master.' Devious nodded.

Harold grinned. 'Come on, Uncle. It's time for us to go to the hospital again. See you later, Devious.'

'Yes, Master.' Devious was grawing at a bone he'd filched from the hole.

***

Jasfoup browsed the contents of the morgue whilst Harold and Frederick dealt with business, treating the place as if it were a trinket shop. His presence unnerved the young man on the desk, and he was having difficulty keeping his mind on his work. He kept staring at Jasfoup.

'Is there something wrong with my friend?' Harold asked.

'Yes... er... no, sir. I just have the oddest feeling about him.' He shrugged. 'Sorry. This place gives me the willies sometimes.'

'It gave me one,' said Frederick, walking behind the desk.

Harold smiled. 'So it was an accident?'

'Yes, Mr Waterman. Your er... uncle suffered a mild stroke and died from wounds consistent with falling off a ladder, just as you wrote on your statement to the coroner. Did you think there might be some other reason?'

'No, but is there any reason for the stroke?' Harold craned his neck to look at the report upside down.

The man shrugged. 'He was old. It happens. One of those things, I'm afraid.'

'Here, they've got me down as 'female',' said his uncle, who was reading over the mortuary attendant's shoulder.'

'You were female once,' replied Harold.

'I most certainly was not, Sir,' said the attendant, his eyes narrowing.

Harold laughed politely. 'Sorry,' he said, 'I meant Uncle Frederick.'

'I see. Yes, we have him marked down as a non-operative transsexual.' The attendant frowned. 'We don't get that many, and it's usually the other way round. Men dressed as women, I mean. It's a bit easier to tell, these days, with the operations being easier to get.'

'Still expensive, though,' said Harold.

'I can give you a card for a surgeon I know,' offered the attendant. 'Very reasonable.'

'Ah. Um... no, thank you. I'm happy as I am, thanks.'

'Good for you, sir. There's precious few that are.' The man smiled. 'If you'd just like to sign for the personal effects. Here's the death certificate.'

Harold signed and received a brown envelope and a package of clothing. Jasfoup returned and stood next to him, smiling.

The young man began to fidget. 'When will you arrange to have the deceased collected, sir?'

'Today, definitely.'

'Which funeral directors?'

'Our own,' said Jasfoup with a smile. 'Waterman's.'

The attendant frowned. 'I've not come across you before. Have you been in business long?'

'About seven thousand years,' grinned the demon.

***

It took them the best part of the afternoon to register the death. Harold had to fill out numerous forms in triplicate to apply for permission to bury his uncle in the family mausoleum at the Manor and the office had no carbon paper for copying facilities. It was only with Jasfoup's help that Harold was able to by-pass the full procedure and obtain permission the same day. The demon was also happy, having secured several contracts over tea and cream buns.

'I never knew that working in a registrar's office could be so rewarding,' he said. 'I thought it would be a miserable place.'

'There are births and marriages as well, though,' Frederick pointed out.

'You can't have everything,' Jasfoup replied.

***

By the time they had detoured to check that Harold's mum was all right, it was after midnight when they returned to the Hall. Harold went to the former green room and was pleased that Devious had done as he was told. The coffin stood on low trestles awaiting Frederick's corpse.

'Last job of the day, then, Devious. Go down to the hospital morgue and when there's no-one to see you, fetch Frederick's body back and put it in the new coffin. Mark off the records to show it was collected, too.'

'Yes Master. Are you going to be a necromancer now?'

'Certainly not!' Harold waved him off. 'I've got a girlfriend.'

***

Frederick stood up. 'Time to do the vigil,' he said.

They followed him to the Aqua, Cerise and Lemon Yellow room (formerly the Mouse room) where Devious had set out the coffin and sat down.

'That was thoughtful,' said Harold, indicating the vases of lilies that dotted the room. 'I didn't ask him to do that.'

'I can't bear lilies,' said Frederick, mournfully. 'They always remind me of death. Father used to have them all through the house.'

'This is a funeral, Uncle,' Harold pointed out. 'Admittedly, though, since it's your funeral, you don't have to have them if you don't like them.'

Frederick shrugged. 'They're here now,' he said. 'Better lilies than nothing. What are those supposed to be?' He pointed to a metal vase containing glowing rods.'

Jasfoup coughed. 'They're from me,' he said. 'Ada said that she had red hot pokers in her garden, so I nipped down to my own garden and got some from there.'

'Mum's are plants, though, Jasfoup,' Harold told him. 'Yours are red hot pieces of iron.'

'Sorry,' said Jasfoup. 'I didn't realise. I thought it was odd that your mother was growing plants from the lower planes.'

'It doesn't matter,' said Frederick. 'It was a nice thought. Thank you.'

'I brought you roses.' The voice was soft and feminine, and they turned to find Jedith standing in the doorway.

'What are you doing here?' Jasfoup asked. 'You didn't know him that well.'

'You were fond of him in life,' Jedith replied, nodding to Frederick. 'If you thought highly of him, he is worth my respect.'

'That's very sweet of you, Jedith,' said Harold. 'Welcome.'

'Thank you for the roses,' added his uncle. 'I don't think I've ever seen black ones before.'

'I brought roses too.' Gillian stalked into the room. 'Blood red ones.'

Harold laughed. 'That was thoughtful,' he said. 'Sit here, next to Jasfoup and me.'

Gillian sat, staring at the coffin thoughtfully. 'Why are we here?' she asked. 'Why are we watching the coffin?'

'It's called a vigil,' explained Harold. 'It's to ensure that the deceased is, well, dead and not just in a catatonic state.'

'I know what a vigil is,' said Gillian patiently. 'My point is that Frederick has been autopsied, so I doubt he's asleep, and secondly, since his ghost is sitting next to you, I believe he's definitely dead.'

'She's got a point,' said Jasfoup. 'Shall we get on with the interment?'

'Might as well,' agreed Frederick. 'It's depressing sitting her, all mournful.'

'I'll get Mum, then,' said Harold. 'She likes a good funeral.'

***

Jedith left on pressing business before Ada arrived, soaring into the night on leather wings. Harold was almost sorry that she had gone before meeting his mum, but glad that he didn't have to explain the presence of the Angel of Pestilence.

They carried the coffin to the tiny mausoleum in silence, Jasfoup and Harold at one end, Gillian and Ada at the other. Unseen by anyone, Devious struggled along underneath, carrying most of the weight, causing Ada to comment upon how light her brother had been.

'Well,' Frederick replied, 'I've had half of my bits removed and put into little plastic bags. You can't tell me that that's good for you.'

'You're dead, Uncle,' Harold pointed out. 'It really doesn't matter. Even cremated people still lead useful lives, or after-lives, anyway. I don't think it really matters whether your body is in one piece or not.'

'I were buried under the apple tree in the orchard,' added Molly, who had tagged along with Frederick at the back. 'I doubt there's much left o' me' mortal remains now, an' I still work all right.'

'There you go, Uncle' said Harold with a smile.

***

An Ungodly Child

The internment was a quiet affair. Harold had half expected to meet his great-grandparents, but the only person there at the mausoleum was an old woman knitting a long scarf who nodded to them and moved her chair a little so that she didn't get trodden on. It was odd to slide the coffin onto the dais and he shuffled his feet, trying to think of something profound to say.

'Um,' he began. 'Rest in peace, Uncle Frederick, and I hope you enjoy your new-found freedom.'

'That's not a very good eulogy,' said Frederick. 'Can't you thing of something uplifting?'

'It's a bit disconcerting when the person you're giving a eulogy for is standing next to you criticising,' said Harold, crossly.

'He was the best brother I could have wished for,' said Ada suddenly. 'He was a genius out of his time, and I'm glad that he's stayed on to look after us all.' She thought for a moment and added: 'And bless all those who sail in him.'

'Thanks, Ada, love.' Frederick murmured.

Jasfoup cleared his throat. 'Frederick was a troubled soul who has now found rest,' he said. 'He was always half a step out of time with the rest of the world and was abandoned by his parents to fend for himself too early. He struggled through life as a gentle soul in an unquiet world and has now, finally, found the peace that he was denied in life. Long may he walk the path he has chosen without having to decide which way to go.'

Harold clapped.

They all looked at Gillian, who shrugged.

'He was a bloke who died,' she said.

Frederick nodded. 'I can't argue with that,' he said.

***

The three angels watched the procession return from the mausoleum, protected from sight by the cornices of the tower.

'Where are the armies of the undead?' Senoy asked. 'Where are the legions of the damned, come to conquer the earth and bend it to the will of Lucifer?'

'You promised us this.' Sansenoy turned on Semangalof. 'You said that when Frederick died Harold would be filled with the unholy power of his father.'

'I though he would be.' Semangalof narrowed his eyes, picking out the object of their discussion in the small party. 'All my studies showed that Frederick was the paternal influence on Harold, and when he was removed...'

'By your nudge against his stepladders...'

'...Then Harold would turn to his real father.'

'The problem is clear.' Senoy pressed his fingers to his temples. 'Frederick didn't leave, thus Harold has not had to replace his influence.' He turned to Semangalof. 'You must destroy Frederick,' he said. 'That will force the issue.'

Semangalof nodded. 'Right away,' he said, drawing his sword.

***

The mourners paused at the stable yard.

'Didn't we just bury that?' asked Harold, pointing to the Beetle.

'We did.' Frederick grinned. 'It was the cup of tea that gave me the idea. If that could be reduced to a spirit, then so could my car.

'This is the spirit of Betsy?' said Harold, looking at the car. Even in the darkness he could make out the stable doors behind it. 'I'm impressed.'

'Well done, Brother,' said Ada. 'I wouldn't have thought of that.'

Frederick beamed.

***

'Who did you leave the manor to?' asked Ada as they settled in the kitchen for a toast to the departed. 'Not me, I hope. This place still gives me the willies.' She looked toward the door to the hall. 'I remember when that bloke turned up, the one with all the heads.'

'What bloke?' Frederick asked. 'I don't remember that.'

'Yes, you do,' Ada insisted. 'You wrote a poem about him.'

'Oh, the headsman.' Frederick laughed. 'He was funny. He kept trying to cut off people's heads, and his axe would go straight through them.'

'It wasn't funny at all.' Ada said. 'I could feel every cold inch of it. He's not still here, is he?'

'No, Ada.' Jasfoup set several mugs of tea down. 'I moved him on myself.'

'I'm glad to hear it.' Ada shuddered. 'He used to come through that door...'

The door opened and Ada shrieked.

It was Molly. 'Careful, sirs,' she said. 'It's Mr Mange. 'E's manifested, and 'e's got such a temper on 'im.'

Molly turned to face the hall. Harold could see through her body as the black-cloaked figure darted into view. Molly raised the knife that she carried at her belt.

She slashed wildly but Mr Mange darted backwards, grabbed her arm and twisted so that the knife fell into his hand, then thrust it into her abdomen. She spun under the momentum so that Harold could see her intestines spill out as he moved the knife upwards until it was blocked by her sternum. As a coup-de-grace he withdrew the blade and sliced open her neck as well, and Molly fell limply to the floor. The spirit smiled, looking directly at Harold as he pulled a sword from its scabbard.

Harold stood and drew his sword from the cane, stepping in front of his mum.

'No, Harold!' cried Jasfoup. 'It won't work against him!'

Harold gave no sign that he had heard, and continued to advance upon the grinning ghost

He dropped into the protective stance that Jasfoup had taught him and inched forwards, all his attention upon his opponent. Semangalof advanced slowly, nonchalantly, his sword not even at a guard since he knew that Harold was out of measure. As they closed, his sword rose and he smiled.

'I'm faster than you, Harold,' he said. 'Invincible. All I need is to push a handspan of steel into you and you're dead, whereas you can bury your pathetic sword to the hilt and it won't slow me a jot. Are you so sure that you want to step the dance macabre?'

'Goad all you wish, Mr Mange,' Harold said, his heartbeat heavy in his ears. 'Your days are numbered and you know it.' He lunged, his sword high for a chest strike as he had been taught, but the angel, with a mere flick of the wrist, deflected the blade easily.

Harold scrambled backwards to return to his defensive crouch.

'I could have had you there, Harold,' the angel said. 'A simple riposte and it would have been over for you. But you would have learned nothing. Try again. Take your best shot.' He raised his sword up and over his back, point downwards and his arm held slightly bent over his head, leaving his whole body exposed.

'No, Harold!' Jasfoup shouted. 'It's a trick!'

Harold didn't hear him, so intent was he upon pressing forward the attack, but his lunge fell short. Semangalof stepped backwards with his left foot to avoid the thrust, bringing his own blade down in a whistling arc, delivering a classic cut to the side of Harold's neck.

Harold fell forwards, his legs crumpling beneath him as blood sprayed from the severed artery. Feebly, he tried to clap a hand to his neck, and fell to the ground, his vision dimming.

Semangalof stepped nimbly out of the way and smiled.

'No!' Jasfoup shouted, genuine distress showing on his face at the death of his protégé.

'Do something!' shouted Gillian. 'Kill the ghost'

'I can't.' Jasfoup could only watch the horror unfold. 'It's not my place to actually kill anyone. I can only influence things to my advantage.'

'You've influenced this situation right the way up the creek, and we're all out of paddles,' said Frederick calmly. 'Now come on, Mr Mange. We've been friends for a long time. Knock it off, would you? You've just killed my nephew.'

Semangalof edged slowly around them, leaving Harold to die on

the ancient stone floor, blood seeping freely from the neck wound.
'He'll survive, Frederick. I've seen the future in him. He will be the
antichrist and lead the legions of Hell into the glorious final battle.' He
edged around to the other side of the table.

'My Harold?' Ada laughed. 'You must be barmy. He wouldn't hurt
a fly.'

'Influence something,' Gillian whispered to Jasfoup.

'The demon can't attack me since he's bound by the ancient laws,'
Semangalof continued. 'I can deal with him at my leisure.'

'See?' Jasfoup whispered back.

'The vampire can also be disposed of. How does one destroy a
vampire?' Semangalof picked up a wooden spoon from the counter
top. 'Oh yes. I remember.' He grinned and advanced towards Gillian,
his sword in one hand and the stake in the other.

Gillian backed off as he closed in on her. Jasfoup looked on
helplessly, flapping his wings and looking from one to the other.
'You're not allowed to affect mortals either,' he said. 'How can you
do this?'

Semangalof laughed. 'I am an angel of destruction,' he said. 'My
brothers and I are not bound by the promises made by our Father. We
have rained fire upon cities, sundered the earth and raised tsunamis.
What is one mortal's life among millions?'

Jasfoup frowned. 'You're one of the three?' he said. 'Senoy,
Sansenoy and... the other one?'

'I am Semangalof!' the angel snarled. He lunged with his sword,
catching Gillian in the arm and she spun away, losing her balance and
falling to the ground.

'Why?' asked the demon. 'Harold has done no harm to anyone.'

'He should,' Semangalof said. 'He should be the antichrist The
apocalypse should be in his lifetime.'

'It might well,' said Jasfoup, edging toward his charge. 'He's part
vampire now. He'll live a very long time.'

'It must be soon,' the angel insisted. 'His father promised...'

He stepped forward, his sword and the spoon both ready to be plunged into Gillian's heart and she scrabbled backwards, hands flailing, until she was backed up against the saucepan cupboard.

Semangalof was surprised. He had expected a quick bout of killing and the spear that had passed through his ghostly form should not have affected him. The little moons had sliced into him as keenly as if he were made of mortal flesh, and the sword and spoon dropped from his now insubstantial hands. He turned, ghostly stomach lining spilling from the wound in a grim echo of his slaughter of Molly. 'How?' he asked.

'Meteoric iron,' said Ada, pulling back the spear. 'Nobody hurts my lad and gets away with it. Not even an angel.'

The spear clattered to the ground.

'I say,' said Jasfoup admiringly. 'That was jolly well done.'

'Can Harold be saved, do you think?' asked Frederick. 'Now that the excitement is over?'

Gillian scrambled to her feet and rushed over to the prone figure, checking the pulse at his carotid artery. 'He's still alive,' she said, 'but he's very weak.' Quickly she bit into her own wrist, grimacing at the pain, until her own blood was welling freely. She rolled Harold onto his back and held her wrist to his mouth, allowing the blood to trickle into his throat. He instinctively swallowed, and his eyes flicked open, his hand grasping her arm so that he could suck greedily at the blood. She allowed him to continue until she began to feel weak, watching the wound in his neck close and knit together, then ripped her arm out of his hands.

'No more,' she said. 'I can spare no more.'

Harold smiled at her, blood still staining his lips like cherry juice, and she smiled back, grateful that she could save this strange man who had shown her such kindness and consideration.

Harold looked up at her, happy to see the first truly genuine smile that she had given him. Her eyes sparkled, red with unshed tears, and he knew that he had come to like her company more than he let on. He was only dimly aware of the crash and Jasfoup's bark of warning, and was as surprised as Gillian when the blade of a sword jutted suddenly from the centre of her chest

He sprang away as she crumpled, his breath catching in horror as he faced the angel again. His instincts took over as he scrambled backwards into the hall.

'Do something, Jasfoup,' he gasped. 'Get Devious.'

He took advantage of the momentary pause in the angel's advance to get to his feet and back away, looking for his sword. It may not be any use against the newly recovered angel, but at least he could use it to deflect the deadly blade. He spotted it on the floor of the kitchen, his path blocked.

The angel turned again as Devious appeared from the cutlery drawer, flinging knives and silver tea spoons at the angel. To his left Harold could see Gillian struggling to her knees coughing up blood, and was relieved that it had been the sword that had impaled her, rather than the makeshift stake.

'Leave him alone, you cad!' Frederick imposed himself between the two combatants, shouting into the angel's face, but Semangalof laughed, pushing his sword into the ghost and pulling it up through his body, severing his connection to the mortal plane. 'A boy needs his real father,' he said. 'Not a poet who gives out wisdom gleaned from television sit-coms.'

Frederick coughed, trails of ectoplasm streaming from his wounds. He blinked, looking into the cold eyes of the angel, and vanished.

The door to the yard burst open and there was a bark. A growling, spitting ball of black and white fur launched itself at the angel. Semangalof paused to swat at it, his hand passing through the body of the dog that Frederick had last seen attached to a piece of string. It was enough of a distraction for Harold to pick up the spear, using it like a quarterstaff to smash down at the angel, his strength, increased by the vampire blood coursing through him, knocking the sword from the angel's hands.

He reversed the staff and drove the moon-shaped trident into Semangalof's head and the angel dropped. Harold drove the point home.

'Bravo.'

Frederick looked up to see the man in the peaked cap from the park, the little terrier at his heels.

'Who the hell are you?' asked Harold, forgetting about the use of Jasfoup's home as a profanity.

The old man smiled. 'Hell? No. Quite the opposite, as a matter of fact.' His ghostly form shimmered, revealing the classic image of an angel, bright enough for Harold to have to shade his eyes.

Jasfoup staggered backwards. 'Azrael,' he said.

Harold used his hand to shield his eyes. 'What can we do for you?' he asked, trying not to look guilty. He felt like a little boy who has been caught with adult magazines stuffed up his jumper. Not that he'd ever done that.

The angel appeared to smile. 'It's more a case of what you've already done,' he said. His form returned to that of the old man with his peaked cap and cigarettes. 'I find this form less intimidating,' he said.

Harold nodded and dropped his hand.

Azrael gestured to the spear. 'I'd be less intimidated if you weren't waving that about, too. Not that it would affect me, you understand. It's more the principle of the thing.'

Harold grinned sheepishly and put the spear on the ground. 'Jasfoup called you Azrael,' he said. 'Are you really the Angel of Death?'

Azrael grinned. 'Only when I have to be. I've delegated a bit since the Fall, and only do the problem cases these days. Wandering spirits, earthbound ghosts, that sort of thing.' He looked at Jasfoup. 'Contract termination.'

The demon coughed.

'There's always a loophole.' Azrael grinned and took out a fresh cigarette. 'You should know that. You have to have a loophole to allow free will, no matter how small a chance it is. Fairy stories are based upon the principle.'

'I thought that the Angel of Death was a woman.' Harold asked, looking toward the demon. 'Menna?'

'Indeed she is,' Azrael took a long drag of the cigarette 'Hers is the task of taking the souls of all those who are certain of their afterlife. She doesn't trouble herself with the unquiet ones. There's too much paperwork.'

'Ah. Like tax forms, I suppose.' Harold nodded.

'Tax forms?' Azrael grinned, the wrinkled prune of a face looking as if it were about to split open. 'Tax forms are easy. You try filling out an A31E when the dearly departed has been missing, presumed haunting, for a century or more. Then you can argue with me about filling in forms.'

'I'll take your word for that.' Harold looked towards the demon, who was unusually silent. Gillian, being technically dead, was also as silent as the grave she should have been occupying.

'Excuse me a moment.' Azrael bent down and picked up a limp figure no bigger than his palm. Semangalof was not looking his best His form was so transparent it was almost invisible, and he looked more like a piece of cellophane than the vengeful angel they had been fighting. Azrael folded up the angel until it was nothing but a tiny spark and placed in carefully in his jacket pocket.

Harold sighed in relief.

'Now then,' the angel began. 'Harold, isn't it?'

Harold nodded.

'You seem to have several of uncollected spirits hanging about.' Azrael walked over to Molly, who was struggling to collect her intestines. 'Good evening, my dear,' he said, brushing his hand across her wounds and causing them to heal. 'Who might you be?'

Molly looked fearfully at Harold and Frederick. 'I be Molly, Sir,' she said. 'Molly Braithwaite.'

Azrael smiled and took out his black book, flicking off the elastic band and thumbing through pages. 'And when were you born, Molly?'

'Seventeen ninety-six, Sir. But please don' send me away. I likes it 'ere, so I does.'

Azrael paused in licking his pencil. 'You do? You know that you could go to Heaven, don't you? Any minor sins have long since been absolved by your continued work.'

'Tha's kind o' you, sir, but I's 'appy enough 'ere, and who'd take care o' the Master if I weren't?'

Azrael smiled at her. 'As you wish, then, Molly. No doubt I'll be here again, sooner or later, if you change your mind.'

'Thank you, Sir.' Molly curtsied.

Azrael watched her leave, and then turned a few pages in his notebook, walking steadily towards Gillian, who gulped and backed away slowly until she ran into Jasfoup behind her. He smiled benignly: 'And you are?'

'Gillian Du Point. Nineteen thirty-eight.' Her voice was soft and sulky.

The angel flicked through a few pages with a puzzled brow. 'Are you sure?' he asked. 'Not Gilly Jones of Basingstoke?'

Gillian sighed. 'Well, you'd change your name if you were given a name like that. I wasn't going to stick with 'Gilly Jones' all my life. Undeath, I mean. At least you've got a decent name: 'Azrael'. What kind of name is that, then?'

The angel paused. 'Not many people ask me that,' he said. 'It's Hebrew and actually means 'Whom God helps', though to be honest it seems to be the other way around, mostly. It's generally known as 'Helper of God' these days, fortunately. How about you? Are you happy to be wandering in this state of half-death, your corrupted corpse given the semblance of life from the people you kill?'

'I'm fine, thanks. Never better.'

'Oh.' Azrael made a notation next to her name. 'Fair enough then. I'll ask you again at another time.' He moved to where Frederick had died, picking something up from the floor and shaking it until it unfolded like a deck of cards. 'Who are you, then?'

'Frederick Waterman.' Harold's uncle checked himself over, holding his arm up to the light.

'And when were you born?'

'Nineteen forty-seven'.

The angel flicked through his book. 'Are you sure that's your name,' he asked. 'I can't seem to find you.'

An Ungodly Child

Frederick looked about him, seeing the others staring. 'Can I have a quiet word?' he asked, nodding away from the others.

'Hmm? I suppose so. There's no harm in that.'

They walked a few paces away from fire and began to converse.

'What are they talking about?' asked Harold.

'The change of name and gender, I suspect,' said Jasfoup. 'It shouldn't be a problem.'

'Why's that?'

Jasfoup grinned. 'In Aramaic, 'Azrael' is feminine. It's funny how these things work out, isn't it? Everything has been done before, even changes of gender, though you won't see them in the edited Bible.'

Frederick finished his conversation with the angel and they walked back to the others. 'I can stay,' said Frederick, smiling.

Azrael smiled. 'I'm all done here. That just leaves little Jester.' Azrael patted the little ghostly dog fondly and hunkered down in front of it. 'I can't take you with me, boy. Do you want to stay here?' He looked up at Frederick. 'Will you look after him?'

'Aye, that I will,' said Frederick, amiably. 'There's not been a dog here in many a year.'

Azrael nodded. 'Then he shall stay.'

Jester tilted his head on one side, aware that something momentous was happening. Azrael gave him a last pat and passed another package to Frederick.

'You'll want these,' he said, his form already beginning to dissolve. 'Take care of him.' The angel folded into himself and vanished.

Jester looked at the space that the angel had occupied and barked, sniffing all around as if he could find his old friend again.

'What did he give you?' asked Harold.

Frederick looked at the ghostly paper bag and laughed. 'Dog biscuits,' he said. 'Here boy.'

Jester wagged his tail.

Chapter 27
Shopping for the Future

Harold sat on one of the benches that bordered the market, watching the bustle of people while he savoured a cup of cappuccino from a woman with a coffee van. It was this market that had started him off in business when he'd rented a stall once a week to sell memorabilia. He'd graduated to shop when he began to run out of stock by lunchtime.

'Harold!' Jasfoup appeared from the throng of shoppers and sat down. 'Not in the shop today?'

'Sod the shop,' said Harold. 'Thanks to you I don't need the money anymore. I'm getting rid of it.'

Jasfoup raised an eyebrow. 'Won't you be bored? What will you do instead?'

'Open a different shop,' Harold said. 'I want to sell books and antiques.'

'That's a noble occupation. You never know what you might come across.'

'I'm bored with all the junk, Jasfoup. I want to move into the quality stuff; antiquated books and artefacts. It would be a good way of getting hold of some half decent magical texts as well. There's a whole new world opened up to me and I want to step inside and embrace it, but preferably with some decent firepower at my disposal.'

'That's a good idea, Harold.' Jasfoup looked at him with something approaching respect. 'I'll miss the old shop, though.'

Harold nodded. 'As will I, my friend. Do you know any estate agents?'

An Ungodly Child

'Hundreds, Harold. You can't move for treading on their fingers sometimes. If I had an egg for every estate agent rolling in agony on the floor of the inferno, I'd have died of cholesterol poisoning.'

'Except for the fact that you can't die, of course.' Harold grinned.

'Apart from that, yes.' Jasfoup grinned.

Harold laughed. 'I meant live estate agents, of course.'

'Quite so. I know a few, but it would be worth having a chat with Mr Isaacs. He's been a lawyer since before you were born. It's quite probable that he'd know who to recommend.' Jasfoup looked across the market as if he could see the old man through the buildings. 'I know his habits quite well,' he said. 'I'm positive he'll be in Bernard's bar round about now.'

'How can you be so sure? It's daylight.' Harold stood and adjusted his hat.

'There's no sunlight in Bernard's, I've just left him there.' Jasfoup grinned produced a plastic carrier bag with a picture inside. 'Here's something for your new shop, look. A pixie.' Inside the deep frame were three butterflies pinned to a board. It was rather tacky, but Harold could see that the left hand one was not a butterfly at all, but a tiny, desiccated humanoid figure.

'Poor little sod,' he said, handing it back to the demon.

'Yes, they look like insects to those who don't have the Sight. It's a shame that this one is so dried. They're really tasty.' Jasfoup grinned and licked his lips.

'Eww.' Harold grimaced. 'Do you eat everything?'

'No, Harold, I don't. I never eat chicken nuggets.' Jasfoup replied. 'An imp probably would, though.'

'They really do eat anything, so long as it's organic.' Harold took the plastic lid off the cup and drained the remainder of the coffee.

Jasfoup looked across the crowded market. 'Not even that. I've seen Devious eat processed cheese.'

Harold shook his head, lost for words.

Jasfoup put the picture back in the bag. 'Your dad used to have a pitch here,' he said, looking around at the market stalls. 'That was before all the modernisation, of course. It was a field of mud here in his time. He used to sell anything he could lay his hands on, though he never made much actual money. He had this habit of nipping off for a quick smoke, like, leaving his stall untended. He was forever having stuff pinched.' Jasfoup laughed. 'Then he'd wander back and mark the souls for damnation.'

Harold laughed. 'That's a bit rough,' he said. 'When was this?'

'The latter part of the nineteenth century.' Jasfoup smiled. 'Those were good times. They were a bit easier than they are now, of course, because everyone's so aware of the value of things now. I used to be able to pick up a bag of apples for a penny, or half a dozen souls for a shilling.'

'Jasfoup?' Harold tossed the empty coffee cup towards the nearby bin. It clattered as it hit the side with a Styrofoam squeal.

'Yes, Harold?'

'There used to be a building just off the market, up there.' Harold pointed to a side street. 'It's been boarded up for years, ever since I was a boy. I wonder if it's available.'

Jasfoup snorted. 'The council have probably turned it into a careers centre by now.'

'Can we have a look?' Harold set off with Jasfoup following in his wake, nodding and smiling at the shoppers as he walked past

As he turned into the alleyway at the top of the market, Harold saw it: Number 33, Dark Passage. Even the address seemed portentous. A little off to the side, its three storey, stone-clad countenance seemed to be sheltering from the onslaught of the more modern brick-fronted offices. Harold was surprised to see that it hadn't suffered at all since his childhood, and seemed to be in exactly the same state of refined deterioration that he remembered. A pair of bay windows flanked an imposing, almost gothic doorway and the theme was followed up the next two floors. Harold couldn't see the state of the roof from the ground, as the temping agency opposite was too close, but he could always have it repaired if need be. He knew a little chap who could be persuaded to help out. Probably for the price of a dead pigeon.

An Ungodly Child

He walked up the six steps to the front door. It was locked, but he could just make out a small handwritten sign stuck inside the fanlight. He had to rub the grime off the glass in order to read it. *All enquiries to J Isaacs, Solicitor. 12 King Georges Street, Laverstone.*

'Serendipity.' Harold said in a hushed breath.

'Not really.' Jasfoup read the notice over his shoulder. 'This is where he lives.'

'Really?' Harold raised his hand to knock on the door, but Jasfoup stopped him. 'There's no point in knocking,' he said, 'He lives alone and he's at the pub, so no-one would answer. Besides, it's still daylight.'

'Oh. Should we go round to his offices?' Harold ran his hand over the age-worn oak of the door, imagining his bookshop behind it.

'No point in that either,' grinned Jasfoup. 'There's a sign there that says 'All enquiries to 33, Dark Passage', which is here. Perfect, when you think about it, no-one can ever enquire about renting it.'

'Do you think he'll let us rent it?'

'With a little persuasion.' Jasfoup grinned.

Harold tried to peer through the grime of the fanlight, but since the windows were all boarded up, there was no light inside to give him any indication of the interior. He gave the doorknob one last try and stepped away.

'We'll go and see him down the pub,' said Jasfoup.

***

Bernard waved as they entered the bar, and put the kettle on. 'Good afternoon, gentlemen,' he said, 'the usual?'

Harold smiled. 'Yes, please, Bernard. I'll just be having a word with Mr Isaacs there for a minute, though.'

'Right you are, Harold. Tea, Mr Jasfoup? I bought Earl Grey specially.'

'You can twist my arm, Bernard.'

'Only if I'm very brave, or very stupid, Mr Jasfoup.' Bernard laughed.

Jasfoup put some money down on the counter, where it tarnished instantly. The coins were swept into the till with a flourish, and Bernard went to serve Harold.

'Another of whatever Mr Isaacs is having,' said Harold, pleasantly.

Isaacs turned his hollow visage on the trainee warlock. 'Mr Waterman,' he said. 'What an expected pleasure.'

'The pleasure's all mine, Mr Isaacs… Did you say 'expected'?'

'Indeed I did. Today is Thursday the sixteenth of June, is it not?'

'Yes, why?'

'Perhaps because yesterday was Wednesday the fifteenth?' He saw Harold's blank look. 'Just my little joke. I have a letter for you, which was to be given to you today.' He withdrew a yellowed parchment from his jacket pocket, folded into three and sealed with wax. 'I've had it in my possession for a while, as you can see. I can tell you that it comes from your father, who rather typically didn't put on enough postage.'

Harold took the letter reverently. He had never had so much from his father, and here was another letter written years before. He looked at the front, where the address was written in faded brown ink in an elegant script:

J Isaacs, Solicitor.
12 King Georges Street, Laverstone, Wiltshire.

The stamp, which had multiple postmarks, was an original Penny Black. He wondered if Mr Isaacs had seen the irony of having to pay three pence excess postage on a stamp worth over a thousand pounds.

'Yes, I saw the irony of it,' said Mr Isaacs, reading his mind, 'and it was worth perhaps forty pounds then.'

Harold turned the letter over. The wax had a seal embedded into it, with several more spots of the dried ink. The seal, under which was a message, was the symbol of a pentagram surmounted by a crown.

An Ungodly Child

To be delivered to Harold Waterman
C/o The Tattered Moon,
On Thursday June 16th

Harold was impressed. How had his father known exactly when and where he would be? He had obviously had access to the planar travelling tunnels, but Jasfoup had always been adamant that it was impossible to travel forwards in time. Reverently, he split the seal and opened the letter.

> *My dear son.*
> *Today you looked at a building in the Dark Passage. Consider it a gift, for I bought it as a retreat before I even met your mother. Johim is using it at present and will probably still be a tenant by the time you read this, for I gave him leave to stay for as long as he needs it. In return he looks after the building and has ensured that it remains in trust for you. I'm sure that he will be pleased to have the company.*
> *Your new image suits you, by the way.*
> *Louis.*

Harold read the letter twice, and then looked on the back to see if he'd missed anything.

'That's all?' he asked.

'I have the relevant paperwork,' Mr Isaacs told him. 'It's already in your name.'

'No, I mean… Didn't he write anything else?'

'No, I'm afraid not, Mr Waterman.'

Harold gave the news to Jasfoup.

'So we have a new building to move your new shop into, only hours after deciding that you want it?'

'It certainly seems that way, Jasfoup.'

'Impressive. Somebody knows you better than you know yourself.' The demon smiled. 'Here's your Earl Grey. I put milk and sugar in already.'

***

Harold spent the rest of the day at the shop, tagging any items that he wanted to be transferred and disposing of the rest by the easy method of telling Devious to get rid of it, though he didn't like to think where all the old tables and wardrobes were ending up. He was joined by Jasfoup, who insisted on rummaging through boxes on a seemingly pointless quest to ridicule Harold, pulling out old clothes and items that Harold hardly remembered buying.

'Is this a dagger I see before me?' Jasfoup held up the blade theatrically.

Harold spared him a withering glance. 'No, Jasfoup. It's a knife. Engraved Damascus steel, twenty-four carat gold borders and stag horn handle. Now put it back in its box and finish packing that cabinet.'

'Yes, Boss. Ouch.'

'You just had to see if it was sharp, didn't you?'

'Sorry. It'll be worth more now, though. Genuine Demonic Blood on the blade. Well, on what's left of the blade, anyway. The bit that hasn't dissolved. Oh.'

'What?' Harold looked up from where he'd been sorting through collectable tea cards.

Jasfoup grinned sheepishly. 'Is this a stubby handle I see before me?'

Harold shook his head. 'Throw it in the rubbish pile,' he said, 'and leave the rest of them alone.'

As the shop emptied, Jasfoup gave Harold another lesson on the art of fencing with his sword cane.

'Look, you do it like this.' Jasfoup demonstrated a thrust with Harold's new cane sword, spearing an imaginary target through the heart. 'It's a little lighter than the rapier I learned with, but it's certainly adequate to the task.' He grinned and spun the blade in a circle, narrowly stopping short of cutting off Harold's head.

'When did you learn to use a sword?' Harold asked.

'In Florence in 1514. You were nobody if you didn't have a rapier at your side, although in those days it was closer to a side sword than what you'd think of as a rapier these days.'

'That's fantastic, Jasfoup. Did they know that you were a demon?' Harold sat on his haunches, glad of the break.

Jasfoup laughed. 'Of course not! I was young then, and still in my apprenticeship, learning everything I could about the mortal world and trying to fit in with the humans that were knocking about. The number of duels I was challenged to because of stupid errors of judgement on my part was incredible.'

Harold laughed. 'Did you fight them?'

Jasfoup grinned. 'A few of them yes. I tried to avoid duelling when I could, but once in a while I would accept, especially if there was no contract in place.'

'Why?'

Jasfoup demonstrated a lunge. 'A contract is voided if the subject is killed by a demon, or an angel for that matter. If it wasn't we'd just go on a sign-and-slay killing frenzy, so it makes sense. The problem with fighting duels was that in the early days I was dreadful with a sword. I couldn't get the point.'

'Ha-ha,' said Harold, politely.

Jasfoup grinned. 'If you think about it, in the time it takes to swing a sword for a cut, and remember that in those days a sword was designed for cutting rather than point attacks,' he demonstrated with the sword cane, 'I could have whipped my claws out and taken their face off. It took an old man, and a mortal one at that, to point out that that was not necessarily the best way to remain inconspicuous, so I had to learn the delicate art of defence. The first few duels I should have lost, but luckily for me a hand's length of steel into the throat just makes me focus, and by the time I was into my twentieth or thirtieth fight I was pretty good with a blade and if I was really stuck I just moved out of the way.' Jasfoup vanished and re-appeared outside, so that Harold could only see him through the window. He re-appeared in the room. 'Of course, that was a little obvious, too, so I had to moderate the procedure so that I only moved out of the way of the incoming sword.' He leaned backward, his body almost horizontal to the floor.

'My,' said Harold. 'That's impressive.'

'I feel alive!' Jasfoup grinned. 'We've had a sombre time recently, with Frederick dying and needing to be buried and fighting with angels. With the change of premises for your shop I can see light at the end of the tunnel.'

Harold raised his eyebrows, and the demon laughed.

'Not that sort of tunnel.'

'What was wrong with the old shop?' Harold asked. 'It served me very well.'

'Don't get me wrong, Harold. It was a nice shop. The trouble with it was that it was so big that you couldn't look after it properly. All those pieces of heavy furniture gathered the dust and blocked the light. It was just dingy. I felt like I needed a wash if I'd rummaged through any of the boxes.'

'It wasn't as bad as that,' said Harold defensively. 'Just be glad that you never had to brave going to the toilet. There were things living in there that would have given you nightmares, whatever you've seen in Hell.'

They returned to the Emporium and worked until it began to grow dark. By then the shop was almost empty, the imps moving furniture faster than a whole company of removal vans could have done so. Their strength was incredible, particularly one that Devious referred to as 'Terminal', who happily carried a six foot high, solid wood bookshelf on his twenty-four inch tall frame. They were making extensive use of the tunnels, and there seemed to be a constant stream of imps with huge items on their backs. Harold was put in mind of a column of ants building a nest

'Right, we're all done.'

Harold surveyed the remnants of his old shop. What hadn't gone across to the new one had been dropped off at the local council tip. What they would make of it, he had no idea, but he'd spent a good twenty minutes instructing Devious and the rag-tag members of his demonic workforce that he'd brought with him on the environmental delicacies of placing wood in the wood skip, paper in the paper skip, and so on, but suspected that the council workers would be somewhat amazed to find, when they unlocked the gates and barriers the next morning, that they had acquired several dozen pieces of general household and office furniture overnight; never mind the dozens of heavy cardboard boxes full of paperbacks, videos, toys and crockery. He and Jasfoup wandered through the empty building, checking that they had forgotten nothing. Although he was excited about the new shop, he felt a little sad about leaving the old one where he had spent almost twenty years building up a business. He remembered the excitement he'd felt when he first took the tenancy of this shop, then the one next door and the one behind, gradually expanding the business and furnishing his own house at the same time.

They arrived at the yard, and Harold saw the garden bench he'd meant to take home, and the two remaining stone statues he'd bought when the church was selling off assets. He clicked his fingers.

'Yes, Master?' Devious looked tired, if that was possible. 'I'm off duty in ten minutes, you know, so nothing too taxing, if you please.' He scratched at his skin, which had dulled to a scaly appearance, reminiscent of fish scales.

'Just those three items to go to Mum's garden, Devious. You might need some help with the statues.'

They left him to it and went back inside, locking up each connecting door as they went through it. Jasfoup welded the locks closed, because he knew it would annoy the landlord. When they reached the street Jasfoup looked up at the sign painted across the front of the building.

'Do you want the sign, Harold? For oldtimes' sake?'

'No thanks, Jasfoup. I shan't be an 'emporium' again and it's too big to go in mum's garden. The new shop will be 'Obscure Items of Desire' I think, or perhaps 'Things you never knew you wanted until you saw them'.'

'That's a bit of a long name for a shop, Harold. How about plain old 'Harold's Bookshop'?'

Harold shook his head. 'That's a bit boring, and doesn't describe the collectibles and occult objects.'

'What occult objects?' Jasfoup looked at him quizzically.

'The occult objects that you're going to bring in for me, Jasfoup, old bean.' Harold grinned.

Chapter 28
The Subtlety of Demons

Harold looked out towards the bright lights of the city. The cupola on top of Laverstone Manor was a place with stunning views. It was almost a shame that the only time they ever came up here was to use the altar stone for rituals.

'What are we doing again?' he asked, taking off his leathers and stripping to his underpants.

'It's a ritual to sanctify you as a member of the infernal plane,' Jasfoup said. 'That will stop you being attacked by our lot for your power, since you'll be marked as one of us.'

'Ah.' Harold clapped him on the back.' That's good then, isn't it? What about angels? Won't they attack me on sight?'

'No more so than they do already.' Jasfoup pattered the altar stone. 'On you get then.'

'Are you sure this is safe?' Gillian looked out over the moonlit grounds.

'Of course it's safe.' Jasfoup grinned and crossed his fingers behind his back. 'Trust me, I'm a doctor.'

'Now I'm really worried.' Harold lay down, looking at the tangle of spider's webs in the corners of the ceiling.

Jasfoup laughed and uncrossed his fingers. 'It's true,' he said. 'I had a licence in 1794.'

'That's encouraging.'

'Want a leech?' Jasfoup grinned. 'Gillian's right here.'

'Very funny, I don't think.' Gillian glared at him.

'Can we just get on with it?' Harold asked. 'I'm cold and I need my bed.'

'Sorry, Harold.' Jasfoup retrieved the two containers of blood. 'This will be a bit messy, I'm afraid. We have to be careful, because this may attract some unwanted visitors.' He opened the jars of blood and they heard a shrieking sound, followed by the frenzied barking of Frederick's ghost dog, Jester.

Gillian looked over the parapet to see a stream of creatures materialising and coming towards them. She could make out various features of the creatures: claws and teeth, bat wings and spider's legs, and she gulped.

'I don't like this, Jasfoup,' she said. 'There're an awful lot of demons coming towards us.' She looked up as well. 'And a few angels, too.'

'I was afraid of this,' said Jasfoup, pouring the blood over Harold's chest 'What we're doing isn't really sanctioned, you know.'

'You don't say!' Gillian's claws extended. 'How long will this take?'

'A few minutes,' replied the demon. 'Keep everyone busy, would you?'

'How?' Gillian jabbed at the first demon that came clawing over the parapet and was satisfied to see it drop to the roof below.

'Keep hitting them. Knock them off!'

'There're too many!' Gillian replied, running from one side to the other, doing what she could. No matter how fast she was, she couldn't hope to keep up, and soon one had managed to climb the parapet and gained a foothold. It reached for Harold, and Gillian's hopes fell.

The demon was suddenly yanked back over the parapet. 'You look to need a little help,' said a familiar voice and she smiled as Devious climbed in, clubbing the demon that attempted to follow him with a thermos flask. 'I thought you might like some tea,' he said, shaking the flask like a maraca.

'I can't tell you how glad I am to see you!' Harold exclaimed from the altar.

Jasfoup risked a brief glance upwards. 'Not long now,' he said. 'What's happening with the angels?'

An Ungodly Child

'They're being politely asked not to interfere,' Jedith's voice came from the tiny roof. 'I have a vested interest in this, after all.'

Jasfoup grinned. 'Thanks, babe,' he said. 'Hold them off a bit longer.'

Gillian grunted. 'That's easy for you to say,' he said. 'You don't have to fend off dozens of demons!'

'How could I?' asked Jasfoup in return. 'You can't have one demon fighting another: that would be chaos. I'd get drummed out of Hell.'

Jedith laughed. 'A demon can't fight another? What would happen if I dropped a soul into their midst, do you think?'

Jasfoup swapped the spear to the other arm. 'That's different. That would be natural selection by superior prowess in combat. That doesn't count.'

'Hurry up, Jasfoup,' shouted Gillian. 'There're too many of them. We can't hold them off much longer!' She dodged the sharp fangs of a devourer beast and sliced open its neck with her claws, then turned to face a walking horror.

'Need any help?' asked Frederick, floating his way through the melee.

'We do, Uncle, but you can't affect demons, can you?'

'I can't, no,' admitted Frederick. 'But my cricket bat can.' To demonstrate he swung the bat at the walking horror, crunching bones and knocking out several teeth. The horror fell slowly backwards, taking with it the demon that was climbing up behind it.

'Hurry, Jasfoup! There are more arriving, and even with Frederick's help they're going to get through us soon.' Gillian stabbed another demon in the eye and was rewarded with fluid all over her arm.

Jasfoup held up his arms. '*Aselohim, grn fedlig ap afga ufi l'grg*', he chanted.

He and Harold were bathed in a ring of red light and the sounds of battle became muted. Harold looked up into the demon's glittering red eyes.

'What's happened?' he asked. 'I can't move.'

'All part of the process. I've shifted us half a second temporally.

Nothing outside can get in.' Jasfoup poured a little more blood onto his face. 'Lucifer, I summon you in the name of the son, blood of your blood, life of your life.'

'Dad? I get to see my dad?' Harold smiled. 'Excellent.'

The red light flickered and was broken by a shadow as a cat jumped through. Harold was reminded of a laser show. 'It's the cat,' he said. 'I thought you said nothing could get in?'

The cat shifted, its form blurring as it grew to human proportions. White feathered wings sprouted from its back, turning dark and then blood red. The figure was truly beautiful and would make the forms of angels pale in comparison. It smiled at Harold.

'That's because Jasfoup calls me by name in the old tongue, and uses power I gave him to do it,' said Lucifer. 'We meet at last, my beloved son.'

'Dad!' Harold struggled against the bonds of time. 'Sorry I can't get up.'

'That's all right, Harold.' Lucifer moved forward and placed his hand on Harold's brow. 'There. I have marked you as my own.'

'You haven't written 'fool' on my forehead, have you?' asked Harold.

Lucifer laughed. 'Perhaps,' he said, 'but it is invisible.' He turned to go.

'Just a minute, your Infernalness,' said Jasfoup. He extended claws over Harold's neck. 'I want a promotion or the son gets to live with his dad.'

Lucifer raised an eyebrow. 'Really, Jasfoup? What if I decided that I liked the idea of having Harold with me? Have you been planning this for thirty years?'

'Of course. It's not long to wait for a promotion.' Jasfoup grinned.

Lucifer laughed. 'I'm impressed,' he said. 'Very well, you are now a lieutenant in the legions of Hell.' He clicked his fingers and Jasfoup's skin darkened with two parallel marks on his left cheek. 'Let him free now.'

Jasfoup grinned and stepped back. 'Thank you, my lord,' he said.

An Ungodly Child

'It was a pleasure.' Lucifer raised his hand. 'Now I shall blast you into Abaddon for your impertinence.' Jasfoup's face fell.

'Wait!' Harold's shriek paused his father's arm. 'Let him go.'

'Why?' Lucifer looked down at him. 'He was going to kill you if I didn't accede to his blackmail.'

'I know, but...' Harold's eyes flicked to the demon. 'I'd have been dead without his help and he's proved to be a good friend.'

Lucifer raised an eyebrow. 'Only if you relish treachery.'

Harold rolled his eyes. 'He's a demon. Treachery is only natural.'

'You would forgive him for it?'

Harold grinned. 'Sure. Wouldn't you?'

Lucifer nodded. 'A long time ago, perhaps. Very well.' He turned to the demon. 'Think yourself fortunate that you made a comrade of my son, Jasfoup, but if you try that stunt again, I will destroy you so utterly that the angels won't bother to spit on you come Judgement Day.'

Jasfoup nodded. 'Yes, your Despoilership, sir.'

Lucifer's form collapsed into itself, shrinking back to the size of a cat. He jumped back out of the time shift and went hunting for tuna.

Jasfoup shifted them back into phase again. The battle still raged. Harold leaped up from the stone, rubbing his arms and legs. Gillian looked across at him, her hand embedded in the throat of a small dinosaur.

'It's done,' he said.

He leaped into the fray, punching and stabbing with his sword; a semi-naked man covered in blood and looking like an ancient warlord. Frederick whaled about with his cricket bat and Gillian opened arteries with her teeth and claws. In every lull of noise, Jedith's calm voice could be heard persuading the congregated angels that it was in their best interest not to interfere.

The enthusiasm left the assembled hosts of Heaven and Hell as they began to recognise Harold's mark and the fighting ceased, each devil and angel returning to their own plane.

Harold wiped the gore from his sword and sheathed it again, rubbing his arm. 'That was a little tiring,' he said.

'You're telling me,' agreed Jasfoup. 'Still, all's well that ends well.'

'What happened?' Gillian asked. 'You seemed to be frozen in time.'

Harold looked at Jasfoup. 'Nothing much,' he said. 'I met my dad and Jasfoup got promoted.'

Jasfoup looked at him and nodded, the events a secret between them. 'You need a bath, old son,' he said. 'You're covered in entrails and you smell like Gillian.'

***

Harold bade his uncle goodnight and went out to the stable yard. He began to walk towards the van, but was arrested by the sight of someone sprawled over the bonnet. 'What on earth is that?' he asked.

Jasfoup hurried up. 'It looks like a corpse,' he said. 'I wonder if he had a contract?'

Harold looked at the body. 'Who is he?' he asked. 'Why is he splayed across my van? Did the demons leave it?' He looked up. 'Or the angels?'

'It's a gift for you.' Gillian strode out of the darkness, her gothic chic perfectly matched by the neo-Georgian architecture of the Manor. 'Now that you're part vampire, you'll need to ingest a little blood now and again. Look more closely, he's not quite dead.' She smiled.

'That's not funny.' Harold glared at her. 'It wasn't my choice to take your blood. You attacked me, remember? I don't have to, do I, Jasfoup?'

'No, Harold, you don't have to.' Jasfoup picked up the injured man and laid him onto the tarmac. There were no wounds upon him; at least Gillian had been efficient. He tried to revive him. 'She is right though. You will have to ingest blood on a regular basis. That's the disadvantage of being part vampire. If you don't take blood occasionally, you'll lose the ability to regenerate tissue, as well as your increased reactions.'

Beneath him the man moaned, and Jasfoup helped him to sit upright. 'Can you hear me?' he asked. 'What's your name?' The man mumbled something, and Jasfoup smiled. 'It's all right,' he called out.

'He's going to survive?' Harold stepped a little closer.

'No,' replied Jasfoup, dropping the man again so that his head banged against the tarmac. 'But he's already got a contract. He had the ability to seduce any woman he wanted.' The demon looked across at Gillian. 'He got more that he bargained for with you, though.'

She shrugged.

'I don't want you to bring me presents like that, Gillian, thank you,' said Harold crossly. 'Roses or chocolates would be more than sufficient in future.'

She shrugged again and walked over to him. 'You will have to drink sometime,' she said. 'The craving will drive you mad if you deny it.'

'That won't take long, then,' chortled Jasfoup.

'Are you so sure that you want a girlfriend, Harold?' Gillian touched his hand, a mocking smile on her face. 'You do seem very attached to your mother, and your father is out of the way.'

Harold laughed. 'You've met my mum. How could you possibly entertain the idea that I'm oedipal?' He grinned. 'I'm not an evil man. If you want out of this relationship I'm sure that we can find a way.'

'How can you say that you're not evil?' Gillian argued. 'Your father is the Lord of Hell, your best friend is a demon, your girlfriend, for want of a better word, is a vampire and you have an undefined entity as a servant.'

'Devious, you mean?' said Harold. 'You have a point. I'm probably not in the top one-hundred of saintly personages, but I'm not evil. Flamboyantly neutral, perhaps, with a side order of selfish, but not evil.'

'Talking of Devious,' interjected Jasfoup. 'Would you mind summoning him so that we can dispose of this corpse?'

Harold clicked his fingers. 'Where's his wallet?'

Jasfoup checked his pockets. 'Here,' he said, displaying a black leather pouch. 'But there's no money in it.'

Gillian shrugged. 'A girl has to shop,' she said.

Rachel Green

***

'Close your mouth, dear, whilst you think of something to say.' Ada shrugged herself into her dressing gown, closing it as best she could with the tie. 'Is that my tea? Do be a dear and fetch a second cup for Louis. I expect he's parched.'

'What?' Harold closed his mouth and tried to make sense of what his mum had just said to him.

'Fetch a second cup, Harold. Have you gone deaf?' Ada opened her bedroom door a little further and took the tray from Harold's unresisting hands. 'Some biscuits, too, if you don't mind. Louis likes chocolate digestives best'

'Yes, Mum. I... er... I'll go and fetch some.' Harold walked slowly down the stairs, stopped, turned back, thought better of it and went into the kitchen.

Jasfoup looked up from the morning paper. 'It says here that they've introduced a new bill to make the incitement of violence toward any religion an illegal activity,' he said through a mouth full of biscuit crumbs. 'I say, Harold. Are you all right? You've gone as white as a sheet.'

'Um...' Harold tried to remember how to form words. 'I need another cup. My father is upstairs in Mum's bed.'

Jasfoup shrugged. 'So? He usually is. It's a good job you were always nice to the cat.'

'Is he?' Harold opened the cupboard and took out a cup and saucer. 'I never knew. All this time I've wanted to see him, and it turns out that he was here all the time.'

Jasfoup put the paper down onto the table. 'I think you ought to sit down,' he said. 'A nice cup of sweet tea is good for shock.'

'So is finding your mum in bed with your long-lost dad,' replied Harold. 'How long has he been coming here, with never a word from either of them? Not a single 'Harold, could you nip to the shop for me and by the way, your dad's back and we've been having a shagfest for the last eighteen years.' She could have at least mentioned it. A simple

'Harold, get your dad a father's day card' would have been sufficient to at least warn me.'

Jasfoup nodded. 'It's a bit of a surprise, isn't it?'

Harold turned to him, his eyes screwed up and gleaming. 'You knew, didn't you? You knew he was here all along and you didn't tell me.'

'I did try to tell you,' replied Jasfoup, primly taking a sip of his tea. 'You just thought I was making it up.'

'When did you try to tell me?' Harold mentally reviewed all the recent conversations. 'The only time you even intimated that mum was... you know... was when that orange cat was hanging about.'

Jasfoup nodded. 'Do you need some bells?'

'The cat? The cat was my dad? I've been feeding it milk and tuna for months.' Harold shook his head.

Jasfoup smiled and turned the page, one hand absently tracing his new mark of rank.

'So everything that I've done, I've done according to some plan? I've been following in my father's footsteps not because I have some natural talent, but because he's been planting my feet in the right places. This is a lot to take in. Did Uncle Frederick know as well?'

'I don't think so,' said Jasfoup, pouring Harold's tea for him. 'Although with the benefit of being dead, he might well have had a good idea. I don't think that either of them ever actually told him.'

Harold sat down slowly, dozens of questions running through his brain. 'He's black,' he said. 'Like you. Not just dark-skinned, but ebony black. How come I'm ordinarily coloured, like mum?'

'I gave you enough clues,' a rich, sonorous voice said from behind him, 'Good morning, Harold.'

Harold turned around. His father had dressed in a conservative business suit and, to Harold's surprise, Cuban heeled boots. Jasfoup coughed. 'Morning, your Disgrace,' he said.

Louis sat down at the table and reached for the spare cup and saucer that Harold still hadn't taken upstairs. He filled the gap in conversation by pouring himself a cup from the pot of tea on the table.

'How…?' Harold began.

Louis let him catch his train of thought, taking a moment to add milk and sugar, then regarded his son through dark glasses.

'Did you never wonder about my name, Harold? All those years?'

Harold shook his head. 'I knew you were foreign,' he said, 'so a French sounding name didn't give me pause for thought. Mum always referred to you as 'Louis' anyway, so I always envisaged a Frenchman. I never thought that 'Louis de Ferre' meant 'Lucifer'. You could have buggered me with a cactus when Jasfoup told me.'

Louis laughed. 'If you ask nicely,' he said, 'it's a delightful sin.'

Harold laughed. 'How come I don't look like a demon?'

'You're also part human, Harold, and Ada kept my identity a secret so that you wouldn't suffer the prejudice that other half-caste kids do. That was probably selfish of us, I know, but this was the late sixties, remember, and the world was nowhere near as accepting as it is now. Not that I'd recommend that you make your heritage the subject of public knowledge. You'd get every exorcist and hit-priest in the country gunning for you.'

'Am I the antichrist, then? And is Mum a virgin?'

Both Louis and Jasfoup laughed. 'No and no,' said Louis finally, when he'd managed to stop. 'No, the antichrist would have to be a girl. It'll be a few years yet before Big G and I plan the apocalypse.'

'And Ada stopped being a virgin long before your dad met her,' Jasfoup added.

'A simple 'no' would have done,' Harold said, huffing.

***

Ada moved the chair out of the way of the dressing table and pulled out the bottom drawer, stretching her arm into the space behind it and feeling for the two boxes. Working out which was which by feeling the carvings on the sides, she snagged her memento box, then pulled it out and placed it onto the bed.

She used a hatpin to prick her thumb. The lock sprang open as soon as she smeared a drop of blood over it. Inside was a layer of soft velvet, which she set to one side and withdrew a small packet of photographs. The first was a copy of the one downstairs of her and Louis, his face blurred as if in motion, on the pier at Blackpool. Ada smiled at the memory and the muttered apologies of the photographer when he couldn't catch a likeness. She'd got both photographs for nothing.

There were several pictures of Harold when he was a baby, his silvery scales playing havoc with the little cubic flashbulb that she'd had to fix onto the top of the camera. There was one of when he still had his wings, feathered with innocence, and one of him on his changing mat, big for his age and possessing qualities of his father that any man would have killed for. The final photograph was a studio portrait taken not long after he'd shed his first skin: his wings shorn, his tiny horns gone and his skin as pink and scale-free as any other healthy human baby.

She put the photographs onto the velvet and spent a moment admiring Harold's first tiny pair of bootees. It was hard to think that his feet had once been that small. Smiling, she put them next to the photographs and unwrapped a silk parcel. Here was Harold's original skin, still inside out from when he'd shed it during his first growth spurt. She stroked it, remembering how warm and dry he used to be before this first shed made him appear more or less human.

It was amazing, the way that baby demons camouflaged themselves to fit their environment. Other silk-wrapped packages contained Harold's vestigial wings, still with their down of soft feathers, and his stubby tail, both shed at the same time as his skin, at two weeks old, to leave him pink and as human-looking as any other newborn. It was fortunate that no-one in the hospital, apart from Doctor Duke, had had the Sight.

Ada put everything back into the box and got dressed. Harold had had enough time to chat to his dad on his own. Now it was time to face the music.

***

Harold was still asking questions.

'So why am I as pink as anyone else, when half of my heritage is black and scaly?' he asked.

Louis grinned. 'You didn't know any better, so when you were tiny you subconsciously chose the form you have now as protection, a little like a chameleon blending in with its background. Now that you know your heritage, you'll be able to subtly change your form at will, when you've had a bit of a practice at it. Jasfoup will teach you how to do that.'

Harold looked at the demon who grinned. 'No trouble at all,' he said. 'You've seen me do it often enough.'

'Did you know?' Harold glared at Jasfoup.

Jasfoup blanched. 'Of course. I knew you when you were born.'

'But you didn't think that I could be entrusted with the knowledge of my own parentage?' Harold moved the plate of biscuits out of Jasfoup's reach as a punishment.

Jasfoup sighed. 'Your father is my employer, Harold. His wishes come before yours, and I knew that he'd have a good reason to keep this secret from you.'

'What was all that with Reverend Duke?' Harold asked. 'And Jedith?'

Louis smiled. 'I had to look after you somehow,' he said. 'They thought that you could be the antichrist, so they protected you until you gained your powers.'

'Why? Did they want an antichrist?'

'Of course.' Louis laughed. 'You can't have an apocalypse without an antichrist'

'But they didn't want that, did they?' Harold frowned.

'Those three did. They miss the killing.'

Harold grimaced. 'It's hard to think of angels that want to kill,' he said. 'Why did Semangalof attack me at the end?'

Lucifer shook his head. 'He was just going through you to get to Frederick,' he said. 'To avenge his death you would have brought all the power you could muster to the fore.'

'But I'm not the antichrist,' said Harold. 'I'm not female.'

'You got sent a lot of dolls as a child,' Jasfoup pointed out.

Louis glanced at the clock. 'Have you any more questions, because I need to leave very soon?'

'Why was Isaacs out when we tried to find him?'

Louis laughed. 'You're tied to a vampire,' he said. 'Would you rather it be Gillian or him?'

Harold blushed. 'Good point,' he said. 'Thanks for planning that. One last question then. How did you and Mum meet?' Harold paused. 'If it's not privileged information. Did you ravish her while she slept?'

'Once or twice,' said Ada's voice from the doorway, 'but that wasn't the first meeting.' She placed Harold's baby box on the table. 'I summoned him, just as you summoned Jasfoup.'

'You're a sorcerer too, Mum?' Harold asked. 'You never said.'

Ada winked. 'I was aiming for an incubus.'

***

Harold sat in the deckchair. Typically for British weather, it wasn't nearly as warm today as it had been recently, but Harold had felt that his head would explode if he stayed in the kitchen any longer. He heard the kitchen door open followed by soft footfalls upon the grass and a hand was laid gently upon his shoulder. He patted it, expecting the dry skin and long fingers of Jasfoup, but was surprised by the firm soft skin under his fingers and looked up.

The woman standing there smiling at him was in her twenties, long dark hair, almost black, feathered in the slight breeze, and her soft skin framed eyes as bright as chocolate. Her high bosom rose gently in time with her breathing, and she smelled of lavender.

He barely recognised her.

The only reason he did was because he'd seen her in photographs; the one that had a blurred image of his dad in front of Blackpool pleasure beach and the ones with her elder sister.

'Mum?' he asked.

Ada smiled and sat on the edge of the sun lounger. 'Yes, Harold, it's really me. This is how I look to myself, and to be honest, with the sort of powers that we have, a little vanity goes a long way to promoting a decent self image. You'll be able to do this, too, soon.'

'But you look lovely, Mum.'

Ada laughed. 'Thank you, Harold, I'm glad that you approve. I have to keep up the usual appearance for the benefit of the neighbours. Even in this day and age, a woman who never ages is bound to cause comment and unwanted attention. You find that you need to do that too. It's just a matter of imposing your will over your flesh.'

'How did you become a sorcerer? Did someone leave a box for you to open, too?'

The smile she gave him was one he would have recognised from his earliest memories, and invited an honest smile of his own. She shook her head slowly. 'I'm not a sorcerer so much as a witch,' she said. 'The powers I get come from the spirits and the earth. You could just as easily have been the son of the Forest Lord, or of a water sprite. I was lonely and summoned the first thing that came into my head.'

'How can Satan be the first thing that comes into your head?' Harold asked

'The night that I summoned your father for the first time was the night I was supposed to go out with the son of the local vicar, only he stood me up. I had the Bible on the brain and when I did a summoning, poof! There was your dad. Don't get me wrong, though, I have no regrets.'

Harold chuckled laconically. 'I was a revenge pregnancy, was I?' he said.

Ada smiled and patted his knee. 'Never that, Harold, never that. Not for one second have I ever regretted having you.'

'How did you become a witch, then? Somehow I doubt it's something that you learn from a website.' Harold sat back in his deckchair, seeing this woman for the first time as someone who had an independent mind and will; a woman in her own right, and not just his mum.

An Ungodly Child

Ada laughed again, and Harold was surprised at what a delightful sound it was; far removed from the guttural belly laugh he was used to hearing. 'I come from a long line of witches,' she said. 'My grandmother Margaret married and had three daughters; Maggie, Lydia and Sophia.'

'That was your Mum, wasn't it?' Harold smiled, trying to recall a time when his mum had last talked about her family.

'That's right. Lydia and Sophia were the daughters of Margaret and her Fairy lover, though my grandfather never knew they weren't his.'

'Social camouflage again.' Harold nodded and then frowned. 'Fairy lover?'

'Yes Harold. Don't interrupt.' Ada patted his arm. 'When my mother met Henry Waterman she moved into the Manor, but he treated her appallingly. I remember the fights they had like they were yesterday.' Ada swallowed and went on. 'When your uncle Frederick and I were still quite young she disappeared, leaving us to cope with Father on our own.'

'She went back to Fairie,' Harold said.

Ada nodded. 'I like to think so,' she said. 'The other explanation is too horrible.'

'No, she really did.' Harold sat upright. 'Jasfoup told Uncle Frederick.'

'Really?' Ada laughed and seemed even younger, if that was possible. 'I'll ask him. I never dared hope that she would still be alive somewhere.'

'I'd like to meet her.' Harold held Ada's hand.

'Then you shall.' Ada squeezed his fingers and Harold fought not to yell at her strength. 'We're descendants of Fairie. When we used to say that Frederick was away with the fairies he probably really was. He and I are one-quarter fairy.'

'Which makes me one eighth faery, and half demon.' Harold looked up and gave a bark of laughter. 'I'm not even half human!'

Ada stood and kissed him on the forehead. 'You're still my little Harold,' she said, 'and I'm very glad about that.'

She began to walk to the kitchen and turned back for a moment. 'Harold?'

Harold sat up again. 'Yes, Mum?'

'I'm very fond of Gillian, you know.'

He smiled. 'So am I, Mum. You're about to say 'but', aren't you?'

Ada grinned. 'I still want to see my own grandchildren some day. There's plenty of time for us both, I know, but I know what Gillian is and I won't get any from her.'

'There's room for miracles in this world, Mum.'

She laughed. 'There is, yes. And this is just one world of many.' She turned back towards the house.

'Mum?'

Ada stopped again. 'Yes, Harold?'

'I'd love a cup of tea.'

She laughed. 'I'll make it myself, just this once.'

Harold watched her go indoors, her hair turning white and her springing, confident step slowing to the shuffling gait she'd had for all the years he could remember. She gave him a wave as she went inside.

Chapter 29
Freedom from Fear

Harold awoke in the middle of the night to see Gillian sat looking out of the bedroom window. She turned as he rustled the sheets and smiled. The bedsprings creaked as he swung his legs out and stood.

'Hey, sleepyhead,' she said, taking his hand as he approached. He reversed the gesture, and kissed her palm with genuine affection.

'What are you looking at?' he asked, following her gaze towards number nineteen across the road, where the dim glow of a television could be seen through the closed curtains of a bedroom.

Gillian shrugged. 'Nothing really,' she said. 'Just thinking about what you told me about your dad. It's pretty momentous, being the girlfriend of the son of Lucifer.'

'Are you?' asked Harold with a half smile.

Gillian raised her eyebrow. 'Am I what?'

'Are you my girlfriend? That's the first time you've really called yourself that.'

'Is it? I didn't realise.' Gillian thought about it for a moment. 'Are you quite sure about that? I thought I'd at least not contradicted you once or twice.' She grinned suddenly. 'I'm hungry. Do you want to come out hunting with me?'

Harold grimaced. 'Must I? I'm not a real vampire, remember. I don't have the natural urge to slaughter the innocent like you do.'

'No-one is truly innocent, Harold, at least no-one that I take. The only truly innocent are children and the insane, and I don't hunt those. Show me someone who's truly innocent and I'll show you a liar.'

Harold barked a laugh. 'Don't get me started. People say that Dad is evil, but his deeds are nothing compared to a mortal man in a position of power.'

'You're not thinking of anyone in particular, of course.' Gillian smiled ironically.

Harold shrugged. 'If the cap fits,' he said. 'Dad may cause the deaths of hundreds and thousands, but at least you know that he can look any one of them in the face and know their name and the reason for their death. Even though he's Lord of the Pit he's a people person, really.'

Gillian nodded. 'I can't say that I'm looking forward to meeting him, I don't think that anyone can, except you of course, but I'm certainly seeing him in a new light.'

'I'm glad,' he said. 'Only a week ago I thought I was an ordinary man. Today I find out that I'm half demon; my mother's an immortal witch with faery blood and my father is King of the Fallen. I need some consistency in my life at the moment. There's been so many changes that I'm in danger of becoming adrift.'

Gillian nodded. 'They say that death is one of the top three stressful things that can happen. I suspect that your own death is probably the top of those three, and finding out that your father was once the Chosen of God would definitely be in the list'

'That's true. Not many people have dads that are in the Bible,' Harold agreed. 'Although anyone can have a star named after them these days, for a modest sum.'

Gillian laughed. 'That's a scam, Harold. It might look official, but who's going to remember, in a hundred years that PX21134 Alpha is actually called Jenny Picton because her widower husband thought it would make a more worthy memorial than a park bench?'

'You're going to pooh-pooh the fact that I own forty acres of the moon and am officially a Scottish Laird because I own three square feet of Scottish land next.' Harold sighed.

'You need to get out more, Harold. EBay is not the way to life-long happiness.'

Harold smiled. 'Perhaps you're right. I'm still going to bid on that soul for sale, though.'

'When does the bidding end?'

'Tuesday.'

'What's the bid now?'

Harold laughed. 'Five pounds at the moment. It'd make a great present for Father's day.'

Gillian laughed as well. 'I bet the seller will regret it when he finds out who owns his soul'

'You think?' Harold grinned.

'I wonder if you could bind them to your bidding?' said Gillian. 'You must have some natural abilities in that department, being who you are. It might serve as some decent protection if you're attacked by forces from either side.'

'That's a nice idea,' Harold mused. 'I'll look into it. I could place 'wanted' ads all over the internet and once I have the contracts, just wait for them to die naturally. It's not like anyone is going to outlive me, after all.'

Gillian smiled. 'True,' she slipped off the edge of the windowsill and stood to hug him. 'You've filled out,' she said. 'You were scrawnier and fatter when I first met you. Now you've lost your paunch and you've got muscles in all the right places.'

'All the right places?' Harold grinned.

Gillian smiled. 'You know how I love the flow of blood.'

She folded her arms around him. 'When did you get to be taller than me?' she asked, suddenly.

Harold's grin faded. 'Have I?' he said. 'I don't know how that happened.'

Gillian stood back and looked at him fully. His pyjamas looked over-tight. 'You've begun to develop your shape-changing abilities,' she said. 'You've changed your legs to look like the traditional image of your dad.'

Harold looked down. 'Oh, no,' he said in dismay.

Gillian laughed. 'I rather like it,' she said. 'It's only because you're full of lustful thoughts. A satyr is the epitome of lust'

'I suppose so,' he replied doubtfully.

'Besides,' she said, pulling him back to the bed. 'Hooves are adorable.'

***

When Harold arose the next morning, he found a letter on the doormat in the perfect calligraphy he'd come to associate with his father, but unlike the others he had received, this one was fresh and stamped correctly, indicating that it had been posted before the events of the previous night. He carried it into the kitchen.

Sat at the table, Stinky was reading a copy of 'Ladies' Prattle', a magazine that his mum subscribed to, hideously expensive and full of absolute twaddle. The imp looked up as Harold entered, a mug of steaming coffee in his hand and a half-eaten croissant on a plate in front of him. he gulped.

Harold sat at the table opposite and laid the envelope down, carefully, if subconsciously, aligning its bottom edge with the table. 'Tea, please,' he said. 'And two slices of buttered toast'

The imp nodded silently and put the magazine down whilst he carried out the request Harold turned it towards himself and glanced at the cover. *'My husband killed me and drank my blood,'* proclaimed the lead story. Harold shook his head and turned to the directed page. This would be a new twist on the term 'ghost writing'.

Harold gave the story a cursory read with a bark of laughter and pushed the magazine aside. Stinky stood respectfully at his elbow and Harold accepted the tea.

'Finish what you were doing,' he directed, taking a sip and picking up the first piece of toast. 'Why are you sat in the kitchen drinking coffee?'

'Um…' Stinky looked around the room as if searching for inspiration. 'You're up early,' he said. 'You're never up before eight, and it's only just after seven now.'

Harold took a bite of the toast. 'That doesn't answer the question.

I'm going to get cross if you're not careful.'

The imp gulped again. 'I was on my break.'

'Break? I wasn't aware that imps got breaks.'

'We don't, Sir. Not as a normal rule, but the Mistress said I could always stop and finish the coffee in the mornings.'

'The Mistress? That would be Mum, I suppose.'

'Yes, Mr Harold. Your mum. I've been working for her for thirty-seven years now, and I've never missed a morning yet.'

Harold grunted. 'How well do you know Devious?'

Stinky smiled, showing his blackened teeth. 'He's one of my own broodlings.'

Harold nodded. 'That explains how Mum knew everything about me, then. What about Jasfoup?'

'What about him, Sir?'

'You're not his son are you? Or by some twisted fate, he's not yours, is he?'

The imp shook his head. 'I'm afraid I couldn't comment upon his parentage.'

Harold sipped his tea. 'Fair enough, Stinky. Carry on with your work, then.'

'Thank you, Sir.' The imp finished his coffee.

Harold looked at him and picked up the envelope from his father. 'Has my mother ever mentioned hygiene to you?'

Stinky shook his head.

'I thought not.' Harold sliced the envelope open with his thumbnail.

The content of the letter was short enough, and Harold read it through at a glance.

Dear Harold.

Just a little note to apologise for not being around for the last thirty-odd years.

Rachel Green

I have been keeping up with the news about you. That was a lovely model of the Titanic you made when you were five. I especially liked the trapped figures on the lower decks. Congratulations on playing the part of Mary in your final year nativity play at St Magdalene's, and well done on your eleven plus and your O and A levels.

You coped with my absence all through your adolescence very well, though I think that even you realise with hindsight that Sally Whitehouse was not the best object of your unrequited love. You might be interested to know that she got married and now enjoys a quiet life basking in the lake of boiling blood reserved for serial killers.

I was impressed when you got your degree. Well done. I knew you had it in you, lad. With your heritage you couldn't fail at theology and anthropology. It's probably a good job you didn't know that you were the son of Lucifer at your Bible classes, though.

Well done on your trading expertise and your acquisition of the shop. I'm glad that my skills at bargaining were a decent inheritance for you. If I had been around, you'd have ended up relying on me too much to become as successful as you did, although I was pleased to lend you a helping hand when you wanted to move upmarket. Call it 'Alexandrian Gold'. It seems fitting.

Jasfoup has been a trusted lieutenant for many years, so don't be too hard on him for threatening you. He may well be the epitome of evil, but he's got a good heart. He'll show it to you if you ask him, he has quite a collection of them, I believe. That was an old joke, Harold. Feel free to borrow it.

That's all for now, son. I'll contact you again soon. I must say, though, that I'm bored of tuna. Would you get some salmon in?
All the best,
Love, Dad.
AKA Lucifer, Lord of Lies etc etc

An Ungodly Child

Harold looked up at Stinky, who had just finished cleaning out the coffee pot. 'Any chance of another cup of tea?' he asked. 'I need to go out shortly.' The imp nodded and refilled the kettle.

Harold shook his head and re-sealed the envelope. The letter was as much of an apology as he was ever going to get, but a dad now was better than no dad at all. Harold wondered how he'd feel the next time that Louis turned up as a cat. Would he still be able to say 'kitty want some milk'? He doubted it somehow, and decided that he would probably stop stroking his dad whenever he came to the back door. He clicked his fingers and after a momentary delay Devious appeared from under the table.

'Yes, Master? What can I do for you today?'

'Shopping, Devious. Something for dinner tonight, lunch for Jasfoup, Mum and myself, and a few tins of salmon. Better get some tea, milk and sugar too, whilst you're at it.'

Devious made a note of the items required. 'Got it, Master. Is there anything else?'

'Washing up liquid, breakfast cereal and bread, lad.' Stinky came around the edge of the table wiping his hands upon a tea towel.

'Hello, Dad,' said Devious, cautiously. 'What are you doing here?'

'It's not eight o'clock yet,' replied the elder imp, nodding towards Harold. 'I'm usually gone by the time he gets out of bed.'

'There was something I wanted to ask you,' Devious said. 'If you work for Ada, how come it's me that does the fetching and carrying for her half the time?'

'Delegation, son.' Stinky grinned.

Devious nodded thoughtfully. 'Thanks for the advice, Dad. I'll be off then, Master.'

'Right you are, Devious.' Harold took a sip of his fresh cup of tea.

'Is there anything else you require, Sir,' asked Stinky.

Harold shook his head. 'No, Stinky. You get off if you've finished your tasks.'

'Stinky?' Devious chortled.

Stinky cuffed his ear. 'Never you mind.' Both imps vanished through the same doorway.

Harold smiled to himself at the dissention he'd just sown into the impish ranks. It didn't do to treat them too well, Jasfoup always said, as it made them uppity and complacent. He took another sip of his tea, flicking through Stinky's magazine.

Devious came out of one of the kitchen cupboards and began putting groceries away. 'You look busy,' he said.

'I'm calculating the parameters of a spell to increase the lifespan of light bulbs, if you must know,' said Harold, pointedly.

'Ah.' Devious drummed silent fingers on the tabletop. 'How many demons does it take to change a bulb?'

Harold looked at him coldly. 'One, of course, because as soon as it's in they see the light.'

'Ha-ha,' replied Devious.

'What do you want?' asked Harold.

'I wondered if I could introduce my kids to you.'

'What?' asked Harold. 'That was quick. You only mated a couple of days ago'

Devious shrugged. 'We work fast,' he said.

***

Regent's Park was overcast and drizzly, but Jasfoup stood under one of the plane trees by the duck pond nonetheless, his wings open and providing a passable imitation of an umbrella. It was sheer bad luck that one of the vagrants, drunk on medicinal ethanol, had been able to see him, and his conviction that a demon had come to claim his soul upon death was the precise thing that caused him to have a heart attack. His spirit had stood there for a moment in shock and Jasfoup, ever eager to avoid paperwork, directed him to the stairs down.

'That wasn't very fair, you know.' Arty stood off to one side. 'He should have had the chance to go and be judged first'

Jasfoup shrugged. 'You saw his face,' he said. 'He was obviously guilty of something, else he wouldn't have been expecting to see a demon.'

Arty frowned. 'That's hardly a basis for an impartial judgement,' he said. 'Surely you should assume them innocent until proven sinner?' He walked forwards until he was standing next to the demon.

'It saves paperwork this way.' Jasfoup extended a wing to provide shelter for the putto as well.

'Don't talk to me about paperwork!' Arty shuffled on his bare feet, grass and mud bubbling up between his toes. 'What did your superiors say? Will I be allowed to defect?'

Jasfoup nodded. 'Yes, they're quite pleased about it. One in the eye for His Lordship up there.' He looked down at the face full of puppy fat. 'Are you sure about this?'

Arty nodded and Jasfoup leaned down and touched the putto on the head. Like a flame creeping across paper a tinge of darkness spread from the crown of Arty's head and engulfed him, turning the skin as black as the inside of an oven. 'There's no going back now,' he said with a chuckle.

The former putto looked at his darkened hands and watched the claws grow with a sense of wonderment.

'What's the big secret, then?' Jasfoup wasn't supposed to ask, but he'd done all the recruitment and it was only fair that he should be privy to the information.'

Arty looked up from his body. 'God is gay,' he said. 'Misogynistic, too.'

'That was obvious,' said Jasfoup. He looked at the new demon. 'Tell me; why did you want to defect?'

The former putto laughed and spat. 'It was unfair,' he said. 'You ought to try being as old as Eternity and still never reaching puberty.'

***

Harold was just unlocking the door of his battered van when his uncle's VW beetle came through the side of it. Since it was a spirit car, there was no damage, although Harold's heart would have suffered had he not been all but immortal.

Frederick left the car partly through the van and parked. Harold shook his head. It was just like his uncle, who had spent thirty years restoring and repairing this car, to keep it in his afterlife. The driver's door opened and Frederick got out, closely followed by his ghostly Jack Russell, who leaped over the seats to escape and promptly cocked his leg over the wheel of Harold's van. As he stared defiantly at Harold the ectoplasm streamed out.

'What ho, nephew,' said Frederick, jovially. 'Is my sister up yet?'

'Hi, Uncle Frederick. She's in the bath, I think. Go on in.'

Frederick scooted round to the other side of the car and opened the passenger door. Harold was most surprised when Molly climbed out.

'Mornin' Mr 'Arold,' she said. 'Master Frederick's bin' takin' me for a ride in 'is car. It ain't 'alf excitin' you know. It goes ever so fast'

Harold creased his brow trying to reconcile the statement with his own knowledge. A fast VW Beetle was surely an oxymoron. He smiled. 'Indeed it does, Molly,' he said. 'How did you escape the Manor boundaries?'

'Well, Sir, Master Frederick reasoned that as the car was part o' the 'ouse, I could travel in it. 'Appens 'e was right.' Molly grinned.

'Clever, eh?' said Frederick. 'It gives her a little extra interest in life.' He smiled and put his arm around the maid.

'That makes sense, but then, how is she able to get out of it?' Harold asked.

'It's like the Manor. She can go about twenty feet outside the hall grounds before she loses cohesion, so I'm hoping that she still has the same range in relation to the car. We'll soon find out, though.'

Harold nodded, watching the ectoplasm slowly fade from his tyre. I hope that you're right, Uncle. I'm off to the shop. Drop by later if you feel like it.'

'Right you are, lad.' Frederick waved and led Molly into the house. Harold suspected that something might be going on between the two ghosts. He started up the van and carefully backed it through the Beetle and out into the road.

***

An Ungodly Child

Ada, Frederick and Molly were seated around the kitchen table. Stinky had made tea for Ada, and Frederick and Molly were sharing the spirit cup that Frederick had brought with him. Wafts of ectoplasmic smoke drifted towards the ceiling from Frederick's pipe.

Ada looked round, through the open kitchen door.

'What's that dog doing?' she asked. 'That's the trouble with dogs, they're always upto something. He's gone into the lounge now. He'd better not wee on the furniture.'

'He won't do any harm,' said Frederick reassuringly.

'That remains to be seen. You know I've always been a cat person, Fred.' Ada was probably the only soul who could get away with the contraction of Frederick's name.

'There's lots of cats at the Manor, Ada,' he replied. 'You'd love it there. Now that Mr Mange has gone you're free to move in whenever you like.'

'I don't know, Fred.' Ada was thoughtful. 'I rather like it here. This has been my house since before Harold was even born, and I like it here. Besides, who knows what's going to turn up now that you're gone. There'll be something worse than that Mr Mange, you mark my words.'

'It's me, Ada. I'm filling his place. It's given me a whole new lease of life, has dying. There's so much to do. It's the best thing that ever happened to me.'

Ada laughed. 'If only you'd know when you were alive, eh? What do you think about it, Molly? You always gave me good advice when I was a child.'

'I think you should do what your 'eart tells you, Ada, an' no mistake' said Molly. 'You stay 'ere if you want to. The Manor's not goin' nowhere. Take a bit o' time an' see how you feel.'

Ada smiled. 'I'll do that. I'll stay here for a year, Frederick, and see how I feel then. At least I feel welcome at the Manor now. Not like the old days.'

'What was the problem between you and the ghosts?' asked her brother. 'You never did tell me what happened to drive you away.'

Ada shook her head. 'It was a long time ago, Fred. That headsman told me he could see demons around me, and it frightened him, I think. He used to stage all kinds of horrible things to frighten me away. After he started killing my pets, I had to leave. I hope that he gets what he deserves.'

'How did he kill your pets? He couldn't affect the physical plane.'

'He could change the little electricity flashes in their brains and give them aneurisms, he could freeze them by making the room as cold as ice, and he could scare them to death.' Ada had her eyes squeezed tightly shut to recall the horrors. 'Of course, him telling me about the demons was where I got the idea to summon one of my own.' She laughed suddenly. 'I suppose it's him I have to thank for Harold, if you look at it that way.'

Frederick laughed. 'I suppose so,' he said.

'Ada,' Frederick said hesitantly, 'Me an' Molly want to get hitched, like. I want your blessings on the matter.'

Ada looked at her brother's hopeful face, lined with age, and then across at Molly, who stared at her with the bright, youthful eyes of a twenty-something.

'Don't you think that the age difference is a bit of a problem?' she asked. 'Not that I'm averse to an age gap, of course, since I'm in my fifties and Louis's older than the world.'

Frederick grinned. 'We thought that too, Ada, but Molly died four hundred years ago, when she was in her twenties, and I died recently at sixty, so it sort of evens out, really.'

Ada laughed. 'As if I'd say no. Even if I did, you wouldn't listen to me. You never did before.'

'Nobody listens to their little sister, Ada,' Frederick grinned.

''Ain't that the truth,' added Molly.

**

Harold sat quietly in his office at Alexandrian Gold studying the instruction booklet for his new state-of-the-art computer. Whilst most small businesses happily ran the accounting software on a little streamlined business machine, Harold had ordered every bell and whistle it was possible to obtain, right down to the deluxe customised transparent case with the live mouse running around a little wheel inside.

Jasfoup was fascinated with it. 'It's got everything,' he said. 'Even the new premium one tetrabyte processor. That's even better than the one I've got downstairs.'

Harold grinned proudly. 'It was a present from Dad,' he said. 'A belated birthday present. He also sent me a new rattle, a bucket of building bricks and a train set.'

'Aren't you a bit old for a rattle?'

'I don't think so.' Harold considered it. 'This one still has the last foot or so of rattlesnake attached to it. It's for sanctifying magical work areas, apparently.'

'What about the bucket of bricks?' Jasfoup looked over Harold's shoulder at the instructions for the computer, which were written, like most instruction manuals, in the Tongue of the Abyss.

'It's in the kitchen at the back of the shop. Devious has got his kids in there. According to him they're his responsibility to bring up to full functional capability. He's letting them play with the bricks.'

'So I see.' Jasfoup nodded towards the flood, where a small imp was carrying a solid yellow lump of bricks towards Harold.

'Which one is that?' he asked in a whisper. 'I can't tell the difference.'

'That would be John, I think,' answered Jasfoup, the hesitation in his voice plain.

'Hello, John,' said Harold. 'What's that you've got there?'

'It'th a cup of tea for you, thir,' said the little impling, holding up the block of plastic.

'Is it?' Harold took the proffered gift and pretended to sip from it. 'It's delicious! Thank you, John.' He turned to Jasfoup. 'Aren't they delightful at this age?' he said.

'If you say so,' the demon replied suspiciously.

'My name'th not John, it'th Deliriouth,' said the impling. 'Only I've lotht a tooth. Up yer bum and tho on.'

'Well, thank you for the tea, Deliriouth. Er... Delirious,' said Harold, handing back the block of plastic bricks.

'You're welcome, idiot. It wasn't a cup of tea at all, it was a bunch of plastic bricks. I'm not Delirious and I don't really have a lisp and you look really stupid now!' The impling began to giggle, and Harold's face flushed beetroot red.

'You were right,' he said. 'It is John, after all.' He clicked his fingers to summon Devious. The imp took one look at his hysterical offspring and turned to Harold.

'I'm terribly sorry, Master. Whatever he's done, I will offer an appropriate punishment.'

Harold nodded. 'Fetch them both, Devious,' he said. 'I need to work out the differences between them.'

The imp vanished, returning a few seconds later with the two implings. Delirious and John, who had by now stopped his giggles and was switching places with is brother.

Harold stared at them. 'So which of you is which?' he asked.

The two imps looked at each other before speaking simultaneously. 'He's Delirious.'

Harold pondered, and picked up a hammer.

'I'm going to flatten Delirious,' he said. 'I have a fifty percent chance of picking the right one.'

'That's him,' said John quickly.

Harold grinned and cut off the tip of John's right ear.

'That solves the problem,' he said happily.

Delirious heaved a sigh of relief. 'Up yer' bum,' he said weakly. 'Testicles! Dingoes gonads!'

'Is he all right?' whispered Harold. Jasfoup nodded cautiously and poked him.

'Ductus deferens!' the little imp said, glaring at them both and stamping his little hoof. 'Internal spermatic artery!'

'I think he's talking in code,' confessed Jasfoup. 'We'd best get Devious.'

Harold nodded. 'He's good at breaking imp codes,' he said. 'He's like a native.'

Jasfoup's brow furrowed. 'He is a native, Harold,' he said. 'He's an imp.'

Harold clicked his fingers and Devious appeared again. 'We're worried about Delirious,' he said.

Devious looked at the imp. 'Don't worry about him,' he said. 'He's talking bollocks.'

Jasfoup laughed.

'Away with them both, then,' said Harold, crossly. 'I've been the butt of enough jokes for one day.'

'Yes, Master,' said Devious meekly, taking an impling in each hand.

Jasfoup watched them walk slowly back towards the kitchen. 'I know something that will cheer you up,' he said.

'What?' asked Harold. 'I'm not in the mood for any more jokes.'

'Not a joke,' promised the demon, 'but you'll have to come with me.'

Harold looked resignedly at the computer. 'Will it take long?'

'Ten minutes,' said Jasfoup. 'Fifteen at the most'

Harold sighed and set his computer to scan for viruses. 'Very well, if you're quick.' He stood and followed the demon through the kitchen and out of the back door, where Jedith was waiting.

'Harold.' She dipped her head in greeting.

'Hello, Jedith.' Harold looked about. 'So what is it you wanted to show me?' He looked at the angel and the demon standing next to each other. 'Are you two getting back together?'

Jasfoup leaped a foot away from Jedith. 'Nothing like that, Harold. What we wanted to show you hasn't arrived yet.'

'Here it comes now,' said Jedith. 'Stand back a bit, Harold.'

Harold stood against the back door of the shop and watched the air ripple. His mouth fell open when a moment later a racing green van stood where there had been empty space a moment before. It was far smaller that the old van, since he no longer needed to transport heavy furniture around, and had obviously been custom-fitted with an engine larger than standard, judging by the four exhausts rising from the hood of the bonnet and sweeping back over the roof.

He walked round it admiringly. They had even arranged to have the name of the shop, Alexandrian Gold, painted onto the two side panels. He looked at the grinning pair.

'Thank you,' he said. 'I love it.'

'Her,' said Jedith, handing him the keys. 'It's a 'her'.'

Jasfoup grinned and pointed to the number plate. 'Since Frederick no longer needs it,' he said, 'we had the registration transferred.'

Harold looked at BET 5Y and smiled.

Chapter 30
The Ventruvian Man

Harold closed the curtains against the night rain and sat at the kitchen table. Ada had left her tarot cards out for him to try and he began to shuffle them. It had been a helter-skelter of a week; one that he was somewhat relieved was over.

Thinking about his future, he dealt out three cards and stared hard at them, trying to discern their meaning. In the past lay The Hanged Man, symbolising the troubles he had undergone up until now. In the present was The Devil. That made sense. It represented both Jasfoup and his Father; both major influences upon him. The future was what troubled him: The Lovers.

Did it mean Gillian? Jedith? Jasfoup?

Each of them had pushed him to the very edge of himself, and changed him in some way. What next?

'Devious wants you,' said Jasfoup, entering the kitchen from the back door and grabbing a tea towel to dry himself. Harold nearly had a heart attack.

'What?' he said. 'I really don't think I could have sex with him; he's all scaly and has the most disgusting eating habits that I've ever seen.'

Jasfoup paused and looked at him oddly. 'What a horrible thought,' he said. 'You do have the strangest mind, Harold. Besides, he's too small.'

'Oh, I don't know,' replied Harold, thoughtfully. 'I've seen him without his loincloth on.'

'I meant,' said the demon emphatically, 'that he's only eighteen inches high.'

'Oh.' Harold backtracked. 'What does he want me for?'

'He's picked up that manuscript of the Prophesies of Nostradamus that you wanted to see.'

'Good,' said Harold, packing away his cards. 'Tell him to bring it here.'

'Sorry, I've sent him out for some dinner. He put it on your desk at the shop.'

Harold nodded. 'I'll go through it tomorrow then.'

'That's good, because it's the original copy and Nostradamus is on a deadline. He said to just cross out the bits that make a direct reference to you and he'll edit them out.'

'Did he like the battery-operated minidisk player and history CDs?'

'Apparently so. He said there was a whole second book in it.'

Harold laughed. 'Wait until he finds out there's only three hours of battery life.'

Jasfoup laughed and poured himself a cup of tea from the pot. 'What's in store for us, then?' he asked, indicating the closed deck of tarot cards.

Harold shrugged.

'Who can tell?' he said.

Jasfoup smiled engagingly and nudged his shoulder. 'You can,' he said. 'You're the prince of Hell.'

Epilogue
An Angel's Grave

Ada laid a lily across the stone.

It was half hidden under grass that objected to the smooth piece of obsidian in her garden. Harold had played on it as a child, fascinated by the reflective sable surface. There were no markings upon it; no hint of what was buried beneath.

It was a small grave, hidden at the back of the garden and dug with a trowel at daybreak. The box inside had been placed with a layer of salt between it and the earth, then another layer between it and the grass on the top. She had never decorated it with flowers since it had been dug, and it had remained untended for years.

Only now, with Louis beside her, could Ada shed tears for the baby that had died while still in her womb: Harold's twin sister.

'Why did she die, Louis?' Ada asked. 'I would have loved to have a baby girl.'

Lucifer placed his hand on the back of her head and drew her to him, muffling her sobs against his chest He gave her no answer, for he had never yet dared let a daughter live.

Enjoyed this book?

Find out more about the author,
and a whole range of exciting titles at
www.discoveredauthors.co.uk

Discover our other imprints:

DA Diamonds traditional mainstream publishing

DA Revivals republishing out-of-print titles

Four O'Clock Press assisted publishing

Horizon Press business and corporate materials